The

GREATEST
TAMIL
STORIES
EVER TOLD

The
GREATEST
TAMIL
STORIES
EVER TOLD

selected & edited by
SUJATHA VIJAYARAGHAVAN &
MINI KRISHNAN

ALEPH

ALEPH

ALEPH BOOK COMPANY
An independent publishing firm
promoted by *Rupa Publications India*

First published in India in 2021
by Aleph Book Company
7/16 Ansari Road, Daryaganj
New Delhi 110 002

ISBN: 978-93-90652-29-7

5 7 9 10 8 6

Printed in India

CONTENTS

FOREWORD

SUJATHA VIJAYARAGHAVAN

The last few months I have been journeying through the story land of Thamizh writers, taking in its terrain, both familiar and unfamiliar. It was this indulgence, taken at an unhurried pace, that culminated in the selection and editing of this volume.

Some years ago, I happened to embark on a marathon reading of more than 800 stories within a span of three months to shortlist a few for expression in dance. Reluctantly I had to set aside some brilliant ones, which defied interpretation through the performing art of Bharatanatyam. When I was invited to make selections for this volume, I was thrilled that I could include some of those that the previous assignment had obliged me to drop.

It was a daunting job to select, or rather decide on, which ones to keep, as we had a burgeoning number of excellent writers and fascinating stories. The present collection covers nearly a century, dating from the 1930s till the writers of today. The colours, scenes, moods, and the characters would give a fair idea of the ethos of the Thamizh people and their vibrant culture. People from all strata of society, from the educated classes to the marginalized, all have their voices here, recorded with energy and the entire range of lived and learned vocabulary. Verisimilitude works for some, ornamentation and imagery for others. Neither loses sight of the core truth that needs to be told.

One may boldly say that every one of the writers here would merit the epithet 'modern'. The most modern among them, remaining contemporary through the decades, would be Pudumaipittan, whose story is one of the earliest examples of magic realism, written decades before the term was coined.

Stream of consciousness with a blurring of borders between the mystical and the tangible set apart C. S. Chellappa and Mauni in this collection. Mysticism in a rural setting draws strength from legend and lore in Thenmozhi's 'Paychi Tree'. Thoppil Mohamed Meeran's tale weaves the real and the magical into a fabric of faith and wonder.

Within these collected stories, grounded realities, with their dichotomies and resolutions, cry out in several voices from all corners of the land. Conflicts internal and external pulsate with drama and suspense. Religion, caste, class and gender-based issues are played out within four walls and out in the open in Fr Mark Stephen's 'Penance', Anbaathavan's 'Certificate!', Poomani's 'Change', and Sa. Kandasamy's 'Slaying of Hiranya'. Sons and daughters of the soil with their hopes, fears, pains, and passions people the stories of Ki. Rajanarayanan, Imayam, and Perumal Murugan.

The resilience and intrepid disposition of the Thamizh woman is legendary and Sangam literature speaks of the likes of women who would ward off a charging tiger armed with nothing more than a winnow. Poomani's Muthupechhi, whose soft voice ignites a revolt, Ambai's pregnant young woman, who spurns a bridegroom with demands of dowry, La. Sa. Ramamirtham's orthodox mother, who defies social taboos to reach out to a woman victimized, even the teenager Vatsala in Sujatha's story, who fearlessly handles a snake, exude feminine power in diverse backgrounds. Bama's 'Ponnuthayi' emerges invincible as the rustic prototype of a women's libber.

The Thamizh people love a laugh and are endowed with the sensibility to perceive the lighter side of life and its absurdities. This spirit of humour has had several votaries through the decades and finds representation in several stories in this collection such as S. V. V.'s 'A Village Experience', Kumudini's 'Letters from the Inner Palace', Indira Parthasarathy's 'A Disciple's Offering', Dilip Kumar's 'The Solution', and Sujatha's 'Snake'. Satire is the mode of Subramania Bharathi's 'The Story of a Crow Learning Prosody', and Kalki's 'The Governor's Visit'.

Values and principles, ethics and morals make a strong statement in the pen portraits of two schoolteachers in the stories of Thi. Janakiraman and Sundara Ramaswamy and in the question of justice raised by Amma in La. Sa. Ra.'s 'Rivulets'. Many are the hurdles between a man and woman in love, in courtship and even after marriage. The situations in urban and rural ambience are related with great empathy by Ashokamitran and Ki. Ra. The self-esteem of a differently abled person in Chudamani's story leaves a lasting impact. Agonizing inner conflicts, ego, arrogance, and irreverence lead to realization and revelation in the stories of Aadhavan and Maalan.

Ramakrishnan's 'Pigeon Fever' infects the reader with its strange obsession while Balakumaran's retelling of the poignant story of Ekalavya, in a multi-layered lyrical rendering, transcends the boundaries of time and space. The panorama of these stories vividly paints the people of the land on a vast canvas that keeps unfurling.

The translators have been faithful to the authors' originals and have achieved commendable success in conveying the essence of the content as well as the flavour of the rich language. It is noteworthy that several of the translations have been commissioned specially for this collection and have not been published elsewhere earlier. I thank Malini Seshadri for translating them with a sensitivity to the nuances of the originals while maintaining the natural flow of the English language. Given the inherent limitations of translation, this volume goes a long way in trying to capture the music and cadence that are part of the timbre of Thamizh and its varied dialects.

I am grateful to Mini Krishnan, co-editor of this book, who not only initiated this project but also followed through with sustained help, advice, and guidance, and liaised with authors, translators, and the publisher tirelessly. I thank the publisher Aleph Book Company for inviting me to select and edit this collection.

INTRODUCTION: A GAMUT OF VOICES
VASANTHA SURYA

Like a flute hollowed out of a piece of bone or bamboo, a story is fashioned out of any existential circumstance that comes to a storyteller's mind. A theme is blown through it, the sound shaped and modulated to reach the listener's ear. The narratives in this collection flow through the instrument of the modern Tamil short story. Moulded from an alloy of old and new ways of telling a tale, this flute plays fresh tunes, in ageless ragas.

These short stories, selected and edited by Sujatha Vijayaraghavan and Mini Krishnan, are by modern writers, many of them household names in Tamil Nadu. What strikes one about these thirty storytellers are two defining features. The first is their common ground as heirs to 'the only language of contemporary India which is recognizably continuous with a classical past.'* Now, once again, in its two thousand-and-some years as a distinct language, Tamil is proving itself more than equal to the challenges of accommodating a gamut of voices. There are close to seventy million Tamil speakers in India,** and ten million more worldwide, for most of whom it is the first language—the mother tongue. Its ever-evolving usage, both written and oral, absorbs the idiom in various regions, castes, and communities. Tamil also

---

*A. K. Ramanujan as cited in Kamil Zvelebil, *The Smile of Murugan: On Tamil Literature of South India*, Leiden: BRILL, 1973, pp. 11–12. Ramanujan (1929–1993) was a Mysore-born philologist at the University of Chicago. A polyglot and path-breaking translator of Kannada and Tamil classical poets, a folklorist, and a poet himself in English, Ramanujan wrote 'Three Hundred Ramayanas: Five Examples and Three Thoughts on Translation' to illustrate the irresistible fluidity of the storytelling process, especially when it comes to hoary myths.

**Tamil speakers in India number almost 70 million, according to the Census of India, 2011, available at <https://censusindia.gov.in/2011Census/Language-2011/Statement-4.pdf>. Other Tamil speakers in the world, according to some estimates, could number up to ten million more.

bears with aplomb, as it always has, the imprint of other languages. These include, not only Sanskrit and sister languages of the Dravidian family such as Telugu and Malayalam, but many others like Arabic and Persian, Urdu and Hindi, and English as well. Yet, supple as it is, this language has a strong spine. It has refused to yield to the asphyxiating embrace of purists.

The second quality these writers share is the part they play in nurturing a literary aesthetic premised on a no-holds-barred ethic of doubt and questioning, which has claimed and will not be denied its space in Indian minds. Over the past century of epochal social change, behavioural norms have been examined, hailed from the rooftops—and shouted down, too—as never before in Indian literature. In modern Tamil fiction are re-enacted the drama and the melodrama, the conversations and the cacophony concerning relationships of all kinds. As one ardent enthusiast of Tamilness puts it: 'As we approach modern times, in the Tamil world, a certain stridency enters both public and scholarly debates...It is not easy to escape this acrimonious, impassioned tone.... Notions of self, and integrity, as also the disintegration of self...cognitive disharmonies and dissent, irony, self-parody...shifting models of the mind, and the person...nuanced theories of what is real'—all these and much more go into the meaning of the word 'modern'. 'All sorts of amalgams and confusions become the norm.'*

Tamil prose has reflected many of these ever since it found place in the print culture, some decades after the first Christian missionary tracts appeared in the early nineteenth century. It was in 1882 that *Swadesamitran*, the first Tamil newspaper, came out with a kind of 'standard' written language for a general readership. That 'standard' had undergone significant transformations even by 1926 when the

---

*David Dean Shulman, *Tamil: A Biography*, Cambridge, Massachusetts: Harvard University Press, 2016, p. 249. Shulman is an American-born Israeli linguist, peace activist, and poet in Hebrew. A scholar of many languages, he has described his experience of Tamil as 'love at first sight', comparing the language to 'the rapid rushing of a rivulet...a delicious, bewitching, incantational music'.

iconic periodical magazine *Ananda Vikatan* appeared. As the demand grew for news and views, fact and fiction, new writers, men and women from a variety of social backgrounds, began writing for a number of periodicals,* which were throwing open windows for people who had limited access to formal education.

This is especially true for women. It can safely be said that the majority of college-going women in Tamil Nadu today do not have grandmothers who finished school, or mothers who finished college. My mother's education (she went to school only till the age of eleven), was mostly through stories and serialized novels, poems, articles, recipes, and jokes in Tamil magazines. Imagine a woman curling up with a magazine after her daily chores...and finding a short story which gives her a peep into the clash of values taking place within every family, every class, caste, and community. Mytheli Sreenivas has suggested that these magazines developed 'new notions of subjective interiority that displaced such conventional identity markers as kinship or caste' and presented 'a paradigm of emotion in which a discourse of love, affection, and pleasure prompted radical critiques of women's oppression.'**

The colonialist dispensation, which saw Indian society as 'backward', had resulted in a close encounter with Western civilizational tropes. The Self-Respect Movement emerged in the 1930s, along with the rediscovery of long-lost or ignored literary treasures of the Tamil. language Even as the call was given to cherish the Dravidian identity, a fiery rationalist discourse decrying superstition and obscurantism arose within the movement. Ever since, writers in Tamil Nadu have addressed patriarchy, caste, and communal issues as rarely attempted with such directness in literature before, armed with some new,

---

*Some names of periodicals, old and new: the *Vikatan* group, *Kalki*, *Kumudam*, and *Kalaimagal*, *Amudha Surabhi*, and *Mangaya Malar*, and today, *Aval* and *Snehidhi* among others, several aimed at a female readership.

**Mytheli Sreenivas, 'Emotion, Identity, and the Female Subject: Tamil Women's Magazines in Colonial India, 1890-1940', *Journal of Women's History*, Vol. 14, No. 1, 2003, pp. 59-82, available at <doi:10.1353/jowh.2003.0016>.

some renascent values articulated by these and other social reform movements.

Stereotypes traceable to hallowed myths were consciously examined. Like inherited furniture, some were cleaned up and refurbished, and some are still being heaved up and thrown out. Several writers have tackled some of these 'social evils' with wit and passion, expressing the rankling sense of injustice felt by many, as Tamil society pulls itself out of medieval mindsets and exerts itself to 'adjist' to the modern age—to use an often-heard Tamlish word. With wit and irony, they turn over and expose the layers of acculturation, between which ideas are ripened to become actions.

The short story, in particular, gives the reader a deftly assembled machaan, from which to survey opinion and action in the jungle of the real world. These writers do not fight shy of stimulating their beloved Tamil to make it display its adaptive and assimilative plumage. As for the translators, they do not hesitate to do likewise with a bird of a different feather. For English is a bird to which these Indian speakers have taught a trick or two. India is estimated to have the second largest number of English speakers in the world.* For the literary genre of translation, this has significant implications: as Sujit Mukherjee has observed, Indian translators into English are native speakers of their source languages, unlike most translators into English of non-English literary works.** Ever since Indians gained proficiency in English under the Raj, they have made bold to translate into it from their own languages. This language that has no geographical base in this country has found an ever-growing space in the minds of millions. The native languages, especially Tamil, have wisely accommodated this newcomer, and set it to work for them.

---

*According to the 2011 Census, English is the first language for 259,678 persons, forming 0.02 per cent of the total population of the country. For 83,000,000 persons it is the second language, and for 46,000,000 it is the third language. Together, these groups form 10.6 per cent of the total population. Available at <https://censusindia. gov.in/2011Census/Language_MTs.html>. Only the USA has a larger number of English speakers than India.

**Sujit Mukherjee, *Translation as Discovery*, New Delhi: Allied Publishers, 1981.

Two of the earliest stories translated here are Subramania Bharati's 'The Story of a Crow Learning Prosody',* an ironic modern fable about the idolization of language, and 'Kalki' Krishnamurthy's 'The Governor's Visit',** about how small-town big shots fawned on the rulers during the Raj. Whether they are about the 'first night' in a marriage, or meeting God on a Madras street, or carving up a rapist with the claws of a man-lion, or finding out how to sanitize a well in which a rat has drowned, or gaping at a basket of snakes emptied on an office floor, or Krishna meeting his end at Ekalavya's thumbless hand—these stories speak for themselves, here, in our kind of English.

Such stories don't need to be saddled with commentaries. They roam free in the wilderness of the shared imagination, and give birth to others like themselves, and yet, unlike themselves.

---

*Originally 'The Crow and Prosody' (date unknown), this was written by renowned poet, writer, and freedom fighter Subramania Bharati (1882–1921).
**'The Governor's Visit' by 'Kalki' Krishnamurthy, the founder of *Kalki* magazine, famed for his historical novels. This story appeared in 1925 in the magazine *Navashakti*.

A VILLAGE EXPERIENCE
S. V. V.

Aweek ago I went to a village called Keezhpulivai. My daughter's mother-in-law's father had died and a condolence visit was required. The man must have been around eighty.

'When an old man of eighty dies what is the need for condolence? It's not as if it was an untimely death,' I reasoned with my wife.

'What are you saying! Our daughter is married into that family, and there has been a death in her family. Won't people talk ill of our daughter if we as her parents don't make a condolence visit? And that too, for her mother-in-law's own father. Important death. If we don't go, it will give room for criticism for all time to come. It may be okay to skip a wedding; how can one skip a condolence visit? Plus, he seems to have left his entire wealth to his grandson, our son-in-law....'

'Well, he has already left it. It's done. If we don't make this condolence visit, is he going to rise from the dead and change his will? After all, even our son-in-law is not at the village. He's away in Delhi earning a living, and is not going to visit the village now. So whom are we going to express our condolences to? Our daughter has already been taken to the village by her in-laws. So what does it matter if we don't go? Forget it, di. You're saying people will talk. What people? What are they going to say?' I said.

'Don't be deliberately obstinate. It won't look good if we don't go. It will be humiliating for our daughter. What's the problem? If we leave on the four o'clock train early in the morning we will be back home by half-past six the same evening. We must go,' said my wife.

'But it's all just a meaningless ritual! Why don't you take someone else along as an escort and visit them? Leave me out of it. Since you seem to be so overcome with grief at his death, you go,' I said.

1

'You have to come with me.'

'Let's take all our children, servants, sweeper…everyone in our house. That way we can demonstrate even better to them that our whole household is in deep grief.'

'Forget all the smart talk and get started,' she said.

So the two of us set off with just a small shoulder bag of essentials for the day trip. We got off the train at seven o'clock in the morning. The distance between the station and the village was three miles. One and a half miles of it was along a paved road and the rest was through a narrow byway. The jutka driver informed us that he would take us only as far as the end of the road, because the horse-drawn cart could not negotiate the byway. 'What about the remaining one and a half miles?' I asked. 'You have to walk, Saami. Everyone who visits the village has to walk that stretch,' said the man.

'Oh, this is going to be *some* experience,' we told ourselves as we settled ourselves in the jutka. Sure enough, he pulled up at the roadside not long afterwards, where the path to the village branched off.

'You told us that a cart can't travel on the road but I can see cartwheel tracks there,' I protested to the jutka driver.

'This cart won't go, Saami,' he explained. 'A two-bullock cart could make it, but one-animal carts like this can't. You see, ruts have been made in the road by the wheels of carts. Two bullocks pulling a cart can walk along the flattened ruts of the wheel tracks comfortably. But a single animal would have to walk on the thorny, stony ground at the centre. No way my horse would walk on that.'

'Can't we get a two-bullock cart?' I asked. 'Where can you get that here, Saami' was his reasonable reply. 'You can reach the village in no time at all. See that clump of trees over there. That's where the village is.' Then he was gone.

A young cowherd was nearby, and we took the boy along with us to show us the way. There were stones and pebbles underfoot everywhere, and thorny bushes sprouted with abandon. The blazing heat of the summer month of Chithirai had set in with full fury. My wife had decided that it was not the right thing to wear footwear when visiting a village; she had left her slippers back at home and was barefoot now.

'Look at this, a road to a village in this pathetic state! And they talk of Taluk Board, District Board, Gram Panchayat...fancy talk, like tying fancy silk tassels onto a broomstick. They squeeze the public for taxes...that's all they do.' As I was shouting this in frustration and indignation, I saw my wife hobble over to sit on a rock. She had a thorn in her foot.

'We seem to be heading for the same place where the old man has gone. That's a good thing in a way. We can meet him directly and convey our condolences. He would be very pleased.' I remarked.

My wife was not prepared to join my chorus. Instead she said, 'If only we had some coffee we wouldn't feel so exhausted.'

'Very true,' I told her. 'I agree with you. Let me look around and see whether I can spot a coffee stall...no, there doesn't seem to be a coffee stall anywhere in sight.'

'Okay, let's keep going. What else can we do?' She rose with a weary sigh. Stumbling and staggering, we finally arrived at the village.

Even as we entered the street, I started adjusting my facial expression, giving it a suitable mournful cast. My wife too had started shedding tears at the leisurely drip-drip-drip pace of a Mambalam water tap. A casual glance told me that she was gearing up to express grief in a suitable manner. Deciding that it would send the wrong message if we were seen to be casually chatting as we approached the bereaved family, we walked forward in silence, heads bowed.

My daughter's father-in-law was sitting outside the house. The moment he spotted us, he donned his own mask of grief to greet us. His wife was standing in the doorway. On seeing her, my wife opened the floodgates and her tears gushed out like the storm-driven waters of a lake overflowing its banks.

I was left wondering where in her body she had stored that much water. The way those tears were pouring out, I even had a passing concern lest she shrivel away with dehydration. Women's eyes are like pools—always brimming and ready to overflow.

Our expressions of condolence were all done within the first five minutes. After that the talk turned to topics of general interest: the weather, price rise, the new cattle disease in the village, and the theft that had taken place a week or so ago.

'Getting to your village is like going to hell and back,' I remarked. 'Why don't you all demand a proper road on which carts can come?'

'That's what we have been demanding for the last twenty-seven years,' said my daughter's father-in-law. 'But who's listening? When it comes to collecting the taxes we hear all kinds of threats. Pawn your wife's thali if you have to, but pay the tax, they tell us. We've been putting up with this all our lives.'

'I have a lot of work pending at home. I need to leave this afternoon itself. Please get us back to the station,' I requested.

'The 2.45 p.m. train, right? No problem.'

We had lunch. At noon, I put in a gentle reminder. 'Please ask your people to get a cart ready for us. We need to start soon if we are to get to the station in time.'

'Oh, you have plenty of time. I will see that you get there. De, Ammavasai! Go quickly and fetch Murugan. Run!' Ammavasai went. He did not return. The clock showed 12.45 p.m.

'It's very late already. Even if we leave right away we may not make it in time,' I said.

'No problem, that won't happen. The fellow will come any minute,' was his response.

By now I was very agitated. Maybe we should just walk? But the afternoon sun had turned the place into a cauldron. Also, wouldn't it sound rude if I told him we would walk when he had already taken the trouble to send for the cart? So I sat there choking on this dilemma, unable to either chew it or swallow it, getting more agitated by the second.

I kept checking the time. One o'clock now.

Murugan arrived. My host abused him: 'Enda, you lazy dog! Strolling at your own sweet pace when we have to get the cart ready to go to the station! Run, you donkey. The two bullocks will probably be grazing somewhere around. Find them and bring them. Wait, wait...come here. It's been some time since the cart wheels were oiled. Just burn a handful of hay and use the ashes to oil the cart wheels. After that, run and fetch the bullocks. It's getting late for the train. Do it at once!'

I couldn't decide whether I should laugh or weep. My wife came to the doorway. 'Isn't it getting late? Shouldn't we leave? It's already half past one,' she said as she glanced at her wristwatch.

There was a storm raging inside my mind. But I was able to mask my emotions and respond calmly, 'Yes, we should leave right away.'

Murugan fetched a handful of hay, set fire to it, and made ash.

'I can't apply this unless the cart is lifted. There's no one to lift the cart,' Murugan pointed out, scratching his head at this unexpected obstacle to the proceedings.

'Why don't you go to the threshing mound, da? You can get hold of some fellow there and bring him here to lift the cart. Run, run! It's getting late for the train. Bring some fellow fast!'

By the time the cart was oiled and ready, it was two o'clock.

'Run, da. Go and find those grazing bullocks and bring them here. I give you half a second!'

'The bullocks were tied to the plough this morning, Saami,' mentioned Murugan helpfully.

'Oh, then run to the clump of trees near the river's edge, get those two other bullocks and bring them here. Don't just stand there like a fat fool. Run!' ordered his master.

The clump of trees in question stood three quarters of a mile away.

I stood up, walked to the passageway of the house, and stretched myself out on the floor, face downward.

'Isn't it late?' my wife wanted to know.

Four tight slaps in reply? No, no, not here. It wouldn't look good.

Translated by Malini Seshadri

THE STORY OF A CROW LEARNING PROSODY

SUBRAMANIA BHARATI

Quite close to Kutraalam a massive banyan tree stood on a hill. One evening, a sad crow was sitting on one of the branches. The crow's wife moved a little closer to her husband and asked in an affectionate tone: 'What's worrying you, dear?'

'This morning I ate more than what my stomach could hold. Now I don't feel the need to hunt for food. But I can't afford to sit still. My friends too have not yet returned from their search. If they were here, it would be easy for me to while away the time by chit-chatting with them. I thought of wandering in the sky and enjoying the scenes below...but my wings, legs, body, and head are heavy and painful. I'm sure I have a fever. My throat too is hoarse and unbearably painful. I have a severe cold. Both yesterday and the day before I didn't get enough to eat in the woods nearby. And so, I had to fly east for a long distance into areas populated by humans, all for the sake of food. Yet, until sunset, there wasn't enough to fill even half my stomach. It rained night and day without a break. It was summer rain and I was drenched to the bone. This may be the reason for my ill-health. Indigestion is added to it from this morning. And I don't know how to kill time. This is why I am sad.'

The crow's wife said, 'Years ago when you married me you cooed to me that nothing on earth was more pleasurable than speaking to me intimately. You said that the time you spent with me was very productive. I recall that you said so over and over again. But now, even while I am beside you, you say you find it difficult to pass the time. By saying this you are insulting me. Every day I look at my image in the water in the spring. My face looks more beautiful than when we married. I also consulted my friends. They also agree that I'm more beautiful now than before. I don't know why you have turned away from me.'

'Who said you are more beautiful than before? Was it your girlfriends? Or your boyfriends?' asked the crow.

'My dear friends are the ones who told me. I don't have "boy" friends,' replied the crow's wife.

The crow reacted by fluffing its wings. It took off from the branch of the tree and started flying southwards. 'Caw…caw….' The crow heard the sound from behind him. He turned his head and saw it was his wife. 'Why are you following me?' he asked.

'You are not well…yet you are going all alone. If your head reels in pain, you may fall. If I am there with you, I'll be able to avert your fall at the right moment. This is why I am following you.'

'Oh! I see! So you are here to safeguard me, are you?' asked the crow.

'Yes! Of course,' replied the wife.

'If that is so, you don't have to go with me. I am hale and hearty now. All my ailments are gone. I will neither feel giddy nor fall to the earth and become food for a fox. So you don't have to escort me. Please stay at home.'

'Where are you going?'

'Quite nearby…Vikrama Singha Puram.'

'Huh! Vikrama Singha Puram? It is near Papanasam…Quite a distance.'

'But I can cover the distance in a jiffy. You don't have to worry about it. Go home now,' instructed the crow.

'Why are you are going there? Tell me,' enquired the wife.

'I know of a man named Veera Maagaala Pulavar who lives in Vikrama Singha Puram. He is a king of poets. He chooses this time to teach his children the art of Tamil prosody. And you know that I understand the spoken language of man, even though I can't speak it. So I will go there, perch on the roof of his house, and learn from him all the nuances of the language. I will then apply it to our crow language to formulate our own prosody. My main purpose is to compose songs and epics in our language. Is it appropriate to call a crow a crow if it has no love for its native land and tongue? It can only be called a little living black carcass. No wood in the world is as clean and fertile as our wood in Kutraalam. It is deathless. No other language is as great as our crow language. As I am born in this wood, I should contribute my share to the growth of this wood and my language. If I happen to die before my desire is fulfilled, I will have to die with regret. Hence, I have decided to prepare our crow language and develop its potential for poetry.'

'What?' retorted the wife, 'Just a few seconds ago you said no other language is as great as our crow language. But now, you say you want to adapt the nuances of the Tamil language into ours to compose songs. So you support the view that our language is inferior to Tamil?'

'Tamil is the language of human beings. Don't be so stupid as to compare our bird language with that! What I meant was our crow language is superior to all other non-human languages. All right, it is getting late. I should leave now. You go home,' said the crow.

The wife tried another argument 'You don't have to go all the way to Vikrama Singha Puram for this! Let us go home. I will teach you, because I know.'

'What do you know?' demanded the crow.

'All the rules for composing poetry.'

'Where did you learn them?' asked the crow in astonishment.

'You may think you were the first to whom such an idea occurred. Not so! My father too nurtured such an idea. He sat on the roof of a master-poet's house and learnt the nuances when the master taught his students every day. He never missed a single one of the classes which ran for six months. At the end of the course, my father mastered Tamil poetics and prosody. Following those rules of grammar, he formulated several strict rules for composing a thousand variations of poetry. Unfortunately, he did not live to present his work for acceptance in the learned assembly hall of the crow king. And so, the new theory of poetry in our language languished in our home itself. I am my father's only daughter. He had no other child, male or female. Our law forbids the female from presenting this new theory before the learned assembly and give a new outlook to our language. But I am ready to teach *you* the theory. You can learn it from me and then present it before the assembly. You will be rewarded for that in the king's court. You will become world famous. So come home and I will teach you for two hours every day. In two months you will receive the highest honours from our crow king,' said the wife.

'I am a supporter of the Republic party. I do not care for the honours and awards of the king,' said the crow curtly.

'So let it be...' replied the wife, 'as you said earlier you can contribute to the growth of our language and you will be remembered even after your death. For the sake of that at least, come with me. I will teach you the art of writing poetry.'

As the crow couple flew back home, that is to say, towards their nest, Manmadhan was moving in the sky, a little distance away from them. It was drizzling on the Western Ghats, a command from Nature to compel the male and the female to unite in love.

In such weather and in such a place, the god of love would be extremely busy. And so, he had already spent most of the arrows from his quiver and was rushing to his own world to unite in love with his beloved Rathi Devi. There were only two arrows left in his quiver. He drew out both of them and sent the love darts to the crow couple, one for each.

Before the crow couple could reach their nest, they began fondling and kissing each other. No sooner did they enter the nest that they, unable to control their passion, began to make love. The very thought of learning the art of poesy left the crow's mind. They were so deeply immersed in their passion that they were awake till daybreak. Then they slept like logs and woke up only on the morning of the next day. Before the thought of hunting for food flashed across the minds of the crow couple Manmadhan passed that way again. All that had happened in the nest a day earlier began to repeat itself. Several days passed in this manner.

The male crow completely forgot all about learning the prosody in crow language. He did not study the art of poesy. He began, instead, to study the art of love.

Translated by P. Raja

THE GOVERNOR'S VISIT

KALKI

Sriman Sivagurunathan Chettiar relaxed on his easy chair after lunch as usual and picked up the newspaper. As he scanned the headlines he was startled by the announcement, 'Poikai Dam: Governor to lay foundation stone'.

Chettiar had goosebumps all over. His heart began to race. Controlling himself with some effort, he read on. The report gave details of the Governor's arrival at the railway station on the twentieth at 7 a.m. He was to take a car to the site of the dam.

Chettiar at once summoned his clerk Jayarama Iyer and asked him, 'Have you heard the news?'

'No, sir, anything special?'

'How is it that you always seem to know nothing? Haven't I told you again and again to read the papers? Why do we spend 250 rupees every year on their subscription? What would have happened if I hadn't followed the news carefully?'

'Sir, please give me the news.'

'The Governor is visiting our town on the twentieth.'

The clerk gaped in wonder. He was too astonished to do anything except break into incoherent exclamations.

'All right, what do we do next?'

'We must get everything organized.'

'I must be at the railway station on the morning of the twentieth. Make sure our car is shining and spotless.'

'Didn't I insist you should buy a motor car? Wasn't it an excellent suggestion?'

'My good man, it is that foresight which makes you so valuable to me.... Well, shouldn't we get our house decorated for the occasion?'

'Why, is the Governor going past our home?'

'I'm not sure. He may go straight to the site from the station. I must persuade the Collector to take him through our street.'

'It doesn't matter. In any case, the fact that our house is being decorated will be reported in the papers.'

'True enough. But will the news of the Governor's arrival escape the eyes of Kurmavataram Iyengar? Doesn't he read the papers as keenly as I do?'

'Don't worry. Even if he gets to know, there is nothing much he can do about it. First of all, he has no motor car, only an old-fashioned coach. Don't you remember how the whole durbar burst into laughter when Iyengar accepted the Rao Bahadur title from the Collector, dressed like a clown and bowing as if he would never stop? The same thing will happen again.'

Chettiar chuckled as he recalled that old scene. 'Still, he must not know our plans. Keep everything ready and put up the festoons on the night of the nineteenth after 10 p.m. Let Iyengar get up and blink in the morning.'

Chettiar and Iyer held long discussions about the necessary preparations. Finally, they were struck by a bright idea. Chettiar sent a message to the president of the town council saying that at their next meeting he would propose the presentation of a citation to the Governor. After that the clerk went about his usual business.

Sivagurunathan Chettiar was a prosperous businessman. He owned the only three-storeyed mansion in his little town. He had started life as a poor clerk in a hardware store. But soon the goddess Lakshmi glanced at him from the corner of her eye, and Chettiar opened his own shop and business. His wealth increased day by day. His large pre-war stock of iron doubled and tripled in value during the World War. Chettiar became a millionaire overnight.

He began to crave social recognition. His next-door neighbour, the advocate Kurmavataram Iyengar, became his role model in social graces and sartorial style. Chettiar engaged a tutor to teach him English. He adopted all the ostentations of high living. He threw frequent parties for government officers. He squandered an enormous sum to become town councillor. Presently, his entire ambition was focused on obtaining the Rao Bahadur title.

A sneaking fear plagued him. What if Iyengar became Dewan Bahadur before that? He intended to overtake Iyengar by hook or by crook in securing the Governor's favour. That was the reason the advocate figured repeatedly in his conversations with his clerk.

The next day Chettiar attended the council meeting with a beaming face. His well-prepared proposal to present a citation to the Governor was tucked into his shirt pocket.

His speech was divided into three parts. Part one described the benefits of British rule in India. Part two traced details of the Governor's ancestry, family history, character traits, and individual merits. The third part listed all the contributions of the Governor, real and imaginary, to the welfare of the state.

At the end of his peroration, Chettiar drew the kind attention of the esteemed Governor to the single regrettable act of omission in his regime. Loyal subjects of the crown were not given sufficient recognition or reward. He humbly prayed that the Governor show discrimination in the conferment of titles on deserving persons.

The clerk sent copies of the proposal to all reporters with the assurance that Chettiar would bear the cost of telegraphing the whole speech to their respective headquarters. The reporters were also invited to Chettiar's home the day after the Governor's visit.

But alas! The moment he took his seat in the council Chettiar's joy turned to grief and anger. He came to know that Rao Bahadur Iyengar had sent his claim to make a similar proposal before Chettiar had. He would therefore get precedence in the matter. But Chettiar was not a man to be stumped by reversals. Life had taught him that determined effort achieved results. He successfully manoeuvred the right to second Iyengar's proposal. After that it was but an easy step to read the entire speech in the guise of seconding the proposal. Poor man, how could he know Iyengar had made arrangements to prevent his speech from reaching the newsrooms?

As Chettiar cursed God and man, his clerk brought him information which consoled him a little.

'The Governor arrived at the station at 7 a.m. He has to travel fifty miles to be at the river Poikai by 9 a.m. to lay the dam's foundation stone. He has no time to receive the citation at the town council or at the railway station. This message came just now from the Governor's personal secretary.... Good thing you did not propose the citation. You have been spared a loss of face.'

Chettiar was very glad. 'Ah, Kurmavataram Iyengar got what he deserved. Didn't he try to steal a march over me?'

'All the same, shouldn't you be at the station on the twentieth morning?'

'Of course. All our other plans stand as before.'

At last, the appointed day arrived. Chettiar was up at dawn. After his bath and breakfast, he stood before the mirror for a good half-hour making his toilette. His beloved wife was beside him, smoothening the folds in his garments and polishing his ornaments. As soon as he was ready, he sent the clerk to fetch the car from the garage. Chettiar's wife took a look at the street outside to check if the signs favoured her husband's trip. When the omens and the time were deemed auspicious, Chettiar stepped out of the house and entered his car. A big flapping Union Jack graced the car's bonnet.

Chettiar felt a pang when he saw his neighbour's house. Iyengar too had played a waiting game through the previous day and had put up flags and festoons in the dark. The car began to move and there was little time for more speculation.

It took five minutes to reach the station. Chettiar saw that Iyengar was there before him, ready for action. Their fierce competitiveness remained strictly hidden. To the world they were the best of friends.

'What brings you here so early?' Chettiar enquired.

'A small errand. I heard you were leaving for Madras. Is that why you are here?' Iyengar asked mischievously.

'Never mind. But tell me, your house has been festooned with decorations overnight. Any special occasion?'

'I saw festoons in your house too. Is it true that you are celebrating your sixtieth birthday?' Iyengar's query had a sarcastic ring to it.

Chettiar wished to give him a severe set down but suddenly the station was filled with people. There were members of the town council, taluk and zillah board; graduates and those who were struggling to become graduates; advocates, officers, members of the security force; volunteers who had come to stage a political protest and watch the fun at the same time; representatives of the secret police who shadowed the volunteers. All of them stood cheek by jowl, their eyes straining to remain unblinkingly fixed on the railway track.

Finally, the Governor's special train arrived. Police officers strode up and down to establish peace. The honourable governor disembarked. A path was cleared for him. All those who had come with manifold dreams stood breathless in adoration—with pounding hearts and earnest eyes. They trembled lest the honourable governor leave without a single glance at them. Later it was learnt that an ardent soul among the multitude had fainted in rapture, but so great was his loyalty to the crown that, determined to cause no disturbance, he stood upright even in such an extreme condition, clutching the pillar which hid him.

Meanwhile, the Governor took off his hat as a mark of civility and held it in his hand. His sweeping glance surveyed the crowd from one end to the other. Everyone present knew it was the moment of fulfilment of their lifetime ambition.

Petrified by the thought that the Governor might miss their salute at the precise moment his eye rested on them, they continued to salute him until he left the station. For five whole minutes their hands kept touching their foreheads and dropping down, like forest branches swaying incessantly in the west wind.

Having brought everyone under his royal glance, the Governor swiftly strode out and got into the waiting car. And those who had come to be exalted by the 'gracious sight' returned to their respective homes.

Sriman Sivagurunathan Chettiar reached home safe and sound. He was immediately surrounded by an excited group of wife, children, clerk and staff. Chettiar was a kind man. He did not wish to disappoint so many eager souls.

'We must call the priest to arrange a special thanksgiving puja to the temple deity. Things went very well today.'

'Did the Governor speak to you? What did you say to him? What actually happened?' everyone wanted to know every detail.

'As soon as he got off the train, the Governor spoke to one or two officials like the zillah collector and came straight to me,' Chettiar told them. 'Do you think I felt the slightest fear? Not at all! He shook my hand and said, "Chettiar, I have heard a lot about you. How do you do? Are your friends and relatives doing well?" You know me. Once I start talking I cannot stop. I said, "Your Excellency, under your rule we have no complaints. But I am forced to express my discontent over the fact that your government shows no discrimination in awarding titles."'

'Ayyayyo! That was quite severe! Didn't the Governor get angry?' the clerk asked with concern.

The words gushed forth from Chettiar's lips. 'Angry? What do you mean? As soon as I said this, the Governor shook my hand again and said, "Chettiar, thank you very much for bringing this to my attention. I will take steps to rectify the matter." The crowd broke into applause. But you should have seen our Rao Bahadur Iyengar. He was dumbstruck. He was standing in an obscure corner. No one took the slightest notice of him.'

At that very instant, if anyone had eavesdropped in the women's quarters at Rao Bahadur Kurmavataram Iyengar's house, he would have heard Iyengar say to his beloved spouse, 'But the Governor did not waste a single glance on Sivagurunathan Chettiar. Poor thing! He stood in an obscure corner and slunk away quite unnoticed.'

Translated by Gowri Ramnarayan

LETTERS FROM THE INNER PALACE

KUMUDINI

When did women first become especially enamoured with advice on managing a home? Were women in olden days also eager to learn about making new varieties of sweets? From the letters given below, it appears that these were concerns of women at least during the Dwapara Age. Some of the advice given in that age may be useful even today.

SITA'S LETTERS

I

This letter is to the beloved consort of Mithila's Lord Janaka from Sita Devi of Ayodhya.

I, SITA, prostrate prayerfully before Amma with a submission.

All is well here, and hope it is so with you too. The people and the chariot you sent have arrived. The messengers told us that you have instructed us to come to Mithila for Deepavali. Considering the state of affairs here, I am sure you will understand that it will be difficult for us to visit you now. My father-in-law is always at Mandavi's mother-in-law, Kaikeyi's house. My mother-in-law is furious. She conceals it well though, and is engrossed in prayer and serving food to Brahmins. I have to get up early in the morning, bathe, and help her with chores. Work fills the day. There is not a moment's rest.

As soon as the wedding ceremonies were over, my brother-in-law Bharathan was taken away by his uncle. You know Shatrugnan, he always tails his elder brother. Only after they return can we seek permission for the journey, and after all that, I don't know if we will be able to reach Mithila before Deepavali. I have great doubts about the whole thing.

After thinking it over, your son-in-law has decided that it is best we spend Deepavali in Ayodhya itself. Father will soon receive a letter about this from my father-in-law.

Do send the gift of silks to us. Your son-in-law likes only yellow silk. So, buy only that for him. Here, for Deepavali, a new design in gold bracelets is being fashioned for the son-in-law of the house, Rishyasringan. It is lovely! Do make a similar one for your elder son-in-law and send it. Along with the people who bring this letter to you, I am sending a goldsmith who excels in that kind of workmanship. No one need know that I have written to you about this matter.

You wrote that a sindhur-coloured, deep red sari is being woven for me. Here in Ayodhya, people are very fastidious about the way they dress. I believe that their silks are brought by traders from foreign lands; those narrow borders look so elegant. My sister-in-law Shantha wore one such in blue. I long to have one like it! All the saris that you bought for my wedding have broad borders. I feel so embarrassed to wear them now. Everyone makes fun of me. Don't send me any more of that kind.

Salutations to my esteemed Father.

Ever your humble,
Sita

II

PRAYERFUL submission to mother.

All well here. After writing to you, I met my sister-in-law Shantha. It seems the blue colour is not fast. Fades soon. So, I don't want a silk of that colour. Send the sindhur-coloured silk as planned earlier. Or else, if you can find a copper-coloured one which is guaranteed to be fast, send that. It is boring to wear the same colour over and over again. Anyway, do what you feel is most convenient. I don't want to trouble you much. However, don't buy the blue shade.

Affectionately,
Sita

III

PRAYERFUL submission to mother.

All well here. Quite suddenly, Father-in-law has had an idea. A plan to perform the coronation of your son-in-law! This means a sari—with your blessings—in the pandal! What kind of sari do you plan to send? Do you think the white navamallika colour will be nice? Since it is going to be displayed in the pandal, it has to be a grand one. How quickly will you be able to get one with spots like a deer's worked all over it? Or will it be possible only if ordered well in advance? My mother-in-law does not like cuckoo- or peacock-colour. Tiger-stripes will look as if I'm in puli-vesham, disguised as a tiger. I really don't know what you are going to do. My head is spinning thinking continuously about these saris. I simply cannot decide. Do as you think best.

Your loving Sita

P. S.: Or else, buy a very grand sari for both Deepavali and the Coronation Function combined.

IV

MOTHER,

No need to send any sari. All is over. We are going away to the forest. The coronation will now be for Bharatan. The person who is bringing this letter will tell you everything. I have only one dress made of bark-skin. If it rains in the forest and I get wet, I will have nothing else to wear. Therefore, if possible, send a bark-skin. Your son-in-law says that only your appalams taste heavenly. We are going to Chitrakoot. Nobody need know this.

Yours in haste,
Sita

P. S.: There is no need to worry any more about the colour of saris. Peace of mind is now mine. How helpful it would be if all women were to go to the forest! Half our worries would disappear.

Sita

GRANDMOTHER'S DESIRES

Letter written by Hidimba's grandmother Sammarjanakesi (she-with-hair-like-broomsticks) to Srimati Pisachavadani (Mrs Ghoul-face).

MAY all propitious things come to my dear friend Pisachavadani.

Are you keeping well?

We have not yet found a groom for my granddaughter, even though she has grown as tall as a tree. I think about her wedding all the time. I have rolled out appalams for it. She does not even know how to use the upper cloth to cover herself. She is always running around with the Hidimban.

Because of this cold weather, my feet are in a lot of pain. I am unable to digest anything. I ate only one goat the other day, and my stomach churned all night. I was very uncomfortable. Hidimba wants only a swayamvara—all because of modern education. Who listens to what we say? If you have any, send me a couple of barrels of chukku-thippili medicine.

Kumbakarna's great grandson Vakranasi (Crooked-nose) is a gem of a boy. Perhaps a little dark skinned. You know his mother—our Tataka's own aunt's daughter. I saw her the other day on the riverbank. 'I want an alliance with you. My granddaughter must be married into your family,' I told her. She was agreeable to this.

I have rolled out 5,000 appalams. Who listens to us? I showed the horoscope to the astrologer. 'It will happen, but the right time has to come,' he said. I have made arrangements for prayers to be said to Lord Brahma. Do drop hints that she will receive many gifts at the time of the wedding.

Both my legs have become useless. Who is to say anything and, anyway, what can be done? Do today's children listen to us? This Hidimban is forever taking her away to roam around. Do you think a decoction of rose buds will help with the gas problem? Or will it bring in some new devilish trouble?

Hidimban growls that the marriage will take place when the time is right. It preys on my mind constantly.

Appalam...

Sammarjanakesi writes to Saubhagyavati Hidimba Devi.

I

MANY blessings to Saubhagyavati Hidimba.

Why did you marry Bhima? I never want to see your face. I had chosen a groom like Manmatha for you!

Does one marry a human? You have done this in the middle of the night without so much as a squeak! You have brought ruin to the family! Never visit my house again!

Kunti has five sons. She will be prejudiced. I raised you so carefully, giving you an oil bath every other day, but she will keep your stomach empty. Why did you marry Bhima?

What do I care what happens to you! I was hoping to see a child of your womb. Does one marry out of caste like this?

In preparation for your wedding, I rolled appalams, made vadams, and went to so much trouble! Why did you marry Bhima! Everything is wasted now! Never again do I want to hear you call me grandmother; I will not come anywhere near your house.

II

BLESSINGS to Saubhagyavati Hidimba.

I saw Pisachavadani yesterday. 'Your granddaughter is very well behaved. She is obedient to her mother-in-law,' she said.

'After all, my granddaughter takes after me! I have taught her whatever skills I have,' I told her.

Be good. Make sure you pull the upper cloth firmly over yourself. If they snigger that you are like this or like that, I will be very ashamed. It seems Dharmaputra praised you. Kunti is a very good person. Such a large family; poor thing! Be helpful to her.

I heard someone say that Bhima and Hidimba are made for each other.

What do I want from you? If I hear that you are doing well, that is enough. No stigma should come to your grandfather's name, that's all. Be good.

III

ALL manner of auspicious thing should happen to Saubhagyavati Hidimba.

Pisachavadani gave me the news, saying, 'She's lost her appetite, she has morning sickness.' I am setting off right away to come over to your house.

Your beloved grandmother.

DAMAYANTI'S LETTERS

I

Prostrating at the hallowed feet of mother, this is Damayanti writing.

We stayed in a grove on the outskirts while returning to the city. When we were there, the king invited Pushkaran to gamble. The king, too, played, and in the process lost his kingdom. We got back our kingdom once again. We are all well. The elder boy was a little feverish. Now he is better. Everything is quite satisfactory. The king also is affectionate to me.

But, mother, we are unable to go on like we used to. All because of this cursed Kali. You know that during my swayamvara, some of the gods gave boons to Nala. One of them was the ability to make delicious food without too much exertion. Earlier, he had no need to make use of that boon. But when he was with Rituparna, he had to cook for a while and became quite the connoisseur. Now, he is constantly finding fault with whatever the cook makes. These days it is so difficult to find a cook. I gave so many extras to the cook you had sent me from there, I even gave him an advance for his marriage—all to make sure that he would stay here. Yesterday, he snarled at this cook saying that he had put too much fenugreek powder in the pulihora. The cook ran away in the middle of the night. Do they put fenugreek in pulihora? What would I know about such things? You brought me up indulgently and I have ended up not knowing anything. Now I have to go through all these troubles.

Can you make four or five new varieties of sweetmeats and send them to me? He pushes away all items served on his leaf. When he is going hungry, I too don't feel like eating anything. I worry constantly about trying to serve him something that he will like.

Awaiting eagerly the sweetmeats that you would be sending so affectionately to me,

Your daughter,
Damayanti

P. S.: Ask the messengers to come straight to the antappuram without being spotted by the king. If he learns that I have troubled you, it may gnaw at his heart.

II

Salutations at Mother's hallowed feet.

The messengers you sent reached here. Trays, baskets, and pots filled with paniyarams, bakshanams, panakams, and modakams were delivered. There was no need to have sent so much! I just cannot describe the pleasure I had looking at them. I derived so much joy merely gazing at them.

But what to do! Unlucky me! I was unable to please my husband.

I learnt the names of all the sweetmeats correctly from the messengers. For the last two days, we have had no cook. I tried saying that I would give half the kingdom for a cook. Everyone is terrified of cooking for *him*. I am myself doing the cooking; I don't know why the king does not come to the antappuram many more. Today I asked the maids to beseech him to come to the inner palace, and in response to that he very kindly came. I myself served him everything and eagerly awaited his praise.

'What is this?' he asked. As soon as I said 'Mysorepak', the response was 'insufficient ghee'.

'What is that?' he asked. As soon as I said 'suruvari', he said 'incorrect proportion'.

What is the use of all my prayers! He pushed aside everything. How am I to satisfy his hunger? I think the best thing would be to lose the kingdom again so that he can himself take up cooking once more. Apparently, now that he is king, it is beneath his dignity to cook.

Why do these cursed gods give boons? Can't they keep their mouths shut?

You have written that an old great-aunt has come from your natal home, and that she is giving you a lot of trouble. Wallowing in my misery, I completely forgot to write about that earlier. Send her here. I will look after her. She is sure to be of assistance to me. I have no time to look after my children. If she comes, it would be very helpful.

Your dear Damayanti.

III

Mother,

The king tried fasting for a whole month. He got sick and tired of
it. His body became emaciated. These days, he secretly cooks and
eats in the middle of the night—hunger is merciless! I am terrified
that the palace staff will get to know of this. The shame will be
unbearable. God alone knows how this is all going to end.

Your dear Damayanti.

IV

Mother,

A million salutations to you.

The ancient great-aunt has arrived. That very day I attained
freedom. She has taken over the kitchen. The king eats silently and
goes away. The reason is that one cannot figure out what it is that she
has cooked. Only if you *know* what it is can you find fault with it!

Aunt is extremely close-fisted. She does not waste any leftovers
from the previous day. Soup, spinach: everything is combined to
create a new brew. No one can make out the ingredients or the
reason for the aroma—quite impossible to guess. All through the
meal, until he washes his hands, the king silently speculates on the
origin of hitherto unknown tastes and on how the dish was cooked.

We are all quite comfortable now.

Your dear Damayanti.

Translated by Ahana Lakshmi

GOD AND KANDASAMI PILLAI

PUDUMAIPITTAN

Melakaram M. K. R. Kandasami Pillaiyavargal, otherwise known as Chellappa, only son of Melakaram M. K. Ramasami Pillaiyavargal, was standing at the junction of Broadway and Esplanade in a relatively safe corner, thinking furiously. Were he to take the tram, it would cost an anna and a quarter, leaving him with a quarter anna. He could then buy betel leaves from the stall next to the bus stop and walk home, chewing blissfully. If, on the other hand, he were to board the bus, somehow avoid the bus conductor as far as Central, and then buy a ticket to Triplicane, he could drink half a cup of coffee and go home, though he would have to forgo the betel leaves.

'When the conductor virtually pleads with me to deceive him, it really goes against the grain of dharma to disappoint him. Now if only I had given him the fare, exactly as he asked, just from Central onwards, I might have enjoyed a cup of coffee...a cup of coffee right now would certainly put life into me.' It was while Pillaiyavargal of the above mentioned town was engaged in such serious philosophical matters that God manifested Himself to him.

He didn't appear all of a sudden and stun him into a state of ecstasy by insisting, 'Here take this boon.' He merely asked, 'Ayya, how do I get to Triplicane?'

'You could take a tram, you could take a bus, or you could walk all the way by asking passers-by—the way to Madurai lies in your mouth,' answered Kandasami Pillai.

'I'm not going to Madurai, I only asked the way to Triplicane, so what is the shortest way?' asked God. Both of them doubled over with laughter.

They stepped away from the animated crowd as it pushed, jostled, and shoved, and stood to one side, near a cobbler offering shoe repairs.

Melakaram Ramasami Pillai's son and heir was forty-five years old. His build was that of one deprived of food for forty-five years, his head was covered in grey with a sprinkling of a few black hairs, his face had not been shaved for the past two weeks, his eyes were keen enough to always pick out his friends, however distant they were and in however dense a crowd. He wore a shirt of unbleached cotton and a dhoti and angavastram, a stole, of the same material.

Kandasami Pillai looked intently at the person who had asked the way. It was impossible to determine his age. He might have been sixty years old. But equally, he might have been sixty thousand years old. Anyway, he had a well set-up, even opulent figure, as if he had never had to worry about his meals in all those years.

His hair, completely grey, without a single black strand in it, had neither been combed nor tied back, but fell upon his neck like a lion's mane, spreading out on all sides. Right at the centre of his throat there was a big black swelling. His brilliant black eyes darted about sharply, in all directions. Sometimes they drooped, as if they belonged to a madman. And his smile? At times it terrified Kandasami Pillai, at times it was like that of a fond child.

'I'm terribly thirsty,' said God.

'You won't get any water-geeter here. If you want, you can have some coffee. There's a café over there, look,' replied Kandasami Pillai.

'Why don't you come with me? Let's taste and see what it's like.' Now Kandasami Pillai was a great abedavadi, one who does not differentiate. Not for him the fine distinction between himself and the Supreme. He certainly didn't bother about the trivial differences between strangers and friends.

'Very well, come on, let's go,' he said. A doubt passed through his mind: supposing he were to be stuck with the bill? But then he resolved it thus: unless one dares, there's only torment.

They went into a spacious restaurant. God followed Kandasami Pillai, trailing close behind him. They sat down at a table. Without allowing the young waiter to reel off the cafe's menu, Kandasami Pillai said, shaking his head vigorously, 'Two cup coffee, hot and strong.'

'Don't forget your Tamil. Say two *coffees*,' reminded God.

'Not so, one ought really to say two cups of coffee,' said Pillai, raising the flag for Tamil.

Outmanoeuvred, God now looked about him. 'This is a fine, tall building, there's a lot of light,' he observed.

'Well, did you expect a restaurant to be like a hen coop? I suppose you think it's as easy as building a temple? The hygiene inspectors these days won't let you do as you please, you know,' said Pillai, following up his victory smartly.

As soon as the word 'temple' fell on his ear, God began to tremble all over.

'Meaning...?' he asked, not willing to let go, even when he had lost. 'Please explain what you mean by hygiene.'

'Oh, that? It means washing down the tables with antiseptic liquid so that the inspectors don't fine you. It's also a subject that children are taught in school, in order to make them fail exams. According to it, flies and mosquitos are equal to the rakshasas of old. If such creatures enter restaurants like this, it's an absolute disaster. They say you cannot hope to escape with your life,' said Kandasami Pillai. He himself was astounded by the turn in the conversation. He began to wonder whether the Goddess Saraswati had suddenly graced his tongue.

God didn't take much notice of him, though. He was observing a fly that was caught in a puddle of coffee spilt by a previous customer. It was struggling, flailing about, straining to free itself from the sticky liquid.

'Here we are,' said God. He stretched out a finger to aid the fly. It flew away. God's finger touched the spilt coffee.

'What are you doing, Ayya, you've gone and touched someone's leavings. Here, take this water and wash your hands under the table,' urged Pillai.

God muttered to himself: *Mustn't allow flies to come in. Hygiene means you should wash your hands under the table.*

The boy brought the 'two cup coffee' and placed them on the table.

God picked up his cup and drank. A divine glow spread over his countenance, as if he had supped on soma, the heavenly drink.

'Our lila, the work of the gods,' he said.

'Nothing of the sort. It's not your lila, it's the restaurateur's lila. He's made it with a good pinch of chicory. Your lila will be necessary in the final chapter of paying the bill,' said Kandasami Pillai in God's ear. He was delighted with himself for clearing up the matter of the bill so subtly.

'And chicory powder means...?' God asked, raising his head, full of doubt.

'Chicory powder looks exactly like coffee, but it isn't. It's like people deceiving the whole world in the name of the Deity,' said Kandasami Pillai.

When he heard the word Deity, God was startled.

Then, they went to the counter to pay the bill. Kandasami Pillai was shocked as God pulled out a new hundred rupee note.

The proprietor who was at the till said, 'If it was change you wanted, wouldn't I have given it to you if you had asked? Why do I have to write out a bill for three annas? To wipe my eyes or salve your conscience?'

'We really did come here for the coffee,' said God.

'Surely you would have thought to keep some change ready, in that case,' said the manager. But because there was a long queue waiting, and because he didn't want to make trouble, he counted out the change.

'There, that's ninety-nine rupees and thirteen annas. Is that right? Please check it, Saami.'

'If you say so, I'm happy to agree; I was never good at sums,' said God.

The manager congratulated himself on having passed off a counterfeit ten rupee note.

They came out together. There wasn't such a crowd now, at the entrance. They stopped there for a moment.

God pulled out the fifth note from the stack in his hands, tore it into shreds, and flung down the pieces.

Kandasami Pillai wondered whether his companion had suddenly gone mad. He stood there aghast, his mouth wide open.

'A counterfeit note. He tried to deceive me, but I caught him out,' said God. His smile was fearful.

'If you had given it to me, I'd have caught that pappaan* by his top knot and made him change it,' said Kandasami Pillai.

'You consented to drink his chicory powder, didn't you? Let's say I agreed to this in the same way. Ten rupees is a big deal for him, that's why I allowed him his deception,' said God.

Kandasami Pillai was now embarrassed to abandon this stranger who had so graciously bought him a cup of coffee.

'You're bound for Triplicane, aren't you? Come on, let's get on the tram,' he said.

'Let's not,' said God, 'Those things make my head spin. We could walk there slowly, couldn't we?'

'Ayya, I've been on my feet all day. I can't manage a step further. Why don't we take a rickshaw instead,' suggested Kandasami Pillai. He told himself in defence, after all I'm going to show him the way, why shouldn't he pay, if he can afford to tear up ten rupee notes?

'A vehicle pulled by man? Those are the best of all,' said God.

They climbed into a rickshaw. 'Saami, wait a second, I'll light my lamp,' said the rickshaw puller.

The daylight had dimmed, now there were only electric lights.

'How quickly we have struck up a friendship! I don't know who you are and you don't know who I am. That we should meet like this, right in the middle of the city's commotion...'

God laughed. His teeth gleamed beautifully. 'Never mind who I am for the moment. Tell me about yourself.'

Kandasami Pillai always took a special delight in speaking about himself. Was he likely to miss an opportunity like this, when he had a captive audience within the rickshaw? He cleared his throat and began.

---

*Derogatory form of addressing or referring to a Brahman.

'Have you ever seen a medical journal known as the *Siddha Vaidya Dipika*?' he asked.

'No,' said God.

'Then I take it you are not familiar with the *Vaidya Sastras*, the classical medical treatises,' remarked Kandasami Pillai.

'I am familiar with them,' said God.

This is really embarrassing, thought Kandasami Pillai to himself. Aloud he said, 'Let us agree that you are familiar with the *Vaidya Sastras*, but that you don't know the *Siddha Vaidya Dipika*. If that's the case, I must say that your knowledge of the medical treatises is not complete. I have all the issues of the past seventeen years at home, in bound volumes. I have to insist that you come sometime and read the lot. Only then can you...'

All the issues of seventeen years! Twelve times seventeen is 204. God quailed at the idea. A fond hope came to him. Perhaps it is a quarterly?

'The *Dipika* is a monthly magazine. The yearly subscription within the country is one rupee, two and three quarters for countries abroad. A life subscription will cost you twenty-five rupees. If you become a life subscriber, you'll find it really handy. If you like, I can send it to you on trial for the first year. After that we'll consider a life subscription,' said Kandasami Pillai, trying his best to persuade God.

Does he think he can force me to read all seventeen volumes, collect twenty-five rupees on top of that, and then drive me out? I shall never allow that, thought God. Then he asked, 'Whose life, by the way?'

'Your life, of course. Not mine. Nor the journal's, it is indestructible. Even when I am gone, someone else will take it up and run it, all arrangements have been made for that,' said Kandasami Pillai.

Just at that moment, the rickshaw puller slackened his pace and looked back over his shoulder.

Kandasami Pillai was afraid that if the rickshaw slowed down, the other passenger might jump out and run away.

'Why are you turning around, da? There's a car coming at you, don't crash into it. Go on, quickly,' said Kandasami Pillai.

The rickshaw puller said, 'What Saami, are you both men or ghosts? The vehicle feels as light as the wind, as if there are no passengers in it.'

'We'll also give you a fare that's as light as the wind, if you don't watch out. Go on, just pull the rickshaw,' Kandasami Pillai scolded. Then he went on, 'Besides, I'm also a practitioner of medicine. I deal only in Siddha medicines and methods. What I make out of it just barely covers the costs of running both the journal and my family. In the current issue, I've written an article about rasakattu, the use of mercury in medicine. You see, I came across an old palm leaf manuscript which explains many rare usages.'

What's this, thought God. It doesn't look as if our friend is ever going to stop. Then he asked, 'How many people do you treat on an average, each day?'

'Not so many that I can brag about it. Keep in mind that I make my livelihood from medicine. The illness mustn't go away altogether, nor must the fellow be finished off. It's only in that way that the patient's illness can be maintained as a means of income. If you go for an aggressive treatment thinking it's got to be either the patient or the disease, you won't have viable employment. The illness must come down gradually and then be cured, and at the same time, the medicine mustn't cause any harm either to the man or to the disease. That's the way of commerce. Otherwise would I have been able to run the journal for these seventeen years?' asked Kandasami Pillai.

God nodded as if he understood all this.

'Come, let me check your pulse,' Kandasami Pillai went on, taking hold of God's right hand.

'What, while this vehicle is actually moving?' God laughed.

'All that depends on the doctor's skill,' explained Kandasami Pillai.

He listened carefully to God's pulse for some time, and then remarked with some concern, 'Your pulse rate indicates a high bile content. Are you in the habit of taking poisonous substances?'

'You really are a clever fellow. Yes, you'll find all kinds of things in here,' laughed God.

'Well, I've been talking away about all sorts of things. Never mind all that, where are you bound for, in Triplicane?'

'Number seven, Office, Venkatachala Mudali Lane,' said God.

'Adede! But that's my address. Who did you want to see there?'

'Kandasami Pillai.'

'Here's a fine thing! I'm that very person. You see, it's the Deity who has brought us together. And who are you, sir? I don't think I recognize you...' said Kandasami Pillai.

'Who, me? I am God,' said God casually, taking his time. He looked up at the sky and stroked his beard.

Kandasami Pillai was startled out of his wits. God? Here?

'I came to visit the earth, I'd like to be your guest for a few days.'

Kandasami Pillai spoke with agitation. 'Please stay as long as you wish, I have no objection at all. Only, please don't tell everyone that you are God. It doesn't matter if others take you for a madman but my wife mustn't take me for one.'

Then he said to the rickshaw puller, 'Just stop by the streetlight, da.'

The rickshaw stopped. They climbed down.

God took a crackling clean, bright, one rupee note and handed it to the rickshaw puller.

The man, his heart filled with satisfaction, said 'May you be well, Saami.'

He was blessing God! Really!

'Watch it, da. Is it your business to bless a respected elder?' said Kandasami Pillai, speaking sharply.

'What if he does,' God remarked. Then he said, 'You speak well, Appa. It's many days since I heard such words, words so comforting to my ear and heart.'

'You might have heard different words if you had given him two annas less,' said Kandasami Pillai.

'Sir, I only care about what is just. I don't bother about what's unfair. Saami, you'll always find me sitting at that particular spot.

Look out for me if you are in that vicinity.'

'You only care about what is just! I know all about it, da. Go away, you only care about the toddy shop.'

'You'd know about it if you had run about all day in the hot sun, pulling this rented vehicle. What can I say to you? God has no eyes, he allows you to speak such words, and makes me listen to them.'

God burst out into loud laughter. He laughed and laughed. He was happy, at ease.

'Well, well, such is this world,' said Kandasami Pillai.

'Is that all it is?' asked God.

They walked on to the house.

As they came up to the lamp post just in front of the house, God stopped.

Kandasami Pillai too stopped and waited.

'Bhakta!' said God.

There was no longer an old man standing there.

God revealed himself in his tiger skin, his matted locks, with his deer and his axe and his crescent moon. His eyes shone with ecstatic joy. There was a smile on his lips.

'Bhakta,' he said once more.

Kandasami Pillai understood it all in an instant.

'Oi, God, I'm not going to be taken in by your tricks of throwing boons at me. I know you, you'll grant me a boon and push off on your business. After that another deity is likely to come along and demand my head. I'm not such an easily fooled simpleton as to accept a boon from you and voluntarily put my head in danger. All right, so you came down to have a look at the world, you wanted to be my guest. I don't have any objection whatever, to any of that. But if you want to move around with me, then you must behave like a man, like me, in fact. You must stay within the limits of human behaviour. Now please come into my house properly, keeping in mind what I've just told you,' Kandasami Pillai said.

Silent, God followed him. He thought that Kandasami Pillai's argument was fair enough. It struck him that truly there was no answer to the question; who on earth, in all this time, has received a divine boon and profited by it?

Kandasami Pillai stopped again at the threshold of the house.

'Swami, what name should I give you? Paramasivan or Ammaiyappa Pillai?'

'Paramasivan would be right. Paramasivan the elder.'

'Well then, I shall call you Appa, as if you were in the position of a father to me, please agree to this, too.'

'Don't do that, call me "Periappa", that is, "Uncle". My property won't be in any danger then,' said God, laughing. Since he had decided to act according to the ways of the world, he thought he ought to be somewhat prudent.

'So what is this wonderful property of yours?' asked Kandasami Pillai.

'Only the entire universe,' said God.

'You don't need to worry, I'm not as greedy as all that.' Saying so, Kandasami Pillai climbed the front steps of his house.

⌒

A single lamp burning in the front room made it the sanctum sanctorum of the house. Beyond that lay the long, darkened central hall. What lay further? A small child, looking to be about four years old, was playing in the front room. Her beauty was such that it filled the onlooker with joy. Her eyes seemed to sparkle with perpetual happiness, and for no particular reason. She stood there pulling at her hair which hung in two rat tails fore and aft, plaited from a crosswise parting in the old-fashioned way. The banana fibre which had been used to tie the front plait had slipped; it fell into her eyes, bothering her as she bent down. She had a piece of coal and a broken tile in her hands. A ragged skirt hung from her waist, reaching down to her knees. She had been trying to draw lines upon the floor, but had straightened up to tug at the bothersome banana fibre with both hands as hard as she could. She wasn't successful; it hurt her. As she was deciding whether she should cry or tug at it one more time, her father came in.

'Appa,' she shouted, flinging her arms round Kandasami Pillai's knees. She looked up at him and asked, 'What have you brought me?'

'I've only brought myself,' said Kandasami Pillai.

'What's this, Appa, every day you only bring yourself. Couldn't you at least bring some fried gram?' the child pestered.

'Fried gram isn't good for you. But look, I've brought you a grandfather.'

'Is this your daughter?' asked God. He simply couldn't take his eyes off her.

Kandasami Pillai hesitated.

'Say what's in your mind. These days I'm a complete vegetarian. I only like what is cooked in a mud pot. I don't even take milk or curd,' smiled God.

Kandasami Pillai said, 'She is like a curry leaf sprig that sprouted long past the season, just to give us joy.' Then he disappeared into the darkness, saying, 'Come and sit here. There won't be any water in the tap at this time, I'll go and fetch some in a water pot.'

God took off his upper cloth, shook it, and laid it down on the floor of the front room and sat down. His mind was full of a certain liveliness, and a profound peace at the same time.

He held out his arms, saying, 'Come here, little one, come here you little curry leaf sprig!'

In one leap she came and clambered into his lap.

'My name isn't curry leaf sprig, it's Valli. Only Appa sometimes calls me Darkie. Why, do you think I'm so dark?'

She didn't expect an answer. Her eyes fell on the dark swelling on the thaatha's throat.

'What's that in your throat, Thaatha, black as anything, just like a jamun fruit? I want to eat it up.' Her eyes blinked as she spoke. And now she stood up in his lap and pressed her flower-like lips into his neck. Her tiny teeth tickled him. God shivered all over.

'I feel ticklish,' said God, pulling away.

'What happened, Thaatha? Did some fire-gire touch you and

burn you? Look it happened to me too.' She held out her finger, with a darkened scab at its tip.

'Paapa, it is really a jamun fruit. Once long ago, some people gave it to me, so I accepted it and put it in my mouth. But some others came and grabbed me by the throat demanding their share. Since then, it just got stuck there. But never mind that. Don't you have any friends to play with?'

'But I have this tile, haven't I, and this piece of coal? Will you come and play hopscotch with me?'

The child and God began to play.

One leg bent right back, hopping on the other, God took a flying leap.

The child clapped her hands and laughed out loud.

'Thaatha, you've gone and lost!'

'How?' said God

She pointed out that his foot had touched a black line.

'Couldn't you have told me right at the start?' asked God.

The child asked, arms akimbo, 'Should you say you'd play when you don't know the rules?'

At that moment, Sri and Srimati Kandasami Pillai emerged from the darkness, Srimati following Sri, the water pot at her waist.

'This is my Periappa from Kailasavaram. You remember the girl from Karisangkulam was given in marriage to the son of his first cousin once removed? Can you make out who it is?'

'Oh, it's that maama, isn't it, who became a sadhu and disappeared on his pilgrimages? Welcome, Maama, let me greet you,' she said, and setting down her water pot, she fell at his feet, making a full obeisance. The old-fashioned heavy ear ornaments, the paampadam, swung against her cheeks.

God blessed her with the words, 'May you and your children live long, in good health and prosperity.'

Kantimatiammai—this was Kandasami Pillai's wife's name—felt a sense of total contentment such as she had never experienced before.

God asked as if reminding Kandasami Pillai discreetly, 'are you going to leave the sack of rice right there, in front of the house?'

'I just can't tell you how forgetful he is,' Kantimati exclaimed. 'I asked him a moment ago whether he had bought the rice. He said he hadn't remembered to buy it. He dispenses medicines to the whole town, only he hasn't got a medicine for his own forgetfulness. The god who created him should stand next to him and look upon him.'

'I am sure he is standing by him and looking upon him,' said God, putting on a rural accent.

'Well then, perhaps he should look upon him and laugh. Perhaps he'll come to his senses then.'

God laughed.

God and Kandasami Pillai went towards the entrance of the house.

'I told you I didn't want any conjuring tricks,' Kandasami Pillai whispered.

'No more after this,' said God.

Kandasami Pillai heaved and shoved as hard as he could, the sack wouldn't shift.

'A fine young man you are!' said God laughing, as he picked up the sack and tucked it against his waist.

'No, no you mustn't pick it up,' said Kantimati in some agitation. Then, to her husband, 'Look here, I'm talking to you, can't you at least give a hand with it. You're just looking on and doing nothing.'

'Don't bother, Amma,' said God, 'just tell me where I should put it.'

'Just let it lie here in the front room. Just put it down,' said Kantimati, intercepting him.

By the time God and Kandasami Pillai had eaten, and returned to the thinnai in the front veranda, it was eleven o'clock.

'What is your plan now?' asked God.

'Only to sleep,' said Pillai, yawning.

The child came running up and said, 'Thaatha, I'm going to lie down next to you.'

'Go and ask your mother to spread out the mats and pillows,' said Kandasami Pillai.

'Are you telling me to go to sleep too?' asked God.

'If you are going to move around with human beings then you must do as they do. If you don't like to sleep, just lie down quietly. Otherwise, you'll earn a bad reputation because of your goings-on at night,' said Kandasami Pillai.

Kandasami Pillai sat on the floor of the *Siddhanta Dipika* office in Pavazhakkaara Street, writing out a detailed textual commentary. A commentary on Boganathar's Treatise was being serialised each month and published in Pillai's journal. He wrote the final words, 'And here is one last thing. To boiling water, add such medicinal plants as garudapicchu, kalluruvi, pulluruvi, and unmatthai which you might have at hand (garudapicchu can also be read as garudapacchai)....' He watched the postman go past his door without coming in and muttered, 'The journal won't go out today either.' He rolled up and put away what he had just written, then flexed his fingers.

A rickshaw came to a stop at his door. God and the little one got out. Valli was wearing a silk skirt, and a paper package of sweets filled her little hands.

The child jumped up and down. 'Thaatha and I have been all around the zoo and the natural history museum.'

'Why do they build a mansion, oi, just to house bundles of skin and bone? Are they wanting to ridicule me or what?' asked God. There was a certain severity of tone in his voice.

'Do you think people have the wit to think it through like that? No, no, they've arranged things in that way because they imagine they are demonstrating the uniqueness of creation. Let that be. Just hand me twenty-five rupees, will you? I'll make you a subscriber for life. The journal must go out today.'

'Who do you think you are fooling? For whose good is it supposed to be?' laughed God, referring to the subscription.

'I don't wish to accept charity, and I certainly don't want to get into debt, that's why I'm saying, let it be a commercial deal. You talk big about Goodness. In this world everything—from ghee to

sesame oil—is adulterated. Don't you know that much?' Kandasami
Pillai hit out.

God was plunged into deep thought.

Kandasami Pillai went on, 'Anyway, let that be. You know Bogar
mentions a garudapacchai, is there a medicinal herb by that name,
or is it meant to be garudapicchu?'

'My responsibility lies only in creating a thing, but you seem to
be charging me with naming it as well. Is that fair? What do I know
about it? I created you, your father named you Kandasami Pillai. So
am I to be blamed for that?' countered God sharply.

'You two have been wandering about in the heat of the day
and that seems to have roused your temper. Don't reprimand me
and put me down on account of that. My only concern is that if
you go and curse me now on a sudden impulse, then twenty-five
rupees might go down the drain unnecessarily.'

The child meanwhile, had undone the packet and was eating the
sweets. 'Why are you talking to Appa, Thaatha? Just taste this and
see, it's as sweet as anything.'

God took and ate small pieces of the laddus that she offered
him. He said, 'Little one, the broken bits are for me, the whole
laddus are for you.'

The child took out a laddu, held it in her hand, and thought
for some time.

'Thaatha, the whole ones won't go into my mouth. But you say
all the broken bits are for you. So is there nothing for me?'

God laughed and laughed. 'It's all for you and only for you.'

'All of it? For me?' she asked.

'Oh yes. For you, and you alone.'

'But then I won't be hungry later! Amma will beat me if I
don't eat my dinner. Appa will give me yucky lehiyam.' The child
was anxious.

'You are sure to be hungry later. Don't worry,' said God.

'While it is true you bought it, all the same it is restaurant food.
Bear that in mind,' Kandasami Pillai cautioned.

'But I am here with you!' said God.

'Did I ever say you weren't?' replied Kandasami Pillai. A few minutes later, he asked, 'How much is left of your hundred rupees, after your expenses of today?'

'Well after I've given you twenty-five, I shall have fifty rupees left,' said God, smiling.

'So what do you plan to do, after that?'

'That's what I don't know, either.'

'You could practise medicine, like me.'

'I have no wish to enter into competition with you.'

'Please don't think of it like that. You would not be in competition with me, but with the world's folly. Still if you don't care for that idea, you could give lectures on Siddhanta philosophy.'

'You are trying to counsel me on a means of livelihood. Would I really make any cash that way?' laughed God.

'So what then?'

'You know, I can dance very well. What do you think? If necessary, I could contrive to have Devi with me as well.'

Kandasami Pillai thought for a while. 'Somehow, I don't care for the idea,' he said.

'So how else am I to survive? Come on. After all, the entire universe survives only through our dance.'

'As you wish,' said Kandasami Pillai. He thought for a little while longer. 'Come let's go,' he then said, taking his upper cloth from the nail on which it hung, shaking it out, and putting it on.

'The little one…' said God.

'She's fast asleep, let her be until we return,' said Pillai.

A quarter of an hour later, three people entered the mansion belonging to Diwan Bahadur Brihadisvara Sastrigal. One was Kandasami Pillai, another was God. The third was a woman, Devi.

'I make thangapaspam for him, a medicinal powder of gold turned into ash, on a regular basis. He'll certainly listen to me if I ask for a favour.' Pillai was explaining all this at length as he climbed up the steps to the front veranda. The other two followed him. There was a small bundle in Devi's hands.

Kandasami Pillai spoke with authority to the servant. 'Is Saami at home? Tell him I've come to visit him.'

Diwan Bahadur, affable in speech, his shrivelled body clad in a fine cotton dhoti and upper cloth, and wearing gold rimmed spectacles, was hastening towards them. 'Oh, is it Pillaiyavargal? Please come in, come in. The powder was finished with yesterday's dose. I was getting really anxious because you hadn't turned up.' The apparition greeted everybody effusively, and seated itself in an easy chair.

'Please sit down, do sit down,' invited Diwan Bahadur.

Kandasami Pillai felt Diwan Bahadur's pulse and said, 'Not bad. I'll have the medicine sent round this evening. But the reason for my visit is actually to introduce these two to you. Between them they are an absolute ocean of knowledge concerning the *Natya Sastra*. If you could arrange for them to dance in your Nritya Kalamandali, it would suit them very well.'

All Diwan Bahadur's enthusiasm suddenly withdrew like a tortoise's head and feet into its shell. He joined his hands together, placed forefingers and thumbs against his nose and chin respectively and nodded his head, muttering, 'Mm...mm.'

'This gentleman's name is Kuthanaar, the lady's name is Parvati. They are a married couple.' Kandasami Pillai explained.

'I don't recognize the names. Have you given any performances before this?' The Diwan Bahadur addressed the question to Kuthanaar, but kept his gaze on Devi.

Devi answered, without giving God an opportunity to open his mouth, 'There isn't a place where we haven't danced.'

'Somehow it hasn't come to my notice. Never mind. But the lady appears to be very dark, it seems to me she may not show up very well to the audience,' remarked the colour conscious Diwan Bahadur.

'Are you interested in looking for a bride, or did you want to see us dance?' asked Devi.

'Amma, don't be annoyed. But listen, let me tell you something. It is true there is no correspondence at all between culture and colour, except that the two words begin with the same sound. But I've been president of the Kalamandali for thirty years. I know when the eyes of the spectators darken with displeasure.'

Devi made as if to go, saying, 'You are welcome to keep your mandali and your sundeli.'

'Please don't get angry,' cried Kandasami Pillai and the Diwan Bahadur, rising to their feet together.

Once again Kandasami Pillai spoke up in their favour. 'These two can dance in completely new modes. It's impossible to see such virtuosity in these parts. The Sastras themselves are put to shame by them. Why don't you see them perform, just once?'

'Very well, I'll see them perform. What objection can there be to that,' and the Diwan Bahadur lay back in his chair. 'Well, all right then, let them dance,' he said, and shut his eyes.

Devi stood up and said, 'Where's a good, wide space?'

'Why not go into the central hall?' asked God. They agreed to this, went in, and shut the doors. Within a few minutes a melody sounded, sung in a majestic voice, clear as a bell.

He is Rudra of the cremation ground
He is Rudra...

The doors opened.

God stood there, still as a statue, eyes closed, clad in tiger skin, the trident in his hand, his locks of hair entwined with snakes, Ganga tumbling through them.

Once again, that music. As he turned his neck sharply, in a swift movement as if the tangles in a bolt of lightning were being shaken out, the trident in God's hand sparkled and leapt, with his eyes full of frenzy, a smile playing upon his lips, he raised his foot.

Kandasami Pillai was extremely uneasy at heart. Thinking that God had surely forgotten the promise he had made, he rose to his feet in his anxiety.

'Oi, Kuthanaar, stop your dance for a while.'

Then the Diwan Bahadur began to remonstrate. 'Chut! This is nothing more than a street performance. What's this? And what sort of ridiculous costume is this, you look like the Wild Man of Borneo.'

God stopped in the very pose that he had assumed, and stood leaning against his trident.

The Diwan Bahadur continued, 'Oi, do you know anything at all about Art? You've gone and tied a real tiger skin about yourself. Does anyone go and bring a real snake on to the stage? You should wear a snake ornament, for goodness' sake! You need a piece of silk that looks like a tiger skin. The first thing you should know about Art is that it should look pleasant to the eye. Even if Parvati and Parameswaran themselves were to carry on like this, it won't be in accordance with *Natya Sastra* rules. This is not what the Sastras tell you to do. First take off all those snakes and put them away carefully in their basket, and then get rid of your costumes. Watch out now, this is a place where little children play.'

He didn't let Kandasami Pillai get away lightly either. 'Look Pillaivaal, just because you prepare certain medicines for me, it doesn't mean that I'm obliged to watch this stuff, and you certainly may not book a performance. I have to maintain a position in public, haven't I?'

Yet another quarter of an hour later, two people were sitting together at the *Siddha Vaidya Dipika* office, without Devi. The child was still asleep on her mat.

Both were silent for a while. Then, God said, 'It looks as if it is impossible to survive in this world by doing the work one truly knows.'

'You didn't appreciate what I told you, neither did the world appreciate what is dear to you. Well, why don't you try your hand at running Tevaram classes?'

God made a sound of repugnance, 'Chut!'

'Has the world gone sour on you already?'

'Having seen you is like having seen the world,' said God.

'And what of my having seen you?' laughed Kandasami Pillai.

'It's all very well to grant you people boons from a distance. It's impossible to live amongst you,' declared God.

'True, your sort are fit only for that,' said Kandasami Pillai.
There was nobody to reply to that.

On the table lay twenty-five single rupee notes, a life subscription.

Kandasami Pillai wrote in his account, 'Income, Rupees twenty-five, a life subscription in the name of Paramasivan Pillai, the elder of Kailasavaram.'

The child sat up, asking, 'Has Thaatha gone back to his hometown, Appa?'

Translated by Lakshmi Holmström

THE FAMILY CHARIOT

MAUNI

One day, at about three o'clock in the afternoon, Krishnayyar sat in the rezhi, his living room, writing down the daily accounts which he had neglected for the past five days.

He was perhaps fifty-two or fifty-three years old. A man of robust health, and prosperous and well-respected, he was considered by the villagers to be an ideal man, a man to emulate in the way he presided over his family and dealt with the outside world.

It was now a month since his mother had died after a brief illness. For the old woman, her eighty years of life had not exactly been a bed of flowers. She had been born into a wealthy family and then had come to live in a large one after her marriage. This had protected her from certain worries. All the same, her life had not been free of such experiences as the loss of a child, anxieties from time to time that the family might fall into ruin, and other such problems. Yet she had accepted it all serenely. The natural good sense and wisdom with which she had conducted her family's affairs had been like a bright light that filled the house.

Krishnayyar reminded himself of the expenses, writing them down one by one: the amount paid to the farmhands, that given to the labourer for his toddy, the carpenter's fee, the Amavaasai offerings for the dead, given three days ago on the night of the new moon, the sum he had owed for the street procession of the deity. Yes, everything had been accounted for, yet he was three and a quarter annas short. Without hesitation, his practised hand wrote, 'Amma's expenses…0.3.3' and balanced the accounts.

He looked at what he had just written. As if suddenly aware of its meaning, his eyes welled up, two teardrops falling on to the accounts book. He wiped them off absentmindedly. The last line he had written, 'Amma's expenses…0.3.3', not yet dry, got smudged and left a stain on the paper.

It was an old habit of his—if ever he was left with a small sum of money that he could not account for, and if, after he had scratched his head and pressed the cap of his pen against his nose, he still could not remember what it had been spent on, he would note the amount down as 'Amma's expenses'.

Before coming to sit on the swing in the main room for his coffee, he always pulled the doors together and locked them, then pushed against them twice to make sure they were secure. His mother would be lying down in the hall, next to the stone used for grinding sandalwood, lost in her own thoughts. After he had drunk the coffee his wife brought him, he would chew on his betel leaf and then say, 'Amma, today your expenses came to one anna.' From within the house his wife's laughter would be heard. As for his mother, though she had grown hard of hearing, she would hear well enough what he had just said. 'Very well! We all know that I am a birdbrain. I forget where I put things. But, what about you? Shouldn't you check on your own expenses? Because I am here, you can put it all on me, blame me. You're old enough now to shoulder the family responsibilities.' She would always come round to that. Krishnayyar was a peaceful man by nature. Yet there were times when his mother's words would make him very angry. 'Oh yes! The way you carry on, one would think the whole family has gone to ruin.' She would then say, 'We've got to have the means in the first place, da, everything follows after that. Do what you like. I say what I say because of what falls upon my ears.' By this time her eyes would have filled with tears of distress. But if you were to see mother and son a little while later, you would see them talking together and hear the chatter of a happy family in conversation!

Yes, his mother's expenses had been a mere three and a quarter annas. In front of him, the notebook lay on the table, outspread, staring at him. Although his tears had dried, his heart continued to melt within him. The supporting wall of the family had crumbled. As her substitute, was he capable of bearing the weight? It was a pity, he thought, that he could not leave the routine affairs of the family to the next generation, and take up that unique position that his mother had occupied. His eldest son had finished his studies, but was concerned only about finding a job. The others were still quite young. As for his wife…she was such a simpleton!

He rose all of a sudden, and went inside. The whole house seemed desolate. His wife placed his coffee beside him. It was as if everything was happening in a dream world. The space next to the sandalwood grinding stone stood empty. He finished the coffee and began chewing on his betel leaf. When his wife came to take away the coffee things, he was still sitting there, looking straight ahead of him, as if gazing into nothingness. The lamp was hanging in the hall, without its chimney. Having picked up the vessels, his wife was about to leave the room, when she noticed him and remarked, 'It's been three days since the glass broke. You keep forgetting, however often I tell you.'

It was true. She had been saying this for the past three days. Her words had made no impression at all on Krishnayyar. But if it had been his mother speaking—what if he had forgotten then? His mind was swamped with all sorts of thoughts. Four years ago, in the sudden upsurge of devotion that they tended to experience intermittently, some of the townsfolk had gathered together and planned a night of devotional singing at the Perumal temple on Ekadashi. The lamp from Krishnayyar's house went on loan for the occasion. His mother had not been told about this. That evening, while he was eating his dinner, she sat by the pillar, making a light meal. Krishnayyar began to speak without even being aware of it, the words breaking out with the same force that had suppressed them till then, 'Amma, they wanted the lamp at the temple for….' Before he could finish, his mother said, 'Yes, give away everything! After all, why do we buy anything? Is it not just to lose it?' He had felt a little angry then. At the same time, he had wondered whether she was not right, after all. Why had he spoken to her about it in the first place? After all, she had only commented on what he told her. It was an odd thing, that—his informing his mother about all matters. But what could you really fault? Everything was right in its own way. Suppose his mother had not known about the loan, or that he had not bothered to inform her...but to run the family in such a way would have been ruinous! He was aware of his mother's sense of responsibility and understood that there had been nothing wrong in her words. So he had not said anything further then. The next day, when the lamp was returned, the glass chimney was cracked—the tanpura, when it was being held upright to be tuned, had struck the lamp. He had told his mother about this too. As if she could read his mind, she had comforted him, 'Never mind. It's a trifle in the service of the gods. Buy another one this evening.' It was this cracked chimney that had been there till recently. He gazed at the naked lamp that hung before him, stirring up memories of his mother.

He got up and went into the inner room. The accounts book had been closed and placed on his desk. He sat down on the chair beside it. The cowherd drove the cattle through the front gate and left, calling out, 'Amma, tie up the animals.'

He remembered now that he had not locked the front doors. A western breeze blew the dust in through them. Insects flew out from the stocked harvested paddy into the house, swarming about his face. He did not even notice them. The shutters of the windows banged in the wind. On windy days, his mother would say, 'You'll get aches all over your body. Sleep in the rezhi.' She herself hardly slept during the night. She was old, hard of hearing. When the coconut thatching on the hall roof rattled in the wind, she would call out, 'Who is it...who?' Then, realizing what the noise was, she'd lapse into silence. In the middle of the night, imaginary sounds would somehow reach her finer awareness. She would not be satisfied then by simply calling out, 'Who is it?' To drive away her night-time fears with the banging of her walking stick, she'd get up and walk about, groping at things in the darkness until she had reassured herself and could return to sleep. The cold of the December months never bothered her. She would wake up at dawn and, muttering a sloka under her breath, would begin to work, sprinkling cow dung in the backyard, right up to the entrance, as if she were purifying the whole house.

For Krishnayyar, the grief caused by her death was almost unbearable. He realized that his mother—now lost—had enabled him to run the family affairs without any worry, and he could not see how anybody else could take her place nor how he could possibly manage without her. If he were to take her place himself, then his heirs should assume his own responsibilities. And there was no one who could do that. And even if there were, would he be as good a guardian of the family as his mother had been? At night she would always be in the hall, sitting there in the half-light of the oil lamp. When she heard the children tormenting their mother, she would call them to her side and tell them stories. Often she would worry about them growing thin and upbraid her daughter-in-law. As he wondered again and again whether he could care for them all like that, he realized that the entire house had been filled with a sense of his mother's presence. Whenever he thought of her absence, he became even more aware of his weaknesses. His mother, who had been a touchstone for him, enabling him to present himself to the world as a wise man, had now left him forever.

Krishnayyar rose and locked the door and went to the backyard where the carpenter was still at work. One of the cows, not yet tethered within the shed, had been eating its bran for the past half hour. Whenever his mother used to say, 'The cattle have arrived, tie them up,' he had wondered nonchalantly, 'Why does she always say that unnecessarily? As if they wouldn't do it!' Now the importance of her words appeared self-evident. The manservant was washing his clothes in the backyard, at his leisure. His wife was lying down, somewhere inside the house.

When Krishnayyar returned to the backyard after tying up the cattle, the carpenter was sitting about idly, chewing betel nut. He reprimanded the carpenter, and then sat down there, facing the rear entrance to the house. He had to keep an eye on the front door, even when he was supervising work in the backyard. He reminded himself of how he had, till recently, been able to leave the house without any worries, and how his mother had always been ready with a retort or an answer for all those who came and went.

He had often spoken of her as being old-fashioned. But it was not so. It was not that she could not see the advancement of civilization nor people's progress along with it. The difference lay in the way she understood and made use of these things. Modernity could not show its force to her, nor attack her brutally at animal speed, as if her mind were a vacant space. She was, after all, the embodiment of certain customs and ideals which had been painstakingly nurtured through endless generations, softened and smoothed by experience. It was not the notion of progress that flowed at a violent speed through open spaces and valleys that gained her approval, but rather one that was modest, beautiful, quiet. Was it possible for families to accept or practise raw notions which were thrust upon them too suddenly, or customs and habits which were not seasoned?

But no one had known better than her, the best aspects of the modern progressive world. Long ago, upon her urging, they had bought a clock that struck each hour. Actually, it was not of the slightest use to her. The shadow that fell across the front yard was her means of measuring the passage of time. At night she observed the movement of the stars. She knew very well how many hours had to pass before sunrise. But after they had bought the clock, many people would come by, to ask the time. Her satisfaction lay in that. She would tell the children, from an early age, about the family's honour and prestige. Passing on old memories as she sat by the pedestal lamp, telling the little ones ancient tales hidden in the cloak of time and beyond understanding…the way her aunt's grandmother was…how her eldest uncle ran away to Kasi…she had nourished their minds with healthy notions of self-worth and family regard as if she were feeding them milk!

It was now evening. He locked the back door and returned to the thinnai in the veranda. At that instant a distant relative arrived on a condolence visit. Krishnayyar felt his throat choking as he spoke to him. The visitor was taken aback. 'What is this Krishna? You're like a child pining for his mother. Where is your famous strength of mind?'

But only Krishnayyar knew who, hidden within the house, had been the reason for all the virtues for which the outside world knew him.

After the relative had left, Krishnayyar sighed at the uselessness of thinking any further. His grief was not merely that of a child that had lost its mother. His mind tossed about restlessly. He had been given a high goal to achieve—he had to shoulder the responsibilities for the whole family and hand them over to those who would come after him. He knew that it is the family that is the foundation of society, and that the notion of family and family life would always be painfully associated with his mother in his mind. With great clarity he realized that it was because of the lack of peace within the family that the world was falling into ruin and decay. The responsibility of the family did not rest on any one person alone. Nor was it easy for a single person to bear it. On the other hand it could not rest with them all. Then it would be the beginning of disorder. He had just been nominally responsible for the family. It was only by discussing everything with his mother and listening to her advice that he had managed to act as the head of the family. What a wonderful device then, this thing that we call family!

Gradually, the evening grew dark. Krishnayyar went outside and stood by the canal to say his evening prayers, and returned home. He lay back against the sloping plank in the thinnai, tapping on one of the pillars with his foot. He muttered a prayer automatically but his mind was chanting something else, something that was unintelligible. Above his head, in a niche in the wall, a little lamp shone with an auspicious radiance. He lay there thus for a long time. He did not realize that his wife had come out and taken away the lamp. He woke up with a start when his youngest child called out to him, 'Appa, it's getting late. Come and eat.'

Krishnayyar went out into the street, made a brief obeisance to

Perumal, then went in at last and locked the door. A great burden had dropped away from his mind, and he had actually gained strength. The future seemed easy. He felt infinite joy. Unfathomable, his thoughts raced, 'A family is a wonderful mechanism. It does not come to a standstill because one part of it is damaged, but of its own accord creates another part to take place of the impaired one.'

Translated by Lakshmi Holmström

THE DOOR CLOSES

C. S. CHELLAPPA

Tomorrow! Tomorrow I will be set free. Not that this has happened out of the blue. Oh, no! The months, weeks, days, hours, minutes, why, even the seconds, have measured themselves out meticulously before bringing me here. And now that moment approaches…that lightning moment that will set me free forever. Throughout one's lifetime, Death repeats the same message that falls like hammer blows on one's ear: one day I will come for you. I have that feeling now.

On the opposite wall, the days, bundled into months, marked and crossed out, stand row upon orderly row. One final slash cleaves the array from top to bottom leaving them darkened and dead. A mere stub of a pencil begged from someone…that is what has made the days bearable. It has wiped out time, day by day, on my wall. How slowly time passes. Does a child in the womb grow faster than this? Or slower?

That first day. The memory of it is firmly implanted in my mind. I marked it as Day One. Day Two, Day Three…all the days thereafter are planted out in rows.

Today is Day 165—the day before Day 166! A little child could tell you that. But no child can ever tell you about the relationship between me and that number. This was the last night those markings on the wall would warn me, 'Be careful! You are a prisoner.' Tomorrow night will have the honour, the privilege, of being the first night of my freedom.

The door is locked. This is no ordinary iron door. It can speak even without a mouth. It has been practising for countless years. It can speak the language of the warders, but it knows the language of the prisoners too. The first time I set foot in that prison block, it growled its trademark growl in greeting. That was how Day One began.

'Hey, you! Number 623...move. Go!' it rasped. As a prisoner, I knew its language well. I knew what it was telling me. I laughed softly. Let me get through these last few days, I thought. Why should I hurt it now with words? 'After tomorrow, you will not have to take the responsibility of guarding me,' I said humbly. 'I'm sorry for all the time you had to put up with me.' The very next moment, the door clanged its mouth shut like an enraged rakshasa. I was about to move out of its grasp. It's only natural, isn't it, to resent one's meal being snatched away?

I sat down on my bed. Yes, *my* bed. Who can deny me ownership of this bed? After all, I received it with my own two hands. And what immense satisfaction it brought! No other bed has ever given me the peace of mind that this one has. That rough sack...wait, wait, one should not be so rude...the bedding made of jute fibre instead of cotton, and the blanket with its myriad holes and its sickly stale odour.... But why go into such details now?

Bed, blanket—these things have been given names. They belong to me, only me. If I had wanted to, I could have torn them up and cast them away. I had the freedom, the right, to do that. But then, I could be given penalty points adding an extra week or ten days to my sentence. No, I will hoard every day I can save. And my plate and tumbler? Those too I will treat well. Who knows how many other owners all these things are destined to have in here? Let them live out the full span of their natural lives. I will not be the one to cut short their existence.

As for these clothes I'm wearing, these too are all mine. If I'd been careless with them they could have been torn and discarded, making them useless to anyone else. This is not attire that bestows pride on the wearer. This is prison garb. In the world outside, people would hesitate to wear them even if they are donated for free. Most likely, they would reject such a gift. But I wear my prison clothes with pride, because they are mine. In fact, if they would allow me (which they won't) I would unhesitatingly wear them outside these walls. Let anyone dare to come up to me and say, 'You're a jailbird.'

Let's see what happens then!

These clothes were not made for me. It's like I was made for them. Truly. They've given me a distinctive identity. When one talks of identity it is not just the outer appearance, it is the inner self too, the persona. The man and his clothes—an inseparable package. The way your skin defines who you are.

623. That is my number. No, no, it's my name. Bestowed on me at a naming ceremony with the prescribed rituals. Don't be upset that you were not invited to this cradle ceremony of mine. If you wish to seek revenge for having been slighted with a non-invitation, please feel free to address me as 623 from now on. It may give both of us some satisfaction. After all, it is my identity, stamped boldly on my prison garb.

Tomorrow they will take these garments away from me. That's what happened with those who were released earlier. This 623 will leave me and go into the prison store room. Maybe it will be laundered first. Will the wash totally erase the number stamped on the back? Or will it survive the wash in a faded but still legible avatar?

If the number is still there, faded or not, he will read it. Are you asking whom I am talking about? I forgot to mention him, my heir. The man who will inherit this precious property, my prison dress. When he deciphers the faded numbers, what will go through his mind? I wonder who this 623 was, he may think. Would he just accept that it was a legacy from an anonymous elder brother? Or would he wonder further? Let his thoughts go where they may wish. After all, I will not be here to argue with him.

I will be a free man. I will be somewhere other than within these four walls that comprise my prison cell. Why should a free man concern himself with the condition of a prisoner? Except that he was once a prisoner himself.

To be honest, I had never been in prison before this. There is more than enough room in the system to accommodate the ills and wrongdoings of society. Anybody can get away unpunished for their crimes, lie low, and live out their lives without ever having to see the inside of a prison. Only the unfortunate few…no, only those who are not crafty enough to slip the net and get away, land up inside. As for me, I was a political prisoner. I openly confessed my crime. The prison experience was a change for me, even a welcome change from a flat and boring life. I think I have spent my prison days as a willing inmate and have enjoyed my time here.

Tomorrow the law will release me from the grasp of its arms. Perhaps it has reasoned that I have been sufficiently punished for my crime and should be set free. Or perhaps it is just casually tossing me out. In any case, I will be a free man tomorrow. Instead of clutching these prison bars, I may be clutching the bars at the ticket window in some railway station, awaiting the ticket clerk's arrival.

And later I may stare through the bars of my upstairs apartment window at the bustle of the street outside.

As these thoughts tumbled through my mind, I suddenly remembered—I had missed my last view of the sunset from prison. The darkness had already set in. How often my eyes had attempted to pierce that impenetrable darkness. Darkness is the only friend of a lonely soul. I know you won't agree with me. 'No,' you will protest, 'light is essential for moving forward.' 'And for going backwards too,' would be my counter argument. Even if I am unable to grow, at least I will not wither into dust. That would be satisfaction enough for me.

My last night here. In the enveloping darkness appears a pinpoint of light. The warder with his lamp is going about his duty. He has to walk the corridors like this for two hours, till the relief warder arrives. After that he has to get ready for his next round of duty. Though he cannot leave the prison, tomorrow I will. The warder, a scarf wrapped around his neck against the cold, will be going on these same rounds tomorrow night. And the next night. And the night after that. Not for him any thought of liberation.

I can hear my fellow prisoners snoring in deep sleep. They are at peace, with no thoughts of impending freedom to interfere with their rest. They are doing long prison stretches, not a short one like mine. But even for them the time will come when they realize that their days in this prison are running out; that they will be outside these walls soon. That thought will rob them of their peace of mind. They too will be in the state of mind I find myself in now.

The night grew darker. The clang of the prison gong shattered the silence. I counted each blow patiently. It stopped at the count of twelve. Midnight. Tomorrow this prison gong will not assault my ears. It will not order me to stop my dreaming and lie down. Instead, some clock on some wall in some room will strike the hour timidly, as though apologizing for disturbing my sleep. But how can it disturb my slumber? Won't I be snoring away peacefully in my new-found freedom?

All these things, this bed, this plate, this tumbler, this number, these iron bars, these surroundings, all these will retreat into the world of the past. Once I am a free man, these memories will blend and meld into the memories of all those other past days and years of mine. Thoughts of the here and now will take over. That is why I want to embed the memories of these things, this experience, deep in my mind now.

I must have fallen asleep at some point. I opened my eyes to a familiar sound. The summons from a single voice that commenced its call from a low register and climbed up the scale to the very zenith. The summons for prayer time. I leapt to my feet—my last prison prayer! I went and found a vacant spot among the assembled prisoners. I was to be one among them for the very last time.

The prayer ended. Back in my cell, I held the bars of my window and watched the dawn light up the sky. The bars were cold to the touch. Maybe they could feel the warmth of my fingers. Only one more day. I could watch the radiant sun emerging from the dark womb of the horizon. I sensed that the sun's rays had already acknowledged that I was soon to be a free man. Now, it only remained for the High Priest to confirm it.

The daily routine of the prison was going on all around me. But all I heard in my mind was, 'Last day! Last day!'

I would have preferred to be the last to leave this world. But of course that's not possible.

The warder approached. He stood at the entrance to the block and bellowed, '623! 623!'

'That's me,' I said, presenting myself. 'Bring all your stuff and come along,' he ordered. Yes, the things were still mine. I bundled them all up and followed the warder. They were checked and then a prisoner on duty threw the whole bundle into a corner. They had ceased to be mine. Maybe those battered items could take some pride in that fact. Instead they gave me *my* things. The possessions they had taken from me 165 days ago became my property again. I put on my old/new things. Someone nearby remarked that now I had an identity. Yes, these were the things that bestowed identity upon a liberated man.

Then came the inevitable hassles, the bureaucratic rituals of being released from prison, or, of being launched into freedom, if you prefer to see it that way. These kinds of hassles are societal, systemic. None can escape them.

Finally, all done. I was walking towards the gate. One day it had swallowed me; today it was going to vomit me out. Apparently it doesn't have good digestion! I had earlier taken leave of everyone. I remember how that went. 'I'm sorry to be leaving you all,' I'd said. What an idiot I was to talk like that! Unnecessary sentiment. The warder was walking alongside. He would open the gate for me and then go back to the cell block. Not *my* cell block, *his*.

Out of the blue he threw a question at me. 'Will you be coming back?' I was stunned. Could the fellow read my mind? Otherwise how could such a question occur to him? Then I understood. He didn't know everything, only bits and pieces. He was just wondering whether something would bring me back to prison the way it once had. A fair enough question. A trivial question, in fact. But I hesitated to reply. Then I said: 'I myself don't know. Who can tell?'

He seemed satisfied with my response. We were at the second gate. It opened with a gentle sound, as though to dampen the harsh connotations of the word 'prison'. I passed through. It shut with a sound that emphatically declared that prison was finally behind me. That warder, my companion—where had he gone?

I went on towards the third and final gate. 'Let this man go out,' ordered a stentorian voice. I had become a man, a person. I was still within the prison compound, but already I had been accorded a human identity. I listened carefully to that voice. It was the same voice that had earlier barked orders from within the prison gate, 'Take the prisoner away.' But 'a man' retains some dignity.

The final gate was about to open for me. I would soon be a free man. It would happen once I stepped through that gate. My heart was full. Was it light with joy or was it heavy with apprehension? No, neither. Rather, both. A screeching noise. The sound of the final gate opening, to my ears, was a sympathetic voice from the bottom of a dear friend's heart. It is possible to find words to describe anything. But that one last moment…that moment belongs to the soul alone, and is beyond words.

I took a step outside. Something made me turn to look back. 'Oh, free man, oh sinner! Never come back here again,' the gate said with a growl (or so I imagined) as it clanged shut.

Only then did I take in what was in front of me. A long road disappearing into the distance. Houses and, behind them, a dense thicket of trees. Further still, a wide arc of tall mountains. And beyond all these, the blue of the sky merging with the horizon. Was this all?

No, no. There must be more. My eyes frantically searched into the far distance. What did I see?

Yet another closed door.

Translated by Malini Seshadri

RIVULETS

LA. SA. RA.

How is it that Anna's* curd rice is always so white? Even when kuzhambu is spooned on to the rice, the brown liquid stays self-contained on the white background, like a decorative bindi on the rice, instead of mixing with it.

He wears only very light, fine fabrics, like mull. He can't bear the weight of heavy clothes. But how come not even a speck of street dust settles on his dhoti? It's true, you won't find a single speck!

When I asked Amma about this, she simply said, 'Some people are born that way.'

A long loose shirt cut close to the neck, a turban, an angavastram around his shoulders, dhoti worn in the traditional style with a loop of the fabric tucked between the legs, a wide smear of vibhuti on the forehead...off he would go, striding briskly, delicately holding up an edge of his dhoti.

We were all in awe of Anna's permanent state of pristine purity.

My uncle, that is my father's younger brother, had stayed with us for some time after he finished his studies and before he landed a job. He is ten years older than me and fifteen years younger than Anna. I have always used the more familiar form of address when talking to my uncle rather than the more formal form usually reserved for elders. I shouldn't have, but then I was rather impish at the time, and he was just a boy still.

Whenever my uncle went to the river for a bath I would accompany him. After washing his dhoti he would wring it dry and then go through elaborate manoeuvres to try and give it a neat 'ironed' look before he hung it on the line to dry. By contrast, Anna

---

*In some households, children address their father as 'Anna' rather than 'Appa', as is the case here.

would simply wash his dhoti, wring it dry, and hang it up on the clothes line with no fuss. But when they wore those dhotis, it was Anna's dhoti whose whiteness and neatness would catch the eye. Was this also some kind of natural gift?

The river was where baths were taken, and on the edge of it stood a washing stone. On the bank grew low bushes and different kinds of trees. Further back were lovely, lush green fields with bordering ridges, wells, and irrigation channels through which the water leapt and splashed as it sped along.

I saw all this only after we had moved here from the city.

But more than all this…there was the sky….

"'On which tree does rice grow?' Aren't you the one who asked that question?' Murugan would recall, doubling up with laughter. 'So now look and learn. All these fields belong to us.' His arms would spread out to indicate all that one could see up to the far horizon.

Sometimes I would let my annoyance get the better of me, and I would try to outwit him with questions of my own. 'Have you ever seen the sea? Have you ever seen a tram on a street?'

But here there is a sky. I tell you, it is a source of never-ending wonder to me. Wasn't it there even when I was living in the city? How come I never noticed it there? Possibly because I never thought to look upwards. It was only after I came here that I thought of lifting up my gaze. I looked; I learnt. I continue to look and learn every day.

Up above is another ocean. Instead of waves, there are clouds. Instead of fish, stars.

What's more, the sky looks especially large above our home because in front of it is a very big open ground and the bustle of the street is well away from us. Try to capture in your mind's eye that expanse of ground, with its huge canopy of heaven above and all its hidden treasures.

Wealth, virtues, vices, differences, changes…everything has been shuffled and thrown up there, beyond anyone's reach. Which person, using which tall ladder gets up every day at the crack of dawn to paint the heavens? What paints does he use? Does he wield a brush? Or does he just splash a blend of colours directly onto the sky from an enormous vat?

What's happening up there? And who's in charge? Something is going on in the sky all the time. It never pauses to rest. Sometimes the sun disappears from the sky…well it doesn't entirely disappear. It's more like someone wiped the sky with a damp cloth and blurred the sun, dimming it slightly. It's neither bright, nor dark. It's a beautiful feeling, even joyful; and also sad, a garment caught on a thorn and ripped; weighing on the mind, yet uplifting…I don't know how to describe it!

When it rains…well, that's another kind of sorrow…or even a fear? Like large puppies brawling, the clouds collide and pummel one another, reducing each other to nothingness. And then it rains. Water pours down in sheets.

The house is soaked. It's a large house, true. There is a central courtyard and a rear courtyard open to the sky. And all around the courtyards run verandas; the front one alone has a sort of partition wall which is the only protection for the kitchen. Two wide thinnais and a large paved area adorn the front of the house. But in that entire house there is only one proper room.

And it was in this one room that we all huddled for protection against the rain and cold. An ominous rumbling starting somewhere in the distance would suddenly rush towards us and break in a thunderclap above our heads. Did some huge thing just fall from the sky? Not daring to look, we would cling to our mother.

'Arjuna Palguna Kreedi Savyasachi….' Mother would chant.

'What's that, Amma?'

'It is the thunder mantra.'

A bright spear of lightning would make us scramble to cover one another's eyes. Anna has told us never to look at lightning.

In the midst of all the tumult from above, our baby sister would sleep on peacefully in Amma's lap. And despite all my nervousness and fear, I was also conscious of the pleasure and excitement of huddling together, sharing the experience....

Bright sunny days come bearing their own moments of magic. At midday the temple mandapam, the trees behind it, even the leaves on those trees quiver and tremble when you look at them from a distance. But when you go closer, they become perfectly still. If that isn't magic, what is?

Murugan's mother says, 'No one should go outdoors at midday. There is something blowing in the air....'

Blowing in the air? A breeze? What breeze is she talking about? The air is so still, it's difficult to even draw a breath!

But she doesn't explain. She only says, 'You don't know about such things. Better you don't know. Come here.' And she pulls me along and smears some dirt from the ground on to my forehead.

'Now spit!' she commands. 'Spit at once!' I spit.

'Now everything will be all right. You can go.'

But what was not all right to start with? And how has it been set right now? No idea.

Oh, it's too much, too much....

And now it's the moon...the entire expanse in front is a huge courtyard basking in moonlight. Bathed in the moon's power. Playing a game of baleen sadugudu in the moonlight.

'...gudugudugudugudu, dagudagu, dagudagu, dagudigudigudagu, dagu...dag-u-tt...' Oh, no. They've pinned me down. Can't hold my breath any longer....

'Hey, boys, let him go. This fellow from Iyer's house will soon become mashed pudding if you don't stop,' remarked Ramu Murugan, while patronizingly patting me on the back. 'You eat rice and sambar and you're such a wimp. Imagine if you were to eat koozhu. How will you be then, eh?'

Boiling in fury I burst out, 'I won't drink koozhu.'

'Idiot! Ignorant fellow! The koozhu drinker is the robust one; the rice-sambar one is the weakling. Understand?'

I lash out and land a blow on Murugan. He just laughs. He knows that if he retaliates I cannot take it.

Where are you now, Muruga? First of all, are you still on this earth?

An intense yearning overtakes me. It's not a new feeling, it's something that keeps recurring. There's some relief in talking about it, though.

What is the meaning of this existence? Nothing is in our control, so what is it all about? Why are we born? Only to meet and part, meet and part, endlessly, till one day we part permanently? Is parting the goal of existence? Is that the only purpose in being born?

Oh creature who is born into this world, if you use your gift of reasoning you can become a Columbus, an explorer. Yet you are a living example of a worthless and wasted creation. It would have been far better for the world if you had never been born. What greater shame is there than merely existing instead of seeking the meaning of life?

Short, sweet, sudden. That's life. Everything happens just once—grief, joy, everything. But the experience of these we taste again and again, like the flavour on spittle. When there is just one, there should be no sequel, no flip side. But what actually happens? 'Going once, going twice…anyone interested in bidding?' We are not even auction pieces—we have been reduced to the auctioneer's chants.

The true meaning of this existence eludes me. But at least I can think about it, can't I?

There is a well in the veranda adjoining the rear courtyard. I am peering into its depths. Amma has come looking for me.

'Enda, what are you doing? Don't lean over like that. What if you lose your balance?'

She joins me and also starts peering into the well. The sun's rays pierce through the skylight and strike the surface of the water in the depths of the well. The water shimmers.

'Amma, why is the water shivering like that?'

'Oh, that? That's what are called "dharais", rivulets. Water seeps out continuously from the underground spring nearby in a thin thread and flows into our well. That's why there's always water in the well though we keep drawing it out. It keeps coming…no beginning, no end. Come away from here, now. I don't want you to be here alone.'

Amma has gone away. But I linger there, reluctant to leave.

Those slender rivulets of spring water. Forever flowing. Day and night, whether people are asleep or awake, whether someone's there or not, whether someone's watching or not, whether anyone knows about it or not, they flow, flow, flow….

Isn't that so?

Suddenly, there was some commotion beyond the rear compound wall. Anna had left early for school this morning. Inspection day at school, he said. Our maid, Mari, who had been scrubbing the pots and pans, got up and ran to investigate without even waiting to wash her hands. I desperately wanted to go and see what was going on, but Amma said no. Anna himself was also pretty firm about such things, so there was no question of disobeying her.

After a long time Mari returned. The expression on her face revealed her inner agitation.

'What…?' asked Amma.

Mari was just starting to say something when she spotted me and stopped talking abruptly. She signalled to Amma to send me out of earshot.

'My boy, go to the front of the house,' Amma told me.

I pretended to do that, but instead hid behind the rezhi door from where I could hear what they were saying.

'Amma, what can I tell you! The city is going from bad to worse. You know that rubbish heap on the other side of our wall? It seems a stray dog was rummaging there and it pulled out a baby wrapped in a cloth. Beautiful baby with such lovely nose and eyes… like a little prince. But what's the use…he's dead. Born in sin….'

'What are you talking about?'

'They tracked down the mother also. They used the same dog and it followed the scent to the slum and they nabbed her. Now she has to face the people's court—street justice.'

'Street justice? What will they do?'

'Amma, it's not your concern. Let it go. If you go on probing, you will only feel more anguish.'

That was Mari's way of offering a lure to Amma. She was hoping that my mother would ask for more details so that she could carry on with her story. But my mother did not take the bait. She didn't ask anything else, and so Mari went away. But I could see that Amma was agitated. She was going around doing her chores, but you can always tell when someone is just making a pretence of keeping busy.

The clamour from the street swelled and subsided periodically. Amma gave us lunch. She scooped out a shovelful of raw rice from its barrel and picked out the stones. She took up a book at random and flipped its pages. She could not put her mind to anything. The midday heat was building up.

Anna was not going to come home for lunch because of the inspection. A boy from school came by to pick up Anna's lunch.

Amma always ate lunch from a proper plate. But that day she ate off a 'plate' of dry leaves stitched together. Absent-mindedly, she put some rice on the leaf plate and ladled sambar on to it. Hardly had she done so that the noise from the street grew to a crescendo. Amma got up, placed a stool next to the rear wall and climbed on to it. She looked through the opening in the brickwork, then abruptly turned her head away. Her expression changed.

She got off the stool, came back, and picked up the leaf with the food on it. She folded it and made a rough packet. 'Child, come with me. You will be my male escort to the street.' And so we went.

As soon as they spotted us, the crowd parted to let us through. The woman was on her knees, head bowed. Her hair had come loose and was trailing around her shoulders. Amma stretched out her hand and offered the food packet to her. The woman did not move. After trying a few times to make her accept the packet, Amma just placed it in her lap. That was when the woman raised her head for the first time. Her face and neck were splattered with blood. Then something lying nearby caught our attention. It was a thick knotted rope, a couple of feet long.

Oh, so this was the 'street justice' Mari had talked about. The crowd was silent.

My mother asked, 'Where's the baby?' After a long silence someone said, 'The grave digger has already taken him for burial.'

Amma spoke out, 'In this kind of case, doesn't the man have an equal role? Haven't you got hold of him and questioned him?'

Someone murmured something indistinctly. Amma went on, 'You won't confront the man. I know you all won't. Instead you are adding his punishment also to this poor woman's, and piling all the blame on her. The police station is three whole miles away. Too far for you to go, right? But even if the police station were right next door you still won't go there. Because if they start investigating, the man you are trying to protect will be exposed. This is street justice!'

No one uttered a word. Silence. Amma's face was burning with fury.

'Let me tell you all something,' she said. 'If you apply your version of "justice" every time, you may end up suspecting your own mother…doubting your own paternity. The mother cuddles the baby in her lap and teaches it how to speak, how to say the words "appa" or "amma" or "thaatha". Whoever she points to as she teaches the baby to say "appa"is the child's father. The child must accept it, and the child does. Only she knows the identity of the father. Just because you have dirty minds don't automatically assume that all women are liars and cheats. You know what I say is true….'

Outrage. Protests.

'In this woman you have found an easy target. Her secret has come out. She is poor. She has no one to turn to. You are punishing her for all our sins, for the sins of society. This is what I see going on here. Come, da, let's go.'

I saw a new side of Amma that day, a sort of dual personality that I had been unaware of till then.

For a whole hour after that, silence reigned. Amma climbed onto the stool again to see what was going on.

'What's happening, Amma?'

Amma replied tonelessly, 'There's no one here. And the woman is still sitting where she was.'

After a while I ventured outside to take a look. She too had left.

When Anna returned in the evening and heard about all this, his reaction was sort of half mocking—it felt kind of unsatisfactory to me. He told my mother, 'Ammapenne, you may be a brave woman, prepared to go to war. But remember one thing. We must think of our own safety, our survival. It won't help to make enemies of the people around us....'

Amma retorted: 'Your idea of fairness and justice comes from logic, from the mind. But the idea of justice does not live in the mind alone. It also dwells in the heart.' As she spoke she placed a hand on her chest. 'And in the gut'—her hand moved to her abdomen. 'These are types of justice too....'

Amma's face was flushed bright red, like kumkum. She was sort of beautiful to look at...and sort of frightening....

We were both stunned into silence.

Translated by Malini Seshadri

CROWN OF THORNS

THI. JANAKIRAMAN

'Sir, with your permission I'll take my leave,' said Kannusamy, rising from his seat. Immediately, everyone else in the crowded hall also rose. 'Goodbye, sir.'

'I'm also leaving, sir'.

One of the boys stepped forward, touched his feet, and reverentially pressed his palms to his eyes. Anukoolasamy stepped backwards involuntarily. 'Wha…what are you doing, young fellow?'

But Kannusamy told him, 'Don't stop the boy, sir. These boys are lucky to have someone like you. Just give them your blessings. Your good wishes will work wonders for them.' Then the rest of the boys also came up to Anukoolasamy, one by one, to touch his feet and seek his blessings.

Anukoolasamy was visibly overcome with embarrassment and discomfort. 'This kind of thing is…' he started saying, in a halting voice.

Kannusamy interrupted him. 'Anukoolasamy, listen. You are a true Christian. I'm not saying it just to flatter you. For thirty-six long years you have been a teacher; never once have you wielded a cane on a student, never once have you even spoken a harsh word to one of them. What is wrong if they show their respect for such a divine soul?'

'No, no, don't say things like that…'

'It's not just me. The whole town is saying these things. I listen to the talk on the streets. Once in a way even parents smack their own children or scold them. But, you…never. How is it even possible for someone to be like you? This is a place of joy in which both child and God are cherished and celebrated. These children—and so many others before them—you have given them the respect that every human being deserves.'

All this while, the boys continued to come forward to offer their respects by touching his feet. Anukoolasamy found himself unable to utter a word. He was sure that if he tried to speak his voice would break and his tongue would tie itself into knots.

'So...shall I take my leave?'

Anukoolasamy was making an effort to respond. 'Yes...all right,' he managed to say, dragging the words out with difficulty.

'May we also leave now?' asked the nadaswaram player, bowing respectfully from the courtyard. Anukoolasamy could only manage a nod in assent.

It took a couple of minutes for the hall to empty out completely. Meanwhile, two or three of the students had been talking among themselves in whispers. Now one of them said, 'Sir, we will leave these two lamps here. We will come and collect them in the morning.'

Anukoolasamy saw off the last few at the door and turned back into the hall. This feeling of utter emptiness, this unfocused yearning tugging painfully on the heartstrings...he was no stranger to this emotion. It had washed over him once earlier; ten years ago, when he was returning alone after leaving his daughter Louisa at her husband's home.

Ssssss hissed the two petromax lamps boldly; but they could not pierce that enveloping emptiness.

They had all gone away and left him alone. Tomorrow would be Wednesday. Not that it mattered any more; tomorrow, the next day, any day...it was all going to be the same. Every day was going to be a Saturday/Sunday. No more school. He had turned sixty. Retired.

He lowered himself on to the swing. On it lay a few framed letters, formal expressions of gratitude. Also a silver plate, and a pen. A four-rupee pen from the local shop; but what was its value to him? Four lakhs...maybe even four crores? All one and the same, because it was priceless. Nearby lay a pile of three or four discarded rose garlands, threaded with kornapattai and silver thread.

And suddenly, there she stood in front of him, clasping the chains of the swing on either side. Mahimai. She stood in silence, her steady gaze fixed on him. A look that spoke without speaking, revelling in the acclaim and felicitations as though she herself had received them all. One moment she was right there next to him, drinking him in with her eyes, and the next moment she had moved to the doorway. She bolted the door and came back. She picked up the garlands one by one and placed them around his neck. She placed her hands on his shoulders and looked into his face.

'You have never struck me in anger either,' she said, 'or even spoken sharply.' She laid her head gently against his chest.

'We are here on this earth only fleetingly. Like winged termites that appear after a rainstorm and die quickly. Why should we waste any part of this brief existence of ours in beating and scolding others? How can you correct anyone by beating them?'

'I'm not asking you to behave like a rakshasa. But, surely, being a man, you must get angry sometimes....'

'Who says I don't get angry...' began Anukoolasamy. Mahima cut in: 'You should show it once in a way.'

'As it is you often tick off the woman who brings the milk and speak angrily to the maid. You want me to join in and show my anger also?'

'But how can you avoid showing your anger when you are dealing with schoolchildren?'

'Well, I managed to do just that!'

Glancing lovingly at him and tweaking his moustache playfully, Mahimai asked, 'Would you like some coffee?'

She got up and went inside. Anukoolasamy felt instantly bereft, as though his very soul was now part of her...and was leaving with her. He gazed at the opposite wall. A face looked back at him; a face overflowing with beatific love, on His head a crown of thorns. Anukoolasamy's eyes moved to a spot a few pictures away. Again the same personification of gentle love, holding a lamb tenderly in His arms.

What Kannusamy had said earlier that evening was absolutely true. Never in all his thirty-six years as a teacher had he ever scolded or beaten a schoolboy.

It was not in his nature to be violent. Once, when his daughter Louisa was six years old, she had got into some mischief at school, and the teacher had struck her with a ruler. The impact of the hard ruler on an already painful summer boil under her blouse made Louisa writhe in agony. From that day onwards, Anukoolasamy decided that non-violence in word and deed, already part of his nature, would also become his unwritten rule for life. He who had sacrificed His own life on the cross to redeem the sins of others—was His sacrifice not meant for everyone and for all generations to come?

That commitment he had made to himself thirty-six years ago had stood the test of time without a single slip. Why else would a retired teacher be given the honour of being escorted back home on his last day of work and felicitated with traditional nadaswaram music?

The school had organized a felicitation function to bid him farewell. But his own class of about forty students had obviously wanted to do more. The ceremonial escort to his home and the meeting to honour him there with further expressions of their affection had been their idea. They garlanded him over and over again. They read out warm messages by the dozen and presented them to him. While all this was going on, suddenly a loud 'Mmm' emanated from the veranda. Instruments were being tuned up. And then began the resonant beat of the thavil. A full traditional music ensemble had turned up just for him!

'Thambi, why all this...' Anukoolasamy stuttered protestingly.

A senior student stepped forward. 'No one can possibly deserve this more than you, sir,' he said. This was Arumugam, a hefty twenty-three year old fellow with a manly build. He was still at school because he had not managed to clear his exams. A student at school still, it was true, but otherwise very worldly-wise. Anukoolasamy decided it was best not to demur; the alternative was to set Arumugam off on a monologue about the other teachers! But still Arumugam did manage to get started down that path. He said:

'We know, sir, of course we understand. It's not as if you declared

"Look, I am going to retire, so raise funds." Nor did you pawn gilt covered ornaments to borrow money after pretending they were of solid gold; and it was not you who stood shamed in front of the whole town for forging a letter to raise loans....'

Anukoolasamy deftly cut short Arumugam's flow of words by interrupting him and asking him to fetch some drinking water. Yes, he had stopped Arumugam's elaborate listing of the litany of misdeeds he had been witness to, but whatever he had said was true. Slapping a student in the face, or slapping society in the face for personal gain...weren't they equally shameful acts? Anukoolasamy could tell himself, with a clear conscience, that he had been guilty of neither.

Anukoolasamy's thoughts turned to Naranappaiyyar. A person like himself in many ways. Not a very large family, just a son and a daughter. And yet, he was up to his neck in debt; he owed people money all over the place. Things had come to such a pass that no one, from the fancy jeweller right down to the roadside vendor selling fresh coriander, would trust him for even a few paise worth of anything. Even this extreme plight did nothing to abash Naranappaiyyar. He prevailed upon a relative in the office of the Directorate of Education to forge a letter addressed to him. It claimed that he, Naranappaiyyar, had been selected as one of the examination officials that year, and that the formal letter of appointment would follow in two weeks. On the strength of that forged letter alone, the fellow had gone ahead and borrowed various sums of money—fifty to seventy-five rupees—from several people. Even if it had actually been true, the salary would have been only two hundred odd rupees for the job.

When it became clear that the letter had been forged, all hell broke loose. Naidu, the money changer, confronted Naranappaiyyar and snatched away his bicycle. He was burning with the fury of one who has been tricked and cheated. So Naranappaiyyar lost the bicycle. But was that all he lost? He was a schoolteacher and had brought disgrace to the whole teaching community.

And what about the bank agent, Ayyangar? He had a reputation for shrewdness. It was said that if you showed him some buttermilk that had been churned to the limit, he would find a way to extract yet another ounce of butter from it. Would anyone imagine that he, of all people, could fall for a con? And yet, Saminathan had the temerity to try just that. He pledged a 'gold' chain at the bank to take a loan; except that it was not solid gold, merely covered with gilt. Because he thought he was dealing with a respectable member of the teaching community, Ayyangar simply weighed the necklace without testing it. Nine sovereigns, so he handed more than three hundred rupees to Saminathan as a loan, and put away the necklace.

Saminathan should have been discreet enough to lie low. But no, he decided to try his luck again. One more trip to the bank with yet another fake necklace. Now, would any reasonable banker go on giving loans on mere trust? This time, Ayyangar tested the second necklace. As the fake jewel gave up its secret, Ayyangar smiled quietly and said, 'What is this Iyer sir? If a student stands up to clarify a doubt in the classroom, the teacher can just cover up his own ignorance by rebuking the child for impertinence and ordering him to sit down. But does that sort of thing work in the commercial world? Am I being naive here? Hold on a moment, sir. Let me fetch the goldsmith.' As Ayyangar left the room, Saminathan's stomach began to churn. Why had Ayyangar gone in person to fetch the goldsmith instead of sending for him? What explanation should he offer to Ayyangar?

Before he could sort out his thoughts, Ayyangar had returned with the goldsmith, the head constable in tow. In the presence of these witnesses, Ayyangar opened the safe and took out the necklace that Saminathan had pledged earlier. That one, too, loudly proclaimed that it was a pretender, not gold but brass. Even in this situation, Ayyangar upheld the dignity of the teaching profession and avoided humiliating Saminathan publicly. He made him mortgage a part of his land for the amount due, and let him go. Fortunately for Saminathan, the constable had come there in his ordinary dhoti-shirt outfit and not his uniform. Saminathan was able to get away without becoming the laughing stock of the town.

Anukoolasamy's thoughts turned to the behaviour of a few other acquaintances. For instance, Ramalingam who, when he was facing retirement, had brazenly coaxed a student to raise funds for him. He declared, 'Oh well, I have to retire. Can't even hope to eat a full meal any more. When I was a student we used to raise funds to present to our teacher when he retired....'

Anukoolasamy's reverie was interrupted when Mahimai returned with the coffee.

'What, still wrapped up in your thoughts?' she remarked. 'Drink the coffee while it's still hot.' She picked up the messages of felicitation and started reading them, occasionally raising her eyes to gaze upon her husband with a mixture of fondness and pride.

'Don't believe everything they've written,' said Anukoolasamy lightly. 'They are being kind to me so that I don't weep with sadness about my retirement. Just some candy to sweeten the occasion....'

'True,' said Mahimai, 'but they have all acknowledged one thing. They have all said you have never beaten or spoken harshly to a student. So they are speaking the truth, right?'

'Tsk...such a great discovery they have made!' said Anukoolasamy, dismissively.

'But surely it is a skill. To avoid being aggressive and yet be acknowledged as being excellent at your job....'

Anukoolasamy thought about what his wife had said. It's true, he decided, maybe I have earned the right to feel some pride about myself.

'It's not so difficult. One can behave like this with everyone... milk vendor, sweeper, everyone. Tell me, would any human being with even an ounce of intelligence rely on violence to achieve anything?' argued Anukoolasamy.

'Not everyone can live by that principle,' was his wife's response.

'All right, but somehow I have managed it,' he said.

There was a knock on the front door. 'Sir, sir....'

'Who is it?'

'It's me, sir.'

Mahimai opened the door.

'Is sir here?' asked a voice.

'Yes, he is. Who...oh, you're Arumugam, right?' said Mahimai, recognizing the visitor.

But it wasn't only Arumugam who stood in the doorway. Beside him was another boy who was also a student in Anukoolasamy's class, and a woman who appeared to be about forty years old or thereabouts—ears, neck, arms, all totally bare of ornaments.

'What is it, Chinnayya?' asked Anukoolasamy.

'This is Chinnayya's mother, sir,' said Arumugam, introducing the woman.

'Come in,' invited Anukoolasamy.

If Arumugam was bringing someone to meet him, it must be to ask a favour. Twenty-three and still at school, Arumugam had acquired the reputation of a person of influence, someone who could get things done. I wonder why he's here, thought Anukoolasamy. Nothing to do with exam papers or anything like that...

'What's the matter, Arumugam?'

'Chinnayyan wanted to meet you.'

'So tell me, Chinnayya....'

Silence for a full half-minute. Chinnayyan stood mute with head bent. Then, he began to weep.

'Tell him!' commanded his mother.

Anukoolasamy noticed that Chinnayya's face was twitching with emotion and his lips were trembling.

'Come on, out with it,' urged Arumugam.

'This has been torturing him for a year now, Sir,' said the mother.

'What? For a whole year?'

'Yes, Sir,' Arumugam burst out. 'Please say we can talk to him from now on. Please permit it, sir.'

'Enda, explain what you mean. I don't understand what you are talking about,' said Anukoolasamy.

'Sir seems to have forgotten,' remarked Arumugam, glancing at Chinnayya's mother, then at Mahimai.

'Forgotten? Me? But what did I forget?' Anukoolasamy was bewildered.

'Sir, last year this fellow stole Kaayaarohanam's English textbook, quietly changed the name and sold it at the store for half-price. I was the one who discovered what he had done, and I brought him to you.'

This set off a fresh bout of loud sobbing from Chinnayya. 'Shh, quiet,' urged his mother.

'Then what?' asked Anukoolasamy, still mystified.

'Sir, you looked at him silently for a while and then you turned to the class and said, "No one in this class has ever done this kind of thing before. You must all boycott this fellow. Don't talk to him."'

Chinnayyan continued to weep.

Arumugam continued his story. 'From that day onwards, we started shunning Chinnayya, Sir. None of us talked to him. Then when we were planning today's party for you, we collected one or two rupees from each of the boys. Chinnayyan also came and offered one rupee, but we said no. And we told him he was not invited to the party either. He just went away quietly. When I got home from here this evening, I found him waiting for me outside my house. He had brought his mother also along. Both of them requested me to bring them to you, so....' Arumugam gulped, sounding apologetic, and his voice trailed away.

By now, Arumugam's words had triggered Anukoolasamy's memory. He could recollect the occasion clearly. But surely it had never been his intention to inflict such a severe punishment on the boy. He had just said something on the spur of the moment to signal his displeasure. If he had only known that the boys would take his words so literally...so seriously...and go on with the boycott for such a long time....

'Hey, Chinnayya, don't cry, da,' said Anukoolasamy.

'Please allow us to start talking to him again, Sir,' pleaded Arumugam.

Chinnayya's mother spoke earnestly: 'Sir, for a whole year now my son has been feeling very depressed. He used to be always chattering and laughing happily; but then he suddenly went quiet. He speaks rarely, and then too only in monosyllables. How could I know what was in my child's mind? Even with his little sisters he doesn't talk and laugh. Earlier this evening, when the smaller children had gone to play, he told me everything. He insisted that he must meet you today, sir. Sir...please take pity on him....'

Anukoolasamy felt cornered, caught red-handed. His mind was in agony.

Chinnayyan's mother added, 'It seems his classmates refused to let him participate or even take the one rupee he offered. But when the whole class was donating for your party, how could he bear to be left out? Come on, da, give it to sir.'

Chinnayyan's sobs grew even louder as he timidly stretched out his hand and offered a grimy one-rupee note, sodden with nervous sweat.

'Please accept it, sir,' pleaded Arumugam.

Anukoolasamy accepted it without uttering a word.

Arumugam said earnestly, 'Sir, he is a good boy. On that particular day he did something stupid, but ever since then he has been very well behaved. No complaints about him.'

'Sir,' urged Chinnayya's mother, 'Please be kind-hearted towards him. Please allow his classmates to talk to him as before. After all, he is only a child....'

'Sad...I never meant for those boys to treat Chinnayya like this,' said Anukoolasamy.

'They only did exactly what you asked them to do,' pointed out Mahimai.

'That's true...' muttered Anukoolasamy, smiling slightly. The smile itself felt as if it were made of tears. And the crown of thorns in the picture on the wall pressed painfully into his own brow.

Translated by Malini Seshadri

THE FIRST NIGHT

KI. RA.

Mallamma felt as though she had been left in a jungle, blindfolded. She had never seen her husband before; nor heard his voice. The house where she was born, the village where she was brought up, the surroundings in which she had moved about—all of them were entirely different from this.

They used to buy cattle in the fair at Kalugumalai and bring them to their pen; likewise they had her garlanded in the shrine of the Lord of Kaluguchala and brought her home.

Mallamma's father was a man of the world. When he left his daughter in that house and started on his journey home he said, 'I take leave of you.' His voice choked. This tongue…it would let you down at the most critical moment. Mallamma too couldn't speak.

She sniffled as if everything that formed part of her from her birth was about to leave along with her father. And he was reminded of the words of Sage Kanva.

Mallamma was left all alone.

Members of that family stayed away for a while, allowing her to alleviate the pain of separation. Nonetheless, solitude did make her heart heavier. Loneliness weighed her down.

She blew her nose and dabbed at her eyes and nose with the loose end of her sari. Then the cat in the house came close to her legs, arched its back with pleasure, nuzzled, and mewed. What message was the cat giving her?

As the cat mewed and cuddled against her, a smile lit up her face. It is woman's peculiar trait to transport herself easily to the peak of delight from the slough of sorrow.

Everyone participated in that smile and called the cat away from her.

'Baas, Baas, Sangu Baas.'

Basu was the name of the cat.

But it did not move away from her; on the other hand, it nestled closer to her over and over again and miaowed. Giggling grew into a roar of laughter. In this way the cat initially helped Mallamma in attaching herself to that family.

She had hot water ready for her husband to bathe with; she watched him take his bath. In villages like these there was only an open inner courtyard and no separate bathroom. She had to scrub her husband's back but she felt hesitant and embarrassed to do it. At the time of the marriage ceremony they were made to clasp each other's hands. She felt then the touch of a strong palm calloused by hard work. Whenever her husband expected her to scrub his back her shyness increased. A touch of scarlet spread over the ears of the new bride. And bashfully she scrubbed the dirt off his broad back.

Involuntarily, Kondayya's back bent and yielded to her scrubbing. When she scratched and rubbed below the ears on the back of his neck, he felt tickled and ecstatic; she too felt his reaction.

Different customs and manners prevail in different societies. According to the custom of these people, the elders did not fix a particular day for the consummation soon after the wedding. If asked why, they would say in disgust, 'Chei, how repulsive it is! That's something like bringing a cow and letting loose a bull to mount.... Aren't we human beings?'

That is a matter the couple have to arrange between themselves when their feelings develop into a perfect blossom. But to arrive at such a stage it might take weeks and, at times, even months according to the mental make-up of the persons concerned.

Besides, the bride who easily yields to her husband does not shoot up in the estimation of that community. And the male too is in no way behind the female.

These two were aware that the elders of the family were watching this game, acting as if they were barely paying attention at all.

They were a big family living in a small house. Their cattle included buffaloes and cows, sheep and goats. Apart from these, dogs, civet cats, ducks, pigeons, spotted deer, white rabbits, and many other creatures were attached to the family.

Early morning bustle. Mallamma is standing and churning the curd in a large, waist-high earthen pot. Kondayya is enjoying the sight—how beautifully her hips swing when she holds the rope with both hands and draws and churns. The children are waiting to get some butter. Sprays of buttermilk fall on them and make them laugh with delight.

A ball of butter as big as a Seville orange bounces and rolls on her palm. She lets it float in water and then places the small globules of butter wiped from the churn stick on the outstretched palms of the children, one after the other. In the midst of those small palms, a big, strong one appears. Instead of placing a globule of butter on that palm, Mallamma pinches it hard. The children jump and laugh boisterously. The elders act aloof, as though they have not noticed anything, and look on unconcerned.

When Mallamma serves food to him he silently stretches his palm and shows it to her. There are fingernail scratches on it! They are the replies she gave him at night when his hand moved towards where she lay. She sees it and yet, as though she had not seen it, she serves him ghee. 'No, enough,' his hand gestures; but on the scratches drips ghee.

Kondayya helps her whenever she has a heavy load of work. She never turns down such assistance nor does she welcome it. His amorous gestures and her sulks prolong their courtship. This helps them understand each other from several angles and different aspects.

Nowadays they do not feel shy to converse, as they did before.

In their field, strips of land had been allotted to each of them to work on. Today, they removed the weeds with a competitive spirit, becoming drenched to the bone with sweat.

They came to the shade of a black babul tree for their afternoon meal. Whenever the wind passed by that tree it would sough in its own language. When the wind was strong the tree would say something back, bend low, smile, and then stand erect. Like the soil of that tract, the tree was black; and like that tree, the people there were dark-complexioned too.

They sat in the shade, removed the cloths tied around their heads, and with them wiped the sweat off their faces and bodies and relaxed. The sea breeze that blew softly gave them immense joy. The sweaty smell of Mallamma sitting by his side made Kondayya long passionately for her. She was touching a sensitive plant under that tree and playing with it. That plant, as soon as it was touched, folded its outspread leaves bashfully.

She placed before him the small pot of food and sat close to him. What a novel, strange, curious creature Woman is! She need not have cast such a glance at him.

Some women appear attractive from one angle. Some others look ravishingly beautiful at first, but their beauty fades if we see them often. Mallamma's charm was not of that type. She didn't look beautiful at first sight. But if one watched her carefully the charm of every part of her figure became more apparent. Her coral-red lips appealed most to Kondayya. She had a small, pretty, dark-green mole on her lower lip. He was all eyes; he was about to touch the mole. She pushed away his hand and moved aside.

He offered her the first morsel of food he was going to eat. Since she kept quiet without refusing it, he took it close to her mouth. She turned her face and rose; he too got up, returning the morsel to the small pot. He didn't heed her look expressing alarm and surprise; he went and took the hoe and began to finish the work allotted to him. Mallamma's face went droopy and sad; she cursed herself for being a fool.

She waited near the small food-pot thinking he would come back. He understood her and wanted to go to her but his pride did not allow him to do so. After some time she realized he would not come back. So she too went and began removing the weeds with greater earnestness—working with a gnawing hunger. Both of them did their work without uttering a single word.

When he approached her, she sulked; when she approached him, he moved aside. Time passed.

The time when birds turn nestwards.

Night was fast approaching. This was the season when labourers had only a brief daytime to work. Nature has arranged seasons in that way—let people who work hard and become dog-tired go to sleep early.

Mallamma took Kondayya's hoe also and went to bring the small food-pot left under the tree. Her foot slipped into a small hole. She got flustered, jumped, and shook her left foot rapidly. Her anklet flew off and fell at a distance. Kondayya came running, asking what the matter was. When she looked at the hole she saw something wriggling and vanishing into it.

That instant she knew of her approaching end. All her empty pretences vanished in that silent second. Never before had she turned to her husband with so much love in her eyes. He could not understand that look of hers. Firmly holding her foot with both her hands, she looked pathetically at him.

In the face of death, man is weaker than straw. Both felt that the way they had behaved till then was a foolish mockery. At that instant their souls felt connected to each other. He bit the edges of the wound, sucked the blood, and spat out the poison. The urgency and affection he showed to save her touched her deeply. She felt death was nothing.

Gathering her up, he ran towards the doctor's house. Her arms wound around his neck tightened and in that tightness her ego was dissolved.

The vaidyar gave some peppers to Mallamma and asked her to munch on them.

'Do you feel the pungency of the peppers?'

'Yes.'

He gave her a piece of steamed oilseed cake to chew. She said that it tasted bitter. The vaidyar's face showed signs of relief. He assured them there was nothing to be afraid of.

The burning sensation at the spot where she had been bitten

spread over the entire foot and she smarted under the pain. She said she felt as if her foot was in a blazing oven. The vaidyar concluded that she had been bitten by a millipede. He brought the green leaf of a tobacco plant, ground it into a paste, and smeared it on the wound. He then waved a bunch of neem leaves and chanted a few mantras. He gave her a small globule of paste and asked her to swallow it, advising her to start taking a salt-free diet. He looked at Kondayya and said that since he had given her medicine to remove the poison, Kondayya should observe ahapathiam.

Kondayya did not understand what the vaidyar meant by ahapathiam.

'You must leave her in her father's house and bring her back only twenty days later. Do you now understand what I mean?' he said and laughed. Only then did Kondayya realize what the vaidyar actually meant by ahapathiam—abstinence from sexual relations while under medical treatment.

Mallamma's father came and took her home.

She regained her health and was slowly cured. Kondayya's face would flit before her often. A pain like that of a heavy load was pressing on her heart. She felt a tormenting dryness in her throat. Because of separation and her loneliness she became thin and constantly longed for him, shedding silent tears unobserved by others. Monday to Monday eight, Tuesday nine, Wednesday ten—she began counting the days....

Disturbed sleep with dreams at night, pining and distress haunted her like ghosts. The twenty days crept by like twenty aeons.

Kondayya came all of a sudden. She was then drying her hair after a bath. Locks of her loose hair touched her body and stretched towards the ground like a jet-black cascade brimming from her head. Seeing him, she rose, only to stretch out her arms for him. Her eyes glistened; words failed her; there was a flutter on her lips.

'Mallamma!' he called out jubilantly, and ran towards her, pressing her to his chest. Such moments are matchless in life; there are very few occasions when souls intermingle.

The woman in her was vigilant enough even when she lost herself in him. Instantly she wriggled away and stepped aside. He saw Mallamma's father crossing the courtyard and coming indoors. Kondayya looked at her as if saying, 'You have the ears of a snake.'

His father-in-law welcomed him. He looked around, and though his face showed signs of surprise seeing Kondayya alone there, he smiled inwardly. Kondayya told him why he had to come alone. That greyhead knew that it was not at all true. Once he too had been young like them. Spring comes every year, but in life it comes only once.

The old man knew this only too well.

Yet, there were grounds enough for this world to keep Mallamma and Kondayya apart for even longer. Besides trivial reasons, the month of Adi posed a stumbling block. For the young couple this was a pitiless month. Mallamma could not understand why a man and his wife must remain separate during this month alone.

Poor souls! They became very dejected when they heard of this. The month of Adi pressed its hands together, put them between those two young ones, and pushed them apart—him on one side, her on the other. They began to count the days. Again.

Half of Adi seemed to them like half a year.

The month of Avani dawned. Cohorts of rainy clouds began to scud across the sky. Rain fell wherever necessary, like a gardener with a watering can sprinkling the plants. Like a beehive the black-soil tract began to hum with activity.

Mallamma's father brought her back to her husband's house one early morning in a wood-topped bullock cart. With her came hampers of dainties. She saw Kondayya and smiled ecstatically. Her teeth gleamed like full-grown maize grains.

They had an extensive piece of dry land. Including the children, all the people in the house, except Mallamma, had gone there. She remained at home, attending to the cooking.

Pebbles were picked; thorns collected, heaped, and set aflame; small plants were cut and removed; the rough parts were dug and fences were mended; gravel was smoothed and ridges strengthened. Such bits of work were attended to with zeal. Kondayya was ploughing the land. He gave the plough to his father, made some excuse, and came home.

He came home with the idea of appearing before Mallamma suddenly and giving her a pleasant surprise. Even as he entered the house he smelt the fragrance of the fresh ghee. He tiptoed as softly as a cat, went indoors, and peeked. She was sitting in front of the oven and was carefully straining the cooked rice with a palmyra leaf colander. Even after spotting him she was not surprised; she would have been astonished if he had not turned up like this.

With a faint smile she watched the way he stood near her, losing control over himself. He lifted her chin a little and took her face in his hands. There were drops of perspiration on her nose and upper lip. She stood the pot erect, rose hurriedly, flung her arms around him, and embraced him. She pressed her perspiring lips on his mouth and rubbed them softly left and right. She drew a deep breath and then gave him a loud, salty, first kiss.

The 'first night' of the Kondayyas.

In the food-bowl he mixed the cooked rice with ghee. Her slack body was on his shoulder as she received the first morsel of food from him. Her face beamed with pleasure and peace.

Translated by M. S. Ramaswami

A DISCIPLE'S OFFERING

INDIRA PARTHASARATHY

These were Pasupati's favourite pair of trousers. What do they call them in Tamil? There was the term 'igantha vattudai' in *Manimekalai*. 'Igantha' means 'loose'; 'vattudai' might mean what we now know as pyjamas. But did the Tamils in those days wear such a garment, Pasupati wondered for a moment. Who would understand what 'vattudai' meant? So we might as well use the term 'trousers'.

Pasupati's problem at hand was the matter of the missing hooks on the waistband of his favourite maroon-coloured trousers. These had come off and fallen to the floor as he was trying to put the garment on. He looked down but could not see them. They might have rolled underneath the cot. His age did not permit him to kneel and search for them; perhaps if he had been in politics he might have had enough knee-bending exercises to be able to do it even in his advanced years.

Pasupati held the headboard of the cot for support and sat down on the floor. He bent down and looked beneath. It was dark. The hooks were nowhere to be seen and as a result of the exercise, he got a catch in his muscles. He stood up with much difficulty. Even if he had been able to retrieve the hooks, what use were they going to be? He did not know how to stitch the buttons on. He couldn't even wrap paper around school notebooks.

But he did not want to discard the trousers for their lack of hooks. This pair had been gifted to him by his wife on his birthday just a month before she passed away. He was lucky on the days he wore them. If he went to the post office there wouldn't be a long queue there. The meal carrier from the mess would arrive in time. His next-door neighbour Padmanabhan would not read out his letter to the editor from the day's newspaper. The list of small pleasures afforded to him by these trousers was endless.

Pasupati tried to put on the trousers. But they refused to stay at the waist. The pair was fifteen years old. These days it was difficult to find a tailor who would replace buttons or hooks on clothes. Now ready-to-wear garments were the rage. Brand ambassadors such as Amitabh Bachchan and Pierce Brosnan flaunted designer suits that big companies produced. Who would care to replace hooks on old trousers?

The calling bell rang. Pasupati opened the door. It was Padmanabhan. Pasupati was relieved to see that he carried no newspaper in his hand.

'Going out?'

'Yes, I was about to leave. But the buckles came off my trousers. Let me ask you something. Do you know of anyone who can replace them?'

'In which world are you living, Swami? Remember those workmen like knife-sharpeners and vessel-polishers who used to go round the streets? Do you see them now? Times are changing! Either you sew the hooks yourself or give away the trousers to the watchman. If we keep using old ones after repairs, how can we compete with the Western economy?'

Pasupati merely kept gazing at Padmanabhan without any response. Contrite that he had probably said something that was not to Pasupati's liking, Padmanabhan said: 'Are the trousers new?'

'No. They are fifteen years old.'

'Fifteen years? My God! Do you have a sentiment attachment to them?'

'Absolutely! The woman who presented it to me has been dead and gone for the same number of years.'

'I am very sorry, Pasupati,' Padmanabhan said. 'Here is a suggestion. If you go to George Town you may find a tailor who can do it. But then you don't travel by the public bus. For the auto fare you may as well buy a new pair of trousers. But that is the price you have to pay if you want to still keep your sentiments.'

After he left, Pasupati put the pair of trousers in a bag and set out. He hailed an autorickshaw. The driver appeared to be as old as Pasupati.

'Want to go to Town and back.'

The auto man surveyed Pasupati from top to toe and asked, 'How much will you pay, sir?'

'Two hundred and fifty.'

'Make it three hundred. Get in, sir.'

Pasupati got in and the auto started. After a little distance, Pasupati wondered if the auto driver had dozed off. The vehicle was going very slowly.

'Why are you creeping?'

'In our younger days we don't have enough time for the things we do, so we fly with wings on our feet. Now aren't we old? Perhaps only a few more days to live! Why don't we have a leisurely look at the world? If we cut our haste, we gain some more moments.' The auto man laughed.

What words of wisdom! Pasupati had not expected such a view of the world from an auto driver.

'Well, I don't mind. I too am old and, like you, I am ready to take it easy. But what about those young people going to work? If they get into your vehicle, what would you do?'

'When they get in I would tell them, "Look here, this vehicle will move rather slowly. If you're in a hurry, you had better take another auto."'

Pasupati smiled. 'All right. Why do you have to drive an auto at this age? Don't you have children?'

'My situation is better. Have you seen older men pulling heavy-laden carts, huffing and puffing in the hot sun? These newspapers carry glib reports that India is becoming a rich country. Actually, the rich are getting richer and the poor poorer. They snatch farm lands from the poor peasants and build IT parks, the wretched fellows. Why are so many peasants killing themselves? Poverty is the reason. I am eking out a livelihood so that I may not become as poor as these peasants. Let this vehicle run as long as it can.... Do you agree?'

'Yes, I do,' Pasupati said. The auto man had evaded his question about children but Pasupati did not want to raise the subject again. The auto kept moving at its accustomed pace and the driver remained quiet.

'George Town! Here you go!' Pasupati was startled by the auto man's announcement. He woke up from his doze and looked around.

'Do you have the address?' the auto man asked.

Pasupati took out the trousers from the bag and held them up. 'I want new hooks on this. See if any small-time repairman who can do the job is around.'

'You mean to say you came all the way from Alwarpet just for this?' asked the auto man, surveying Pasupati from top to bottom.

'Odd-job tailors are so rare these days,' Pasupati said. 'All big, big shops! A friend told me there might be small shops here.'

'Admit that you didn't spot the small shops in places like Alwarpet and Mylapore. Can all people buy readymade clothes from City Centre or Spencer Plaza? If you live on the eighth floor you can't see the ants crawling on the ground. You live high up, so you don't see the small shops. It's as simple as that!'

'Not really!' said Pasupati. 'I am not someone in a high place. I am just managing on a pension from a job I was in years ago. I am simply trying to give a fresh lease to an old pair of trousers. If you know of a small shop at Alwarpet, turn back. Take me there.'

'Well, having come so far we will see if there is one here,' the auto man said. After travelling a little further, he cried, 'Look there! A tailor.'

'Seems to be big....' Pasupati said. 'Will they do the repair job?'

'Find out! Nothing wrong in asking.'

It was indeed a big shop. A cool breeze wafted in as Pasupati entered. Most of the customers were young; some middle-aged. They had come perhaps to buy suits or sherwanis. He hesitated to open his bag and proffer the old trousers to the neatly dressed shop assistant who welcomed him with a pleasant smile. He was thinking of retreating when an older shop assistant came forward and said, 'Yes?'

Pasupati began apologetically, 'It's not a big job…some fixing, in fact….' He took out the trousers and showed them to the shop man. 'This is an old pair but with a lot of sentimental value for me. Could you replace the buckles at the waistband?'

The assistant merely smiled at him. Pasupati was not so dumb that he could not interpret the gesture. 'That's okay,' he said. The assistant had the same fixed smile.

When Pasupati went back, the auto man was washing his hands after his lunch. 'Sir, you have had your lunch, haven't you? he queried.

'Yes.'

'What happened at the shop?'

'The moment I took out the trousers, the shopman smiled politely. I came away.'

The auto man smiled. 'At your old age and in this uncomfortably hot weather you're going here and there just to have a pair of worn-out pants repaired. And you've to pay me three hundred rupees. Isn't all this funny?'

'Didn't I tell you? This pair may be old. But it was presented to me by my wife on my birthday fifteen years ago. And it's been fifteen years since she passed away. Now do you understand?'

After a few silent moments, the auto man said: 'When you go out of this world, can you take the pants along with you…I too have had relations, attachments…I can do without these luxuries, I decided. So I gave up everything…I now lead a simple life. No problems….' He started the engine.

'What are you hinting at?' Pasupati asked. 'That I must throw away this old pair of trousers?'

'Not exactly! The trousers may be old but they are not torn. They are still usable. Gift them to someone who can use them. He will put the hooks on and wear them. And it will please your wife, wherever she is.'

After some seconds passed quietly, Pasupati said: 'If you don't mind, shall I make a suggestion?'

'Go on.'

'Why don't you take this yourself?'

The auto man turned and looked at Pasupati, his face betraying no emotion. Pasupati wondered if he should not have made the offer. Till they reached Pasupati's home the auto man did not talk any further. Getting off the vehicle, Pasupati said: 'Sorry! I should not have said that. I acted thoughtlessly. Pardon me.'

'Give me the trousers,' said the auto man. 'I'll take them. But on one condition—this should be for the fare you owe me. I don't take anything from anyone for free. Don't think I am putting a price on your kindness. If I take them for free, I won't be able to sleep at night. So it's a price I pay for my sleep.'

'This is not charity,' Pasupati said. 'This is dakshina—offerings from a disciple to his master. You're my guru. I have learnt many things from you.'

The auto driver took the trousers and drove away, as if he had not heard what Pasupati had said.

It seemed to Pasupati that the vehicle moved faster than it did before.

Translated by C. G. Rishikesh

LET ME SLEEP IN PEACE TONIGHT

ASHOKAMITRAN

When the lift in which Sakuntala stood descended from the fifth floor and stopped at the first, a gentleman wearing a coat, tie, and all, came running up and said, 'Just stop there. Just stop. The Secretary is coming right now. Just wait.' He placed his foot just inside, so that the lift door wouldn't shut. Someone asked, 'Who is this Secretary, sir? Who is he?' The man in the tie replied, 'The Agricultural Secretary, sir. He came today to attend the Council meeting. It's over, they've all got up.'

'Please move aside,' said Sakuntala, getting out of the lift. When was the Secretary going to come, and when would she finally reach the ground floor? The staircase, which she could climb down in ten seconds, was just adjacent to the lift in any case. By the time she arrived at the ground floor, there were several people waiting there for the lift. However, it was still stuck at the first floor.

There were a couple of women standing at the reception, who appeared to have been waiting for Sakuntala. When they saw her, they moved towards her, smiling. Together, they crossed the open space in front of the office building and came to the pavement on the verge of the road. Both the road and the pavement were crowded with hundreds of office employees on their way home.

Although the three of them walked up to the main road together, Sakuntala said nothing further to her companions and instead mingled with the other pedestrians crowding there. At the traffic signal, vehicles stood on opposite sides of the road, in massed ranks, as if ready for battle. Every time one of the traffic lights came on, one of the rows would roar off in frenzied haste. From the gigantic buses to the comparatively peaceful-seeming bicycles, each vehicle seemed to assume a fury appropriate to itself. Even when she avoided it all as much as possible, walking on the very edge of the pavement, the onrush of the five o'clock traffic made her tremble somewhere deep within herself. As she came to the entrance of the Connemara Hotel, she hesitated a little. Should she have come here at all today?

On the street opposite was the bus stand for the Number Sixteen and for perhaps another dozen buses, each of them going off in different directions. Some buses were waiting there already. In spite of all the confusion there, her eyes swept over the entire crowd in a swift movement. She registered a sense of relief; Rajaratnam wasn't there as yet.

It had become an unchangeable custom with her to meet Rajaratnam at this place and to exchange a few words with him before going home. If he missed the 5.18 p.m. bus, he would have to wait another half an hour. He complained that if that happened, it would be past seven before he reached home. So, on many occasions, within the first minute, even before they had exchanged a word of greeting, his bus would arrive and he would run to try and get a seat on it. While a hundred others tried to clamber onto the same bus, Rajaratnam would contort himself and find some window through which he could see her and wave to her as his bus pulled off. After that she would set off from there, wait for the traffic signals twice again, and cross the road to her own bus stand. By the time she reached home, it would certainly be past seven. But she did not complain.

Today she felt tired and fearful from the very start. The fear didn't spring from one cause alone; it had been there for so long that it had grown many branches. Now she was perturbed because she could no longer say which was the tree and which its branches. Like these one- and two-minute meetings.

What delight, what excitement there had been in these meetings in the beginning! Her own elder sister had said to her one day, 'You're suddenly looking very beautiful, Saku.' Her sister too had been beautiful at one time. Even now she appeared lovely when she came out all fresh from her bath. But within five or ten minutes, a certain weariness and lack of interest made its appearance over her face, etching it with fine lines and wrinkles, obliterating its freshness. There were small gaps here and there between the even rows of her teeth. Her front teeth seemed to protrude slightly.

Sakuntala felt a sudden spark of joy. Rajaratnam had arrived. And now he had seen her.

The traffic lights at the street where she stood must have turned green just then signalling to the vehicles to move on. Scooters and motor cycles leapt forward headlong. Following them came cars and buses. Sakuntala, waiting for all this to subside, wondered for a fleeting moment whether she shouldn't just fall in front of the oncoming traffic. She didn't pause to consider why such a thought should even have struck her immediately after that moment of intense happiness. Such thoughts, in fact, had become frequent and commonplace with her. And the days when she had remonstrated with herself for giving room to such thoughts were over too. Many things had happened to her, yet here she was, in the same place.

By the time she managed one way or the other, to cross the road and reach the other side, it was as if all her strength had evaporated.

But he didn't ask her any questions; at least not straightaway. He said, 'I've planned to take the next bus today, must talk to you a little.'

'I only have enough money for the bus fare,' she said to him.

'Did I ask you whether you had any money?' He replied, somewhat angrily. She followed him as he strode on ahead. The crowds on the pavement were such that even if they had wished to, they could not have walked side by side.

The cafe they went to must have been opened very recently. The tables and chairs, the cupboards, the uniforms of the waiters— everything had the lustre of newness about it. And in such a small space, there was even an air-conditioned area. At first, when she walked in, Sakuntala found it extremely dark there. But only for an instant. As soon as her eyes became accustomed to the darkness, she saw Rajaratnam already sitting at one of the tables, 'Come over here,' he said, taking her by the hand to guide her. She felt her own hand resisting him a little.

Although it was only dimly lit inside, the lamps at least allowed them to look at each other. Soft music played; a tune that had no beginning and no end.

'Two ice creams,' said Rajaratnam to the uniformed waiter who appeared soundlessly at his side.

'What sort of ice cream?' the waiter asked.

Sakuntala put in, 'But I don't want an ice cream.'

'Just have it this once. You won't lose anything,' Rajaratnam said to her. To the waiter he said, 'You remember the two-piece double decker you gave me day before yesterday, we'll have that.'

'Two?'

'What else?'

Now it was time for the question that Sakuntala was dreading. 'Well, have you told them yet?'

Sakuntala looked up at him with an utterly helpless expression. All she could make out was that there was no anger in his eyes. But it is not just anger that one fears in others.

Rajaratnam said, 'Chu.'

'What is it?'

'Saku, you must understand one thing. There can be nothing honourable in our meeting like this at bus stands and then waving goodbye to each other, for years on end.'

Sakuntala lowered her head.

'I am not the kind of man who spends a few days with a girl thinking she has dropped into his hands and then abandons her forever.'

'I know that, Ratnam. I know that.'

'If you know it, what's the point of wasting time like this? I too have parents. I too have a family, you realize that, don't you? Don't I have to say something to them when they keep on asking me, "When are you going to get married, da?"'

'I know, Ratnam, I know.'

'Then? You told me, let's wait till January, I'll tell them then. Then you said you'll tell them in April. Now it's September already. What do you say now?'

'But I explained it to you, Ratnam. Even yesterday, some people came to see my sister. What am I to do, Ratnam?'

'You've been saying this for a whole year. This must be the tenth time you've said it.'

'But what can I do, Ratnam? Don't I have a heart, too?' Tears came into her eyes as she said this.

Rajaratnam made a hissing sound in irritation. The waiter brought two mountainous ice creams in enormous cone-shaped glass dishes. As soon as he left, Rajaratnam said, 'Do you imagine that my family will be prepared to agree instantly? They are most certainly going to leap on me, saying, "Why on earth do you want to marry out of caste, da?"'

The tears that had welled up in Sakuntala's eyes slid down her nose and began to drop on the table. She took out her handkerchief and pressed it against her mouth.

'Well, well, don't start to cry now. Finish your ice cream. I must catch the six o'clock bus at least,' Rajaratnam said. The ice cream burnt her mouth like slaked lime.

'Look here, Saku, it isn't as if I can't take you by the hand and drag you away somewhere with me. There are lots of people I can think of who would do just that. Today is Thursday. Tomorrow I'm on leave. So I won't see you again until Monday. Give me your final word then. Don't ask me what will happen otherwise.'

'I've given you my word, Ratnam. Once my sister is married, I'll come to you the very next day. Then I won't need to say anything to anyone. I won't need anyone's permission, either.'

'When is your sister likely to get married, di? If you insist on waiting for her to be married, I'll marry both of you myself.'

Sakuntala opened her eyes wide and looked at him. She saw the look of shame on his face.

'Don't tempt me first, only to let me down later, Saku. I can't bear it any more.'

He put the money for the ice creams on the table and walked out. At once Sakuntala got up and followed him. But without turning around, he rushed away into the press and throng of the crowds. Sakuntala stopped short, realizing it was useless to try and follow him any further. He would have reached his bus stand by now. His mind would be fixed on clambering in and fighting his way towards a seat as soon as the bus arrived.

Sakuntala walked towards her own bus stop. Today, it might be as late as half-past seven or even eight by the time she reached home. Just as she had been fearful of Rajaratnam's question, now she was afraid of what her mother or someone else would say. Appa never opened his mouth. It was Amma, always…. Desperately she hoped that at least this time, the marriage negotiation for her sister wouldn't fail.

ſ

The huge crowds of the rush hour were a little less dense now. All the same, the number of people there would make it difficult to climb on to the bus, when it did arrive, with any semblance of dignity. Standing there, gazing into the distance, didn't lessen Sakuntala's anguish. If the bus were to arrive now, for the duration of forty minutes she would not be able to put her mind to anything other than the experience of the journey itself. If it turned out that there was only standing room, her whole mind would be focused on her own bodily discomfort, nothing else. And certainly, if the bus arrived now there would only be standing room. So if the bus arrived, there would be temporary relief. But after seven, it was always at least half an hour late.

Rajaratnam had called her 'di' once before, in too familiar a manner. Once, when they met during the holidays, he had been drinking before he arrived. But who was there in the whole of Tamil Nadu who had never had a drink in all of two years? Her own uncle was so far gone in his alcoholism he had to be hospitalized. As for her elder brother, words couldn't describe his state. Rajaratnam was always full of remorse immediately afterwards. During the past year, they had been alone together several times. Never once had he taken advantage and overstepped the limits of propriety. He was the favourite son in his family. Because of this very fact, there would be plenty of opposition to their marriage. But for the same reason, he would get his way in the end. Now she too was the favourite daughter in the family. How much leeway favourite daughters had in the matter of marriage was something she had yet to learn. Her stomach churned at the very thought of putting it to the test. Perhaps, after all, such a test would never be needed? Was that the answer?

The notion of a possible escape only increased her inward tumult. She had imagined that she was standing absolutely still, without registering any change of expression on her face. But a woman wearing a white sari, with no ornaments in her ears or about her neck, handed her a few sheets of printed paper, speaking softly but clearly, 'You are in the midst of many trials and tribulations. But there is One who can bear them for you.' Sakuntala accepted the leaflets without a word, thrust them in her handbag, and made her way closer to the waiting crowd. There was one thing that she was absolutely certain about. She alone could carry her own burden.

When the bus arrived finally, it was incredibly crowded. Sakuntala climbed in somehow, and pushed her way forward, near the conductor's seat. The bus began to move. Just then a woman sitting immediately behind the conductor stood up and began to shout, 'Stop! Stop! I have to get out. I must get out here.' Automatically, the conductor blew his whistle in response to her plea and the bus came to a standstill. The conductor's fury was boundless after that. But all the same, because he had actually responded to her wish, he couldn't now call upon the rules and regulations. Anyway, as a result of this, Sakuntala managed to get a seat straightaway. Was this a sign of good times to come?

If there is such a thing as a lucky time, things which seemed impossible even to contemplate, could actually come to be. Great kingdoms fall, while people whose fortunes seemed to be at an end, and who were long forgotten, are suddenly reinstated in high positions. Would this be possible but for such a thing as a lucky moment? As for her, she didn't need an extended good time. Only a moment's worth, a drop. Her sister should get married. That was all.

On one occasion before this, Rajaratnam had said, 'Why do you always keep talking about your Akka? Is she your contemporary and sibling, or are you responsible for her? Let her marriage happen when it must.' She could leave it at that. But, if Sakuntala were to get married first, then her sister would never be sought in marriage. On top of that, the sister of a girl who eloped with a man outside her caste could never ever hope to get married. They would both have to run away with men of different castes. But Akka would never be able to do that.

Sakuntala was overcome with pity when she thought of her sister. She passed her SSLC only after her fourth attempt. Because of that, there was no opportunity for her to go on to further education. She did all the household chores without ever wearying of them. If she really did get married one day, and moved in with her in-laws, her own parental family would never be able to function smoothly. In fifteen years, there wasn't a household responsibility she hadn't borne. Ten or twelve years ago, prospective bridegrooms who had come to 'see' her, had asked in surprise, 'Doesn't she go out to work at all?'

Poor Akka. One young man's mother had commented, 'Nowadays, everyone is joining correspondence courses and passing exams. Can't she do something of that sort?' Must Akka go for career guidance at the age of thirty, listen to notions of success through competition, and attend a typewriting institute day and night? And even if she did that, and got herself a certificate, what employment was she going to get? She could write out receipts, for a stretch of nine hours at a time at a Chit Fund, and earn three thousand rupees a month. A hundred rupees of that would go on bus fares alone. Then, doesn't a woman who is sitting on a steel chair throughout the day need at least a cup or two of coffee? So, after all that, what would be left? No. Akka need not go out to work anywhere. She need never do it.

Sakuntala got off one stop before her usual one. She bought a string of jasmine from the flower seller who sold it at forty paise a muzham. Rajaratnam would be waiting on Monday, just as he said he would. Once again she would repeat her sister must get married first. This time he would go away without replying to her. It was now a whole year that he had been waiting. It would not be right for her to make him wait any longer.

Everything is a matter of dharma, right order. Even the granting of her name, Sakuntala, was a matter of dharma. Why could her grandmother not have given her another name? Why did she have to be 'Sakuntala'? Any marriage she entered into would have to be without the knowledge of her parents.

Nobody said a word when she reached home. Akka had been lying down with a headache. She had been to the optician, apparently. He had said she must wear spectacles. It would certainly be a misfortune, given the state of her looks at the moment.

The question that Sakuntala wanted to ask was on the tip of her tongue many times, but she forced it back. Did the people who came to see Akka send any word? Did Appa go and enquire? She didn't know anything yet. It seemed that nobody remembered that there were two girls waiting to be married, fixed like mountains in the house.

After they had eaten, when she was emptying out her bag, what fell out first were the leaflets that the woman at the bus stand had given her, saying, 'There is One who is ready to bear all your troubles.' There was even a small picture on a card. A woman bearing the crucified Jesus on her lap. It was a cheap print from a poor photograph of Michelangelo's sculpture. Sakuntala had read an essay about it in one of her supplementary textbooks. The young woman who supported Jesus on her lap should have been as old as her own mother. Even in the days when the sculpture was just finished, some people had been scornful. How could this be the mother of a thirty-year-old man? Did she have the gift of eternal youth, in that case?

Michelangelo's answer: Those who are pure in heart never experience old age.

Who in this family was not pure of heart? Yet Akka was already halfway to becoming an old woman. That time was not too distant when she too would be considered old. If she herself were to ask her parents, even without Rajaratnam's urging, they would certainly take the jewellery and utensils which had been stored away for Akka and make all the arrangements for her own wedding. On the other hand, Sakuntala was a working girl. Her job, in a growing company, had been made permanent. However stressful it was to travel there by bus, she worked in an air-conditioned building, where a lift took her up to her office, in comfort.

Yes, it turned out that her father had indeed gone to enquire. They did not say 'No'. They would definitely give their answer tomorrow.

As Sakuntala went to bed, she thought, let me sleep in peace tonight at least.

Translated by Lakshmi Holmström

MY NAME IS MADHAVAN

R. CHUDAMANI

He stood there, a boy at the threshold of youth, about five-and-a-half feet tall, with a wheatish complexion bordering on fair, a half-hesitant, half-expectant expression on his face that was like a partly closed, or partly open, flower, cheeks toughened by a crop of acne, a pointed nose above the grin, small, fixed eyes, a high forehead, and folded hands that shook a bit. He introduced himself as if trying to give a meaning to this form.

'My name is Madhavan.'

'Please sit down,' I said.

His feet haltingly moved two steps, feeling their way forward. I involuntarily stretched out my hand to guide him, but stopped midway. Would he like it? I looked at him with concern. With a little hesitation, but with a practised ease and a sense of pride that he had managed to move around in a strange house, he sat down on a stool; there was a big sigh—it was I who sighed, not he.

'Is the stool comfortable? If not, the chair is close by. You can sit on that.' I wanted to make him aware that he was sitting on a stool and that he should not lean back, believing it to be a chair.

'It's okay, sir. This is quite comfortable,' he, that is Madhavan, said. I had learnt his name just today.

When I first met him five years ago, he was not alone. An elderly man was with him. He was standing behind the older man, hugging a big book against his chest with his right hand. He must have just let go of the hand that had led him thus far. He was wearing crumpled but spotless, loose white shorts, and the brown shirt was dark near the armpits because of perspiration. I thought the smile on his face was meant for me when I shouted, 'Who is that?' He was looking not at me, but at the wall! Was he squint-eyed? The next moment I saw the two glassy eyes.

'Who are you?' This time my question was not so peremptory.

'We are from an organization for sightless people.' The elderly man stopped and looked at me. He could see. He probably worked there.

'Please can you take a look at this?' Even when I took the book from him, I continued to look at the young man—sightless glass eyes, but such radiance in his face!

I looked down at the book: 'Society for the Welfare of the Sightless'. The words written in English were at the crest of the first page and at the bottom was an address in Park Town. On the left was a list of names of important members of the organization. On the right, under the heading 'Request', written in ink in a smudgy and shaky handwriting, was a request for donation from kind benefactors to the society, which worked for the welfare of the sightless. I turned over the pages. The names of the donors and the amounts donated were recorded there.

The elderly man was telling me about the organization, but my eyes were still fixed on the boy.

'Though it is only after learning skills like cane work, carpentry, basket weaving, etc., from the training school on Poonamallee High Road that they come to us, we nurture and develop their skills by giving them training. We keep writing to other organizations, asking them to reserve some posts for the visually challenged. Many get jobs and some even get married.'

The sightless. In the book, the words used were 'the sightless'. For some reason, this sounded more humane than 'the blind'. I felt that the older man's complete avoidance of the word 'blind' was a meaningful omission. The terms 'sightless', 'speech disabled', and 'hearing disabled' did not denote contempt, unlike the words 'blind', 'deaf', and 'dumb'. They did not express scorn or scathing contempt; instead, they seemed to say 'accept your unfortunate friends'.

'We...approach...individuals...like this and...we receive donations from rich people and the government.'

I looked at the amounts written down on the brown, dog-eared pages, which had a grimy feel to them—50 paise, 5 rupees,

1 rupee, 2 rupees. One rupee was the amount that occurred the most frequently. After giving the book back to the older man, I pulled out a rupee from the wallet in my shirt pocket.

'Thanks, sir.'

The younger man followed suit and also gestured his thanks, his smile again directed at the wall.

After that, they started coming every month. And I gave them a rupee every month. I was eager to get to know the young man. But the older man's presence stopped me. When both of them said farewell, I felt like dragging him by his folded hands and bringing him back in.

'Who are you? What is the truth hidden in that "you"? Which is this other world whose leader you are? Which is the inner space that you seem to rule? Will you not reveal to me that inner you? Will you not grant me that vision?' My heart beat hard as I yearned to plead with him for answers,

'See you,' was all I would manage to say.

He was fragile, like a book that one had to open gently and carefully, by blowing on it. How do I approach him?

The opportunity came one day. Looking at the boy, I gave the rupee to the older man. From inside the house, the clatter of the typewriter could be heard. 'Tat tattattattat.'

His face brightened up at once. 'Is it a typewriter, sir?'

'Yes.'

'Do you have one? Do you type?'

'I don't. The machine belongs to my sister's son. He has gone out of town for some training. He has left it with me till he comes back. If my neighbours want something to be typed urgently, they come and type it here. The girl next door asked me this morning if she could type an article for her college magazine. She is here.'

He was silent for a while. His face expressed joy as he bent his head to one side and listened intently.

'Tat tattattattattattatattatattatattatat.'

'I think she has made some mistake. That is why she is scoring it out.' It was only when he said that that I noticed how the keys sounded different from the way they had the last time. I looked at him in surprise.

'Do you know how to type? Do they teach you that too?'

'No, sir. There are separate Braille machines for that. We don't have them. He had learnt to type even before…before he lost his vision.' The older man explained.

'Lost his….'

'I was interested in that, though I was doing odd jobs,' he intervened and picked up the trail. 'My factory owner was a good man. He arranged for me to learn free of cost at an institute run by his friend. He even told me I would get a good job afterwards. I learnt typing for two years at that institute. I liked it very much.' His fingers danced away as if they were typing.

'At first, I would furtively look at the letters and type, and the teacher would yell at me. He would cover the keys with a piece of cloth and ask me to type, or tell me to type with my eyes closed….' He stopped for a minute, as if he was staring at the last two words, and then burst out laughing.

I turned away, forgetting that he could not see the sorrow flooding my face.

Factory…what kind of factory? Was it a factory accident that had bli…that had robbed him of his sight? There could be a thousand reasons—how did it matter? He may have become incapable of working or maybe the owner had died and the factory had closed—how did it matter? The fact of the matter was that he was bereft of all support. He was still lost in thought.

'So even now, you can type on ordinary machines, not necessarily Braille, no?' I asked him eagerly.

'Oh, yes! It is just a touch system. All I need to do is to position my fingers right when I start.'

I did some quick thinking. My wife had caught the literary bug from the girl next door. She had written a pile of stories full of romance and pathos, to be sent to some monthly journals. After reading them, I had sternly resisted the idea of getting them typed, but now found a use for them.

'My wife writes stories. If someone reads aloud, can you type them? They are in English. I will pay at the usual rate. You can come when it's convenient and I will accompany you back to the hostel.'

His face lit up like ten thousand lamps. His body shook as if the dance of his fingers vibrated through it. His wide grin revealed his gums. The smile on his raised face was not for me, but directed elsewhere.

'Yes, sir, I'll come, sir. What is your machine, sir? Is it Remington portable? I am used to that. Even if it is upstairs, I can manage by climbing slowly. If I do it carefully for two days, I'll get used to it.'

That's how it started. The hostel permitted him to come. After all, this was another source of income for him. Then a day was fixed and the elderly man brought him home. He stood in excited anticipation. It was then that I asked him, as a step towards forging familiarity and closeness, 'What is your name?'

He told me. I realized that the name 'Madhavan' stood for this boy and his eagerness, his liveliness, his young age, which was half of mine, and his misfortune and the smile in the midst of it.

He had sat on the stool for merely two seconds.

'Where is the machine, sir?'

I took him to his seat. He leant on the table and stroked and touched the machine with both hands. Then he bent and rested his face on it, and a smile spilled from his lips.

Then he was not there; he was somewhere else. Where? At the factory? Or at the typewriting institute? In those days, eyes meant vision. He could see then—a world that had colour, shapes. He saw people and their forms. He could look at both sides and dart his glance across the road before the distant bus came close.... The black eyes slyly looked at the board while typing with dexterity... tat tattatattattatat. The voice that asked him to type with his eyes closed belonged to a face which had a stern expression. He could look at him with a mischievous smile. He could look at the machine and stop typing before the bell rang to indicate that he had reached the edge of the paper. And then? And what else? What other sights were locked inside the glass eyes?

He was not there but I could not follow him...because I can see.

He looked up and slowly ran his fingers over the machine.

'Is this small machine a Remington?'

'No. Hermes.'

'I must get used to it. Can you give me a sheet of paper?'

With ease and just by touch, he fixed the paper in the middle of the cylinder. His fingers measured the space and were then ready on the keys.

'ASDFGF.'

His face focused inward, the letters came out as though they were religious chants.

After the middle row, he went to the second row from the top.

'QWERTR.'

I kept watching his face. I had called my wife to introduce him to her. She came and stood there looking him up and down, with the manuscript in her hands.

The fingers of his right hand, starting from the little finger, were now on the bottom row, moving over the keys as if counting them.

'Full stop, comma, M, N, B...I've haven't forgotten at all, sir! I remember everything! Shall I now check by typing the alphabet—A-B-C-D-E-F-G?'

His fingers flew over the keys. I looked at my wife, full of appreciation for him. My mother stood behind my wife. The way she looked at him, I could sense that for her it was like a circus trick.

'V-W-X-Y-Z-full stop. Sir, I have come to the end. Will you please check if it is correct?'

I took a look at the sheet of paper.

'Excellent! Absolutely correct.'

Pride and joy flashed across his face.

'Nothing surprising. I have not forgotten anything. But it is a different machine...some keys may be in different places...for example....' The index finger jabbed a key on the top row. 'In that machine this was a hyphen. Is it so here too?'

Emotion choked me, but I steadied myself, looking at his cheerful face.

'Why are you silent, sir? Are you wondering because there are two marks on the same key? Tell me what is at the bottom?'

'This is not a hyphen.'

'See? There may be such minor variations. Just tell me what is on the top row in order, and I will memorize it. The numbers will be in the same places. Tell me the other marks. Even if you do not understand it does not matter—I will.'

He was in his domain and now, assurance, self-confidence, and pride came naturally. This was the real him. It exhilarated me as I called out the keys, and as I did so, he touched them to commit to memory. Then to practise, he typed a few sentences.

'Is it correct, sir?'

I bent down.

'In one place it is "I" instead of "e".'

He typed the sentence again.

'Now?'

'Correct.'

'I'm ready.'

I called my wife and introduced them. He said 'vanakkam' to her. Then he briskly started the work.

'Ma'am, just tell me when I come to the end of the sheet and I will insert a fresh one. Will you now give me the sheets of paper for typing? As soon as I insert one, we can start. Double-spacing, no? One plus one or two.... Oh, sorry! How many copies do you need? Have you bought carbon paper?' He continued to speak excitedly, the sightless one. I looked on at him with a smile. My wife did not answer.

It was my mother who spoke. 'Great! The blind boy is so clever! He can even type!'

He straightened up. Was his complexion wheatish and almost

fair? No. This was just white. The blood had drained out of his face. Just white. The exuberance, liveliness, human dignity, and unyielding self-confidence had all gone—he had died.

The sightless one slowly rose from the chair.

'Sir, take me up to the gate, will you? After that, I will go by myself, I'm used to it.'

I stared at my mother's face just once. Without a word, I held his hand and started walking. What right had I to ask him to stay or even talk to him? He would never come here again.

He reached the doorstep. Then he looked in the direction from which my mother's voice had come. He turned his face.

'My name is not "blind boy".' He took four steps beyond the door and continued in a tired voice, 'My name is Madhavan.'

I crossed the collapsible gate and took him outside.

Translated by Prabha Sridevan

NAADAR SIR

SUNDARA RAMASWAMY

These days I often remember Naadar Sir. I am getting to be quite old, and I have this nagging feeling that Death, which came by and snatched him up, actually brushed me too in passing and is now lurking somewhere nearby, biding its time. I have lost many loved ones over the years…relatives, friends. I have always been nagged by guilt for never visiting Naadar Sir, although he lived barely half an hour away. Yet, the thought that he was still there, living in the village, had given me some solace. Now it's just me, my loneliness, and memories of the past….

These events are from fifty years ago. I was in the tenth class in Sethu Parvathy Bai School. Our maths teacher was E. R. S. (our nickname for him was kaaraboondhi). That month, thirteen students, including me, scored zero in the maths test. 'Good-for-nothing idiots! After this week I'll wash my hands off you fellows! Ekambara Naadar will take my place. From now on, he is the one who will have to put up with you fellows….' shouted E. R. S.

We started imagining this new teacher, creating mental images of this Naadar Sir. He will be riding a bicycle, said one of the boys. The rest of us couldn't believe this. Our teachers had always arrived walking and carrying an umbrella. In fact, it seemed they were incapable of walking except under an open umbrella. True, a few of the scrawnier teachers did arrive in jutkas. And S. P. Sir, with a huge bandage on his leg like someone who had recently been wounded in war, would roll up in a cart drawn by a single bullock. He would crawl onto the veranda and then clamber into a chair with a great deal of effort. Wouldn't it be beneath the dignity of a schoolteacher to be pedalling a bicycle along the road? How come Naadar Sir didn't know this?

Naadar Sir entered the classroom. His appearance was comical.

Our mental images of the new teacher bore no resemblance to the real man. We had imagined cropped hair or a tuft; some sandal paste on his forehead, or a smear of sacred ash; a coat and the traditional panchakachham dhoti, or maybe a double-length dhoti; a turban; a watch on the inner wrist, or perhaps a pocket watch on a chain. A severe expression, wounding words, refusal to be satisfied even with high test scores. And the power to make us cower under his thumb.

As it was, the whole class burst into laughter the moment Naadar Sir entered. Even the girls giggled, covering their mouths with their hands, heads bent. It was as if someone who happened to be passing by on the street had inadvertently wandered in, unaware of the reputation of the premises into which he was trespassing. The hair on his head stood up like stubble. When he placed the thumb and forefinger of his right hand on either side of his forehead and pressed upwards, the stubbly hair would stand up straighter and then ripple forward when released. He seemed totally unaware of what a comical sight he presented. The pointed ends of his twisted moustache arched upwards, and Sir would try to get a glimpse of them by squinting his eyes inwards. Khadi dhoti, khadi jibba, rough rubber sandals. His bare wrist was a curious, unsettling sight. Instead of a pen in his pocket, he sported a pencil sharpened at both ends. (How often our teachers had whacked us for breaking a classroom taboo and doing exactly this!)

'Without any warning they've thrust the maths class on me,' Naadar Sir informed us. 'I've forgotten everything. So now I have to learn it first.' And he laughed.

We laughed too.

'Take out your maths notebook, ma,' he said, holding a hand out towards Vilasini who was in the front row.

His use of 'amma' to address a student sounded bizarre to us. It set off a fresh wave of laughter.

'So, the very sight of me amuses you all so much?' remarked Naadar Sir, joining in the laughter.

He turned the pages of the maths notebook one at a time. 'Enna de, each is more frightening than the last,' he remarked.

Laughter rose in billows and crashed against the four walls. Sir stood staring at us with a bemused expression.

'It's not all that difficult, sir. You can easily work them out with some practice,' Nagarajan reassured him.

Sir observed Nagarajan's face closely. 'How many marks do you score in maths, thambi?' he asked.

'A hundred,' said Nagarajan.

'Always?'

'Yes, always.'

'He has never got less than hundred, sir,' shouted Thirumalai.

'Then naturally you would find it easy,' said Sir.

We were beginning to feel a strange sensation, as if the whole class was being dissolved in some strange fluid.

'How many marks did you get when you were in the tenth class, sir?' asked Chakrapani.

Now, this Chakrapani was the most cowardly fellow in the class. And yet, here he was asking Sir a bold question like this! Did a whole yuga somehow go by in an instant? The student was questioning the teacher about the marks he secured. And that too in Sethu Parvathy Bai School, where Headmaster Rajam Iyer, ruled with an iron fist!

'Too low to announce publicly,' said Sir.

Again the students laughed.

'I don't think I will start teaching maths today. I will tell you about some games instead. Tomorrow we will get started with maths.'

'But are we allowed to talk about games in class, Sir?' Seshan wanted to know.

'Nothing wrong with that. After all, sports are also a kind of education.'

He started talking to us about football. He spoke with great involvement and passion. As he went on, he seemed to forget he was in a classroom. His hands were waving about. He headed away an imaginary ball. As though it had rolled down the stairs and into the garden, he stared into emptiness. He scored goal after imaginary goal, kicking the invisible ball through the goalposts repeatedly, while we sat watching in tension, wondering if his khadi dhoti might get ripped in the process.

We students could not contain our excitement. 'Goal! Goal!' we yelled. Sir sidled towards the classroom door like a child, and peeped around the edge cautiously.

Upstairs, at the front of the building, was an imposing structure resting on a stone foundation supported by massive pillars—the Headmaster's room—flaunting its grandeur and proclaiming its importance to the universe. On three sides, wide windows displayed sturdy curved grilles, each of them having dark green curtains. It even had a tall, wide, green bamboo screen just in front of the entrance door; placed so close to it in fact that one had to slide in sideways to enter.

Sir took in the scene outside our classroom door with a keen eye. Then he looked at us and smiled a mischievous smile.

'De, don't make such a noise. He will pluck out your eyes,' he said, pointing upwards in the direction of the Headmaster's office.

'We couldn't beat Carmel School in the football match, Sir,' said Govindan Kutty.

'Why, de, what's so special about them. Do they have horns growing on their heads or something?' Sir mimed the horns by holding the back of his right hand against his forehead and extending the forefinger and little finger upwards.

'What's needed is coaching. And a strong will to succeed,' he told us.

'Sir, do you think it's possible for us to defeat Carmel School?'

'De, any game requires intelligence and discipline. What do you boys have? Do you have the brains for it? Do you have physical strength? Discipline? Determination?' asked Sir.

Each of his questions fell like blows on our skulls.

'If you show us how, we will play beautifully, Sir,' said Vallinaayagam.

'You all have to get permission from above, de,' said Sir, pointing at the ceiling above which sat the Headmaster's room.

'We're scared, Sir,' shouted all the boys in one voice.

'If that's so, then go and find a game that cowards can play. Then we will see,' declared Sir.

It suddenly dawned on us that Sir was capable of anger. The bell rang. Sir waved at us and strode out briskly.

Naadar Sir had stirred our minds deeply. Time and again, we had been made to swallow humiliations. In a school full of teachers who saw red at the very mention of sports, how could we ever learn a game? We saw that we had lost all sense of pride and self-respect. That is what rankled the most in our hearts.

Every year, on the day before Christmas break began, a familiar humiliation would await us. Carmel School challenged us every year to a football match, because they had the competence and skill to play. But why did our Headmaster have to accept their invitation? That was the question for which none of us had an answer. We went to Kumaravel Sir and pleaded with him.

'Let's not accept the invitation this time, Sir. We can't stand the repeated humiliation.'

'How is that possible? Our school is the largest one in the whole of Thiruvithangur. The Rani Amma, out of affection, sends the silver cup to our school. Isn't it proper that we should present it to the winning team?' asked Kumaravel Sir.

'But does that mean we should accept and then lose dismally year after year just so that Carmel School can win the cup?'

'They play beautifully, they win the cup. You scrawny fellows… are you capable of playing at all?'

'We are not going to play this year, Sir,' we declared.

'The Headmaster has already announced your names on the noticeboard. Is there any among you who has the guts to defy him?' shouted Sir.

'We are too scared to tell him, Sir. Please tell him on our behalf,' we pleaded.

'If I do, he'll ask me "So, then will you take the silver cup home with you or what?"'

The next thing we knew, the date of the match had been announced.

'Sir, Sir, wha-a–t's this?' we protested to Kumaravel Sir.

'I will coach you fellows for three days, de. Enough?'

'But there's no ball, Sir.'

Kumaravel Sir was angry. His voice rose.

'Balls are there aplenty. But the room key is lost. The Headmaster has written to the Inspector's office in Thiruvananthapuram for permission to break the lock, but the wretched people there haven't bothered to reply. You fellows are not even smart enough to get a ball on loan from somewhere and you're standing here arguing.'

'The rival team has had five years of coaching. You're telling us you will give us three days of coaching, Sir. Year after year they come and score goal upon goal, and taunt us by shouting "One more, one more" each time they score.'

'De, I will tell you something and I want you fellows to listen carefully. Those who are good at studies cannot be good at games. And those who play sports well will be hopeless at studies. In the whole of Thiruvithangur, which school tops in academics? Our school!' declared Kumaravel.

We were stumped for a suitable response to this, so were momentarily silenced.

Kumaravel Sir continued: 'Look, I have an idea. Go stealthily to Carmel School, observe the coaching they're receiving there and learn the techniques, de. You fellows can't get anything done, but still you want to win. Hmmhh!'

The next day three of us set off on our quest. Me, Subramania Sarma, and Emanuel. The moment we entered Carmel School, we were confronted by five or six students. The very sight of them brought fear to our minds. Each of the boys was about a foot taller than any of us. We had to crane our necks to look at their faces. Their chests were so broad that their vests were in imminent danger of giving way. Big, muscled thighs like mature banana plant stems. Knees moulded in solid iron. They were wearing special boots. We had heard that the soles of these boots were studded with nails.

'Aren't you the fellows from the Keerathandu school?' demanded one of them who seemed to be their leader.

We stayed silent.

'Did you come to watch our football coaching?' he asked. Sarcasm spread over his face and scorn dripped from his voice.

How did he know? Who could have revealed to this accursed fellow what was in our minds?

He cleared his throat. Then he made a pronouncement: 'I will tear you limb from limb. I will disconnect all your joints. Be wise and run away from here.'

Sarma and I looked at Emanuel. Emanuel had some acquaintance with boxing techniques. His face was flushed.

'Some day you will be at my mercy. Then you will find out what I am capable of,' retorted Emanuel.

'Oh, get lost you son of a bitch!' responded the Carmel School fellow.

I tugged Emanuel's shirt gently. The three of us shuffled away.

The failure of our mission brought us further humiliation.

'You hopeless fellows…you can't get even the simplest task done. But you want to win the silver cup,' scolded Kumaravel Sir.

There were six or seven football fields on our school grounds. They were the best in the whole of Thiruvithangur. We also had a lot of footballs. But because the key to the storage room had been lost, we had not seen a football for a very long time.

We managed to borrow a football, and practised for three days. Even our Sanskrit teacher turned up one day to watch us at practice. He continuously twirled the tuft on his head as he watched us, like someone trying to unscrew the lid of a ghee pot. When we ran he would shout out, 'Careful! Careful! Don't fall and break an arm or leg!' It seemed even the teachers were beginning to empathize with us. Kumaravel Sir stayed with us the entire three days. Because of his blood pressure condition he couldn't join us on the field. But he supplied instructions and admonitions aplenty. 'Slice kick…now tap… no, no, idiot, not there, kick it into the goal…the goal!' Joseph Sir also came by. He had received football coaching at Carmel School in his student days. His football exploits and his goal count were among his favourite talking points. And—surprise of surprises—even the Headmaster watched our training session. Except that he watched from the veranda. When we had finished our practice we went up to the Headmaster.

'You all played well,' said the Headmaster in English.

Grabbing the unexpected opportunity that had presented itself, we said, 'We need a ball, sir.'

The headmaster turned to Joseph Sir. 'Tomorrow itself we should write a reminder letter to the Inspector about the locked room. Don't forget,' he said.

We had been instructed by Kumaravel Sir that each of us should eat a nendran banana before turning up for the evening match. He explained that this input was essential to ensure that we were able to kick the ball hard and well. So we bought a whole bunch of nendran bananas and ate two each before heading for the football field. Just abutting the field was a spacious raised area of ground. The peons Arunachalam and Chokkalingam were arranging chairs on it. The Sanskrit teacher, Joseph Sir, Kumaravel Sir, Malayalam teacher Unnikrishnan Nair, E. R. S. Veerabhadran Chettiar, Sivaramakrishna Iyer, R. L. Kesava Iyer, the Arabic teacher, Sarvottam Rao, Sivan Pillai, Pannirugai Perumal, Achamma Thomas, Kanthimathi Teacher… many of the teachers were there. Near the front gate of the school, the Carmel School team players were standing together in a bunch. They were in uniform outfits: blue shorts and yellow jerseys. As we watched them, their formidable combined strength seemed to leap across from where they stood, turning our insides to mush.

'Only ten minutes left for the game to start. Why are they still hanging around over there?' the Headmaster asked sternly.

'They will come only after Father Xavier arrives. He is their coach,' explained Kumaravel Sir.

'What a big hoo-haa,' remarked the Headmaster, frowning. A motorcycle was heard approaching. It came in through the front gate and onto the raised area, and stopped under the neem tree. From it alighted Father Xavier, the hem of his cassock billowing stylishly in the breeze. His slender frame darted rapidly towards the Headmaster. The latter was still in the process of raising his arms with the intention of greeting the visitor with folded palms, when the visitor grabbed the Headmaster's half-raised right hand and shook it heartily. The Carmel School team fell into line and walked in. The awesome discipline that emanated from the group further impressed us.

'Please be seated, Father,' invited the Headmaster. The two sat down next to each other. We team members stood next to each of them. The student leader we had encountered during our humiliating visit to Carmel School was present, his expression full of menace. But no way would he have the courage even to lay his little finger on us with our teachers watching.

'Shall we have the first whistle now?' asked Kumaravel Sir.

'Go ahead,' said the Headmaster.

The Carmel School fellow turned towards Father Xavier and asked, 'Father, how many goals would you like us to score?'

Father Xavier lifted his head slightly and asked, 'How many did we score last year?'

'Nine,' replied the team leader.

'Then let's make it the same this time also. No more and no less,' advised Father Xavier.

We looked at the Headmaster. We looked at our teachers. The Headmaster wore a sheepish smile. His lips twitched slightly as though a mosquito had settled on them. The rest of the teachers stood with heads bowed, whispering among themselves.

Eight goals were scored against us before half-time. In the interval, the Carmel School heroes opened a large leather suitcase and took out soft freshly-laundered towels, one each, and wiped their faces and hands. They took out juice bottles, flipped open their caps, and gulped down the coloured drinks. As for us, we only had a tin bucket of water. As we dipped a tin mug into the bucket and took turns drinking water, the Carmel team captain came over to us. He said, 'We will score our last goal exactly three minutes before the final whistle. You poor weaklings, don't run around too much and kill yourselves.' He sauntered away.

One must praise his commitment towards keeping his promises. When the game was over and we looked around, the Headmaster's chair was empty. So were all the other chairs. All the teachers had left. Even Kumaravel Sir was nowhere to be seen.

'We must destroy our school, flatten it,' fumed Emanuel. 'My heart won't know any peace till it is reduced to rubble.'

One day in class, Naadar Sir showed us some photographs and certificates. Each photo featured a team he had represented in his college days; and in each photo, Sir held a trophy. One, particularly, which showed him standing next to the Rani and holding a huge cup, made us rub our eyes in disbelief. What a radiant smile on the Rani's face!

Sir said, 'This afternoon, at three o'clock, the H. M. has agreed to meet me. Whoever is interested in playing football, give me your names.'

'What are the requirements, Sir?' we asked him.

'Both legs should be normal, with no knock knees. You should be prepared to work hard. You should have a determination to succeed. Tell yourself, if we lose the match this year, our life is over right there and then on that field. Those of you who can do all this may submit your names.'

Sir arrived in front of the H. M.'s front door screen at 2.45 p.m. We were already waiting. Through the side of the screen we could see that the blades of the ceiling fan were turning hesitantly, as though expecting a reprimand any moment. On the wall hung a large clock with no pendulum, its second hand twitching as it moved around its face. None of us had ever been inside the H. M.'s room before. Before long, our feet would tread its floor; and as we stood with hands respectfully clasped together, the full majesty of the room would disclose itself to us. The momentousness of the anticipated event evoked emotions in us that we could barely control.

At exactly three o'clock, a peremptory summons was heard: 'Ekambaram! Ekambaram!'

'Sir, sir,' said our Sir, as he inserted himself sideways through the narrow opening between screen and wall. Then, turning back to us for a moment, he warned, 'Not a word from any of you in there.'

The Headmaster said, 'Ekambaram, we must win the silver cup this year. I don't know what you will do or how you will do it, but it must be done. Money is not a constraint. I will stand behind you and support you all the way.'

'Sir, I have brought some photos and certificates to show you,' said Naadar Sir.

'I don't need to see any evidence. I know football means Ekamabara Naadar and Ekambara Naadar means football. The whole of Thiruvithangur knows this.' Then, turning towards us, the Headmaster said, 'If you don't listen to Sir and play the way he tells you to, I will break your legs.'

Naadar Sir turned his gaze towards us. 'They are all very fond of football, Sir,' he said. Then, he added: 'Sir, I have a request.'

'What is it?'

'If you look up an auspicious day for us, I will start the coaching on that day.'

'Auspicious…inauspicious…no such thing. Start right now, this very minute.' The Headmaster turned to us and asked, 'What do you have in the last period, da?'

'History.'

'Who's the teacher? Sarvottam Rao, right?'

'Yes.'

'I will talk to him. You boys run to the playing field, right now.

If you lose the match this year, I won't allow any of you donkeys to take the exams.'

Ekambara Sir strode unhurriedly along the veranda. We followed in his wake. We descended the big staircase. Sir came to a halt at a tiny room that stood near the foot of a ladder. He tugged at the padlock. Then Sir took a few steps back, ran forward, and delivered a mighty kick to the bottom of the door. The hasp of the latch shattered. 'Collect all the footballs and throw them out of the room, de,' said Sir. And that is what we did. Big and small, there were seventeen balls in all.

Naadar Sir's house was on the route from my home to school. Before sunrise every morning, Emanuel would come up to Saanthaan Chetty Circle and signal for me with a shrill whistle (which he managed to produce by inserting a couple of fingers in his mouth and blowing hard). Primed for his signal and raring to go, I would leap out. Sir would be standing at the door of his house in khaki shorts and a white vest. The moment he saw us approaching from a distance, he would descend his front steps and start jogging away slowly. This was our running practice. Once in a way he would turn back and look at us to see whether we were using the proper running technique he had taught us. 'Heads up!' he would shout.

By the time we reached the school playing field, seven or eight bicycles would already be parked under the neem tree. At least twenty boys would be present. Sir would join the game and play with us. Sometimes, to get a better view of our on-field performance, he would station himself at the goalmouth.

How that remarkable brain of his could itemize and codify every single movement made by every single one of us remains a mystery to which only God above holds the key. Once our practice session was over we would move over to the wide steps leading down to another field at a lower level. We would sit down on these steps in a neat row. Sir would stand in front of us and talk to us non-stop for half an hour; and during all that time he would keep tossing the ball between his hands. He explained every mistake that each of us had made, and he followed it up with instructions on how to avoid these. No scolding, no censure.

'It's not only the legs that come into play, de,' he said. 'Your whole body has to play. The eyes play, the brain plays, the ears play…everything must join in the game. And another thing. You must anticipate what will happen next. Your mind must work out the strategy…the angles, the approaches, in a split second. De, the ball is willing and ready to carry out your instructions. Finally, always keep some of your strength in reserve. Keep the opposition guessing about your capabilities.'

Solid, powerful words, flowed towards us in a stream from Naadar Sir.

From Christmas right up to the Pongal vacation we did not miss a single day of practice. Morning and evening. Plus training sessions three times during the week. Physical exercises, running. We ourselves couldn't believe how much we had improved. Our relationship with our physical selves was rapidly and noticeably growing more intimate, as was our relationship with the football itself. Sir was fond of saying that the ball was the most emotionally responsive creation of the Almighty. We were beginning to understand what he meant. But whenever we thought we had attained great heights in football, Sir would say, 'De, we have only now placed our feet on the first step. Don't become overconfident. There's still a long way to go.' As a team, we were beginning to instinctively understand one another without actually speaking, and this intimacy strengthened day by day. If one of us tackled an oncoming player and got possession of the ball, we could be sure that the appropriate person would be in place, ready to accept our pass, and take it forward to the danger zone near the goal. There another of us would be in just the right spot to send the ball into the goal with a well-directed header.

On one occasion, Seshan said, 'Sir, this game is not just a game…. It is something else, something more.' He couldn't quite explain what exactly he felt.

'A sport is like a gold mine. You can keep digging, layer after layer, deeper and deeper, and continue to take out treasure,' said Sir.

His words seemed to lend shape to our muddled thoughts.

Sir would invite several of the teachers to come and watch our evening practice sessions. The teachers were astonished at what they were witnessing. They were full of praise and encouragement for us. The Sanskrit teacher told Sir, 'Ekambaram, you have transformed these reedy fellows into the swift arrows of Lord Rama! This is truly some kind of magic.'

Because it was the twenty-fifth anniversary of the school, the Headmaster was busy with preparations for the Silver Anniversary celebrations. He had already decided to invite the Rani, and was going ahead with the necessary arrangements. On the auspicious occasion, our school team should receive the winner's trophy from the Rani's hands. What could give the school greater pride than reaching that pinnacle of glory?

The day of the football competition dawned! That afternoon, Naadar Sir asked us to assemble in one of the vacant classrooms, and started talking to us. We felt detached from our bodies, as though soon some spirit would possess us and we would be able to walk on fire. Sir continued to encourage us. 'Today, you are definitely going to win, de. I don't have even an iota of doubt about that,' he declared. 'Let me remind you again. Strength of mind is the most important thing. Never waver. Within five minutes of the start of the game you should score a goal. It is do or die.'

As we stepped on to the playing field, we had no worries at all about our bodies. We felt we were walking on air. Electricity was coursing through us, from the soles of our feet to the hair on our heads. If we lose, let me die here and now, said the mind.

Within three minutes of the commencement of the match, we scored our first goal. At that moment it felt as if all the things around us...trees, buildings, people, even the sky...were leaping around wildly. Father Xavier, who had been sitting in a chair, jumped up, shouted something in English, and ran around the edge of the field. Our rivals were mere broken cobwebs in our path. They tried their utmost to somehow respond with a goal of their own. But they couldn't even get the ball to our half of the field. Their frantic efforts revealed their desperation. Our hearts were like cores of steel in our chests, and the vapours that emanated from them were overpowering, enfeebling our rivals. Every time their bodies brushed against ours in the course of play, we sensed their weakness.

During the half-time break, Sir was so overcome with emotion that he couldn't utter a word. His eyes were brimming. Stammering a little, he managed to say, 'You played well, de. But you must score one more goal. They mustn't wriggle away by somehow managing to score an equalizer.'

'We are sure we can score another goal, Sir,' said Emanuel.

Sir looked at our faces. It seemed to us that he was reassured by the confidence he read in our eyes.

In the fifth minute after resumption of play, we scored another goal.

The crowd erupted with a roar. Our teachers, oblivious to decorum and dignity, were prancing around in glee. Like small children, they clambered on to chairs and cheered. The Headmaster raised both hands and waved wildly. The moment the game was over, the Headmaster and the teachers rushed onto the field. Totally unembarrassed, they embraced each of us.

'Ekambaram, the entire credit goes to you,' shouted the Headmaster in English.

'The boys played well,' replied Sir.

From wherever they stood, our school students began chanting 'Jai to Ekambaram Sir! Jai to Ekambaram Sir!' The chanting group broke up, fell into line, and approached the field in a procession. Ekambara Sir looked at the Headmaster and at the teachers. Then, in a loud voice, he shouted, 'Jai to Sethu Parvathy Bai School!' But his words did not reach the students, and they continued with their chants praising Ekambara Sir.

That week, school inspectors came from Thiruvananthapuram. Our teachers had given us two or three days of preparation ahead of their arrival. The school was clean enough already; how could we make it even cleaner? The teachers went around looking for tiny bits of dust on window grilles and in the corners of the rooms, and asked us to wipe harder. In the evenings we tidied the garden beds and removed every weed. The black paint on the wooden fence of the garden was fresh enough, but the Headmaster decided it was not an auspicious colour. So we had to paint it green instead.

Our class teacher E. R. S. was in a state of great agitation that day. He told us that the Inspectors would be visiting our class in the first period of the day, which happened to be English. But the bell rang after English class and they had not yet come. When they did come, Pannirugai Perumal's Tamil class was going on. None of the three Inspectors knew any Tamil. One of them asked in English, 'Do you study Thiruvalluvar's *Thirukkural* properly?' 'Yes,' we chorused. We had exactly three kurals in our syllabus. 'Right,' said the Inspectors, and walked away.

That afternoon, during Ekambara Sir's maths class, the three Inspectors paid us another visit. Neither Sir nor we had anticipated that this would happen. Along with the Inspectors, the Headmaster had also arrived.

'We have come to tell you a few things,' said an Inspector, addressing Ekamabara Sir. His tone was stern and disapproving.

'Why is it that all the students are scoring so poorly in maths?' asked the Inspector.

'But that's not so, Sir,' said our teacher.

The third Inspector was holding a large sheet of white paper. He placed it on the table and unfolded it. He continued to consult the contents of the paper as he spoke, 'Earlier there were seven students in this class who usually scored a centum; now there are only six.'

All three Inspectors turned their gazes on Ekambara Sir. The Headmaster was staring at Ekambara Sir in total surprise.

'Earlier the average mark was fifty-four; it is now fifty-one,' added the Inspector.

Sir was looking at the Headmaster, waiting for him to intercede. Nothing.

Why was the Headmaster silent? Did he have nothing to say?

'Many of the students who were scoring above ninety are now managing not more than eighty-five marks.'

Sir stood silent, head bowed.

The first Inspector told Ekambara Sir, 'You must do your job more responsibly and teach better.'

Sir raised his head. Humiliation was writ large on his face. The Headmaster was still silent. Why did he have nothing to say?

'We will give you two months of grace time. You must bring the students back to their previous level,' ordered the first Inspector.

Sir nodded.

After the Inspectors had left, Sir was not in a state of mind to conduct the class as usual.

'De, do you all think I don't do a good job of teaching you?' he asked us, in a pathetic tone of voice.

'No, no, Sir. You are teaching us well,' we said in unison.

Our attempt to reassure him seemed to have made him more despondent. He stood gazing at nothingness through the open window.

That whole day, Ekambara Sir was the topic of discussion among all the teachers. We heard that the Headmaster had sent for him that evening. He seems to have told our Sir, 'The Inspectors have written good reports about all the teachers except you. You are the only one who has received an adverse report.'

Hearing this, Ekambara Sir apparently asked the Headmaster, 'What is your own opinion of me, Sir?'

'When the Inspectors base their comments on some data, we have no choice but to accept it, Ekambaram,' was the Headmaster's response.

The school building was resplendent. Garlands of coloured lights, elaborate festoons of leaves and flowers, arches flanked by lush banana plant stems, not a speck of dust or dirt anywhere. A huge pandal had been put up on the football field. Inside, a wide dais had been erected. The Rani sat smiling in a chair on the dais. The Headmaster stood close to his chair. More than once the Rani had urged him to sit down, but still he stood, lost in his thoughts, unaware of his surroundings.

The items followed one another as per the agenda. Music competitions. Dances. Fancy Dress competitions. Debates. Prize distribution to the children. Suddenly, the Rani turned to the Headmaster and asked in Malayalam, 'Where is Sri Ekambara Naadar?'

The Headmaster looked around here and there. 'Mr Ekambaram! Mr Ekambaram!' he called aloud. He spoke to the teachers seated in the front row. 'Where is Ekambaram?' he demanded sternly. The teachers looked around. Ekambara Sir was nowhere to be seen. The Headmaster spoke directly to E. R. S. Sir. 'I want Ekambaram here in the next one minute,' he ordered. E. R. S. Sir rushed over to where we were gathered. He told Emanuel, 'Go quickly on your cycle and fetch Sir.' When Emanuel got on his cycle, I clambered on too and sat behind him. 'Give the cycle to Sir and ask him to get here at once,' shouted E. R. S. Sir.

We entered Sir's home. He was lying shirtless on a coir rope cot.

'Sir, what's the matter?' asked Emanuel.

'Headache. That's why I couldn't come,' said Sir.

'Who will receive the trophy, sir?'

'H. M. can receive it. Nothing wrong in that.'

'Sir, the Rani asked for you,' I told him.

'Oh, so she remembers me,' remarked Sir.

Emanuel's voice was all choked up when he pleaded again: 'Sir, without you there…how…?'

'Just study hard, de, that's the most important thing,' was Sir's response.

We both studied Sir's expression. His face looked different, wrapped in gloom. It was as if he was in his own world.

'Sir, even if not for anyone else, please come for our sake,' urged Emanuel.

New shadows danced across the doorway. We turned to look. Seshan, Vallinaayagam, Govindan Kutty, Manikandan…all of them were there. We could see more faces through the window. Disappointment was writ large across all their faces.

Sir's wife stood leaning against the kitchen doorway.

'You toiled day and night for the sake of these boys, and now they are asking you to come,' she told her husband.

Sir made no move to get up.

'Then we won't go either,' declared Emanuel.

Sir looked into our faces, one by one.

His wife went over, removed Sir's jibba from where it was hanging from a nail on the wall, and handed it to him.

Naadar Sir rose from the cot.

Translated by Malini Seshadri

SNAKE

SUJATHA

A pile of firewood had recently been bought at Nanu Vadhyar's house next door. It must have come from there, this snake. After a lengthy price negotiation in the morning, punctuated with protests of, 'What, Saami, you're leaving me with nothing to eat… look at the wood, see how fine it is…' the man finally unyoked the bull and tilted his cart to unload the firewood. I knew it would lie right there in front of their house for at least the next one week, drying in the sun.

No one told me there was a snake inside that pile of wood.

In the evening Sivaraman came cycling up in great style. He would pretend these visits of his were to see me, but in fact his purpose was to 'eye' my sister. In his laundered shirt and dhoti, and a cloud of Cuticura talcum powder, and with a broad streak of sandal paste on his forehead, he was convinced that all the young girls would swoon at the sight of him. We didn't want to puncture his bubble, and so Vatsala and I always waited till he had left before sharing comments and laughing at him.

With its green body, metallic handles, multi-coloured decorations at the centres of the wheels, and glittering carrier, Siva's Raleigh cycle looked rather like an ornate Vaiyali horse at a temple festival. When he got off the cycle at the front of our house, Vatsala called out 'Hello Siva'. As though under a spell, he came over and sat next to me on the thinnai, while Vatsala stood in the doorway. In a voice pitched loud enough to carry to Vatsala, Siva embarked on a litany of self-praise. He declared that he would go to Madras to watch the cricket test match; that his uncle was in the Middle East; and another uncle worked in Narayan Company. 'So if you want to catch any of the latest movies, just tell me,' he announced.

When Amma called Vatsala into the house, it was as if a light had been switched off in Siva. That's when I spotted the snake. Well, at first I didn't recognize it as a snake, it looked like some kind of extra decoration on Siva's bicycle. A sort of mossy green to complement the darker green of the bicycle, it was curled around the slanting support bar. 'Siva, what is that new decoration you've added to your bike?' I asked.

'Where, da?'

'Look, on the slanting bar in front,' I said. Even before I had finished speaking it moved. The realization dawned on me that this was no decoration. It was a snake. My hair stood on end. 'Pa... pa...pa...' I stuttered like Janaka trying to learn the musical scale.

'What?' Sivaraman was still mystified.

'Look there, on your cycle wheel. Pa...pa...paambu!' I managed to say it at last—paambu. Snake.

Siva couldn't spot it straight away. 'Where, da, where?' he went on asking, glancing the other way towards the Peshkar's house.

'On the cycle...pa...pa...big pa...' I was back to stuttering. I just couldn't say paambu. In fact it took me a while to even say, 'Look!' Meanwhile, Sivaraman had also spotted the snake. He was still in a quandary about the next course of action, when Vatsala came out of the house. The need to display valour came to the fore in Sivaraman's mind. 'Vatsala, do you have a cricket bat?' he asked.

'Why?' Vatsala wanted to know.

'Pa...pa...pa...' I chimed in.

Sivaraman said: 'Don't be scared, Ranga. You too, Vatsala, no need to panic. A snake has got on to my bicycle.' Instead of being alarmed as we had expected, Vatsala asked 'Where is it?' She went up closer to inspect it. 'Yes, it is a snake,' she declared definitively.

'Endi, Moodevi, don't go near it, di. It may bite you or something....' I told her.

'Vatsala, you shouldn't go near it,' cautioned Sivaraman. 'Why don't you go and fetch something to beat it with.' Since my younger sister herself had walked up close to take a look at the snake, I ventured a further inch and inspected it myself. It was all tangled and twisted like the Sri Lanka issue. While lying there in the middle of the firewood heap in front of Vadhyar's house, who knows what had gone through its snake mind? Maybe it had decided that the evening hour would be a good time to go out for a stroll in the open. And then it couldn't find its way back. And so it climbed onto the bicycle. Bad luck....

'What are you going to do?'

'What a question, Vatsala! We're going to beat it to death, of course,' replied Sivaraman.

'Oh, poor thing, da.'

'What do you mean "poor thing"? If it starts spitting poison around then you'll know. Go inside, di. Do as I say. Go and fetch the bat. Don't tell Amma about this, or she'll collect the whole town here.'

As Sivaraman and I stood there contemplating the snake, the milk depot worker Govindan happened to pass that way. 'What's the matter, Saami?' he enquired.

'Nothing, Govinda, just a snake.'

'Where?'

'Look here on the cycle.' By this time the creature had tangled itself up even more; there was a longish interval between the movement of its head and the subsequent movement of its tail. Govindan threw a brick at the snake. The missile missed its mark, smashed into Nanu Vadhyar's house, and shattered to bits.

'Who's throwing bricks?' demanded Vadhyar, emerging from his house. 'There's a snake, sir,' we told him. He retreated hastily and shut the door. After that no one from the household (wife and four daughters) came out at all. In the meantime, Vatsala made her appearance and handed my much-bandaged cricket bat to Sivaraman. He inspected the item and then approached the cycle gingerly.

It soon became very evident that Sivaraman had absolutely no experience in killing snakes. He swung wildly at it, as though he wanted to split it in two. The bat missed the snake and landed hard on the bicycle seat instead. The seat got dislodged and fell to the ground.

By now, the snake had been alerted to its perilous situation. It speedily untangled itself, slithered to the ground, and within an instant wriggled away into the municipal pipe nearby.

This drain in which the creature had found refuge was just outside our front door where, as a concession to us, the municipality had connected a three-foot-long pipe. Govindan chided Sivaraman, 'Thambi, is that the way to swing the bat? See, now the snake has escaped.'

Sivaraman's attention was on Vatsala as he replied to Govindan's remark. 'Hold on, Govinda…it can't get away. Just don't confuse me, all of you.'

Just then, our grandfather shuffled out from inside the house and further proceedings in the matter of the snake had perforce to be suspended. Thaatha was seventy-seven years old. After his retirement, a kind of senility had set in. Then, his wife, our Paatti died, and nowadays Thaatha was often confused about people, places, and events. Often he was unsure whether he was in Srirangam or still in service in Delhi.

Sometimes he would get my name right…'What, Ranga,' he'd say. But at other times he would call out to my mother, saying, 'There's someone inside…. Oh, it's the butter-seller!' Of late, he imagined that every day was the day of the Panguni Uthiram festival, and that the procession with temple cars would come down the street any minute. Every evening he would set up the string cot outside the house and sit there, awaiting the procession.

Thaatha was preparing to set up his vantage seat right on top of where the snake had taken refuge in the drain. If the whole story were to be explained to him—about the firewood bought by the neighbour, about how the wood pile had harboured a snake, and about the circumstances leading to the snake's journey into the drain—we would have been at it till dawn! So we decided to just lift the whole cot, Thaatha and all, and reposition it on the opposite side. But Thaatha noticed that the cot had mysteriously risen upwards and was moving seemingly on its own. 'I'm not yet dead, da,' said Thaatha.

'Just sit quietly here, Thaatha,' Govindan told him. To which Thaatha responded, 'Has the Panguni festival temple car come by yet?'

We, the valorous trio, left Thaatha in the care of Vatsala and set about the task of finishing off the snake. Just then who should arrive but 'Pathanna' (ten annas) Padmanabha Iyengar. His policy was to 'help' everyone, come what may; he would never take no for an answer. 'Ennada, what's it? A snake?' he asked.

'Yes, Maama. Before we could land a blow on it, it wriggled into the drain. We were just debating how to get it out.'

'Is it a nalla one?' queried Maama. We had no clue what he meant. A 'good' snake?

'Why are you all gaping at me,' admonished Maama. 'If it is a sacred cobra, I won't kill it. Because I'd have to perform a Shanthi Homam ritual afterwards.'

'Well, we don't know whether the snake is a good one. We haven't yet asked it that question.'

'Ennada, trying to make fun of me or what?'

'No, no, Maama. It was sort of brownish and slimy looking. That's all we know.'

Vatsala chimed in, 'Maama, it didn't look like a nalla paambu at all. I had a good look at it. It looked like some harmless variety. I'd say there's no need to kill it.'

'Shut up, you stupid girl! Look after Thaatha properly, that's all you need to do. Don't interfere in men's affairs,' I said to my sister. She made a face at me. Thaatha asked, 'Is the Panguni temple car going to come now?' Govindan was poking the drain in an exploratory fashion with the long, reed-like rib of a palm leaf. He was going about it quite cautiously, standing well away from the drain and holding the flimsy reed at arm's length, as if trying to light a firecracker.

'What, Govinda, is this the thinnest stick you could find?' I asked mockingly.

'If I use a thick one...well, I am alone at this end....'

'But that doesn't mean you have to use such a delicate reed, as though you are going to pick your ear.'

'Well, your Highness, you're welcome to try,' retorted Siva.

'Look, you fellows, this kind of thing won't work to make it come out. Go to the DPG store and buy some incense powder. I will get the snake out in no time.' Since quite a few people had gathered at the scene by this time, suggestions and instructions were flying around from all directions and it was difficult to tell straight away who was dispensing this particular piece of advice.

'No need for incense and all that. There's a snake charmer at the donkey stable. He will lure out the snake just by blowing his pipe.'

'I hope each of you has kept your own snake safe.'

'De! Want me to give you a slap across the face?'

'When will the Panguni temple car arrive?'

Sivaraman spoke firmly: 'Ranga, you have no experience with this. Go and stand near the thinnai. We will kill the snake. If all you spectators will kindly stand aside and give some space for the snake-killer team, it would be much appreciated.'

Padmanabha Iyengar had gone back to his house to fetch a ladle with glowing embers. He arrived at the scene of action, blowing gently on the embers to keep the flame alive. In addition, he was also carrying an umbrella. Someone sped back on Sivaraman's bicycle, having successfully accomplished his mission of buying incense from the designated shop. The moment the incense was tossed on the glowing embers, a billowing cloud of fumes arose. Padmanabha Iyengar, holding the smoking ladle like some ancient practitioner of the magic arts, was waving the fumes encouragingly in the direction of the drain with the help of a folded copy of the *Dinamani* newspaper. On one side stood Govindan, Patta, and Sivaraman, holding a variety of implements to be used as weapons. The whole street was represented in the crowd that stood at a distance of about ten feet, offering advice and suggestions.

That snake must have been in some dilemma we knew nothing about. Anyway, it did not emerge. By then, the smoke had become a smokescreen, like the dream sequence in the movie *Awaara*. It was difficult to make out who was who…was that Thaatha…or was it Patta…? And why was Padmanabha Iyengar holding up an open umbrella?

'With this much smoke, even a crocodile would have come out by now,' he declared. 'De, Ranga, did you actually see it go in there?'

'Didn't *you* see it, Govinda?'

'Actually, there was no snake to see by the time I arrived. Maybe these fellows are making up a snake story,' suggested Govindan.

'Che, che…Saami, I swear I saw it going into the drain,' I assured them. Half past five in the evening—Lalgudi passenger train must have just arrived. The office-goers were returning home. Among them was K. V. The moment he arrived, he took over the leadership of the ongoing catch-the-snake project. He placed his tiffin box on the thinnai ledge. He folded and tied up his dhoti to reveal the edges of his khaki undershorts. 'Where's the snake, da?'

'Here, inside this drain.'

'It's a harmless snake, K.V.,' said Vatsala. 'There's no need to kill it.'

'Whatever kind of snake it is, it's best to kill it. All of you spectators…stand away or climb on to the thinnai. Ranga, I need a thick stick…bring the one from the clothes line. The drain has to be poked with some force. Your kind of namby-pamby approach is no good. Oi, why are you messing about waving smoke like some sadhu or something? Whom are you trying to propitiate? Go and fetch a stick, da, Ranga. Can't even make out the people in the middle of all this smoke…what a silly thing to do….'

When I went into the house to fetch the stick used for hanging clothes up for drying, my mother asked, 'What's going on, da?' I ran out without answering her.

K. V. was a fearless fellow. He plunged the entire length of the stick into the drain and prodded vigorously. The blood froze in my veins. I envisioned the creature bursting out with a *booossss* from its hiding place and rearing its head up menacingly to elbow height with its hood spread wide.

Nothing happened. K.V. continued to prod the drain as though to break up a major clog in it. Finally he declared, 'There's not even a tiny earthworm in there. Someone has been pulling a fast one on us.'

'No, no, K. V. It was on the cycle bar. Sivaraman tried to hit it. It escaped and wriggled into the drain.'

'Sivaraman? Tried to kill a snake? Enda, have you ever even squashed a caterpillar?'

'You're talking big…let's see you do it,' challenged Sivaraman.

'Show it to me and I'll kill it,' declared K. V., as he quickly pulled the stick out of the drain and twirled it menacingly in front of Sivaraman. The latter, momentarily in shock, stepped backward. K. V. laughed uproariously. 'And you say this is the fellow who was trying to beat a snake to death?'

K. V. turned to Padmanabha Iyengar and said, 'Oi, go and light a petromax lamp and bring it back here. It looks like this task will go on into the night.' But just as he said this, K. V. spotted the snake. It must have emerged from the drain under cover of the convenient smokescreen. Otherwise how did it end up wrapped around the leg of Thaatha's string cot? What possible business could it have there?

'Vatsala, don't move. Stand still. Look, it's on the leg of the cot.'

'What, K. V.?'

'Don't even breathe, don't move a muscle. We will make a pulp of the creature right there.'

'When will the Panguni temple car come?' Thaatha wanted to know.

I had expected Vatsala to shriek, leap up in fright, and run away. Instead she picked up a stick that lay nearby, placed it against the leg of the cot, and gently picked up the snake which had been clinging on in its new position rather insecurely.

Now the snake was dangling at the end of the stick she was holding, half its length hanging to one side and half to the other. Its pale underside was visible for the first time. Its eyes had a frightened look, and it was darting its tongue—*pleech-pleech*—in and out of its mouth. It wasn't showing any other signs of aggressiveness.

Vatsala walked over to Sivaraman with the stick bearing the

dangling snake. She laughed as she challenged him, 'Here's the snake. Come on, hit it.' Sivaraman, so terrified that he was unaware of his dhoti having slid off, ran away, and climbed onto the thinnai in front of Nanu Vadhyar's house. K. V. was the only one who stood his ground.

'This isn't a game,' he told her sternly. 'Throw the snake down now.' Vatsala swivelled and exhibited the snake in every direction. In each direction in turn, people shrank away as they sighted the snake. Meanwhile Amma had come out of the house. 'Hey, you monkey,' she called out to Vatsala, 'drop it before it bites you.'

'No, Amma, this looks like a harmless snake. Ranga, fetch a basket. We will take the snake in the basket and go and release it in the forest. There's no need to kill it.'

Just then the snake lost its balance on its stick-end perch. It fell to the floor and wriggled away again towards the drain. K. V. snatched up the cricket bat and slammed it hard on the snake as it was trying to get away.

Vatsala was screaming, 'No, no, please don't K. V., please! Don't kill it. What harm has it done? Don't, don't....' K. V. ignored her wails and pleas; he smashed the bat on the snake again and again. The front of the snake now looked like brinjal paste. The tail, as though clinging on to a cherished memory, waved elegantly and gently a couple of times and then ceased moving. K. V. went on to squash that too. He was laughing as he picked up the squashed snake on the stick. They took it to the corner adjoining the temple car shed and consigned it to the flames.

Vatsala was sobbing aloud as she kept repeating, 'Poor thing. What harm did it do to you all? Why did you kill it?' She sobbed for a long time; I was mystified by her reaction.

After that, Sivaraman stopped coming by to see Vatsala. I, in turn, began to understand my sister better.

Translated by Malini Seshadri

THE SLAYING OF HIRANYA

SA. KANDASAMY

Chinna Karuppu was sitting above the sluice of the canal, swinging his legs. Under his feet were a pair of old chappals. Using his right foot and leaning slightly forward, he shifted the chappals, whose toe-straps hung loose like torn ears. From a pouch in his belt he took out a snuffbox, inhaled the powder into both nostrils, shook the excess off his fingers, and raised his head.

A rat snake slithered towards the water.

Chinna Karuppu climbed down, hitched up his belt, and looked around. The figure of Rajaraman was half-visible, half-hidden, as he approached through the coconut grove.

A flock of storks flew overhead. Chinna Karuppu quickly jumped back on the parapet and sat down. Rajaraman came up and stood before him. Very properly and respectfully, he had lowered his casually tucked-up veshti and covered his bare legs.

Chinna Karuppu turned and gave him a look, as though he had only just noticed him. Reaching for the fluttering end of his veshti, he said, 'Here, Raja! Sit!' with an accommodating gesture.

'That's all right, 'nga,' said the other, moving backwards a little. 'Seems you came to the house in search of me last evening. Paappa told me.'

'Oh, nothing special. Pakkiri of Aakkoor has some tiger claws that can be worn with the Narasimha costume. I thought they'd be good for when we perform for the German visitors. That's what I came over to tell you. But you were not at home.'

'There was a death in Needoor.'

'Those claws are from my grandfather's time. It'll look terrific if you put them on for the dance.'

'Then I'll go at once and get them.'

'The sun's about to set. For tomorrow's koothu we can manage with what we already have. There are still some days left until the Germans arrive.' He jumped off the embankment.

'If I have them, I can practise with them on, right?'

'Yes, yes. But what a long way you'll have to walk, just for that!'

'If by adding something to my costume, the koothu is going to turn out good, then I had better be ready to walk any distance to get it.'

'Spoken like a real koothu actor!'

Rajaraman shook his head modestly.

'If Pakkiri isn't at home, you just mention my name to his wife.'

'All right.'

'You put on those tiger claws and do your dance, and it will turn out perfectly! Even I feel like putting them on! But that would mean a role-change.'

'Hiranyan can be only your role, 'nga.'

Chinna Karuppu laughed a great laugh. That laugh of his spread to the bushes, to the creepers, and the grass. It leaped to the water, rose up and echoed in all the four directions. A kingfisher which was perched on a yellow blossomed poovarasu tree whooshed up suddenly and soared away.

'Come on!' Chinna Karuppu put his hand on Rajaraman's shoulder. Rajaraman fell in step alongside.

'Our Pakkiri used to dance quite well at one time. I expected he would become a big star in koothu in two–three years. But as soon as he got a wife he thought it was enough just to dance to her tune!' As Chinna Karuppu walked along the ridge between the fields he reached out and wrenched loose a stalk from the thuvarai bushes planted alongside. Stripping the lentils from their pods, he strode along, full of grace and arrogance. It didn't seem like what he was treading on was mere earth.

That gait of his was what made him so handsome. Also his commanding presence. It showed in every step he took and scintillated in his voice, in his sweeping glance, and in every gesture of the hand. With every koothu performance he grew more and more dazzling.

After seeing one of Chinna Karuppu's performances his mother had herself said, 'Yes, that demon's role is just right for him. You think it just happened today or yesterday? Hasn't that role been in the family for three generations?'

His every movement bore out the truth of her words. Before him, his father had donned the costume of the demon-king Hiranya Kasipu in the koothu. And before him was his father, Chinna Karuppu's grandfather, the very first in the family to paint his face for the koothu. When he acted and danced the part of Hiranya Kasipu, it was as though the demon-king had indeed arrived on earth in the flesh, to kill and destroy.

Yet Chinna Karuppu's grandfather was not of the play-actors' caste. At the age of ten or twelve the police had nabbed his father in a murder case and hanged him. Leaving his mother behind, he ran away from Usilampatti to Madurai. A koothu performance happened to be going on at the Tamukkam maidan. All night he watched it, squatting in the front row. When day broke he began doing odd jobs for the actors, and then going from town to town with them. He played all the small roles. After about six or seven years he was given the role of Hiranya Kasipu. And he seized the opportunity and held on to it. All that he had seen and heard and learned he polished up to a high gloss, with song and dance. As a result the koothu drew bigger and bigger crowds. Chinna Karuppu's grandfather became the talk of every town....

And now, 'Chinna Karuppu Hiranyan Special!' said the banners on the railway coach bringing the troupe to Madurai. 'His grandfather's legendary elegance and eloquence have found a worthy lodging place in young Chinna Karuppu,' reported Krishnaiyar in the *Times Weekly Magazine* in a special article with photographs. What the article had to say about Chinna Karuppu's accurate portrayal of an ego-ridden human soul, violent and tyrannical, made him known throughout the country.

He became much sought after. Obligingly he showed off his dance to everyone who came to see him. When it came to dancing, he never played hard to get. One had only to say, 'Dance!' and he would dance at once. If there were women around, he didn't even wait to be asked. The flutter of their eyes, the toss of their heads, and even the smallest of smiles could make him dance.

The ridge between the fields climbed up the road and came to an end. Chinna Karuppu flung the stripped thuvarai stalk into the field and turned back. Rajaraman went on ahead into the scrubland, pushing aside the dark boughs of the nochi trees.

'Shall I also come along with you, Raja?'

'What for? I'll just go there by myself and be back.'

'Already it's so dark. Go! And come back soon!'

'Right.' Rajaraman walked on into a grove of oilnut trees.

A bus went by, stirring up dust. Chinna Karuppu stood watching Rajaraman disappear behind the oilnut trees. Then he nodded to himself and let out a chuckle.

The dirt road to Aakkoor went downhill. His feet sinking into the mud, Rajaraman trudged along, swinging his arms and singing a koothu ditty. Was it six years ago or seven that he had first begun to dance? It seemed to him that it was about then that he had visited his aunt at Bargur and seen Chinna Karuppu for the first time, decked out as Hiranya Kasipu, the demon-king. The desire to dance had seized him then.

A year later there was another koothu at Arasur. That, too, was a Chinna Karuppu performance. It went on all night, and Rajaraman never took his eyes off him. The desire, which had already sprouted and taken root within him, now quickly grew into a full-sized tree. For five or six days he brooded over it. Somehow or other he had to catch hold of Chinna Karuppu. To convince him....

One evening, as Chinna Karuppu squatted on his haunches on the edge of the canal sluice, Rajaraman washed his face in the canal and went and stood before him.

'Who...? What do you want?'

'I want to learn koothu from you.'

The great man's astonished gaze fell on him.

'Aren't you one of Ukkadai Thevar's boys?'

Rajaraman nodded assent.

'How will koothu and such things be all right for someone like you?'

'It will.'

'It will? How do you know?'

'Because I want it.'

Chinna Karuppu leapt down from the embankment. He placed an arm around his shoulder and slapped him approvingly a couple of times.

'That's settled, then. Come to the mango orchard tomorrow. We shall start the dance.'

The next day he went to the mango orchard. Five or six boys were rehearsing beneath a flowering mango tree. He stood aside, out of their way. Along came Chinna Karuppu, inhaling pinches of snuff up into his nostrils. The boys stopped dancing. Beckoning Raja to his side, he made him sit down while he told him the story. As he told it, he suddenly got up and began to dance. He was Hiranyan the demon-king. He was Prahalaadhan. And he was Narasimhan. Squatting in front, Rajaraman closely observed him, imprinting every gesture on his mind. When the dance was over, Chinna Karuppu came up to him and enquired, 'Have you been watching?' Rajaraman nodded assent.

'Let's see! Now you dance! I am Hiranyan. You are Narasimhan. You are catching hold of me, putting me on your lap, tearing open my chest, and killing me. Mmm! Dance!'

Rajaraman tucked his veshti up to his knees, stepped up, and began to perform. In a few moments he forgot everything he had watched. His feet refused to move forward, his legs got tangled up as though they had somehow been bound and tied together. At the sight of him standing there, dumbfounded, one of the boys let out a giggle.

Chinna Karuppu looked in the direction of the giggle. With a wave of his hand he summoned the still-giggling boy. The lad came happily enough.

Pa-leer! came a resounding slap on the cheek, followed by an agonized yelp.

Rajaraman could almost feel the pain himself. He turned and stared at Chinna Karuppu.

'Don't be afraid. Just dance!'

He was terrified. But he danced! With his eyes and with his feet, he portrayed all that he had just seen, and heard.

'Shabash! You have passed!' Chinna Karuppu rose and patted him on the shoulder.

Three months later Chinna Karuppu got rid of the old Narasimhan and put Rajaraman in his place. It was quite a risk. But Rajaraman proved brilliant in the role.

'With the advent of the new Narasimhan, the play *Hiranya Kasipu* has been polished up and given a new lease of life,' noted Mythily Aiyangar in the *Times of India* 'Sunday Magazine'. Rajaraman's wife had cut out two of the seven colour photos accompanying the article and pasted them on the wall. It was soon after their wedding. He didn't look much like the bridegroom, with his lion's face, whitish mane, and whiskers, showing his teeth in a horrible snarl.

'Doesn't it scare you?' he asked her, looking across the bed at it.

She shook her head and smiled.

'Really?'

Rising from bed she embraced him so tightly that he could hardly breathe. He rolled her off him with all his strength, and she just got up and laughed.

'Don't go to the koothu any more.'

'Why?'

'Don't!'

'All right.'

But he continued to travel from town to town with Chinna Karuppu, dancing and acting and singing so well that he earned praise everywhere. Gifts of money, ceremonial shawls—he got them all.

Rajaraman obtained the tiger claws from Aakkoor Pakkiri, crossed the bridge over the Kaveri, and entered the town. The moon had climbed overhead. Aware that it had grown very late, he hurried to his house and rapped on the door.

'Who is it?' his wife asked, after he had called out a couple of times. She sounded unusual to him.

'It's only me.'

She turned up the wick of the lamp and opened the door. He looked straight at her. Her face was hidden in her loosened hair. Taking her by the hand he led her to the bed, sat down, and gazed at her. It was obvious from her swollen eyes that she had been weeping for a long time.

'Paappa!' He grasped her shoulders. Clinging to him she wept noiselessly, shaking all over.

'Paappa…say what it is.'

Straightening up, she gave him a look.

'Tell me, Paappa…did he come today, too?'

She nodded her head.

'So that's why he sent me to Aakkoor!' he said, swinging his fists in the air. She went to him and put her arms around him, leaned against his shoulder, and began to weep. She wept for a long time, with him patting her gently on the back. Tired out with weeping, she finally fell asleep. He laid her on the bed and rose up.

His hand stroked the waist-knot of his veshti, felt the tiger claws. Taking out two claws, he turned up the wick of the lantern. The light spread over everything in the room. It made Paappa turn over in her sleep. Hurriedly he pulled in the wick to dim the glare. She stretched out her legs and lay quietly again.

Lamp in hand, he went to the backyard. Tilting the firewood box he brought out a saw blade. He examined its edge, touching it with his finger. It seemed sharp enough. He took the tiger claws from his lap, one by one, and sharpened them against the saw-edge. Slipping the tiger claws over his fingers he brought them close to his eyes and stared at them. Their keen steel points gleamed in the lamplight.

'Hahaha…!' With a fearful laugh he sprang indoors. Paappa woke up, wide-eyed with fright. Gnashing his teeth, he swung his arms through the air, one after the other, again and again.

'What…what happened, 'nga?'

He looked at her, his hands dropping to his sides. Two of the tiger claws fell to the floor. The rage that had risen up his arms and into his eyes appeared to subside. She took his arm and pulled him to the bed, made him sit down. Having run out of kerosene, the lamp went out. Paappa fell back on the bed, embracing him tightly.

The next day dawned brightly, a Friday. He rose, bathed, and went out. She cooked and waited for him to return. He was very late. As he ate he told her, 'You're coming to the koothu tonight.' She was surprised. Usually he was not one to invite her to watch the show; she had only seen two or three of his performances since they had married.

That evening as soon as the sounds of the koothu fell on her ears she called Anjalai next door. They walked together towards the Mariamman temple. It was a very big crowd. Men and women and children were all watching the show, in between snatches of sleep. She sat behind a mango tree, hiding but not quite hidden.

Jil! Jil! clashed the ankle-bells, as Chinna Karuppu came striding in, stepping high and kicking the ground with his feet. Coming to a sudden halt, he threw a bold stare around him, brimming with arrogance and conceit. Then, laughing mockingly, he strutted and pranced from one end to the other and whirled back again, before coming to another abrupt halt before Prahalaadhan. Twirling his big moustache, he sang out the words, spontaneously improvising:

'*The One you call your Hari, is he here? Inside this pillar of my palace?*'

'Yes. He is in this pillar.'

'In this pillar?'

'He is within this pillar, too.'

Ankle-bells clashing, Hiranyan dashed to another pillar and stopped before it.

'In this one? This pillar?'

'The One I call my Hari is within all pillars of this place! In every pillar and every particle dwells he.'

'Ha-ha-ha-ha!'

Chinna Karuppu emitted a jeering cackle, and looked around challengingly at the crowd. Catching sight of Paappa, he took an eager step forward. She pulled her sari around herself and vanished behind the mango tree. But now she completely filled his thoughts. It seemed to him that she had come to the koothu just to see him. How proud he was! How jubilant! Energetically jerking his head up and down, he advanced with long, kingly strides, demanding:

'In this one, too? This pillar here?'

He thrust out his leg and gave the pillar a kick.

Bells, drums, and harmonium made a simultaneous mighty din. Pale-faced and tiger-clawed, the Man-Lion burst out from behind the pillar. Hiranyan stared at the strange creature. The Narasimhan let out a hideous laugh, reached out, and struck him once on the chest. Unable to bear the unexpected blow, Hiranyan stumbled and fell down.

A large chair appeared. The Narasimhan picked up the fallen Hiranyan and sat down upon it with knees spread out, draping him over its lap. It tossed its mane and hit him a couple of times on the chest.

'Ayyo!' Hiranyan wailed.

The Narasimhan let out another laugh. That laugh, that blow… they were something new.

Hiranyan writhed and struggled to get loose. Two more blows descended on him.

The audience watched the koothu in horrified silence. One after another the blows fell, and with each blow Hiranyan emitted loud screams of unbearable pain. The Narasimhan shook its head, showed its teeth. Those false teeth, that false face cowed Hiranyan utterly.

'Ada, you worthless speck of chaff! How dare you commit such villainy?'

The Narasimhan pounded him on the chest, ripped off his clothes, and flung them in all four directions. Hiranyan bounced up, tried to wriggle loose.

'Oomm...!' Another punch on the chest, and blood and flesh lay entangled in the tiger claws. Hiranyan swung his legs and flapped them, but the Narasimhan did not let go. It flung one leg over him and pinned him down, and with both tiger-clawed hands it gored Hiranyan's chest and scattered handfuls of blood and flesh in all four directions.

'Ayyo...Ayyo...!' shrieked Hiranyan again and again. With every shriek the crowd surged forward.

Hiranyan's hands and feet twitched, trembled, then suddenly became still. The Narasimhan thrust aside the lifeless body and stood up. With a shiver of its mane, it glared at the crowd. Blood dripped from its claws.

Paappa pushed her way forward through the crowd. An expression of unbounded joy suffused her face. On seeing her, the Narasimhan became exultant. Pulling off the mane and whiskers, it declared, 'I have slain him!' and descended into the crowd.

More! More! she seemed to be saying, full of greedy delight, as she advanced to meet him.

Translated by Vasantha Surya

ARROGANCE

AADHAVAN

This Sunday too had passed without his paying a visit to Venkateswaran's house.

'At least I could have gone there….' So thought Kalyanam. He had finished his dinner and was chewing betel leaf while patting his child, who lay in his lap, half asleep.

A function had been held to felicitate Venkateswaran. At the end of it Kalyanam took leave of him and said, 'I'll meet you later…I'll drop in one of these days.'

Venkateswaran said, 'Bring your wife too.' Perhaps it was said only as a matter of etiquette. But Kalyanam took it to heart. Every Sunday, some inconvenience or other made them postpone their visit to Venkateswaran's.

Was it really an inconvenience? No. The truth was that his wife did not like to go there. 'Enough! Even on ordinary days that auntie goes on bragging about her husband. And now will there be a limit to it?' There was no exaggeration in these words of hers. He too was aware of the foolish pride of the man who had taught him music. He had impressed Kalyanam with the powerful style of his singing. Kalyanam showed a natural respect for Venkateswaran and regarded him as one of his well-wishers. Venkateswaran's wife demeaned this approach as hero-worship shown by an apprentice towards his master, as the fawning of a boy who desires deeply to be in his teacher's good books. Many times Kalyanam did not like her behaviour for it suggested that she too deserved a share in the respect he showed Venkateswaran. But he would excuse her, thinking 'Poor woman, that's all she knows. So what if she has such an opinion. After all, I am what I am.' He would comfort himself thus.

But his wife was certainly not prepared to excuse Venkateswaran's wife, to grant her such a concession. 'The husband may be a genius and worthy of respect. But does that make the wife, too, a person deserving the same respect? One can respect people only according to their worth. Like me, she too is a wife, a mother, a housewife. That's all. How can I accept her expectation that I should treat her as a person more respectable than myself?' This was his wife's argument—how could he say that there was no substance in it? Of late, even Kalyanam thought that it was a duty, a formality to go to Venkateswaran's house. He too had neither the enthusiasm nor the zeal to go there. Lately, Kalyanam had been noticing that Venkateswaran was cultivating earnestly, just like his wife did, the friendship of people in high positions and of coveted social status.

Many gossiped that only through such friends had Venkateswaran got an award from the Central Government.

Once or twice when Kalyanam had gone to Venkateswaran's house, he had felt slighted. He thought he was a misfit in the midst of the bigwigs there. And of late he had stopped going there at all.

The child was fast asleep. 'Meenu,' Kalyanam called to his wife. She came with a cup of milk, placed it close to him on the table, and took the child away.

Kalyanam picked up a postcard lying on the table and covered the tumbler with it to keep the milk warm. The postcard was the invitation for the function arranged by the local Tamil Sangam to honour Venkateswaran. It contained Kalyanam's name too as one of the speakers that day.

He opened the front door and spat out the chewed betel. The Great Bear shone bright up above in the clear sky. For a moment he stood looking at it. Seven rishis. Seven swaras.

Rishi means control of the senses, penance. Swara is movement, excitement.... An artiste has to arrange the swaras through his effort and knowledge and create several forms and give colour and brightness to the movement of life.

So how can one say that the manner in which Venkateswaran adjusts himself with one and all is not the natural, healthy attitude of an artiste? I try to think of art only as a penance, an exercise in self-discipline. But is that only a cover for my inability, a self-deception?

The celebration in the Tamil Sangam and the speeches made there flashed in Kalyanam's memory. The meeting was addressed by the Collector, the manager of a bank, a female doctor, a principal of a college, and a retired judge of the High Court.

The Collector spoke more about himself than about Venkateswaran. He said that he had no great knowledge of or practice in music or, for that matter, any other sphere, but he had the ability to spot where and in whom such expertise lay. He had the insight to identify the person whom he should consult about a particular matter, to whom a job should be entrusted to get done completely. A good administrator should possess such insight. Regarding music, his only adviser was his wife. (Here the Collector turned towards his wife by his side, and she smiled.) It was his wife who told him first about Venkateswaran's eminence, his genius. Very soon the Collector himself saw this special quality. And he began to enjoy it. Still, he was not one who was afraid of holding an opinion different from that of his wife. (Here all the people present laughed. This made the Collector happy and he explained in a light vein, citing examples of how he and his wife differed in their tastes—items of food, actors and actresses in the world of cinema....) The Collector reminded them all of Bharathi's line 'If there is light in the heart, it will be reflected in the words.' Only because Venkateswaran had this inner light was he able to kindle a spark even in him, a veritable Aurangzeb. This was true art. It should touch one and all at some place or other. A good administrator was one who did not swerve from the rules but at the same time did not cut himself off from the urgent needs of the times and circumstances. Such disciplined observance combined with compassion was all that he expected from a good artiste. (Words, empty words). He concluded his speech by saying that only through Venkateswaran did he get the ability to change himself from an Aurangzeb to an Akbar and recognize the exceptional ability of a Tansen. Thunderous applause followed.

Those who came to speak after the Collector had not only

praise for Venkateswaran's eminence in music but also applause for the excellence of the Collector's address. They prefaced or concluded their speeches with the words, 'As our Collector observed well', 'As our Collector said.' On those occasions they looked at the Collector with a certain amount of deference and gave a new interpretation to some of the words they took from the Collector's speech. The nature of their profession made the bank manager and the doctor like the idea expressed by the Collector: 'A good artiste should be easily accessible to all.' They found in it a view of equality and an attitude of sacrifice and said that this was the need of the hour. Artistes are the public property of the people, of the country. It is of no use if a work of art or an artiste was accessible only to select persons or claimed by a few.

The principal began his career by teaching in the lower classes and gradually got promoted to this position. To please and to attract the attention of the children he would give explanations and examples for each and every item. That practice had become a habit, a part of him. He supported the Collector in his observation about keen insight, pointed out the appropriateness of the name of Venkateswaran and said that the very name indicated musical genius. That name itself contained the word 'swara' and in the original Sanskrit word 'Venkateswaran' there were letters conforming to the seven swaras. And he was amazed by this.

The judge who spoke afterwards said in a jocular vein, 'I thought I should hear the arguments on both sides and then give my verdict. But here everyone is in support of the defence.'

At last when Kalyanam's turn came he found that all the enthusiasm he had for the function had dried up. He was almost in a state of half lunacy. He felt he had started to go somewhere but had arrived at some other place. He wished he could tear his hair out and run away. Now and then he cast a sidelong glance at Venkateswaran in the hope that Venkateswaran would share a mischievous smile with him. But Venkateswaran sat majestically, in exultation, smiling gently, like an idol of Vishnu enjoying the many sacred baths. That appearance gave Kalyanam a shock. With a sad heart he thought, 'After all, you do need all this. Perhaps you need only this.' This doubt did not allow him to speak well. He had thought it over and come prepared to speak at length about the dexterity and classical correctness of Venkateswaran's gamakas, the tautness and finesse of his sangatis, the fine texture of his voice and its capacity to sustain a note, and other aspects of his music. But suddenly all of this appeared to be in vain because of the inability of the audience to grasp these finer points. In an atmosphere where shorter, lighter songs got loud applause, his attempt to elaborate a raga seemed to him to be sheer nonsense. His good luck in getting a genius like Venkateswaran as his guru, Venkateswaran's amiable nature and his noble manners, the few lessons he, as a vidwan, a scholar, and as a man, had taught him, the help he had been rendering to young artistes—Kalyanam had to stop his talk after giving just these superficial details. Sadly he recollected now the manner in which the audience had reacted favourably to his words.

Not for earning the applause of that audience but only out of the regard he had for them had he descended to their level and spoken those words. He did not want to tom-tom his knowledge among those ignoramuses and astound them and thus become a pseudo-hero. So he hid his considerable proficiency, pretended that he was one of them, and thus obtained their acclaim.

Who knows…perhaps Venkateswaran too was doing the same thing? Realizing that the fine characteristics of his genius would isolate him, and afraid of such isolation, on many occasions even he had diluted his expositions, adulterated them, and thus made them popular. As a result, he found himself acceptable to one and all. Why should Kalyanam take it as a compromise? Why should not Venkateswaran's endeavour be a yoga of a very high order and a fine dedication that did not want to drive out anyone from his world but by destroying his ego wanted him to converse with all beings, realizing 'I am the poorest of the poor among you'?

This line of thought attracted Kalyanam immensely. But was this the truth? Could not this thought be an attempt to justify his desire to make his art popular?

Suddenly, he realized that he too was one who was after the acclaim of the majority of the people gathered at that function. Afterwards would not his mind try to belittle, as well as justify, this thought?

That noon he heard one of the old vocal records of Venkateswaran at the radio station. Thoughts began to revolve in his mind. Kalyanam was a producer at the radio station. (This job, too, he had got on Venkateswaran's recommendation. Perhaps whenever he called on Venkateswaran he was being reminded of his low position and his indebtedness to the latter. Was it because of this that he avoided Venkateswaran? Quite possible.) Once he played the records of many musicians for a programme on Thyagaraja. One of them was Venkateswaran's 'Ramabhakti Samrajyamu'. My! How magnificently had he sung that piece! He must have sung it in a state of absolute ecstasy, forgetting himself, forgetting the crowd in front of him....

Nowadays, why are such moments of rapture so rare?

Worse than that, why did he feel angry and spiteful towards Venkateswaran, sensing that he did not feel that ecstasy, that the feeling of this was growing less and less of late, and he was therefore trying to avoid him? In the depth of his heart he too felt that he was anxious to get the applause of the common people. And wasn't that the reason why he became jealous of Venkateswaran who got such appreciation in abundance? Wasn't that the truth?

Kalyanam sat down on the floor at once and began to sing 'Ramabhakti Samrajyamu'. He sang it quietly with plenty of sangatis, elaborate niraval, and svaraprasthara. He finished singing: his mind became clear.

When he stood at the bus stand the next morning, someone wished him 'Good morning'. Kalyanam turned and saw the new tenant of the first floor of his house. With a smile he reciprocated the greeting. He had not yet become fully acquainted with the new tenant.

The tenant said, 'Sir, yesterday night, the music was very good.

You sang it? A fine voice…so refreshing…. It is days since I heard such music.'

Kalyanam was filled with joy. His mind became light, his doubts having disappeared. The tenant said that he had not heard that song ever sung so faithfully and mentioned the names of a few eminent musicians. Kalyanam felt proud. The tenant's bus arrived and he took leave saying that he would meet Kalyanam that evening.

As promised he came in the evening. Then he discussed the voices, the methods of singing of some of the prominent practising musicians of the day. That showed him to be a sound, knowledgeable person. At his request Kalyanam sang three pieces. The tenant left the place after praising Kalyanam's songs.

The acquaintance thus born between the two grew apace. It became a habit for Kalyanam to sing elaborately before the tenant two or three times a week. He was pleased that he also had a rasika. He felt a little proud when the tenant pointed out to him on several occasions, after observing the special characteristics and subtleties of the way he sang, how these aspects were better than the attempts of some of the leading musicians of the time.

For an artiste, realizing the aspects of his achievement and justifiably feeling proud of them could not be wrong. At the same time, it was not good for him to have a superior notion of the enormity of his achievement. Only so long as he did not have the burden of this consciousness could he learn and preserve his art with a humility and a poise that was natural, youthful.

Very soon such a situation arose for Kalyanam. The man upstairs made Kalyanam's achievement a crown, placed it on Kalyanam's head, and made him feel uneasy.

Kalyanam began to try and avoid the new acquaintance.

To forget his crown he began to sing to his child, wife, people in the office, to the boy in the canteen, to all sorts of persons, without any notion of time or place, without any sort of order. He tried thus to distance himself from his achievement and from the huge burden of 'ego' born of it.

One Saturday evening, when he was singing in the presence of his wife and child, he lost his sense of self and imagined himself as Venkateswaran instead. It then became clear to him that what he had thought about Venkateswaran—that Venkateswaran was compromising, even with ignoramuses in music, just to get a high place in society and obtain certain concessions, that he was pledging his art only to get fame—was wrong.

No. He was running after ignoramuses only because he realized the harm that might happen to his art due to the critical estimates of wise men.

How foolish he had been when he thought that Venkateswaran was disregarding him, a true rasika, simply because he did not have social standing, but was rather patiently putting up with people who had a status in society even though they had no taste at all.

Fools could not give him arrogance. Without disclosing his true self to them, without his 'ego' being affected, he could put up shows, could crack jokes.

But I am the one who can give him arrogance. So he is careful about me.

He is not arrogant. Only I am. The meaningless arrogance of 'I am the true artiste'.

'My master, save me from my myself,' muttered Kalyanam.

Next day, without any kind of complex, Kalyanam took his wife and child to Venkateswaran's.

Translated by M. S. Ramaswami

JOURNEY 4

AMBAI

There was still some time before the bus would start. She had already demolished a paper packet of peanuts, following it with a ginger muraba, just to aid the digestion. Still no sign of the driver. Next to her, a pregnant woman, on a seat meant for three passengers. She looked as if she were five or six months gone. Wrists covered in bangles: red, yellow, green, and dark blue. Around her neck, chains, thali, mango-patterned necklace, etc. The middle-aged woman beside her—possibly her mother—kept blotting the sweat off her forehead, shoulders, and neck with a small towel. She touched the younger woman as gently as she would a bird. 'How it's pouring off you! At least when the bus starts there will be a bit of a breeze,' she said, fanning the girl with the newspaper she held in her hand. The pregnant girl accepted all her mother's attentions with quiet pride. At the same time, she was mindful of the young man who stood outside, beneath the window. He, for his part, continued to hand her, one after the other, a tender coconut, gram sweets, murukku, bananas, and so on.

'Come back soon. Don't stay on there,' he said, standing solidly there. Firmly moulded arms and legs. A body like a rock.

'I've told Bakkiyam-anni to send you your meals. Eat properly. And don't go about in the heat, Ayya. It's not good for you,' she told him, again and again.

The same conversation might have been repeated ten times over, without change of tone. Yet it seemed to contain different meanings each time. The expressions on the speakers' faces kept changing too, showing in turn elation, fond reproof, playfulness, laughter, tenderness, yearning, and sadness at parting.

Now and then the mother intervened to say, 'Why don't you let Thambi go home? He shouldn't have to stand there in the sun.'

The driver jumped in and sat down. Noises preparatory to starting the journey ensued. All at once, the man standing beneath the window began to cry.

'Go and return safely. I'll be yearning for you,' he said, sobbing hugely, and crying aloud. The girl was shaken. Greatly anxious, she said, 'Don't cry. I'll be back. I'll be back very soon.' He wept the more. Broken words came from him, 'The house, so lonely....'

The girl rose to her feet. 'Ayya, should I just stay here? Will you go on your own?' she asked piteously, wiping her tears.

'No, no. It's a wedding in your relative's house. You must go. But come back quickly,' he said.

The bus began to move slowly. The girl leaned forward and stretched out her hands to reach him. He touched her fingers, then laid her hands against his cheeks. 'Go safely, Kamalam,' he said, breaking down yet again.

The bus began to pick up speed. The words 'careful', 'heat', and 'food' mingled with the wind and were lost. As the bus left the station and turned into the main street, when they looked back, they could see him standing in exactly the same place; his whole self shaken, his shoulders rising and falling soundlessly. The girl must have caught sight of him.

'He's still crying,' she announced. 'He's like an innocent child. He won't even realize when he's hungry,' she said.

'Oh, really. It's not a year since you married. Did he stay hungry before that? He's his father's only son. After the woman of the house died, his father brought him up, didn't he? What are you talking about?' The mother snapped at her.

'You don't know anything, Ayya. Within four months of arranging his son's marriage, my father-in-law went off on his countrywide pilgrimage. No, he'll be all alone at home. Only a wife knows what goes on inside a house.' The girl's eyes filled with tears.

'As if he's the most fantastic husband around town! I've borne four children, remember? Are you trying to teach me?'

'Let's say he is a fantastic man. He's certainly better than the bridegroom you wanted to tie me to—the one who demanded another half sovereign's worth of gold and a motor cycle before he would put a thali on me.'

'Why do you want to rake up that old story now? You just go to sleep,' the mother consoled her, laying the girl's head against her shoulder.

The girl laid her head on her mother's shoulder and went to sleep, her handloom sari of green with yellow checks tucked conveniently at her waist, her stomach slightly raised, her bangles jingling each time she moved.

When the bus stopped at Nagercoil, several people had arrived to meet mother and daughter. A small girl in a rose-coloured paavaadai skirt, who wore butterfly-shaped slides studded with brightly coloured stones in her hair, hugged the young woman, calling her 'Athe'. A young boy who looked as if he had just begun to wear long trousers came and stood next to her. Love, sympathy, and contentment on all their faces.

When she had finished her work, her friend told her she must not leave Nagercoil without going to Kanyakumari. At Kanyakumari, waves like shoals of whales. Yet as they touched the feet they were as gentle as a kitten's tongue. The sun, smeared in liquid orange. When she turned her head to take in the full sweep of the sea, the girl came within her orbit. The pregnant girl on the bus. She was standing by the waves, at a little distance from her relatives. A round vessel with a lid in her hand. There was a tenderness in her expression as she gazed at the sea. Like a mother looking at her child. A softness played on her face, reminiscent of Balasaraswati when she mimed gazing at the Baby Krishna in his cradle, as she danced to the song 'Jagadhodharana aadisathalu Yasoda', 'Yasoda played with the saviour of the universe'. Was she looking at the sea, or at some illusory form? Even as she gazed at her, the young woman turned sharply towards her, returned her look for a second, and recognized her. She came forward, smiling.

'Watching the sea?'

'Yes, I've never seen it before. How the waves beat against the shore! I want to watch it forever.'

'Did the wedding go off well?'

'Mm. All of us are here together. We'll be leaving soon.'

'You'll go back home soon, won't you? Your husband was in tears, wasn't he, poor man!'

She smiled. 'Yes, he wept. He's got a heart as soft as cotton wool, Akka.' She stopped, then repeated, 'A heart as soft as cotton wool.' She looked at the sea.

'My family looked for a different bridegroom for me. That man worked in a government office. He seemed all right. But when we were about to buy the wedding clothes, he cut in, "So you are going to spend two thousand rupees on her sari, but only eight hundred on my vetti? In that case I must have two vettis." People in our town laughed amongst themselves, "What's this! He's talking like a child!" But gradually the whole story changed. Before he would tie the thali, he claimed that the wedding jewellery was short by half a sovereign's worth, and demanded that it should be made good immediately, besides a promise of a motor bike within the month. It turned into quite a fracas. My sister held my brother-in-law's chin and pleaded, "Let me give her the chain I'm wearing around my neck." Something like a frenzy came over me, at that time, Akka. I rose to my feet and rushed outside. I said, "I don't want this bridegroom. I will not marry him. If there is a man here who is willing to marry me as I am, then let him come forward." My voice was trembling. The base of my throat was hurting. Everyone was stunned. Their party said, "How brazen of her to say all this!" My family worried, "She's gone and thrown it all away by speaking out." Our townsfolk meanwhile, were wondering, "Who will marry her now, when she does this at such a tender age?" But then, his father came forward, bringing his son, his hand on his shoulder. His face was as innocent as milk. His body well set and sturdy. He was smiling slightly.

'The older man said, "This is my son. He is educated. He supervises my lands. There is no woman in our house; I have brought him up myself. He is willing to marry the girl. Ask her what she wishes." I stood there in shock. I looked at my father and nodded assent. I bowed to the departing bridegroom's people and said, "Stay and eat before you leave."

'And that's how this thali came to me, Akka. He has such a good heart. A child-like heart.'

She stopped and looked at the sea. Then she continued, as if she were speaking to the sea. 'He dotes on children. All the children in our town come to him if they need anything. To fly kites, play ball, produce a play, to be taken to cricket matches. But a senior doctor has said that he of all people can't have children. It seems he wasn't looked after properly when he had mumps as a child, and became infertile as a result. He doesn't know this. He would die if he knew.'

Because of a short bus journey together, she was willing to take her entire life apart, and to share it. Responding to the glance on her slightly raised stomach, she said, 'This belongs to his family, absolutely.'

An image flashed through her mind of an older man on pilgrimage, dipping into and rising from many temple tanks.

'He's never seen the sea. If I catch the waves in this vessel, will they still be tossing when I show him, Akka?'

She imagined a wave rising and falling within the small circular vessel. In the evening light, the pregnant girl who stood by the shore seemed one with the sea.

She could only touch her gently and say, 'No, you cannot capture the rise and fall of the sea's waves.'

Translated by Lakshmi Holmström

SPACE TRAVELLERS

THOPPIL MOHAMED MEERAN

This historic and proud town had two guardians of the east, the Chentapallipaarai and the Aanaipaarai, two massive rocks. The splintered Chentapalli was the one which prevented the cholera epidemic from entering from the east. When the sea swallowed the red sun, first-time mothers-to-be would make 101 paniyarams, the dumpling-like snack, and carry them up the Chentapallipaarai. There they would chant the Yaseen Koran and offer God the paniyarams to ensure that they had a safe delivery. The Aanaipaarai stopped the howling storms that blew in from the east.

It was the Aanaipaarai that we scampered up like squirrels during those times, the fasting season, to catch sight of the Ramadan moon. The rock looked just like an elephant, with ears, a trunk, forelegs, and a huge rear. Makkatti Lebbai, the Islamic scholar, had covered the Oosikinaru well with a round stone slab, on the head of the elephant. According to legend, the well sprang when a certain Mastan Sahibu came to the area during a terrible and fierce drought and tapped the rock with a stick. Were ten elephants to join together and push it, the huge stone slab would not have moved even the distance occupied by a mustard seed. But it is said that Makkatti Lebbai just lifted it with his little finger and covered the well.

It seems some men actually saw that…and all of them instantly turned blind.

The younger generation had heard from Maideenadimai uppa, the lone survivor among these blind men, that Israyeel (the messenger of death) was hovering around Mastan Sahibu, afraid to come close and take his life, and that Mastan Sahibu was circling the skies, unseen by human eyes.

The boys would creep, bit by bit, up the elephant's rear to the top, in order to see the Ramadan moon. They climbed cautiously, gripping the rock like squirrels. It was a steep climb; one false step could mean instant death.

If the hands of the clouds did not cover it, the crescent moon could be seen as a faint thread on the western forehead of the blue sky. You stood there without taking your eyes off it. After making its appearance for a split second, the moon vanished. The wretched clouds which knew nothing sometimes covered the moon. But once the moon was sighted, it was a quick dash from the rock to the entrance of the mosque.

Piraikandaacho! Sighted the moon!

The street would go delirious, and the people waiting in expectation near the mosque would be euphoric with joy on hearing this. Heels hitting their buttocks, they would run to do their Perunaal shopping.

Mastan Sahibu, the one whom death dared not approach, flew high above the sky without any wings. He flew above the Aanaipaarai, above Chentapalli, and above Valiyaaru, where the Chettichi community lived. He also tied his matted hair to his toe and went into the deepest part of the ocean. He flew above Chippipaarai, which appeared like a single breast of the Arabian Sea; he flew as he pleased. Only if Mastan Sahibu got caught in Israyeel's hook would the slab covering the well be thrown off and the waters erupt and flow.

And then there would be a deluge, like in Nooh Nabi's times, and the whole world would be submerged. So, to guard Mastan Sahibu from Israyeel's hook, the townsfolk would gather at the foot of the Aanaipaarai on the night of every Rajab, the seventh month, read the 'Fatiha', and distribute sweets.

Before the Rajab moon, Sundan would pluck the tapioca he had planted on the red soil of the public land at the foot of the Aanaipaarai. Sundan knew these dates and months well. He knew that if Mastan Sahibu's life were plucked away by Israyeel's hook, the slab covering the well would fall off and the waters would flow, causing a deluge. He knew that the deluge would drown his tapioca, the red soil, and the mud hut where he and his young children slept at night. Sundan would often think of the devastation that might take place. It was only because Makkatti Lebbai knew all this through his intuitive wisdom that he had placed the round slab to cover the well.

An underground tunnel running from beneath the Aanaipaarai, passed under the Arabian Sea, and ended inside Chippipaarai. Mermaids lived inside Chippipaarai, in a palace of rubies built by one of the gandharvas, mythical beings who live underground. They picked pearls in the morning and strung them together in the evening. When the sea drank the red glow of the sun, the radiance of the ruby palace broke forth. At that moment, the tunnel door opened on its own and the mermaids came out on to the Aanaipaarai, climbing up the crystal steps that were inside. They gazed leisurely at this outside world, fringed by coconut fronds, and were thrilled by the chilly breeze blowing through those swaying trees. They inhaled all the fresh air they needed for the day, and went back down the crystal stairway.

On every fourteenth-moon night, Sundan heard the tinkling anklets of dancing feet, and stood in front of the rock with folded hands till dawn.

'Thaaye, mother, mother of the sea, protect me and my family!'

Once, when the boys who went up the rock to sight the moon came back disappointed, Maideenadimai uppa told them the secret story of how Makkatti Lebbai went down the underground tunnel.

One day, during the chilly months of Ani and Adi when it was raining, Makkatti Lebbai, without even a shirt, went up the slippery rock as if he had seen a vision there. After skipping easily over the Chentapallipaarai, he climbed up to the top of the Aanaipaarai and vanished from sight.

The people were filled with wonder when they heard this.

Then, Lebbai appeared before Maideenadimai uppa in a dream and Uppa told us what he had heard.

When Lebbai's feet touched the centre of the Aanaipaarai, the rock cracked on its own. He peered into the crack. It was pitch black. In the light that emanated from his body, he could see the crystal stairs descending. He stepped onto them and climbed down. When his feet touched the last stair, he saw the face of the tunnel. The radiance from his forehead caused the thick darkness of the tunnel to disappear. He went ahead as the path revealed itself in the glow and soon reached the entrance of the ruby palace. At this time the mermaids had gone to the sea to gather pearls. The light was refracted from the radiant rubies and the whole palace shone. Makkatti Lebbai went around the palace, where no one was to be found, drowning in its beauty. He was about to return, when someone behind him called out to him.

'Elabbey!'

A melodious voice, like the strumming of a veena string.

He was startled at being addressed by his name.

'Who are you?' he asked, though he knew the answer.

'We are mermaids. The king of the sea, Aazhiarasan, has asked us to live in this palace built by the gandharvas. He is the lord of the seven seas. We swim around the seven seas to gather pearls and string them together to garland the king. When the sun sets and darkness spreads on earth, our palace lights up by itself. When we see the glow, we gather here…and you?'

This unexpected question elicited a puzzling response from Makkatti Lebbai.

'I am a servant of Allah, a world wanderer. I now stand before you. At this time, I pray at the mosque in Mecca, and also have my food at Medina, and at the same time, rest in the Jerusalem mosque. Do you understand who I am?'

Stunned by what they had heard, they nodded.

'Yes, Bawa, we understand.'

'I fly faster than the wind in the outer zone, run across the water, and sleep in fire.'

They felt quite small hearing of his superhuman powers, which they did not have.

'How do you live under the sea, without air to breathe?' He asked them.

'At night, we go to the Aanaipaarai and collect our day's requirement of air. We have that ability. God has given the camel the capacity to save the water it needs for many months; similarly, he has given us the capacity to save the air we need.

'We also have the ability to protect the Aanaipaarai and other rocks on the surface of the earth from being injured by human beings. We can lift the Aanaipaarai like an umbrella over the town, so that it is not destroyed by storms.

'We are the guardians of the seven seas and the Chippipaarai. We can protect the world from being drowned by deluges from the rising sea. Our arms have the strength to push down and suppress the waves that rise high.'

When Lebbai attempted to return after listening to this, a question was addressed to him.

'How did you discover this passage which man cannot enter?'

'I did penance for fifteen years atop the Aanaipaarai. It cracked and opened up when my feet touched it.'

Lebbai disappeared with the dream, when Maideenadimai woke up with a start. The secret that he had heard in the dream travelled through the ears of the town, also in a secret way.

After Makkatti Lebbai had shared this secret, no one in the town saw him, nor did he speak in anyone's dreams. Makkatti Lebbai had a slight frame, went around bare-chested, and wore a short vetti that just about reached his knees. The townspeople believed that he had become invisible and was travelling in space. Maideenadimai uppa was of the firm belief that it was only because Makkatti Lebbai foresaw his death that he had revealed the secret to him; and that thereafter, Lebbai had split his chest and offered it to Israyeel for him to snatch.

Some nights, Uppa would light up a Cycle brand joss stick and read the 'Yaseen Sura', so that, with Makkatti Lebbai's blessings, the town would prosper and the Aanaipaarai would not come to any harm.

Once the news leaked that Maideenadimai uppa was reciting the Yaseen, Aithroz, who had a sudden vision, made a startling prophecy, swearing by Chentapalli Sheikh.

'Aanaipaarai, the rock is growing!'

When Maideenadimai uppa heard that Aithroz was insisting that everyone must recite the Yaseen and seek blessings to protect the growing Aanaipaarai, he asked Aithroz: 'Hey! How do you know that the Aanaipaarai is growing?'

'Makkatti Lebbai appeared in my dreams and told me, okay? Do you know that it grew when the warmth of his feet touched it?'

After Aithroz took an oath in the name of several places of worship and many saints, the townsfolk also began to see that the Aanaipaarai was growing.

The people made some calculations and decided that the date when Makkatti Lebbai had vanished from sight was the third day of the moon in Sha'baan, the eighth month. So on the third pirai of Sha'baan, Aithroz, holding aloft the green crescent flag, led his friends and family, all of whom were wearing caps, to the Aanaipaarai. They applied sandal paste at the place of worship, recited the Yaseen, and distributed offerings to the massive crowd that had gathered.

They sat on Sundan's red floor on the fourteenth moon of the month of Rajab and recited the Yaseen for Mastan Sahibu, and did the same on the third pirai of Sha'baan, sitting near Aanaipaarai.

'Fear no more. Mastan Sahibu will protect us and our town. Aanaipaarai will also be protected.'

Just when the people heaved a sigh of relief and gained confidence, Allahu sitting in the seventh sky, became enraged with the people of some other towns because they had forgotten Him. And in a show of strength, He unchained the shackles of a mighty storm and let it loose, like He had during the time of Prophet Hud.

This storm was like the one sent to destroy the Adhu tribe, which had refused to accept Prophet Hud as a messenger of God. It swept away the roofs of the houses in many towns. Flung by the wind, the tiles flew like arrows, and fell on many heads, breaking them and drenching them with blood.

In town after town, the coconut trees, the palm trees, and other trees were uprooted. Unable to face the might of the hurricane, many old tamarind trees, and even banyan trees, were pulled out by their roots. Vessels and other objects flew like balls of cotton. The falling trees and collapsing buildings resulted in many a death. And the Aanaipaarai, with its strong arms, prevented the violent and angry hurricane from travelling west, for which the people were eternally grateful.

Had it not been for the Aanaipaarai, the whole town would have perished. Now the townspeople were doubly devoted to the Aanaipaarai, since it had saved them from terrible destruction.

This is our town's strong bulwark against destruction.

After the hurricane died down, some ran to the Aanaipaarai and kissed it in a show of gratitude.

They were filled with pride, because they felt that they need not fear the wretched hurricane.

Till the end of the world, Aanaipaarai will keep growing without moving. One day, it will touch the sky and that's when the world will end.

It was just when the fame of the Aanaipaarai had spread far and wide that the world was shaken by raging tidal waves.

It used to be a lovely quiet beach where the children of the fishing village romped around and played. Now they cut the coconut trees, the leaves of which would fly in the wind like beautiful wavy tresses, and cleared the ground. Then they built resorts to attract foreigners, just as Ad's son, Sadaat, had built Iramdhat al-Imad, akin to a heaven on earth. The purity of the seashore was violated by intoxicating drinks, gambling, and sex. These resorts hindered the waves from reaching out their arms freely and rolling and sporting on the wet sands.

The sea controlled its anger. But one day, it could control itself no longer and from its depths, its rage erupted, shook everything, and boiled over. Though the mermaids desperately employed all their skill, the sea, dancing like a demon, could not be reined in. The mermaids were devastated by their own helplessness. The sea rose higher than the tallest palm tree and forced its way in ferociously,

breaking all barriers and demolishing the resorts. Whatever it saw—
homes, shops, and everything—it chewed and spat out.

The dance of death lasted a few minutes. Wherever the water
started retreating, piles of corpses could be seen. Men walked around,
sniffing like dogs, in search of jewellery on the corpses of women.
The resorts had been smashed to the ground, and unidentifiable
white corpses were found crushed under the rubble. After much
searching, the hundreds of bodies gathered from the swampy jungle
in the wake of their destruction, were lined up. Thirty-five of the
bodies which could be identified were buried in the same pit in
the mosque.

'You have gone, my son, my child!'

The people realized that the earth had taken revenge on the
heartless men who had caused it so much damage and violence.

In the silence of the shores, the waves that seemed to be made of
tears, dashed and fell apart. When Makkatti Lebbai felt the dampness
of the tears, he went down the tunnel steps, and knocked on the
doors of the ruby palace. And when he saw the weeping mermaids,
he quietly climbed up the steps and went out.

The coastal community had long been requesting the government
to take measures to protect them from tsunamis, and it was indeed
a miracle that wisdom dawned on them after this disaster. Officers
racked their brains to find a means of guarding against the tsunami
waves. The people who had dragged their feet, seemingly in
anticipation of orders from higher-ups, now roamed like wild demons
in search of the wealth that could be 'skimmed' off these deals.

Huge rocks and mountains that are like Mother Earth's roots had
been broken, and the boulders shipped to other countries with the
blessings of the government. Now, when permission was granted to
build a wall against the sea and stones were needed, there were no
rocks in sight and efforts to build the wall floundered.

A giant machine was brought to break the Pipaarai near the
Aatrorapaarai, upon which Nagore Andagai used to sit, enjoying the
sea breeze. When Nagore Andagai saw this from Nagore, he extended

his hands and made the street narrow. As a result, the giant machine retreated in defeat.

The village officer suggested a rock poramboke to the east of the village. Sufficient rocks were available and could be blasted. The machine was redirected there, on his instructions.

The Chentapalli rock! The Aanaipaarai! The officers and contractors were full of glee. Boulders available so close by. These boulders would suffice to build a wall many miles long.

It was the time when the fragrance of neyyappam sweets being fried wafts through the breeze, just before the third moon of Sha'baan. Suddenly, an earth-shattering noise was heard and people were terrified that the sky itself had fallen. Dust and smoke spiralled up the eastern sky and the people near the mosque stood rooted to the spot in shock.

The ones who saw it were paralyzed by fear. When the dust and smoke settled a bit, there was another deafening noise, enough to rip apart one's skull. The earth shook and the sky was covered with dust and smoke.

The terrified people looked above...the curse of Allah was falling on them.

'Ya Allah!'

They cried to the omnipotent Allah, who dwelt over the seventh sky, praying for protection. They cried to Mastan Sahibu, who was flying above the cloudy highway. They cried to Makkatti Lebbai, who moved unseen.

After sunset, when it was less hot, the crowd climbed the rock. They watched carefully, wondering if they could see Makkatti Lebbai's shadow move; Makkatti Lebbai, he who closed the well with a slab to prevent the world from coming to an end because of a deluge. They listened carefully in the hope that the echo of his voice would be heard from the Aanaipaarai.

When they climbed the Chentapallipaarai and looked at the Aanaipaarai, their blood froze and their hearts stopped. Their eyes were plunged in darkness. They tried to drive it away by rubbing them and stared. In whatever little light there was, they looked, and they looked again. They could not believe what they saw, so they looked again.

The Aanaipaarai was missing.

The elephant rear of the growing Aanaipaarai had been broken into big stones. The sandal paste had dried into powder and was stuck there. The round slab that covered the well lay in pieces. The people's wrath overflowed. The giant rock breaker, exhausted after toiling so hard, had been abandoned there. The very sight of it kindled the people's rage and they went immediately in chase of the workers.

The underground tunnel that went to the Chippipaarai?

The well which could overflow and drown the town?

Mastan Sahibu, who roamed the sky above the Aanaipaarai?

Makkatti Lebbai, the guardian of the Aanaipaarai?

Questions, questions, questions.

The townspeople had no answer; they were lost in a cloud of incomprehension.

Now if we want to sight the Perunaalpirai, which rock will we climb?

If a terrible storm blows in from the east, like the one that destroyed the Adhu tribe because they did not respect Prophet Hud, will the shattered and flattened Aanaipaarai grow again to protect us?

The people did not know…a dark cloud of confusion enveloped them.

'It will grow,' said Aithroz.

Translated by Prabha Sridevan

RAIN, ENDLESS RAIN

BALAKUMARAN

He laid his right thumb flat on a nearby stone. With his left hand he raised the sword high. He looked up at his guru, Andanar. The latter indicated his consent by closing his eyes. The young man swung the blade of the sword down with great speed and force on his thumb. The severed thumb jumped up and landed at the feet of the Guru. It twitched a little where it lay. A red tide of blood fountained from the wound. He rose, went over to the Guru and, like water from a jug, he offered the streaming oblation of blood at his Guru's feet.

Andanar raised his hand to signal 'Enough'. In great agony, the man clutched his right wrist hard with his left hand, finished a swift clockwise circumambulation of his Guru as demanded by custom, and sped away. Trembling with pain, he jumped into a nearby pond. The pond water turned red.

Seeing the man's agony, the divine spirits who inhabited the lake shivered in empathy. Unable to bear the pain any longer, he passed out. Gently the spirits pushed him towards the bank. His injured right hand stayed buried in the fresh soil at the edge of the pond, soothed by the cool water lapping around it. The roots of the plants gave out their healing sap. A lotus leaf floated over and covered his hand carefully.

All these creations of Nature knew that a great injustice had been done. Though they could not raise their voices in protest, they could revive him. They could stop the bleeding and heal the injury with medicinal sap. For three full days the man lay unconscious in this manner. His bow and arrows lay beside him, like bereft orphans, at the edge of that pond.

When the group of hunters who had been looking for him found him lying at the edge of the pond, they were startled. The sight of his mutilated hand alarmed them. For a while they hunted around the spot looking for the missing thumb. Finally, thankful for having found the man at least, if not his thumb, they carried him away, along with his trusty bow and quiver of arrows.

The man was astonished that his wound had healed in just three days without a vestige of pain. This must be due to the benevolence of my Guru, he thought to himself.

'Miracle…it's a miracle', he told himself. But yet he asked himself why the Guru had sought this sacrifice from him. From the other forests too, hunters came by to ask how he was getting along. They all wanted to know what exactly had happened. How did he lose his thumb?

He described how it had come about. When they heard the details, the hunters grew very agitated. 'Aa…hoo!' they exclaimed in indignation as they slapped themselves on the forehead. Some buried their faces in their hands and wept. 'Oh God! What justice is this?' they demanded, raising their eyes heavenward. The man was bemused by their reaction.

But where was the injustice in this? He had meditated on his Guru, Andanar, and attained great skills. His Guru's blessings had given him access to powerful weapons and he had attained perfection in his skills as an archer. So, where was the injustice if his Guru demanded a sacrifice from him? After all, would he have asked for his thumb unless there was a good reason to do so? Would someone so wise and learned do something unjust? Why are these ignorant and illiterate hunter friends of mine raising such a hue and cry about it?

'Oh, you wretched fellow!'

'Why did you ever agree to sacrifice your thumb?'

'Why did you not see the evil intentions of that Guru?'

'You could have raised up our whole community of hunters. This miserable existence of ours…roaming the forests like bears and tigers…we could have put it all behind us.'

'You could have become a famous leader and our whole tribe could have got good food, an education, a good quality of life….'

'And you cut off your thumb! Why didn't you refuse to do such a thing?' They went on and on, lamenting his stupidity and their fate.

The oldest man in the group got up and said: 'This is the beloved son of our tribe, our north star. You, Andanar, have hatched an evil plot to rob him of his power by demanding this sacrifice from him. Know then that you too will meet your death through a plot. Just as our blood boils at the sight of our son's plight, so too will you feel the agony of the loss of your own beloved son. As there is a God above, I am sure this will come to pass. Your love for your son will be the instrument of your death, oh Drona.'

Cries of 'Yes, Yes', rose from all sides. Thunderclouds roiled overhead. They seemed to be endorsing the old man's curse, signalling that his prediction would indeed come to pass. When a righteous person in great mental agony curses the one who has done him a grave injustice, it will surely come to pass at some future time. Time always ensures that justice is done.

The young man was upset by the uproar. He did not like the shouting and cursing. He did not endorse their sense of outrage. He picked up his bow and quiver of arrows and walked away. He went into the forest and calmly examined the wound on his hand. He could not string his bow; he could not even pull an arrow out of the quiver.

He used his teeth to string his bow. He tried to use just his forefinger and middle finger to pull back the bowstring and despatch an arrow. It missed its mark. It travelled erratically. His mastery of archery had been such that he could seal shut a dog's mouth by unleashing a single arrow. Even when perched precariously on the branch of a tree, he could land his arrow unerringly on a running elephant; even while swimming in the pond he could shoot down a bird from the sky. And now…he was not even able to shoot down a fruit from a tree to assuage his hunger.

The bow and quiver felt like a burden.

Why, why, why? The question whirled around in his head endlessly. Why had his Guru asked him to sacrifice his right thumb? He

couldn't eat, he couldn't sleep.... At the same time, he couldn't
bring himself to think or speak ill of his Guru. If just the Guru's
statue had been able to teach him such great skills in archery, if just
meditating on the Guru had bestowed valour on him, how blessed
are those who actually learn from him directly, he thought.

He alone is my Guru. Whatever my tribe may say about him,
he is my spiritual guide. With single-minded concentration on his
Guru, the young man once again tried to shoot an arrow using two
fingers instead of the missing thumb. The arrow found its mark this
time, but the shot was weak—the earlier power was gone. The other
fingers could not match the power that his thumb had wielded on
the bowstring.

He practised. Again and again. He managed to shoot a deer.

He practised some more. Endlessly, relentlessly. He shot a leopard.

He persevered with his archery practice. Tirelessly, day after day.
He shot birds out of the sky.

But the intricate skills—shooting an arrow precisely to close a
dog's mouth, or to pursue it with arrows as it ran, or to shoot off
a continuous rainstorm of arrows—all these now eluded him. He
was a good hunter; that was all. Not a champion archer. Not any
more. He could do enough with his bow to hunt food for himself.
But he no longer had the skills to use his bow in battle.

The years rolled on by.

A young woman from a neighbouring forest fell in love with
him. They married with gandharva rites in the forest. When he
explained all that had happened, she advised him, 'Go and see the
one who is known as Krishna. Tell him how you came to lose your
thumb. He may restore your thumb to you.'

'Restore? But how?'

'The Yadavas consider Krishna to be a god. It is said that he
lifted and held aloft an entire mountain to shelter people from the
rain. They say he even went down under the water in a pond full
of poison and slew a vicious five-headed serpent. And when an evil
rakshasa took on the form of a huge bison to attack him, Krishna

grabbed him by the horns and twisted and broke his neck. So it can't be that difficult for him to restore your thumb.'

'Please come with me,' said the young man. 'Come and show me the Krishna you are talking about.'

'Oh, no, no. I won't. I'm scared....'

'Why?'

'They say that he casts his spell on beautiful young women, and they can't resist it....'

'Oh, you're not such a great beauty or anything. Just come along.'

'Oh, so I am not beautiful? Your wife doesn't appear beautiful to your eyes? Just for that I refuse to come with you.'

She was offended. He had to go on his own to seek Krishna. When he reached Dwaraka he was told that Krishna was not in town. He had left just the day before. There was some quarrel between two kings and Krishna was trying to restore harmony.

'When will he be back?'

They had no idea. But they did say that it would be next to impossible to meet Krishna right away because he would be far too busy.

The young man was downcast as he turned back to go home. On his way through the forest he shot rabbits and deer and took them back with him as a peace offering for his angry wife.

Sons were born to them, and he taught the boys archery and hunting. Once one of them said, 'Appa, it is so much easier to use the thumb to release the arrow.'

'Wrong!' he admonished the boy. 'You should use your index and middle fingers only.'

'Why?'

'That is the rule laid down by my Guru.'

The boy was incredulous; he did not look convinced. 'Listen to me, son,' urged the man, 'always do exactly what your elders advise you to.'

The boy became a skilled hunter...using only his fingers.

One day, the man was moving around on a wooded hill in quest of a peacock feather that his wife wanted. A chariot approached through the trees. It was drawn by two horses, like a royal carriage. It stopped as if looking for something or someone. What could they be searching for in the forest, he wondered. He ran towards the chariot, intending to offer his assistance.

When he reached the chariot he bowed in greeting. Out of the chariot stepped a man; his skin was as dark as that of an elephant, eyes as wide as those of a deer, shoulders broad like a tiger's, lips as red as a lotus in bloom. He lifted his soft palms in blessing. The stranger gazed intently at the hunter...and smiled.

The hunter was mesmerized by that smile. 'Ayya, who are you?' he asked. 'Whom do you seek in this forest? The heat of the day is stifling. I am a hunter and even I am finding the heat oppressive. How can you withstand it? Can I do anything to help you?'

'Oh hunter, who wanders fearlessly through the forests like the God of Death himself, did you happen to see a group of five men and a woman pass this way?'

'No, Ayya.'

'Well, then they must have gone to the other side of the mountain. I'll take your leave now....'

As the stranger was about to climb back into the chariot, the hunter spoke hesitantly, in a humble tone, 'Ayya...by the time you reach the top of this mountain in your chariot they may have covered quite a distance. If you walk with me to the top we can descend the other side much faster. I know the way.'

The stranger turned back from the chariot. Again he smiled. And again the hunter stood transfixed by the smile.

'This way,' said the hunter, as he strode out in front, using his sharp sword to slash away the thorny branches in their path. They arrived at the mountain peak. The stranger did not appear the least bit wearied by the exertion. With his peacock feather waving in the breeze, he surveyed the expanse below him with a keen eye.

'There they are,' he pointed. As the hunter started heading in the direction he had indicated, the stranger clapped his hands to signal him to stop. The hunter turned, and his puzzled expression sought an explanation. 'I will go on from here, oh hunter. I am grateful for your help. But please go back to your own task, there's no need for you to trouble yourself further for me.'

What sensitivity! What serene eyes! Did kings have such humility, such a countenance?

'Ayya, who are you?'

'I am known as Krishnan.'

'The king of the Yadavas?'

'Yes.'

'Ayya!' cried the hunter, falling at Krishna's feet. Krishna closed his eyes.

'Ayya!'

'Yes, tell me, oh hunter,' urged Krishna.

'I came to Dwaraka looking for you, but you were not in the city at the time.'

'Is that so? Why, what's the matter?'

'I don't have my right thumb, Ayya.'

'Why?'

'I cut it off as a sacrifice demanded by my Guru.'

'*What...!*'

The hunter briefly related the sequence of events to Krishna. Krishna listened intently to every word.

The hunter pleaded, 'Can you restore my thumb? I have heard that you lifted an entire mountain, that you killed a fierce serpent, that you slew many demons. Can you give me a thumb? Even recently I was told that when someone tried to outrage the modesty of a woman you bestowed on her an endless sari that could never be undraped. I have suffered a grievous bodily injury, Ayya. Can you not help me?' He fell once again at Krishna's feet.

Krishna closed his eyes.

'Why do you need a thumb, oh hunter?'

'I want to regain my artistry and skills in archery. I want to be an expert in the use of all manner of weapons.'

'Why?'

'Because I want to stop having to run around like this. I want to bring down a deer easily from wherever I am standing; I want to be able to shoot down many birds with a single arrow. Look, today I am roaming around so much just to find a peacock. If I had my skills restored I could just sit at home and send out an arrow to fetch me a peacock. My family and I could enjoy a life of prosperity as well as leisure.'

Krishna laughed.

'You don't need weapons, my friend. If you could kill all the birds in the village with a single arrow, soon there wouldn't be any birds left in the world.'

'My other two fingers are very painful, Ayya. That's why I am asking for a powerful thumb to use instead.' The hunter held out his fingers.

'I will give your fingers more strength,' said Krishna. He gripped the hunter's fingers firmly. The hunter's body trembled; power surged through his body. The pain vanished as though it had never been there.

Krishna released the man's fingers and instructed him to wring his hand. The hunter did so. He could feel new strength in his fingers.

'My deepest gratitude to you, Ayya,' said the hunter, bowing to Krishna.

'Don't make any living creature suffer needlessly. Kill instantly with a single arrow, and hunt creatures only for your food.'

'I will do as you say, my Lord.'

'You have love and compassion; of what use are weapons to you? Oh hunter, don't spend any more time in regrets. Don't even ask yourself why Drona did what he did to you. Believe me, it is a good thing that he has done for you. You will come to realize it some day. I will be on my way now.' Like a blue cloud Krishna blended into the forest and was lost to sight.

The hunter returned home in a mood of high elation, gazing at his newly power-charged fingers as he went.

His wife's reaction was very different. 'So even Krishna has refused to help you. Now who else is there to ask? You are an idiot. Why didn't you insist that you should get back your thumb? It is our fate, what can anyone do....' The heavens signalled their agreement with a roll of thunder.

More years passed. The children grew up. The hunter took his sons on trips through many forests. One day they saw armies, chariots, and elephants going through one of the forests. Evidently a battle was taking place somewhere. The sons were eager to taste some of the action. 'We have swords and bows, Appa. Can't we join in?' they asked.

The hunter rejected the idea outright. 'No,' he told them, 'we are hunters, not soldiers.' They begged to be allowed to at least watch the battle. He agreed.

So they climbed to the summit of a hill and watched the battle. Thousands of arrows were flying back and forth through the air. Many heads were being chopped off. There was one particular soldier dressed in white who was hacking through enemies left and right, like a farmer reaping grain. His arrows performed magical feats. When he chanted an incantation and released an arrow, it sent up flames where it landed; with another he set up a strong wind; and with another he brought down rain and poisonous fumes.

What is he using, asked the sons. Weapons, replied the hunter. Hundreds of thousands of soldiers were falling dead, as if they were bugs and beetles.

The hunter lost all track of time. The battle raged on for several days. Once the bugle sounded to signal the end of the battle, he and his sons went down to the battlefield. A sea of death surrounded them.

A ten-year-old boy, a twenty-year-old youth, a thirty-year-old king, a forty-year-old commander, a seventy-year-old man—why even an eighty-year-old general—lay slain. All the bodies were collected and brought to share the same funeral pyre.

Someone asked the hunter to go and fetch wood for the pyres. Dry wood was piled into mounds and the pyres were lit. Many wives whose husbands had died in battle leapt into the flames to join them in death. Other women who had been widowed in the battle tugged off their thalis, slapped their foreheads, and wailed aloud. Children whimpered. 'Amma, Appa,' arose the cries of new orphans. Mounds of corpses everywhere. The whole place was a massive graveyard.

The hunter was appalled. Is this what battle looks like? Is this why people want to master the art of archery? Is this mass butchering of people the true aim of weapons training?

Contemptible wretches! Is this what all those years of training have led to? All those years of learning at the feet of a Guru? Is this what inspired you to study the Vedas? And to spout your lofty commentaries? Oh, pathetic sinners...wretches.... His mind was in turmoil.

He squatted on the ground and wept. 'My mind is not at peace,' he told his sons. 'You go home now. And don't ever leave the forest again for any reason.'

He walked in the direction where his feet took him.

A voice he had recently heard echoed in his ears—the voice of the one known as Krishna, the one with the wide lotus eyes: 'You should not attain skills in warfare, oh hunter. Some day you will realize what I mean....'

'I don't want to master the skills of warfare. No, no...never.' His mind cried out.

And Krishna's other words of wisdom: 'Do not resent Drona for asking you to sacrifice your thumb. He has done you a great service.'

'Oh Guru, by making me cut off my thumb you have saved my family, my lineage. I salute you most reverentially.'

What had started the battle? It appears someone had refused to part with property. No, we will not give you even five houses, they said; we will not give you even five tiny needlepoints of land. But whose land is this? Whom should it be given to? How can someone claim this land as his personal property? Millions of people have lived and died on this land. How can it be parcelled out between you and me, them and us? And for what purpose?

What folly! What sort of people can do things like this? Next, perhaps they will argue about who owns the air above us. Or about which water bubble in a flowing stream belongs to whom. Oh, you utterly stupid, stupid men.

His mind full of questions, he walked on mechanically, aimlessly. For days on end he walked.

He realized he was hungry.

He looked around carefully. He heard a rustle. He detected a new smell in the air. From among the bushes, the head of a deer emerged.

He automatically set his bowstring between his forefinger and middle finger. And then he remembered Krishna's parting words: 'Don't make any living creature suffer needlessly. Kill instantly with a single arrow, and hunt creatures only for your food.'

'Oh deer, I am killing you only because I need to eat. Please forgive me.'

The arrow fled swiftly from the bowstring.

'Aaaa....' cried out a human voice. In shock, he ran towards the sound.

It was Krishna. It was blue-hued Krishna, and the hunter's arrow had pierced right through his big toe.

'Ayya!' wailed the hunter.

'Come, Ekalavya.'

'Ayya, I thought I was shooting a deer. I mistook your foot for a deer....' he sobbed.

'Oh hunter, my chapter has ended at your hands. I took on this mortal form, and so I will have to die. There is no need for you to grieve. It was I who decided that, rather than meet death at the hands of evil schemers and those filled with hate, I would meet my end through you. I am attaining my death from the hand of a good human being, a loving and compassionate man. Your fingers are powerful; your aim is true. The other day when we met, I put an extra arrow into your quiver...an arrow meant for me.'

Krishna laughed.

'I am not a good person like you, oh hunter. I have always

helped anyone who sought me out for a favour, yet I refused your request to restore your thumb. Now I am reaping the consequence of that refusal. Please draw out the arrow gently from my foot and release my soul.'

'Ayya, for this great sin that I've committed I–' the hunter stammered in distress.

'No, no, oh hunter. You took aim only to kill for food. That is no sin. You were sure it was a deer, and that is why you shot your arrow. As long as there is a pure heart like yours left on this earth, there will be rain. Grass will grow, forests will flourish. Please release my spirit now. Draw the arrow out from my foot and leave. Go home, don't look back.'

With trembling fingers the hunter drew out the arrow from Krishna's foot. He flung the arrow and his bow into the bushes and walked away rapidly into the forest.

There was a sudden roll of thunder. Lightning flashed. The sky opened up. Torrential rain fell upon the earth. As though sent to cool the heat of the battlefield, the rain fell ceaselessly.

The hunter walked aimlessly, in a daze, wailing 'Krishna, Krishna' from the depths of a great grief.

Translated by Malini Seshadri

CHANGE

POOMANI

The women strode along briskly as a group, headed for the fields. At their waistbands, weed cutters; in their hands, sickles. Also gruel for their midday meal, in mud pots, in lunch buckets, and a variety of other utensils. As they walked by rapidly, not one of them appeared to have noticed frail old Maarimuthu, squatting listlessly on the thinnai of the house to the west.

It was always like this when weeding season arrived. There would be hardly anyone in the village. Every person, young and old, would be at the fields of the Pannaiyar's Melur farms. At the most, a few who were too elderly or too frail to work would be left to watch the home.

The pot-bellied contractor who had rented fields on labour lease was coming around the curve near the termite hill. Behind him, like a herd of goats, followed a group of workers, their banter and laughter rising and falling in the air.

Old Maarimuthu screwed up his face and glanced westwards. The soles of his feet itched. One by one, people were climbing up the embankment of the Vaguthodai stream.

He turned his face towards the open front door of his house. 'Our girl must have gone past that hollow tamarind tree by now, right?'

From inside the house, old Gomathi's muttered response, no louder than a cooing dove, did not quite reach Maarimuthu's ears. He fell silent.

With his two legs no longer sufficient to do their job, a third had arrived in the form of a cane. What did it matter whether he could now hear or not hear? The days of toiling away, weeding the length and breadth of the black soil of those fields, were done. Now this thinnai was his refuge. He hardly ventured out any more.

The old woman's situation was no different. She rarely moved around. Once in a while she would shake out her small knot of hair a couple of times, tie it up as though getting ready for some activity, and then sit back exhausted.

In these circumstances, it was no easy thing for the two of them to hold a leisurely conversation. With each sitting unmoving at different corners, what was there to discuss or do? If at all, they could sigh aloud while reminiscing about the tough times gone by, when they had tirelessly slogged day and night in the fields.

Both had toiled their whole lives just to keep body and soul together. Now, completely drained, the two old people just sat around. They took some solace from the fact that they had passed on their responsibilities to their only child, their daughter.

Maarimuthu, who had been placidly stroking the top of his bald head, suddenly made a grunting noise, as though clearing his throat. This was a signal that some matters of deep concern were running through his mind.

His toothless face had shrunk inwards to such an extent that it was difficult to spot where his mouth was. When the toothless jaw moved, the chin rose towards the nose, hovering as if anticipating contact.

His thoughts had turned towards the task of weeding.

'They call this weeding? Is this the way to go about it? If one takes these youngsters along, will the job go well, I ask you! In those days, when I was a contractor, was this sort of thing happening? To this day that fellow Sivanaandi will tell you—the poor fellow has been stricken with arthritis—the men and women who worked under me were no soft pushovers. Not a single fault to be found with them. And they always received the full measure of their wages in grain. But these fellows take their responsibility so casually. If you hire people for work, you have to calculate the numbers and pay out the grain correctly. Should the payment not match the high standards of my Muthupechhi? Instead neither the quality nor the quantity of the grain is good. Good at talking big, that's all. What a pathetic breed of contractor!'

Maarimuthu muttered under his breath with disgust.

The sky was growing lighter by the minute. A solitary rooster, perhaps suddenly realizing his earlier omission, decided to crow loudly.

The thought of his daughter lay heavy on his heart. By now she must be in the fields. Among a group of women, weeding tool in hand, amidst cotton plants languishing under the rising heat of the day. Everywhere the *sarrat-sarrat* sounds of weeds being scraped out of the ground…sweat forming beads on her forehead….

'Not much longer, now,' mused Maarimuthu. 'Can't lean on her for very long. The time will come soon for us to find a prince for her and give her into his care, before we close our eyes forever.'

He longed for someone to talk to. He ached to open his heart and speak about his daughter. His glance turned towards his house. The old lady was busy counting something on her fingers.

'…mmm, yes. Before we leave the world, it would be good if we can see our daughter with a thaali around her neck. It's painful to see such a young girl having to work herself to the bone like this, and all alone. Our only child, and we didn't have the time to enjoy her, to enjoy raising her and watching her grow. Hardly had she come of age than she had to go to the fields to work. And to this day she continues to slave away, back and forth, round and round…field to home, home to field, endlessly, like a bullock drawing water out of a well. Perhaps we will not live long enough to see her married….'

His eyes were wet with tears. Every time he had to see his daughter carrying home her wages in grain, he would be overcome like this. To wipe his brimming eyes, his hand groped for the old cloth lying nearby on the thinnai. What's the point of worrying when one is so helpless? No energy left for anything. Better to conserve enough energy just to die.

There had once been a time when he had possessed boundless energy and strength. Many had admired him for it and spoken in awe about these qualities of his.

'Oh, that fellow…he is as sturdy as a roof beam,' people would remark. 'Just with his own hard work he can support so many....'

Whenever grain was received as wages, he would carry the whole heavy sackful back from Melur effortlessly. If he was given a labour contract, he would never speak disrespectfully to the landlord. Unmindful of distractions, ignoring any ranting and raving going on around him, brushing aside annoyances of all kinds, he would remain calm and reasonable and get the job done. Sometimes he would have to hear wounding words when someone spoke in the heat of anger.

'Enough of your sloppy work. Don't bother to come here to work tomorrow. Go and ruin someone else's life.'

Even to such remarks he would not show any resentment.

'He's angry and so he spoke harshly. I just have to take it. If I take offence and stay away from work, how will I eat?'

The next day he would turn up as usual at the landlord's fields with his group of workers.

In the midst of all the hot words and abuses, sometimes there would be no time even to sit and have a meal. Even now when he thought of those times, torturous though they were, he wanted to just get up and run to the fields. He disliked sitting idly on the thinnai. His hand groped for his cane.

*

There's much to be said about Muthupechhi too. It's no small achievement to support three lives all by one's own labour. She was the sole anchor of the family. It was by mere chance that she had been born as Gomathi's daughter. She was now about twenty years old, with well-rounded limbs, a sprightly frame, and a face small enough to be covered with the palm of a hand.

Whenever she walked by on her way to the market to buy spices, eyes cast down modestly and carrying a bamboo basket of the day's wage-grains, the leader of a group of young fellows who were whiling away their time playing cards on a platform at the roadside would pass some snide remark.

'Looks like Pechhi has a crick in her neck....'

She would never even cast a sideways glance at them. But a slight smile would curl the corners of her lips. She never spoke an unnecessary word to anyone. The moment she returned from her day's work in the field, housework took up all her time. In the midst of this, she also had to serve a meal to her parents. Whenever she looked at her aged parents, so totally dependent on their only daughter, her mind was troubled. Her sadness blotted out thoughts of the future. It was this ability of hers to live always in the present that had given her the aura of a responsible adult even when she had been just a child. Yet nowadays she had learnt to step forward and join in the festivities during happy occasions.

Out in the fields, weary hands loosened their grip on the sickles they had been wielding. The bent backs straightened tiredly. The landlord, who had positioned himself comfortably in the middle of the dry field under the welcome shade of a karuvelam tree, broke out into abuses.

'What's all this! Hungry already, eh? No-good creatures! Okay, go and eat quickly and get back to work.'

He turned westwards and surveyed the road from the village. His wife was walking towards the fields in a leisurely fashion, carrying a large food bucket. The man muttered irritably.

'Strolling...as if she is out there to enjoy herself. At this rate when will she get here and allow me to eat....'

It was past noon. Some of the bullocks that had been harnessed to the device drawing water from the irrigation well had been unyoked. In the neighbouring field, the manure cart had come and gone.

The weary labourers headed towards the well to sit and drink their gruel. Some went to check on the babies they had left sleeping.

When they were leaving the fields in the evening, the soil, newly scraped and scoured, glistened in the sunlight. Dotted around were mounds of cut sedges and weeds.

The labourers approached the landlord's house. A separate enclosure had been constructed at the thinnai, and that was where they gathered to wait. A bullock calf tethered in the corner drew back its lips, exposed its stained teeth, and mooed softly. The four bullocks standing in the shed, happy to have a few discarded seedlings to munch on, were breathing gustily and chewing away. At a little distance from one another were two cows and a buffalo. The smell of cattle urine pervaded the whole area.

The landlord led the workers to the first floor. Soon a jute bag containing pearl millet was rolled out. Once it was untied and emptied out at the threshold, grain poured out in a cascade. Interspersed with the grains were several tiny wriggling worms. His wife started scooping up the grain with a measure. The first woman worker who received the grain in her sari pallu did not like the look of it. She ran it through her fingers again and again, then frowned in displeasure.

All the workers had been observing the pile of grain, and none looked happy. Many eyes started searching around for the contractor. As for the contractor, he was absorbed in a private chat with the landlord.

The murmurs from the women workers were growing louder. And then there was a loud outburst:

'Akka, throw down that grain from your pallu and come away. Is this supposed to be wages for our work or some charity? Why should we accept this worm-infested grain?'

No one had ever thought Muthupechhi would talk like this. She was furious.

The landlord and the contractor stopped their conversation and turned to look at Muthupechhi. The landlord's wife continued to be immersed in her task. She measured out the grain and went on measuring it, not even noticing that the first worker had flung back her wage grain into the heap and stepped back.

The landlord's face expressed the frustration of one whose ploy to palm off damaged goods has failed. He glared at Muthupechhi and then turned to the contractor.

'Who's this girl? Seems her tongue won't lie still in her mouth.'

The contractor swallowed nervously a couple of times and said, 'She's from my village.'

'Doesn't look that way. She doesn't talk the way you do, does she?'

'She is our Maarimuthu's daughter.'

'Is that so! His daughter dares to speak in this manner!'

The contractor cast a partly guilty, partly embarassed look at Muthupechhi. What else could I have done, this look seemed to say.

Hot words leapt out of Muthupechhi's lips, like peanut shells popping.

'Tell me, would you cook and eat this worm-infested grain? When we slave away in your fields you are liberal with your abuse. What will come next…a cattle prod?'

Her words stung the landlord deeply.

'Che! What atrocious behaviour! If she felt the quantity was low she could have asked for more; instead of coming into my house and then carrying on like this with complaints about the grain being this way and that way. Look here, girl! Shut your mouth. Hey, you contractor fellow—do you want to keep your contract and bring workers to my fields? Let me tell you, if you bring this kind of troublemaker again I will not tolerate it. Are we clear?'

The landlord snatched up an empty sack and shook it violently… *padaar, padaar*…after which his temper seemed to subside somewhat. Meanwhile, one of the servants, reading the situation, went and rolled out another sack from another location.

Muthupechhi's lips were still twitching with fury. Yet she restrained herself out of respect for the contractor.

As for the contractor, he was not upset with Muthupechhi. He had been observing, day after day, how shabbily the landlord's wife treated the women workers when they came to collect their grain-wages in the evening. But then, these people and their families depended on him for their livelihood; the workers followed him trustingly to the landlord's fields every morning, tools in hand. So he tried to pacify Muthupechhi and calm her down.

'Don't worry, Muthupechhi. Of course we must ask for what

is our due. But they are going to give us good grain now, so why talk like this?'

Muthupechhi's reply was muttered under her breath. 'As if they would have come forward to give us decent grain if we had not protested.'

At this moment, a thought crossed her mind—a spineless wimp like this fellow was not fit to be a contractor.

The women were tying up their grain parcels and getting ready to leave. A fellow who had been smoking a beedi just outside the house was hurrying them.

'Come on, come on, make it quick. I need to get back home soon.'

The house door was shut with a loud bang the moment they had all stepped out.

Muthupechhi had not finished with what she wanted to say to the contractor. She walked up next to him. 'Chinnayya, tomorrow, whether you ask me to come or not come, I am not coming.'

The contractor was astonished. 'Emma, why do you say that?'

'Today it was me. Tomorrow maybe another woman will protest. If it continues like this, he is sure to give you your marching orders. He doesn't have to spell it out. He made it very clear today. Is he donating the grain to us for free? We are putting in back-breaking work for it. If we stand firm, there would be no need for arguments or for making a scene.'

The contractor, despite being much older than her (he would never see fifty again), listened intently to her words. In the corner of his mind arose the thought: there seems to be some justice in what she says.

Those who had gone on ahead down the path bordering the canal had waited for the rest of the group to catch up. Muthupechhi and the contractor joined the others. He asked her, 'So what can we do about this now?'

'Just a simple thing, Chinnayya. Take a stroll along South Street. Describe what happened today. Tell a couple of the elders to spread the word that if that landlord sends for workers, no one is to go.

Tomorrow we will all go the Keezhur fields instead. We have to tell our village people too. After all, we can get paid only if we work. But let us see who is willing to set foot in that landlord's fields and slog only to get paid in rotten grain.'

Muthupechhi put forward a strategy for all of them to follow. Everyone agreed that her point of view made sense.

'That's true. Today it is grain with worms crawling in it. Tomorrow he could give us grain sprayed with poisonous pesticides. What if our children ate it and something happened to them? Please do what she suggests, please....'

One of the women deftly lifted her infant from her hip without allowing the baby to slip, and pushed the sari fold off her breast.

The contractor walked briskly away towards South Street. The rest of the group waited for him. As twilight fell, two kites perched on the pump handle of the well took to the air as an urchin flung a stone at them. As they all watched, the birds flapped their wings and flew to a hollow tamarind tree.

Three days later, the Melur landlord, who had hurried over at the crack of dawn, spotted Muthupechhi entering her house, a full pot of water held on her hip. He scurried up to the thinnai and seated himself next to old Maarimuthu.

'Enna, Maarimuthu, I hope you're in good health.'

'Who...who is it? Oh, is it the landlord? I couldn't make out at first. Is the family all well? What brings you here so early in the morning?'

'No weeding has been done in the fields as per the contract. No one has turned up for work for the past two days. So I just thought I would come by and have a word with the contractor.'

Muthupechhi, overhearing the mention of weeding, hurried to the door and peeped out. Meanwhile Maarimuthu called out to a passer-by in the street. 'De, if you see Sankaran tell him I asked him to come by.'

Through the corner of his eye, the Melur landlord was watching Muthupechhi intently. He spoke in an aggrieved tone: 'Hmm...so this is your daughter. The other day she was full of complaints. She said the grain-wage we give is no good, that we drive the workers too hard. I felt wounded when she spoke that way.'

The old man's eyes turned towards his daughter.

'Yemma, is that so?'

Muthupechhi did not hold back. 'I didn't say anything insulting. The grain was crawling with worms, and so I said I didn't want it.'

'Weren't there any men among the workers to ask the question?'

The landlord's gaze was fixed on the crumbling mud wall in front of him.

Muthupechhi said, 'Yes, there were. Do you mean only they should ask questions?'

It struck her later that she should not have impulsively flung that question at her father.

At that point, the contractor arrived. 'Ayya, you sent for me?'

The Melur landlord cut in. 'Come, come....'

The contractor sat quietly at a corner of the thinnai.

The old man said, 'What is this I hear, Sankara. You've left the weeds to grow wild. What's the matter. The landlord himself has come here....'

'Nothing, nothing. There was some urgent work that had to be finished in Keezhur. Two days got used up in that. If his work was so urgent he could have got some workers from his own village and got it done, couldn't he?'

The Melur landlord said, 'Come on...whether it's them or you, it's all the same. Why don't you just finish the job you have agreed to do as a contractor? The weeds are so overgrown they are threatening to smother the plants. How will other workers agree to do the work that you have taken on contract?'

The old man brought an end to the argument.

'Sir, you go. I will send the workers tomorrow.'

The landlord rose slowly and walked away.

The old man questioned the contractor. 'Ennada, what's this all about? The way he criticized Muthupechhi's behaviour, and the tone in which you spoke just now—what happened exactly?'

'Our girl spoke a few angry words complaining that the grain was of very poor quality. He claims that he has been deeply hurt by her actions.'

'Tell me more.'

The contractor described all the happenings in detail.

Maarimuthu looked at his daughter. There was no disapproval in his look. Both his eyes were wide open.

As he watched the figure of the landlord trudging tiredly back along the path, a laugh bubbled up in his toothless mouth.

Translated by Malini Seshadri

PENANCE

FATHER MARK STEPHEN

The generator on the bullock cart came to life. The next moment, the lights on Mother Mary's procession carriage glowed radiantly. She seemed to be afloat on luminous waves—a heavenly sight to behold.

Next to the carriage, lined up against the wall, stood ten poles with tube lights tied on to them. Gone were the days when oil lamps and petromax lanterns were needed to light Our Lady's path. Nowadays, tube lights had come into use for processions like these. After all, times change.... How can one keep celebrating the festival in the same old way?

The Christians of the village who enjoyed caste privileges were standing around the carriage. The nine trustees of the church, having verified that everything was ready for the procession to begin, went to garland the Parish Priest ceremoniously and formally invite him to start off the procession by invoking heavenly blessings.

The Parish Priest's stentorian voice broke the silence as he proceeded to recite the customary prayers. He ended with the first part of 'Our Father who art in Heaven...', and then started blessing the chariot. Once the blessings were over, the Chief Trustee ordered, 'Mm...come on, it's getting late. Pick up the tube lights. We must get started.'

No one picked up the tube lights. They remained standing in a row against the wall.

'Where are those Dalit donkeys? Why are they making Our Lady wait? Why are they not here to carry the lights?'

The crowd started getting restless and became noisy. The tube lights stayed where they were. For fifteen whole minutes chaos and confusion, raised voices, and frayed tempers marked the scene. And then....

Heaving and panting for breath, ten young men, all of them Dalit Christians, came running and picked up the tube lights to fulfil their duty to Mother Mary.

The Chief Trustee was gnashing his teeth and blubbering in rage. 'Where did you disappear to for all this time, da?' He swung his hand back and delivered a stinging slap on the face of one of the young men. The crowd saw this as a signal. Many of them rushed up and started adding their share of righteous punishment in the form of punches and blows.

The ten young men stood unmoving, heads bowed, as the blows rained upon them. The chaos showed no signs of subsiding.

In a bid to salvage the situation, the Chief Trustee started speaking into the microphone. 'My friends, something unprecedented has happened. For the first time, the procession of Our Lady was unable to start immediately after the blessing. Some people have insulted Her by delaying the procession and forcing Her to wait. For this, there must be a penance. We will decide the details tomorrow after a public hearing. But for now, let the procession begin.'

This announcement produced a degree of order. The procession started on its way. Its route would take it only through the streets where the caste Christians lived, and the lights alone would be carried by Dalits.

The Parish Priest, who had been watching all the developments from the sidelines, went back to his room once the procession had set off.

The next morning, a crowd of villagers gathered outside the church. The nine trustees had taken their seats. Facing them stood the ten young Dalit men, the designated tube light carriers, whose delayed arrival the previous evening had earned them the wrath of the trustees and blows from members of the crowd. They stood accused of insulting and disrespecting Mother Mary herself. With folded hands they awaited their fate.

The Chief Trustee addressed Muthu, the spokesman for the group of Dalit youths.

'Empa, Muthu, since you requested it, I personally went and asked the Parish Priest to come and attend this hearing. But he said "I have nothing to do with the public hearing." He refused to come.'

The Dalit men were dismayed. They had been counting on the Parish Priest being present and ensuring that justice was done in a fair manner.

Unmoved by their reaction, the Chief Trustee continued with the proceedings.

'Muthu, do you agree that you fellows were in the wrong? Our Holy Mother, Our Lady of Lourdes...should she be made to wait? Wasn't that a grave sin?'

'Ayya, I wanted to say this even yesterday when we were being beaten up for being late. I kept quiet only because I didn't want to create problems. But we are telling you now. It's true that we were late and that we should not have delayed the procession. But we came late only because....'

Before Muthu could finish, the Chief Trustee interrupted him. 'Yesterday, you all went to do harvesting work in the fields, and so you came late.'

'That's right. And the field we were working in belongs to none other than the Deputy Chief Trustee who is sitting there right next to you.'

'But why didn't you finish the work quickly and get here in time?'

Muthu replied, 'Ayya, we pleaded with him to let us go in time to carry the lights for the procession, but he refused to release us.'

The Deputy Chief Trustee was enraged. 'Why should I let you fellows go early? Harvesting that field is a single day's work. I said finish the day's work before you go. What's wrong with that? If you deliberately go slow and then want to leave the work half-done, how can I allow it? Lazy donkeys!' he raved.

Muthu addressed the Deputy Chief directly. 'Ayya, don't ever call us lazy,' he told him. Then, turning toward the others, he explained. 'It's true that it is possible to finish the harvesting work in that field in a single day. But it is usually done by a team of fifteen workers.

If you hire only ten instead of fifteen and still expect them to finish the same amount of work, how is it possible? He hired five people fewer, pocketed those wages himself, and then expected us to somehow finish all the work in the given time. Is this fair? Do we not have the right to question this? We were not able to complete the work, and we explained that we needed to reach the church in time to carry the lights in the procession. He refused to let us leave. Whose fault is it then?'

The Chief Trustee was annoyed. He spoke harshly: 'De, Muthu, why are you babbling all kinds of things? We're not here to discuss wages. We're here to decide on the proper penance for the insult to Our Lady who was made to wait. So don't go on and on with your long stories….'

'Ayya, I am not just talking for the sake of talking. I am only speaking about justice. If fifteen of us had been hired for the harvesting work, why would we have been late? Not only that…realizing that it was getting late and the procession would start soon, we went to Ayya and pleaded with him. "Ayya, Ayya, we have to go and carry the lights for Our Lady. Please let us go." We pleaded with him a second time. "We will finish the rest of the work for you tomorrow, and we won't ask for wages. But right now it's not right to make Our Lady wait." But Ayya told us, "I am the Deputy Chief Trustee. How can they start the procession unless I am there? There's still moonlight. Finish the work and then go." That's what he told us. And then he went away.'

'De, why are you repeating the same thing all over again? The point is, you fellows came late for your job of carrying the lights, you made Our Lady wait, you disrespected and insulted her. So didn't you all do a wrong thing?'

'Ayya, please don't keep saying that. It was never our intention to insult or disrespect Our Lady. Ayya, I'd like to say something…don't get angry…if it is disrespectful to Our Lady to delay the procession, you could have prevented that from happening,' said Muthu. His face seemed to have taken on a new glow.

The Chief Trustee was taken aback. 'What do you mean, da?'

'Yes, Ayya...there are two hundred of your people in the village. Many of them are young, strong men. If ten of them had come forward to carry the lights, the procession could have started with no delay and with no insult to Our Lady,' Muthu replied.

When Muthu's words fell on the ears of the caste Christians, their faces reddened with anger, their lips twitched, and their eyes blazed. 'Enda, you scum of a fellow. You think we are pariahs like you...?' A stinging slap landed on Muthu's face. More angry blows followed.

Muthu rubbed his stinging cheek and looked at his tormentors. 'Why...how is it insulting to you to do a service for Our Lady by carrying lights for her procession?'

He lowered his eyes and did not speak again.

Someone from the crowd called out, 'Hey, Chief Trustee, hurry up and prescribe the penance. Let it be appropriate for the offence of disrespecting Our Lady.'

After a moment's silence, the Chief Trustee raised his voice and spoke: 'After this hearing, the truth has emerged. That is, knowing full well about the schedule of Our Lady's procession, these fellows deliberately arrived late, and have therefore disrespected Our Lady. The penance for this is as follows. Today, in the heat of the midday sun, these fellows must carry a lighted candle on the palms of their hands and go around the church. They must keep moving till the candle burns down. And they must go around, not on their feet, but on their knees. Then, as the wax of the candle burns away, so will their sin of having insulted Our Lady.'

'Very appropriate penance,' said the Deputy Chief. 'I have not yet paid these fellows their wages for the work they did in my fields yesterday. I will use that money to buy some large candles.' He set off quickly to do his bit for justice.

At midday, the prescribed penance commenced. The ten Dalit men assembled in front of the church. With bleeding knees scraping across the hot, rough stone floor, the sun blazing down on their unprotected heads, sweat pouring off their bodies, and the wax from the melting candles dripping and burning their hands, the ten paid penance to Our Lady.

Meanwhile, the Parish Priest was busy counting and tallying the hundi offerings from the previous night's procession.

Translated by Malini Seshadri

THE DOOR OPENS

MAALAN

The door to the matam was closed.

The sight of that door made him chuckle inwardly. It would surely need at least four people to tug it open or push it shut. A massive teak door. Some skilled carpenter must have slaved for hours to make that door, planing the wood, then shaping and polishing it to perfection. It was decorated with tiny brass mouldings and miniature bells.

Krishnamurthy continued to take in the sight of that door, and the more he looked, the more his amusement grew. Why all this ornamentation for a mere door? Why such a high polish? He wondered how many hands must have worked for endless hours to achieve this end result. Why does a monastery need a door like this? His thoughts turned to the inmate of the matam, the one who sat somewhere behind this massive door, and laughter bubbled over in his mind. Why would a saamiyar need a door like this? Such a hefty, massive one?

What kind of renunciation is this? For one who dons saffron and claims to have left the material world behind, why this entourage? Why all the showy paraphernalia? Why live in an abode built like a fortress? And why such a gigantic door?

The endless 'whys' continued to rattle around in his mind. It was only in a bid to escape such endless interrogation, questions without answers, that he had cut himself off from his family, his home town, his very roots. Indeed, he had wanted to leave his entire past behind, don saffron robes and find a haven somewhere.

His life had been wonderful till he turned eighteen. Abundant crop yields, a luxurious house, a sparkling river in which to splash and play, Sunday treats, kabaddi games…it was all an ideal existence. Even later, when he left village life behind to go to college, it was still enjoyable in its own way…the seasons marked by trees shedding their leaves, the warmth of a circle of friends.

Abruptly, when he was twenty-three, his life started stagnating. Everything became jarring. His job in an office became a drag; the plastic flowers in vases and the false laughter of Lakshmi at the desk next to his jangled his nerves.

His college degree was in pharmaceutical chemistry, but now he had come to detest the subject heartily. He was horrified at conversations he sometimes overheard on bus journeys, like when fifteen-year-olds discussed abortion. The more he saw the hustle and bustle of people rushing around, the more he felt the inner pain of alienation. Then, one night, as though an unseen hand had grabbed him by the nape of the neck and shaken him, questions flooded his mind. Why this rat race? What is it all for? What is the goal? What is the purpose of this existence?

Amidst the pop music at the restaurant, in the hubbub at the railway station, in the rattle of the vending machine which swallows a coin and spits out milk, the questions went on relentlessly. In this ugly rigmarole, where his intelligence, his training, now went towards producing birth control pills and meaningless calculations, his mind clamoured and demanded: What is the purpose of life? Money? Status? Fame? Fulfilment of desires? Or is death the purpose? What? What?

He tried to find the answers in books. But no book was big enough for life to fit into it. He tried sitting in silent prayer and meditating on God. It brought no relief. He experimented with smoking ganja. He experienced temporary euphoria. One day, with hair uncombed and clothes crumpled, he set off with a backpack. His uncharted journey had taken him through many towns and finally brought him to this door.

The door was dragged open rapidly. The holy man emerged through the doorway, his arms raised in blessing. He was tall, and his face had the glow of burnished copper. A warm smile, gentle eyes brimming with compassion. A single saffron cloth was draped around his whole frame. In one hand he held the traditional staff.

He took careful steps to avoid treading on any of the people who had rushed forward to prostrate at his feet. In that crowd, Swamiji somehow managed to walk among all the people without being jostled, and without shrinking away from them.

The moment he had seated himself on the sacred peetam, the petitions from the devotees began.

'My son is getting married. We ask for your blessings,' said a man, as he reverently held out an invitation card.

'Do you plan to have a grand procession for the groom?'

'No, the boy himself did not want it.'

'What about dowry?'

'Well…just what is required by religious tradition, you know… just the minimum….'

'Oh…is there such a religious tradition? I was not aware of it.'

The onlookers burst into laughter as the petitioner turned red in embarrassment.

'Make it simple without all the frills.'

'Family members will be unhappy.'

'God, too, is family. An important family member, right?' said Swamiji, and gestured that the interview was over.

One after the other, more petitioners came forward—I am going to start a new business venture; my mother is going to have surgery; please send a message of blessing for our new magazine; my wife is pregnant; my daughter's marriage proposals are encountering obstacles; my husband has abandoned me….

It was a lengthy list of pleas. Swamiji spoke with each of them appropriately, handing out kumkum, or pictures of Goddess Ambaal, or pieces of kalkandu, the rock sugar candy. As Krishnamurthy watched the proceedings, a sense of astonishment grew alongside his amusement. What kind of ascetic existence was this? What had this Swamiji actually left behind? In fact, he was immersing himself in hundreds of lives, swimming alongside them in their sea of joys and sorrows. How can he call himself a sannyasi?

Just ahead of Krishnamurthy in the queue, dressed in dirty pyjamas, stood an American. He was about six feet tall, with the smooth, chubby face of a baby and a straggly moustache. With some difficulty he prostrated at Swamiji's feet.

Swamiji uttered a single word. 'What?'

Words rushed out of the foreigner as if a dam had burst. 'My name is Bob McCarthy. But I don't know who I really am. I was born in the US, near Nashville, and studied at Tennessee State University, and yet I can't think of the US as my country. After leaving rural life and moving to a city to study for four years, I could not reconcile to rural existence later. I couldn't take to a farming life like my father and my grandfather before him. Neither could I identify myself with the city I had lived in for four years. There is a kind of mechanical existence there, everything seems artificial, and nothing retains any natural attributes any more. I couldn't readily find a job that suited my outlook, and those that did come my way I emphatically disliked. I became a stranger in my own environment, an alien in my native land. I am orphaned, with no one to respond to my childish babblings or pay heed to my cries. I don't know what my life means....

'Everything I see, every place I go, fills me with aversion and disgust. I wish I could just run away somewhere. Please give me diksha; initiate me into your way of life. I am prepared to don saffron and stay on here in your ashram. If that is not possible, please take me into one of your orphanages. If not, I have no way out but suicide.'

To Krishnamurthy, who had been listening to the foreigner's words, it sounded like an American edition of his own plight. Swamiji had listened to the man's story with a smile playing on his lips. Now he turned towards the onlookers and asked, 'Is it such a simple matter to don saffron and accept all that goes with that life? Hmm?'

Then, looking compassionately at the petitioner he said gently, 'Mm...if you ask me, all the moving parts in life are seeking out their proper places. Everything eventually falls into place—that is how the dynamics of life works. Our responsibility is to realize this, recognize the reality of it. Not only should we know it and understand it, we must also embrace it. To live is to relate to things. We have relationships with every entity, not only with humans. These walls, doors, trees, flowers, stars…everything is related to us. If you think about this calmly, you will realize the truth of it. Then you would not feel agitated, nor would you feel hatred towards anyone.

'In our ashram we have a Veda school, a workshop, an English school, a hospital, a cow protection centre, and many other such places. But what we do not have is an orphanage. Because there is no such person as an orphan. It is a mere illusion.

'One should not don saffron just to get away from it all. Not everyone in this country who took to donning saffron did so as a gesture of renunciation of material life. Many others have done so out of a deep understanding that our relationships extend beyond our families, that they embrace anything and everything. What you call Universal Love…it is the colour saffron. You may not know this, but our Aadhi guru (first sage) took sanyaas at the young age of eight. As he was leaving home, his mother clung to him as a crocodile would to its prey. Do you know what he said? "From now on, I am not the child of just one household. All families are our families." So every home is our home. Then, how can anyone be homeless, how can anyone be an orphan? Hmm? Tell me…'

Even as he was talking, Swamiji was handing out kalkandu as he would to a little child.

Krishnamurthy felt as though every one of those words had been addressed directly to him.

Swamiji turned to Krishnamurthy with a smile and asked, 'Mm… what is your problem…?'

Tears sprang to Krishnamurthy's eyes. He fell at Swamiji's feet, palms joined in obeisance.

The door in his mind had opened.

Translated by Malini Seshadri

THE SOLUTION

DILIP KUMAR

To tell you this story, I am afraid I must drag you out of this compartment in the Nilgiri Express, coming from Coimbatore, which is now arriving in Madras so irritatingly late.

Making my way between porters who are obviously disgruntled that I don't give them my only box to carry, and shouldering their displeasure as an additional burden, I walk past the eagerly waiting rickshaw-wallahs, disappointing them as well. I then hurriedly cross Walltax Road, slip into a narrow lane, and reach Mint Street.

Among the seven or eight lanes trapped and helplessly squirming between Walltax Road and Rattan Bazaar, Mint Street is the only one wide enough to walk on in any reasonable comfort. This is a North Indian, specifically Gujarati, neighbourhood, and is therefore distinguished by a certain blend of ostentation and filth. I mean the ostentation in the kind of clothes these people wear. As for filth, I refer to the garbage that they spew out of their houses. These Gujaratis believe in keeping their houses clean and their thresholds dirty. In accustoming their minds and noses to living in a squalid environment, these people are second to none.

It is 8.45 a.m. Shops and offices are being opened; school children are hurrying along; people look spick and span. Gandhi-capped sethjis and their smartly turned out, stupid sons have begun to fill the lane. Foreign cars, motorcycles, and scooters are lining up along the curb.

The famous Ekambareswarar Temple is in this very same Mint Street. It is a big temple, with a tank and an enormous courtyard, very impressive, with statues and tall, sculpted pillars. Like the city's other famous temples, this one too appears quite ordinary to its inhabitants, and magnificent to infrequent visitors.

At its gates, to the left, is a sethji's snack shop. To the right are a chettiar selling coconuts, a woman selling bangles, and the usual row of beggars displaying their inexhaustible wares of disease and wretchedness. Lord Ekambareswarar himself sits placidly inside, allowing all these people to make profitable use of His address.

The three narrow streets, which run around the side of the temple in the form of the Tamil letter 'pa', are collectively known as Ekambareswarar Agraharam. It is in this eminently respectable neighbourhood that both my uncle's house and the locale of my story are to be found.

I turn into the left arm of the 'pa' and reach my uncle's house, which is a narrow building cowering miserably between two larger ones. On one side is the dirty, red-and-white striped wall of the temple, and on the other, houses, mostly without porches. One of these buildings is a primary school and another a high school. As I walk on, children of all sizes spill into the street, milling around the ice cream man's ubiquitous pushcart.

Absorbing none of these distractions and remembering, one by one, the faces of my uncle and every other member of his large household, I kept moving, walking quickly towards the house. At the gate was a group of young Gujarati women, struggling with a tap that had apparently refused to yield to their manipulations, and mocked them, dry-mouthed.

They greeted me with a solemn silence. I looked at all of them, but not one was really worth a second glance. Thirty families in this building, and not one beauty among them! Except, perhaps, Urmila who lives on the top floor...but that's another story. To understand this one, I must first acquaint you with the topography of this building.

In the centre is a large, open courtyard, eighteen feet by eighteen feet in size, cutting the sky above into a large square. This aperture has seemingly been made not only to admit Varuna, wind, and Surya, sun, into the building, but also to serve as a receptacle for chewed-up Calcutta paans, deposited in it from the upper floors.

Six flats confront each other across this square. Two smaller courtyards lie beyond these flats, one on each side; the one on the left leads to two lavatories, and the one on the right has a well within it. Around each courtyard are ten flats, making a total of thirty in this one building. Thirty flats with thirty Gujarati households in them, connected to one another by filthy staircases stained with paan spittle.

A two-and-a-half-foot wide corridor runs along the six flats of the first courtyard, dividing them from one another. Usually at this time of the day women are to be found sitting within the open doorways of these flats, busily engaged in some household task or other. One might be scrubbing dirty utensils, another washing clothes, a third cleaning rice or wheat.

Though most of these women have the kind of bodies that bloat after a few years of marriage, they are a hardworking lot. Ignorant and stubborn, quarrelsome, they have quelled their world and reduced it to Hindi films, sugar-sweet filmi songs, recipes, and finery. Apart from these, they have another interest: the alarmingly thoughtless reproduction of the species. Each of the housewives in these thirty households has at least five offspring. (My uncle, too, has five.) The rate of population growth in this purely middle-class residential area has the inexorability of a natural law, given the kind of lives these women lead. Mind you, they're not submissive, these women. It's their men who are meek, obedient, and self-effacing. Grieving over the crushing mediocrity of their existence, and imagining that they have inflicted some terrible cruelty on their wives, they slink guiltily along the corridors. The prospect of receiving a salary once in thirty days is the only thing that inspires within them any degree of zest. From force of habit, they go to the cinema; out of a helpless piety they sing at Saturday night bhajan sessions, and once in a while borrow a newspaper and read it.

As soon as I entered the building, a surprise awaited me. The main courtyard was deserted. At its corners hung plastic lines with yesterday's washing still upon them. The passages were empty, and somewhat less dirty than usual. An extraordinary silence filled the place. I crossed the courtyard towards the staircase and caught sight of one of the inner courtyards, the one with the well in its centre. Around it was a crowd of men, women, and children.

My uncle was standing in the middle of this crowd, staring intently into the well. Everyone looked silently at me as I approached. After a second's surprise, Uncle pulled himself together, smiled faintly and told me in Gujarati, 'Go upstairs, I'll soon be with you.'

Suppressing my curiosity, I hurried towards the staircase. Gopal Bhai was coming down, and I asked him what the matter was.

'What to say, Dilip Bhai! The water problem has become acute. Not a drop of water to drink in this entire building! And in this fine state of affairs, a rat has fallen into the well. Poor Babu Bhai! From eight this morning he's been trying to get it out, and can't!' said Gopal Bhai sorrowfully. After the usual exchange of pleasantries, he moved towards the crowd and melted into it.

On the top floor, as I entered Uncle's house, I was met by Chandra, his daughter, who smiled joyously and called me in. My aunt bustled about to make some tea for me.

My uncle's house was small and compact, with a largish hall at the end of which were two rooms. The room on the left was the kitchen and the one on the right was a bedroom-cum-bathroom-cum-storeroom, all in one. The boys must have gone out to play. Uncle had two daughters (Poorna was in the kitchen), and three boys: Kanu, Vrajesh, and Deepak.

Grandmother had gone out to the temple. She left in the morning at five and would not be returning till half past ten or eleven. Extremely orthodox, Grandmother believed firmly in ritual observances of pollution and purity. Every time I came to visit, the first thing she did was push her ritually washed pure clothing to the two ends of the washing line, where it would not come in contact with the top of my head; I am somewhat tall. She would carefully use a bamboo pole expressly meant for handling such vestments. If despite these precautions, I happened to touch any of them, she would promptly pull them down and go off to wash them again.

I looked in the direction of the lavatories. Wonder of wonders! They were empty and waiting to be used. Something was up, certainly. Normally, quarter past nine in the morning is peak lavatory time for the sixty persons who live on this floor, on which there are just two conveniences.

In accordance with the culture of my uncle's household, renowned for its orthodoxy and its scrupulous observance of ritual purity, the use of the lavatories was subject to certain strict regulations. In fact, a trip to the lavatory was an exercise in discipline.

Firstly, one was required to fill a small plastic pitcher with water from a broken cement cistern, and to place this filled pitcher on the narrow parapet beside a waterless tap. Nearby on a low wall stood an empty Dalda tin, placed upside down. One picked up this tin *with the left hand*, set it down at the entrance to the little passage at the end of which were the lavatories, picked up a small plastic bucket *with the right hand*, dipped it into the aforementioned broken cement cistern and filled the Dalda tin.

Carrying the full Dalda tin in the left hand, and gracefully stepping around and across the many little pools of urine produced by the children on this floor, avoiding the first lavatory, which overflows with excrement, and the sight of which is guaranteed to produce nausea for a whole month, one reaches the second, exerts oneself to the utmost to avoid slipping on the slime and then immerses oneself in meditation on the philosophy of J. Krishnamurti or the poetry of T. S. Eliot.

Until the girl next door, in desperate tones, pleads in Gujarati, 'Who's inside? Get out, quick!' inducing one to rise.

Emerging with head bowed, one goes quickly past the waiting girl, straight to the parapet and puts back the Dalda tin in exactly the same position. One then picks up the half-dissolved 501, Rexona, or Lifebuoy soap lying next to it, raises the plastic pitcher full of water using both wrists only, gently pours water on one's hands and scrubs them with soap, makes an elegant mudra with both palms facing each other, as in the garba dance, pours more water and washes them. Then one picks up the pitcher in the usual way, fills it, and washes one's feet.

I performed these rites with the careless skill born of long practice and returned to the house, where my aunt had tea waiting for me. She was wearing a washed-out blue sari. With her fair complexion, she would have looked better in brighter colours, but she always wore insipid shades. I silently cursed my uncle's taste in clothes.

The crowd around the well had thinned. The women had left, and so had most of the men, except for a few youths and some children. The men all wore long-cloth vests with pockets and white pyjamas, except for Uncle. He had on a frayed sleeveless sweater and a dhoti, held up with a cheap belt.

Uncle had worked in LIC for almost twenty years and was among the foremost of the educated occupants of the building. This was his realm, and he commanded such prestige, derived from his old-time school-leaving certificate, as to lord it over everyone else.

Right now he was involved in the matter of the well. A tin sheet had been placed above the well to prevent bird droppings from falling into it. This blocked off the light, leaving only a small gap. Into this gap, a youth was now beaming a flashlight.

Deep down in the darkness bobbed a black shape. The general guess was that it was the rat.

No one was willing to lend his bucket to haul up the dead rat. Uncle particularly was very definite that no bucket belonging to his household was to be thus defiled. And so an empty old fruit basket had been tied to a rope and lowered into the well.

As the rope had been tied only to one end of the basket, it sagged and was partly submerged in the water. Yet, it was confidently asserted that the rat would get caught inside the basket, while the water would drain out without being wasted—an ingenious idea, surely. Behind it was a certain cunning, traceable to Uncle.

The rat had now floated to the well's edge and had been in the same spot for over half an hour. When the crowd told me this, Uncle believed it to be a comment on his competence and became quite angry. Yet, with lowered brows, he doggedly went on with the work of getting the rat out. For him it had become a challenge of the highest order.

From time to time his neighbours, Kantilal and Chandrakant, kept pestering him with questions in Gujarati on the progress of his efforts. Though frowning and drawing his eyebrows together with fierce concentration, Uncle actually enjoyed all this distracting attention.

Finally, losing patience, he resorted to some desperate strategies— lifting and lowering the basket in jerky movements, as though he were pounding chillies or grinding batter or pulverizing grain with a variety of pestles.

These tactics worked. The rat floated to the middle of the well. Enthusiasm bubbled up. Everyone felt that it would be easy to bring it out from this position. Like a ship's captain, Uncle now issued authoritative directions to the youth with the flashlight, and ordered everyone else to stand aside. Then he lowered the rope and, with great deliberation and dexterity, brought it close to the floating rat. The next moment, with dazzling speed, he hauled up the rope. Everyone peeped eagerly into the well but were disappointed. The basket had come up empty.

For the next forty-five minutes, the wretched creature defied him most impudently, bobbing adroitly out of reach of the basket and making him look more ridiculous than ever.

It was quarter past ten before the rat was somehow brought out. Shuddering at the sight of the corpse, both adults and children shrank away. Deeming this an excellent opportunity to demonstrate his virility and courage, a hitherto unnoticed youth bore off the basket containing the rat to dispose of its mortal remains.

Uncle basked in the triumphant pride of a Mahmud of Ghazni, a Caesar, or a Napoleon. Then for fifteen minutes, with a demagogue's eloquence and a strategist's penchant for detail, he held forth to half a dozen fawning Gujarati youths on the methods by which he had forced the rat to vacate the well.

When Uncle's lecture was over, Jayantilal, and some others who were waiting nearby, asked a reasonable but troubling question: Could the water in the well now be considered potable?

Not having given thought to this aspect of the matter until that very moment, Uncle was slightly taken aback. Pulling himself together at once with the realization that any expression of anxiety would lower him in the eyes of these followers, he declared hurriedly, 'No, no, of course the water can't be used as it is. Someone must go to the Health Office; they'll sprinkle some medicine or other into it. Or we'll pour a little chlorine in it ourselves.'

He began to move away. Although heads bobbed in agreement, faces registered not just worry, but sheer terror at the prospect of having to drink not only rat-polluted, but also chemically contaminated water.

The Tanjorian Gujarati Chandrakant said to Uncle in a pleading tone, 'Will you go to the Health Office? We know nothing about such matters, Babu Bhai!'

Uncle replied politely that though he was quite willing to go to the Health Office and it was 'no trouble at all' to him, the fact of the matter was that he didn't exactly know where the Health Office was. Anyway, he said, he was already very late for work, and wriggled away.

Meanwhile, rich, TV-owning, old Govindji Seth, who had come down to see what was going on, strongly advised that fifteen or twenty pitchers should be lightly skimmed from the water's surface and poured off to make the rest of the water fit to use. Standing authoritatively by, he saw to this operation at once.

When it was over, everyone stood around the well, panting with the effort, and stared disconsolately into it, unconvinced of the efficacy of this method of purification.

Just then, Grandmother appeared at the building's entrance, leaning on her cane. Wearing a white sari closely printed over with small black flowers, with a tulsi mala around her neck, she was the very picture of clarity and orderliness.

Yet no one noticed her at first in the confusion. She came up to the harried group around the well and asked what was troubling them. The problem was immediately referred to her for solution.

Grandmother thought for a moment. Then she announced, 'Come, I'll show you a way out,' and led them all upstairs.

In the hall, Kanu and Vrajesh were playing at wrestling. As she went in, Grandmother reprimanded Kanu with a light but painful rap on his buttock with her cane. Then she went up to the teak almirah near the kitchen and seated herself before it.

Slowly, she began to open its doors. Inside the almirah were several small idols dressed up in gold, lace-bordered garments, and reclining on tiny mattresses.

In the corner was a little bundle tied up in saffron cloth. Grandmother took it out and placidly untied it with fat, but amazingly deft fingers. Within it was a very small mud pot, with a clean white cloth tied around its mouth.

Grandmother called to Poorna to fetch a bowl. Untying the cloth, she poured a little water from the pot into it. Utter silence accompanied her movements, although everyone was impatiently watching her. But Grandmother closed the almirah properly without the least bit of hurry, before she turned to face them.

Among those who crowded near the door and outside was Praanjeevanlal. Grandmother now beckoned to him. As she had been sitting with her head lowered for some time, her glasses had slipped down her nose. She pushed the bowl of water a little forward, raised her eyes so that they could look through the glasses, and announced calmly, 'Here you are. There's Ganga water here. Say the name of God, pour it into the well, and use the water.'

Praanjeevanlal nodded humbly and received the bowl. Everyone followed him as he went out towards the well.

In a little while pots once again brimmed with water in every house. The abnormal silence of the building gave way to the sound of households functioning once more.

Grandmother serenely immersed herself in reading *Jan Kalyan*, a monthly religious journal.

Translated by Vasantha Surya

PONNUTHAYI

BAMA

Ponnuthayi was around thirty years old. A very robustly built woman, in the seven or eight years that she had been married, she had borne four sons. Ponnuthayi was incredibly dark-skinned and very good looking, with lovely features. If you were to look at her sons, they outdid ravens, roaming the streets like beggars on their spindly legs—a complexion they had, every one of them, inherited from their mother—so dark that if one could dip one's finger and take a little of that inky colour, one could use it as a bindi.

Ponnuthayi was quite tall and had a build to match her height. When she walked along the street the earth would shake with her each step.

'Who could say she is a woman, looking at her stomping?' the other women would gossip. Even when she spoke it had the same effect. When she went to fetch water from the street tap, her voice could be heard till the end of the street, ringing like a bronze bell. Her tone was nothing if not brusque. It was for this reason that most people could not take to her.

Very few people knew her as Ponnuthayi. But everyone would know who the 'leathery lipped' one was—her lips were somewhat oversized.

'Are just her lips oversized?' they would remark.

'Her mouth is even bigger.'

Many did not at all like the fact that, unlike other women who were earning their wages working for a big landowner, she was running a business on her own.

Although illiterate, Ponnuthayi managed to take a bus to the neighbouring town, buy vegetables and fruits, and earn her livelihood as a vendor. No other woman was earning her living quite like this. Unmindful of all the comments made about her, Ponnuthayi carried on with her trade.

One day, Ponnuthayi brought a basketful of coconuts and went about on the street hawking them, calling out, 'Coconuts...coconuts... three for ten rupees. Come along and take a look.' One of the women, unable to restrain herself, asked for trouble when she remarked, 'If we buy coconuts at the grove we can get one for two rupees. Look how shamelessly she comes here, she thinks she is a big merchant.'

'I am not the one to pick a quarrel; but mind you if it comes my way, I will not leave it be. If you feel like buying, buy them, or else keep mum. Who are you to advise me about running a business?' Ponnuthayi retorted before moving away towards South Street.

The exchange rankled in her mind even after she reached South Street. Instead of hawking the coconuts, Ponnuthayi walked along shouting at the top of her voice, leaving the street in a state of terror. 'I will work or not, as I please. It's my sweet will and pleasure. Who's this whore of a woman to talk like that to me? How the hell does it matter to these women what business I do? If any woman dares to talk about me flippantly I will cut her tongue clean off.' Looking at the way Ponnuthayi was shouting, no one ventured to go anywhere near her to buy her wares. Only after she was out of earshot did the women dare to talk. 'Look how her speech smacks of arrogance! Can't she work in the fields like the rest of us to earn her living? Imagines herself to be one of those big shots from Mekalakudi...venturing to engage in trade! I tell you she is quite domineering....' As Muniyamma was running on like this, Ponnuthayi who had headed west again happened to turn east. Muniyamma promptly held her tongue.

When Ponnuthayi again approached the spot where the women had gathered she started yelling. 'Even the other day...just because I squeezed paste on to a brush and brushed my teeth, these women were shocked out of their wits and spoke in whispers among themselves. It's my money, I buy and I spend it as I please. I don't see how it is any of their business....'

Once Ponnuthayi had moved away, the woman from Akaasampatti said, 'Did you listen to what Leathery Lips said? Because she is so great she won't deign to brush her teeth with her finger! What vanity! As the saying goes, "you live on gruel but wash your ass with soap".'

Aathiamma cautioned, 'Don't ever say anything within her hearing, Sister, if she hears it she'll tear you to pieces. Don't take her lightly. Remember once she made the police beat her own wedded husband black and blue, she is such a bully.'

There was hardly anyone in the village who didn't have a comment on this matter involving the police. For the past two years, Ponnuthayi had been living alone, having walked out on her husband. She lived with her mother and with the money she earned from her trade she managed to make ends meet.

When she got married to Mookkandi she set up house with him, hoping to lead a happy life like any other couple. Mookkandi was pitch dark and his moustache stood out sharply. He was in the habit of twisting his moustache all the time. Being constantly twisted in this manner, the two ends of the moustache stood out belligerently like two pointed horns waiting to gore someone.

He went to work for two days in the week and stayed at home the rest of the week. But not a day would pass without his eating out at the 'club'. Visiting these eateries in the evening, he would stuff himself with idli, dosai, vadai, and what not; returning home he would not forego his rice in the night either. His day wouldn't be made if he didn't eat out at one of those 'otels'. The little that he earned he would spend on himself. On days when he didn't go for work he would bully Ponnuthayi and snatch away her wages. Come Sunday he had to have beef and then arrack from Mariappa Thevar to wash it down, or else he would make life hell for Ponnuthayi.

Ponnuthayi tried her best to carry on with him, holding her feelings in with great restraint. In the early days of their married life she somehow ran the household with her earnings. Later, when four sons were born one after another, even porridge became a luxury at times. She went on trying to survive as she led a hand-to-mouth existence. She eventually managed to get a milch cow, but with the job of maintaining it, looking after the children, slogging both in the field and at home, her vitality was sapped.

One day, to cap it all, not only did Mookkandi sell the milch cow, he also pocketed all the money from the sale without giving Ponnuthayi a single rupee. It was because of the quarrel over this matter that she finally ran away from him, after being beaten and battered.

When she left her husband, she was still suckling the last child. She brought away only this child with her. After about four or five months, when he was weaned from the breast, she left him also at her husband's house and came away.

'Call her a woman? Not even a touch of maternal attachment in her! She struts around like a man, doesn't she? When did we ever see a woman leaving her children in her husband's care and go off gallivanting like this?' Though in the village all sorts of people indulged in all kinds of gossip, Ponnuthayi went her own way.

'So what? Are they not his kids too? It was just for his own gratification that he made me bear children year after year. When I was going in for a tubectomy after two sons, he prevented it forcibly and brought me back.' Ponnuthayi would thus justify her decision to herself.

Mookkandi struggled with his four sons, all of them skinny and scrawny, and reached the verge of despair. Having waited quite some time for her to return on her own, he intercepted Ponnuthayi on the street one day, saying, 'You woman! Come home.'

'You and I have no relationship; whatever there was, it was done with two years ago. I don't want to live with you any more.' Ponnuthayi walked on.

'You wretched woman, how dare you tell your husband that you don't want to live with him? You bitch...are you a woman at all? You roam about like a whore dog leaving your own children uncared for,' Mookkandi shouted at her.

'I roam as I please. Who the hell are you to question me? Do you mean to say that I had those children without you? Try bringing them up. You will know then,' Ponnuthayi retorted in anger.

Mookkandi's fury knew no bounds. He yelled back in wrath.

'You bitch! Shut up...look at those leathery lips, that body of yours! If it had been any other man, he wouldn't have married you at all looking at your lips. I took pity on you, and married you; serves me right. I deserve to be beaten with slippers.'

'Go ahead,' she shot back, 'not only with your slippers but also with a broomstick. Thoo! Good for nothing fellow...even then you will not come to your senses.' Spitting at him, she walked away. Mookkandi pulled her back by her hair and hit her on her face and arms. He dragged her along, raining blows all the way. Ponnuthayi kept writhing and struggling. She wriggled away from him and bit his hand. Stung by the bite, he kicked her hard in the abdomen. Unable to bear the pain she screamed aloud and fell down, her head colliding with the hard ground. Blood poured from her injured head, drenching her clothes. After that she did not shout, nor did she let out a single abusive term. Dripping blood, she ran towards the south.

Someone in the crowd shouted, 'Go, stop her. She is running through the fields. She might jump into a well and take her own life. Look at how fast she's running...she might do some such thing.'

'Let her go to hell! Wretched woman! I'll bury her and marry again. As if there's no other woman in the world if this one goes away!' Mookkandi retorted haughtily.

With her hair dishevelled, Ponnuthayi's mother ran screaming after her. By this time the whole village had gathered. Men and women ran behind Ponnuthayi. A few, after running some distance, gave up.

But Ponnuthayi did not jump into any well as they had thought she would do; instead she cut across the field ridges and ran straight to the police station in the next town. A huge crowd gathered in front of the police station at the sight of Ponnuthayi standing there, dripping blood. The police took her into the station and made enquiries.

'Sir, for the past two years I have been living by myself, minding my own business, having left my husband because he was torturing me. Today he comes, picks up a quarrel with me, and beats me till my head splits open. Sir! You must put him in his place.' As she spoke, Ponnuthayi wiped blood off her face with her sari. There was blood on the floor where she was standing. They enquired about her village, street, and other details, then asked her to go to the government hospital. By then her mother too had arrived, and took Ponnuthayi to the hospital with her. Surely it was God's grace that the policeman was capable of human consideration. He immediately sent two constables to fetch Mookkandi. Ponnuthayi came back after having her wound bandaged. In the station Mookkandi was mercilessly beaten and reduced to a pulp. Then the policeman locked him up and turned to Ponnuthayi, 'What do you say? I will keep him inside for a couple of days, advise him, and send him back. Will you live with him? If he again starts giving you trouble, inform me at once.'

'Sir! You do whatever you want with him; as for me I won't live with him. I've had enough. Let me live by myself for the rest of my life.' Having said this, she left with her mother.

Mookkandi was released the next day after a severe warning. By this time the whole village had come to know that Ponnuthayi had gone to the police station, lodged a complaint, and got her husband soundly beaten up. There arose as many versions of the story as there were people in the village.

Aathiamma said, 'Whatever may have happened, is it wise to have complained to the police about her husband and had him beaten up? Stupid woman!'

Kuruvamma said, 'Don't say that. How long could that woman put up with this? Didn't she take all his beatings? One must hand over such heartless fellows to the police. Surely then other fellows will think twice before bossing over their wives.'

Aathiamma asked, 'Going by what you say if the husband beats the wife, she should have him beaten? Nice logic isn't it? How long do you think this policeman would support her? One cannot trust these policemen either these days, you know? All said and done you must ultimately come back to the husband, and he'll put you in your place then, won't he?'

Kanniyamma, who had been listening to their exchange said, 'Of course you know, for the past two years she is living by herself after leaving him. He should have kept quiet; instead he called her back home, she said no. Now it is he who made trouble for her. If she does not want to go back to him, can't he just leave her alone?'

'Do you think he has called her back because he wants to live with her? Fact is, he is not able to bring up four children. That is why he somehow wants to pick up a quarrel so that he may leave the kids in her care.' When Kuruvamma said this, Kanniyamma retorted, 'How long will he remain single? It is possible for a woman, but certainly not for a man.'

Even as the womenfolk were talking among themselves the men too gathered in small groups and gossiped. 'Call him a man? No better than a woman. The wife who dared to go to the police station and had him beaten up—he has let such a woman go scot-free. What a shame! Useless fellow! If I were in his place, I would have strangled her to death right there in the police station,' Kuppusamy said hotly.

'You are a fool. It's no big deal killing a woman. He failed to keep her in her place, right from the beginning. Now he is paying for it. If a man can't control a woman what kind of a man is he? Why should he sport a moustache?' Govindan laughed as he said this.

When the men started deriding Mookkandi thus, it stung him to the quick. Grinding his teeth in fury, Mookkandi paced about restlessly. Then, with his mind firmly made up, he went to Ponnuthayi's house. He spoke to her father. 'I shall never call your daughter back to live with me. Let her also keep the children here with her. I will marry another woman and go my way. Thanks to her I've faced many insults.'

Ponnuthayi's father patiently replied, 'Please bear with her, Maaple. Woman's wit, as the saying goes, is given to folly. Like a fool she went to the police station the other day. Give me time. I will put good sense into her and bring her around.'

'That won't work, I don't need her any more. I will come and leave the children. That's it.' Mookkandi turned to leave. Ponnuthayi, who had so far silently listened to the conversation, said, 'Why leave the children here? You take care of your children. I don't want to have anything to do with you or your children. What law says that only a mother should bring up the children? Don't bring them here nor show your face anywhere here, I warn you.'

Mookkandi left with his pride injured. It was Ponnuthayi's mother who cried aloud saying. 'He might bring another woman as he threatened. That woman will harass the children. Listen to me. A husband is a husband, be he a stone or a blade of grass. Whether he kicks you or beats you, you should still be with him; instead what have you done coming over here like this, you sinner! Let us at least bring the children and keep them here.'

'Stop wailing and keep quiet, Mother. As if a father doesn't know how to bring up his children. Let him try that; I've had enough of stones and blades of grass.' Ponnuthayi stepped into the house, only to emerge with a razor blade. Sitting on the chicken coop railing in front of the house, she cut the thali thread around her neck and pulled it off.

Seeing this, her mother shouted, 'You foolish woman! What are you doing? Why do you imagine that what has befallen you is something exceptional? Does anyone cut away the sacred thali tied by her husband? It would have been better if I had borne a grindstone instead of you.' Her mother wept as she picked up the thali.

Hearing her wailing, a few women gathered around and hurled abuses at Ponnuthayi. Ponnuthayi could not care less. She scolded her mother, 'Amma, will you stop this lament now? What has happened here for you to cry loud enough for the whole village to hear? I'll go to the town and be back. You fetch some tender leaves from the tank bund for the goat, poor dumb creature, it is starving.' She took the gold thali and tucked it in a fold of her sari, picked up a basket, and left for town. The next morning, she set up a petty shop in the village centre and started her business. The thali which had hung around her neck for ten years had filled her shop with many things for her to sell.

Translated by C. T. Indra

THE BINDING VOW

IMAYAM

From earliest dawn, the area surrounding the Pottai Tank started coming alive. Unusually for them, crows, kites, and small birds all started to flock there in large numbers. Meanwhile, many families from the surrounding villages had already arrived. Almost at once, they sought out a place in the shade, and began their preparations for cooking pongal. A few were digging out holes for makeshift cooking hearths. Others were selecting hearthstones. Women set off to gather sticks for the fire. Old women and children kept guard over the bundles. Without exception, they all warned each other, 'The wind and rain will come soon; set about your business smartly.' The families continued to gather, one by one.

More than half the crowds surrounding the Pottai Tank came from other villages. As for the local folk, they had heard that the government was donating television sets, and had all gone off in the morning to sit in the offices of the local government official. 'The deity isn't going to run away. If we don't manage to get to the shrine in the morning, we can always go there in the afternoon. The TV isn't like that. Unless we all receive it together, in a crowd, the official will ask for something extra. If we miss the time allocated, he'll charge us a hundred or even a couple of hundreds.' So the entire village population sat waiting at the office. At the same time, at the back of their minds there was the thought that however late it was, the pongal offering had to be made to Ponnuruvi Saami.

Pottai Tank's surroundings began to take on the air of a festival. Bangle sellers were setting up their stalls. The astrologer, with his parrot, and the palmist, both spread out their mats. The potter carried his wares out of the bullock cart in which he had brought them. Another stall was displaying baskets and winnowing fans. The ironmonger was undoing bundles containing knives, chopping gadgets,

224

pestles, and other tools made of iron. Coconut sellers had already arrived at dawn. Others selling camphor, incense sticks, puffed rice, and toasted gram were all arranging their goods on coarse canvas spreads. Balloon sellers, the ice cream man, flower sellers, and gypsies with needles and beads, all began to thread their way through the crowds. As the crowds increased, so too did the noise; and this in turn made for more and more excitement.

A man wearing a red cloth on his shoulder, warned, 'It will rain soon. Hurry up and get on with cooking the pongal. Once the rain and the wind arrive, it won't be possible to do anything. Last year, it started to rain by twelve or one.' The woman standing next to him replied, 'You get on with digging out the hearth and don't waste time chattering or stargazing. There isn't anywhere here to take cover under once it begins to rain.' She opened her bundle and began to take out all the materials she had brought with her. A man hurrying past said to his wife who was following him, 'Go to the shops and get back quickly. We must finish everything before it pours.'

Towards the west of the Ponnuruvi shrine, at a distance of about twenty or thirty feet, under a neem tree, a man was digging a hole to make a hearth. A woman sat next to him, cutting up a pumpkin. In front of her was a woman breastfeeding a baby. The child was streaming with sweat. The woman fanned the child with the end of her sari, and then fanned herself. Suddenly she said, 'Heaven knows why the sun is beating down so early in the morning. Even under this tree, there isn't a whisper of a cool breeze. If this carries on for another ten days, it will be the end of us.' At this, the woman cutting up the pumpkin returned, 'It's going to rain today, definitely, before sunset. By tomorrow, the heat will lessen. Isn't it for the rain that we're here? It could arrive at any minute.'

'Looking at the state of the skies, I have to say, it seems doubtful. The child has boils because of the heat. When even adults can't bear it, how can a child's tender body manage?'

'Yes, it's like that now. But the rain will arrive by the evening.

It's a promise that has held for twenty years. How can it not rain? All these people have come here today because they believe this firmly. Can't you see them around you?'

'Of course it will be a good thing if it rains. It's just that I'm not sure it will happen. Who knows what is in that Amma's heart, today? Everything is happening the wrong way round, today. Four or five years ago, too, the rains failed.'

'You tend to doubt everything. But of all things, should you doubt the deity's power? It's because of the rain that this Saami has such a reputation in all the villages around here. You know, don't you, that this Amma's life was lost in the brimming tank? Whatever happens, the rains won't fail today. The Saami will test us, certainly, but she will come to our aid in the end.'

'It's no good talking to you,' the other woman said, just as two children ran towards her and threw their arms around her neck. 'Don't go and fall on the baby!' she warned them, 'Why can't you sit still in one place for a bit? Why are you wandering about in this burning heat?' But they wouldn't listen to her and instead began nagging her for money to buy ice cream.

The woman cutting up the pumpkin put the pieces into a large vessel and rose to her feet saying, 'No sign of the man who said he was going to buy a coconut, and the girl who went to fetch water has disappeared as well. I'll just go and take a look. If you come to a place, don't you have to stay together? There's going to be a big downpour today. What sort of man is he that doesn't know this much?' She went towards the Ponnuruvi shrine, trying to see if her husband was among the crowd there. Everywhere she looked, she could see saris, coloured bright red or yellow. There were at least sixty or seventy places where families had gathered, making preparations for their pongal. A large crowd was bathing in the Pottai Tank. Men and women were walking about and criss-crossing everywhere. Taking in all the sights around her, the woman arrived in front of the shrine. She raised her eyes to the deity and lifted her hands in obeisance.

The banyan tree wasn't a very old one; it had grown for only about twenty years. But it had the sturdy growth of a tree that had been well fertilized and its shade spread over a good quarter kaani of land. A wide cement stage had been built around its base and, resting against the tree trunk, the shrine stood like a three-foot high cage. An oil lamp burned inside. About twenty tridents had been fixed into the ground, surrounding the tree. That was all it was, the Ponnuruvi shrine. As the woman stood gazing at the lamp burning within the cage, she was moved suddenly; she prostrated full length on the ground. At the same time, a couple of women arrived, their clothes wet from their bath in the tank, to worship the Saami. The pujari who sat on the raised stage gave them sacred ash. They received the sacred ash and the kunkumam, touched the red sari wrapped around the tree, and made obeisance. Then they helped themselves to the bangles heaped up beneath the red sari, slipped them on to their wrists, and melted into the crowds.

The woman, having watched all this, began to move northwards, as more and more women arrived for worship. Walking along, gazing about her, she stumbled against an old woman who sat in her path. Full of remorse for what she had done, she addressed the old woman, 'Where are you from, Amma, which village? You are sitting here alone in the heat, do you need some water or anything? Do you know where your family and kinfolk are?' She tried asking her a number of questions, but there was no reply from the old woman. 'It seems there's something wrong with her head,' she told herself and continued her search for her husband and daughter.

People walking past her did indeed glance at the old woman who sat a little to the north of the shrine in a certain kind of way. Her form and her appearance certainly gave the impression to passers-by that she might be mad. Her gaze was fixed on the red sari wrapped about the banyan tree. Nothing distracted that look, neither the comings and goings of the crowd, nor the din surrounding her. It was doubtful whether she was even aware that people from many villages from afar had gathered there, that they were making their offerings to Ponnuruvi Saami. Had she been the old Nagammal, she would have been totally aware of everything.

⌣

It had now been more than twenty years since Nagammal was her real self. She and her husband, Chinnasami, used to work for Samidurai Padayachi. Chinnasami's parents, too, had been labourers there, for that family. During harvest time, the labourers belonging to all the families of the village used go and keep guard over the fields. On one occasion when they arrived, there were seven or eight thieves beating the grain off the paddy. In the bright moonlight, it was plain to see what they were up to. Chinnasami was in a hurry; he called out loudly to the other labourers, 'They are stealing the paddy, come on, doy!' Immediately the thieves were alerted and surrounded Chinnasami. In order to shut him up, they thrust his head into the irrigation channel nearby. The mud entered his nostrils and he choked to death. The thieves were shocked by what they had done, and fled, leaving behind even the grain they had gathered. Chinnasami's death became known only on the following morning. Ponnuruvi was an eight-month foetus in Nagammal's belly at the time.

From the time she was a little girl, Ponnuruvi worked in Samidurai Padayachi's house, along with her mother. She went home only to go to sleep. The rest of her time was spent at Padayachi's house. And that is how a relationship began, between her and Padayachi's grandson. As a result, Ponnuruvi's stomach began to swell. Six months went by. Nagammal tried to take care of the business secretly, wanting to cleanse her daughter's womb, without, at the same time, antagonizing Padayachi's family. She wanted to take Ponnuruvi elsewhere, since everyone would come to know if the baby was aborted in the village. She couldn't manage that, however; so she tried to do it locally. With all the indecision, a month went by. And one way or another, the news spread. Step by step the affair slipped out of Nagammal's hands and was taken over by the village. In turn, the village divided into two factions.

The foetus in Ponnuruvi's womb became a matter of discussion for the entire village. The people of the Dalit Colony, remembering everything done to them in the past by those living in the upper-caste streets, kept guard over Ponnuruvi, refusing to allow her to abort the infant. Besides this, they determined not to work for their employers until the matter was resolved properly. They stopped anyone who tried to go to work, besides. It was at that point, when matters came to a head, that the caste people united. Inviting two or three Dalits to go with them, they took the problem to their panchayat. The Dalits were insistent that there should be a marriage. Matters worsened when the Dalits threatened to go to the police if the caste people refused to comply with their wishes. Gradually, Ponnuruvi's problem became the concern of many villages in the area. Ponnuruvi, thinking that because of her, her own village, as well as many others, were in trouble, and that while she was alive the problem would never be resolved, decided to commit suicide. She was rescued twice, and beaten up for her pains. Nagammal too, received her share of blows, with the abuse, 'Why did you give birth to a whore who wanders all over town?' Nagammal hit herself on her head, saying, 'If this village is to return to normality, she must die; she must die.' She lamented aloud, 'She has committed a sin which will not be forgotten for seven times seven generations.' Ponnuruvi, for her part, struck her stomach, crying out, 'All this is happening because of this saniyan.' Desperate to get rid of her burden, she tried several remedies: raw papaya, sesame seeds, jaggery. But the foetus stayed firm, as if a piece of granite were bound inside her womb.

For six or seven days, the colony people were resolute in their decision not to work for the caste houses. This news spread to the neighbouring villages. Some began to say they should allow an abortion. But most of the villages thought they should not allow it. By now, the people of more than ten villages were losing their sleep because of Ponnuruvi's unborn child. The caste people considered how best to put an end to the affair. In the end, the caste people from three or four villages put their heads together, and summoned

Nagammal and Ponnuruvi to come to them secretly, and counselled them. 'A wrong has been done. Now it looks as if it is going to cause difficulties in several villages roundabout. Before our reputation suffers further, it is better to get these two married secretly, take them towards Mayavaram, and settle them with our kinfolk there. Let them find employment and live out their lives there. We are people from three or four villages advising you; trust us. We speak for your own good. If you refuse this, it's your daughter's life that will be ruined. Besides, the village will turn into a bloody battlefield. We are upper-caste people, speaking to you. We are not a caste that speaks false words. Do you think this is the first time this kind of thing has happened? Haven't we dealt with such affairs in the past? These fellows are getting all agitated, as if something exceptional has suddenly sprung up. Let them carry on; we'll see to it. This is women's business. It's for you to decide, now.'

Neither Ponnuruvi nor Nagammal could go against them. Anxious only that there should be no further trouble in the village, they nodded their heads to everything the caste people told them. And they did believe what they were told, absolutely. The caste folk gave details of everything clearly: at which temple the marriage would take place, where they were to travel after that, and by what route. Nagammal brought Ponnuruvi to the designated place, at the designated time, just as agreed, in great secret, and handed her over. Barely three or four hours went by, after that. In the morning came the news that Ponnuruvi's corpse was found floating in the Pottai Tank.

The colony people were extremely perplexed. They kept asking each other, 'How could it have happened?' Nagammal was not the sort to go against the decision of the village. And how did Ponnuruvi even come out of the house, and escape the villagers' surveillance? Had she been found hanging, or poisoned by eating arali seeds, they might have believed she died at her own hands. But nobody believed that she could have drowned herself in the Pottai Tank. She knew perfectly well the Pottai Tank was out of bounds for the colony people. Even if she had climbed in to wash herself, it was difficult to believe she had somehow slipped and drowned. They said to each other, it wasn't credible that a twenty-year-old who knew how to swim would die in that tank. Nobody knew quite what to do and how. There was further confusion as to who would take the initiative to go beyond the law. They tried taking hold of Nagammal, shaking her. She lay curled up, as if she had fainted.

The caste people would not allow the Dalits to remove the corpse. They said that Ponnuruvi had climbed into the tank either to drink the water or to wash herself, and then slipped and drowned. How could a woman from the Dalit Colony dare to approach the tank? Now how was it possible for the upper castes to use the tank water when a corpse lay there? Hereafter from which tank were they to fetch water for their cattle? Where must they wash their animals? Most importantly, how were they to wash after they relieved themselves? The caste people began to make a lot of trouble. While they appealed to their panchayat, the colony people found themselves unable to make their case. There wasn't a single one among them who didn't curse Ponnuruvi. 'Just see: when she was alive she was trouble, when she died she continues to make trouble, the whore!'

They had to submit to the upper-caste panchayat decision, but affirmed that they could pay only half the fine imposed on them. The caste folk agreed to this and only after the money was paid would they allow the Dalits to claim the corpse. As they carried the body out of the water, night was beginning to descend. When they saw that swollen body, seven months pregnant, the entire colony gathered together and wept. Only Nagammal would not weep. Not a single tear would she shed. Above all, she would not even look at the corpse's face. She would not give in, however much they insisted.

After Ponnuruvi died, many stories began to circulate through the village. First there was a rumour that the sound of a woman weeping endlessly could be heard by the edge of the tank, at midnight. Then there was talk of her wandering about as a ghost. Many events occurred, too, all in keeping with the people's imaginings. The upper-caste folk were now absolutely prohibited from climbing into the tank. Nobody could be certain why a small boy of five had wandered into the lake to wash himself, forgetting the rule, nor how he had slipped and drowned. But the entire colony was certain that Ponnuruvi had caught him by the leg and dragged him in. Before that story was forgotten, three young goats fell into the same tank and died. More important news came that as Mutthusami Padayachi was grazing his goats at midday, he was overcome by chest pains, and died under the tamarind tree that stood close by the tank. And that wasn't the end. There were three upper-caste men who took the lead in the dispute over Ponnuruvi. Of those, one began to suffer from diarrhoea, was taken to the Chidambaram Hospital, only to return as a corpse. A second person's wife hanged herself, because of a trivial altercation, leaving behind four children. And two cows belonging to the third man were bitten by something poisonous in the jungle.

Unusually, a woman from the upper-caste streets became possessed. On the same day three women aborted their babies spontaneously. At the same time two or three pregnant women gave birth to stillborn babies. In this way, because there was a death every day, or an inauspicious event every week, the entire village was shaken and overcome with fear. Everyone believed that all these events happened because of Ponnuruvi's curse. There was a pervading dread as to what might happen next and to whom. And it did indeed seem that things kept happening for the very purpose of fanning that fear.

Now the men began to say, 'Why on earth did we chuck a stone on shit?' Women insisted, 'A sin against a woman will never vanish. It will demand redress from all seven gotras.' The women pleaded that some way should be found to escape Ponnuruvi's anger and her curse. What's more, they said that if they made pongal offerings to her themselves, her fury might abate. Only Chidambaram Pillai, who owned the house opposite the Sivan temple exclaimed, 'You've gone and deified a parachi, somehow.' But his words didn't have any effect on the panchayat's decision. The caste people couldn't make the food offering themselves. So the panchayat determined that the responsibility for making the offering should be handed over to Ponnuruvi's kin, and the expenses would be borne by the caste people as a whole. It was consequent to that decision that the first offering was made to Ponnuruvi close to the Pottai Tank.

From the very day that Ponnuruvi's corpse was found in the tank, the caste people stopped going anywhere near it. They did not even draw water from it for their goats and cattle. They didn't bathe their animals there nor did they allow them to drink from it. Even if they were caught short when they were up and about, and had to relieve themselves hurriedly, they never washed themselves there. In this matter, even the small children didn't dare to go against the ban imposed by the village elders. The very next day after Ponnuruvi died, they sought out an old tank which lay to the west of the Perumal temple, dug it free of silt, and began to use it for their needs.

Nagammal performed Ponnuruvi's eighth month rites and all the other funeral rituals around the Pottai Tank. She drew the water for these rites from that very tank. She herself bathed there. Thereafter, the tank became Nagammal's.

From the time of Ponnuruvi's death, Nagammal left off going to work and spent her entire time sitting on the sides of the tank. Or she would walk around it, going round and round. At first, her kinfolk insisted on dragging her back home. In time, they left her to her own devices. Night and day, she stayed by the tank. She didn't go home even to escape from the cold and the rain. When she was surrounded by crowds, she was just the same as when she was on her own. The expression on her face was always the same: as if she was carrying a huge burden. She never spoke an unnecessary word to anyone. She came into their street only when she was overcome by an unbearable hunger. Then she would go and stand in front of one house or another. She'd accept whatever was given to her and return the next minute, to the tank without exchanging a single word. Many people would realize that she was still alive only when they caught sight of her. Whatever relationship she had with the village people had been severed a long time ago. But stories about her were told in the village, nevertheless. Night or day, she never slept a wink. People said that she talked to someone all through the night. Besides this, they began to refer to her as a madwoman, crazy, cracked in the head.

Gradually, all these stories too dwindled. As if she were indeed mad, Nagammal brought different kinds of plants, pulled up from elsewhere, planted them around the lake, watered them, and created a veritable temple garden. She gathered around the lake fifty to sixty trees: neem, banyan, peepul, pungu, and others.

In time, Pottai Tank became an important place in the village. It turned into a place where travellers could rest, where gypsies gathered and dispersed, where the panchayat met, a place where card games, or board games such as 'goats and tigers', were held. Everything seemed to happen casually: the caste villagers requesting the pongal offering to Ponnuruvi; Nagammal making the offering on the Tank's edge for the eighth month ritual and the completion of the funeral rites, and thereafter, on every Amavaasai night, and on the occasion of each death anniversary; Nagammal gathering and planting the trees and shrubs; lighting an oil lamp underneath the banyan tree for worship; making a heap of stones around the lamp and guarding it from dying out. Following Nagammal, children who grazed goats and cattle, and travellers passing by also began to worship there, and light camphor at the lamp. It was they who turned Ponnuruvi into a deity.

Ponnuruvi was dead. But her story became established as a myth. It became a story told endlessly by young and old. If Ponnuruvi had not floated as a corpse in Pottai Tank, had the upper-caste people continued to use the Tank for the needs as was their custom, had her death been like all the other deaths that befell the villagers, it would have been forgotten easily. But today, Ponnuruvi was no longer Nagammal's daughter. She was a deity, a goddess. A goddess who never failed to grant the prayers and vows made to her. A goddess who brought the rains on the day she died, because she was murdered. You couldn't point to a single person from the surrounding

villages who had not prayed to her, asking for help in arranging a
marriage, for a boy child, for an illness to be cured, for the crops
to flourish. Ponnuruvi, in fact, became Ponnuruvi Saami, to whom
even thieves made vows. In the villages surrounding Cheeti Kattalai,
these days, there was at least one Ponnuruvi in each family. In some
there were even two, called 'Little Ponnuruvi' and 'Big Ponnuruvi'.

Only the older people knew that Nagammal was Ponnuruvi's
mother. For the little ones, she was a wanderer. A woman whose mind
was impaired. All the same, even though she seemed like a stick of
firewood clad in a sari, she was still alive. Samidurai Padayachi's house,
on the other hand, was like a house that had burned down. On the
very same day of the eighth month offering, following Ponnuruvi's
death, as if a curse had come upon him, Samidurai Padayachi died
of a heart attack. Not even a month had gone by after his death,
when his second son died, struck by lightning during a summer
storm. His eldest son left the village on the day Ponnuruvi died.
To this day he had not returned. Nor had there been any news
of him. In the past three or four years there hadn't been a single
grown man in that household. And for twenty years no boys were
born into that family, either.

*

A middle-aged woman approached the pujari and handed over a
dozen bangles and a small box of kunkumam. The pujari accepted
them and offered them to the deity. Next, three women came
together, also bringing bangles and kunkumam boxes. The pujari
offered them up as well. Then he handed the women some sacred
ash. The women took the holy ash, smeared it across their foreheads,
helped themselves to what they wanted from the heap of bangles
lying next to the shrine, and then went on their way. More and
more women began to arrive, with bangles and kunkumam boxes.

There was a much bigger crowd now, compared to the morning.
People from the local village had begun to gather, at last. As the
crowd grew, the noise grew louder and louder. A small crowd had

gathered around the astrologer with his parrot, sitting beneath a punga tree, to the west of the shrine. He was making money, steadily. A little further north from him, the row of bangle stalls drew the densest crowds. Little girls were jostling and shoving to try and buy bangles and small kunkumam boxes. These were the objects most pleasing to Ponnuruvi.

Suddenly another small crowd gathered in front of the shrine. A woman was swaying and shaking, possessed by the deity. Three or four men tried to hold her down, but could not control her movements. The deity was moving about in a frenzy. From the crowds a woman called out, 'Amma, tell us what is your wish, we'll do it. We have brought you bangles without stinting. We have brought you kunkumam. We have sacrificed a rooster. We have chosen a red sari for you, fine enough to make all the other gods jealous. Tell us what more you would like. What is the reason for your coming here?' But the deity would say nothing. A man from the crowd asked, 'Will it rain today?' The entire crowd joined in and asked whether it would rain that day. But the goddess would do nothing more than shout, 'de, de'. She gave no predictions, no words of mercy. There was no reply whatever, throughout the possession, and up to the moment the god left the woman. After that, when the first woman was resting, the god entered another woman. The crowd now gathered around her, instead. Once again, the crowd asked the god if it would rain that day. But there was no word: it was as if the god's mouth was locked up. All that happened was the frenzied swaying and straining of the neck. One woman said, 'Give the god something to drink.'

The crowd's hopes were thwarted; the god had given them no words of comfort. There were also doubts as to whether it was going to rain or not. Everyone began to look slightly tense, anxious. Which god would tell them whether the rains would come or not? A look of yearning spread across their faces, as they waited to hear these words from some woman's lips.

The sun was at its fiercest now. The heat bore down with its full force. The wind burnt like fire. But the crowd took no notice. They began to make their pongal offerings to the deity in good time, in the hope that the rains would come. As time went on, the number of people gathered there grew even more. The pujari struggled to keep up. His assistant was completely confused. It was difficult to make out who said what, to keep in mind each person's gift. It was the noise that contributed most of all to the pandemonium. As more and more people came to make their offering and the crowds thronged around the shrine, Nagammal got up and began to walk away. Nothing seemed to affect her, not the people rushing to and fro, nor the children playing and shouting. She walked on, looking for a tree beneath whose shade she might sit. There were families gathered beneath each tree. She walked on, some distance away from the shrine, towards the west. Here it was less crowded and she sat down in the shade of a neem tree, leaning against its trunk. In front of her, three families were making everything ready to cook their pongal offering. A robust looking woman, sitting facing south and tucking firewood into a hearth, remarked to the man sitting by her side, preparing a coconut, 'Every year the sky starts to darken, usually by midday. This year, on the contrary, it's like a white sari up there. Heaven knows when it will rain!'

The man answered, 'There's not going to be a drop of rain today. The astrologer has said that if it does, by some chance, he is ready to give up predicting the future.'

'Where does that astrologer come from?'

'Can you see that neem tree over there? Look there, towards the north. Can you see him sitting there under the tree, with his udukku drum? He said so.'

'You can hit that prediction with a shoe. Just because that black-tongued man says so, do you think the rain will hold off? A promise is central to the god; diet is central to good health. Is it likely the rains won't come today? We'll have at least a single drop. There will be rain and wind, most definitely, you'll see.'

'How can you say that?'

'I know it. This Amma always grants a boon when you make

a vow to her. It was only after I came here and offered myself to her, that your fifth child was born a boy. Last year, when my father lay in bed, unable to lift his limbs, didn't he get up the very next day after I brought the sacred ash from here and smeared it on his forehead? Are you the sort of man to forget all that god has done for you? For how many people, from how many villages, has that Amma granted favours? Doesn't she know what is in the hearts of all the people gathered here? Can she be blind to that extent?'

'If a king admires her, a woman becomes a beauty to all eyes.'

'Chi, shut your mouth. Those words come from a male heart. That Amma gave up her life, not just for her own sake. After her death, didn't every farm labourer stop working, as if protected by a fence? By whose grace do women from these villages all around dare to walk safely, night or day? You yourself had a series of girl children born to you. How can you forget all that?'

As the woman was scolding her husband, two little girls aged six or seven, came running up. Panting for breath, they said, 'Appa, we need some money.' The man merely scowled at them. The children began to wail.

'Why are you crying, di?' the woman asked them.

'We need to buy bangles to offer to the god. He won't give us the money,' the elder girl said, through her tears.

Immediately, the woman turned into a fury. She shouted, 'Are you denying them the money to make an offering to the god? Your hands will become empty. Give them a rupee each, Ayya.'

He protested, 'You took five rupees from me yourself, as soon as we arrived, to make an offering.'

She returned, 'Chi, are you a man? How can you keep count of what you give to the god!' At this, the man took out a five-rupee note and handed it to the children, without a word. As soon as it reached their hands, they flew away like little birds.

Two people walked past, talking, on their way towards the coconut stall. 'How the sun is striking down, today of all days! Will it rain? People have begun to make their food offering. But there are no signs at all of rainfall. We were disappointed like this six, seven years ago, when it looked as if it might come down, but didn't. It might happen again, today.'

What had happened to the skies? Usually, on the day of the pongal offering to Ponnuruvi, the skies would darken by midday. Sometimes, even as the pongal was placed on the leaf for the offering, the rain would come down. People were happiest when they made their offering, soaking wet from the rain. In fact, some people came to make the offering, with the very purpose of getting wet in the rain. But it was doubtful, looking at the skies, whether on this occasion it would happen. The sun's heat threatened to turn their faith into a false belief.

Now, family by family, people were returning after making their pongal offering. As soon as they returned to their own spaces, they sat down to eat. Every family, without fail, set out a leaf containing the food, for the crows. Now, there were people sitting down in small groups and eating, under every single tree. A few were still going up to the shrine to make their offering. In front of Ponnuruvi Saami's shrine, there was quite a hubbub. Everyone, both those who were eating already and those who were still making their offerings, looked less happy than they did in the morning. Everyone spoke wearily. Whatever they were doing, everyone stopped and looked up at the sky, now and then. Often people came there more to enjoy the rain than to cook the pongal, or pray to the deity and take vows. It was the rain that people desired most, and prayed for. A good ten days before the day of the pongal offering to Ponnuruvi Saami, everyone's heart filled with the belief that the rains would come. It was that belief that inspired people to walk ten miles, twenty miles without getting tired. But it looked as if today that belief was being turned on its head.

Four or five families sat eating their pongal beneath a peepul tree which stood next to the potter's stall. The bald man who sat leaning against the trunk, spoke up, expressing his deep disappointment, 'The gods are just like human beings. Just as the times change, so do the

gods. For twenty years things went as they should. Today, though, the
air is like fire. Someone in this crowd might have done something
wrong, or might not have done what they should; who knows. The
god hasn't shown mercy; the skies have not darkened. There's no
point in sitting here any longer. Collect your things. Let's go. This
morning, as we were setting off, a cat crossed our path. I thought
immediately that it was an ill omen. My fears have come true. Now
we are not going to have any rain or anything. Get ready, let's go.'

But a woman who was rinsing out a large cooking vessel said,
'No, don't say that, Maama. She lost her life in the water, will she
deny us water? You see whether it doesn't come pouring down
before sunset. She brought us rain for twenty years, won't she do
it today? Is there anything in the world the gods can't do? It will
rain today. I can promise that on the heads of my three children.'

All the people sitting nearby turned and gazed at the woman
as she spoke. A middle-aged man who was with a family sitting
towards the west asked the woman, 'Every astrologer has said even
if you beckon to the rain, it's not going to come today, there isn't
the planetary force. Are you saying they are telling lies?'

Without hesitation, the woman snapped back, 'Is the god's word
more important or the astrologer's?'

'The god's.'

'In that case, it must rain today.'

'What makes you say that?'

'The god is what she is because of your faith in her. Otherwise
she is chaff. You can doubt even the child you gave birth to. But
you must never doubt god. She is a god only if you have faith in
her. If you have faith, it will happen.' She went on scouring the
vessel and washing it.

'There have been so many times when this god didn't bring us
rain. Have you forgotten all the times we came here hoping for it
to fall and were disappointed?'

But the woman swore at him and turned her face away, sharply.
The sun began to sink in the west. There wasn't a single cloud

in the sky. The wind was still burning hot, like a hearth fire. The crowds in front of Ponnuruvi Saami's shrine began to lessen. Finding the heat unbearable, a number of people were bathing in the tank. A couple of families began to bundle up their belongings. Some, who had arrived very late, were still making their preparations for the offering. Two or three families began to move off.

It was getting late. The belief that it would not rain now began to spread. A short, stout man came from the direction of the shrine and joined the others beneath the neem tree, saying at once, very loudly, 'Don't you realize it's getting late? Can't you see that people are starting to go home? Don't we have to get back in good time? It's not going to rain now. Today that Amma has smeared all our faces with charcoal. If the god doesn't keep a promised word, then what's left? When all's said and done, she was born just a human being, after all. The money you see in your dreams isn't money you can spend. The dog that gnaws a bone can never bite iron. Hereafter, who among the farming people is going to respect us? A fine god she is!' Saying this, he began to pack up all the goods they had brought.

An old woman who was also sitting there tried her best to pacify him, saying, 'Wait, Thambi, let's give it a little more time. Is some thief going to run off with our house? It will stay where it is; it's not going to walk off.' But it didn't seem as if he heard a single word she said.

The old woman then turned towards the shrine and said, 'Ei Ponnuruvi, Mother, stop all these people's mouths by allowing a single drop of rain to fall. Let not your reputation go to ruin, Amma!' She looked up at the skies and folded her hands.

Just then a middle-aged woman ran towards the shrine, weeping and exclaiming, 'Oh, I've lost the chain which was around my neck!' Two or three other women ran after her.

The old lady asked, 'What is going on, Thambi, the crowds seem to be running somewhere?' But her son didn't answer; he just bundled up all their things silently.

Now they were all going home, family after family. The crowd that had gathered in front of the shrine and in the tank had lessened by more than half. As the people left, crows and dogs began to gather in greater numbers. They fought over the leftovers on the leaves on which people had eaten. Monkeys, too, turned up to join them. As for them, their only targets were the bananas in the little children's hands.

The pujari who officiated at the Ponnuruvi shrine, a kinsman of Nagammal, spread out a sari that had been given as offering, threw on to it all the coins which people had gifted, and tied them all up in a bundle. His assistant gathered up all the red and yellow saris into a sack. The pujari yelled at the assistant to tie up the coconuts and limes separately. He seemed to be the only person there who looked happy. Every now and then he glanced at the crowd that remained and up at the sky. He scowled at a woman who arrived there just then saying, 'What is this, di, why have you come so late? It might still rain and spoil everything. Don't we have to take everything home before that? Look at her, beggar's daughter, arriving just at the time of the washerman's departure!' He ordered the assistant, 'Lift one of the bundles on to her head and send her home.'

As the sun sank lower and lower in the west, the crowd thinned out more and more. There were only a couple of families or so still in front of the shrine. The noise and bustle had quietened. In all, there were, probably, no more than a hundred people left. There was not much expectation of rain; people spoke to each other wearily. Trade had decreased during the afternoon as soon as the idea took hold that there would not be any rain. Now the coconut stall keeper began to bundle up his wares. The potter loaded his cart with all the unsold pots. The bangles seller took down his stall.

All of a sudden, Nagammal left the shade of the punga tree, came out, and looked up at the sky with her dim eyes. Then she went straight to the Pottai Tank, dipped her head into the water, and came up to the Ponnuruvi Saami shrine. She made an obeisance to the deity. Neither the pujari nor his assistant said a word to her. They were totally absorbed in packing up the gifts and offerings. Nor did Nagammal appear to pay them any heed. Having worshipped at the shrine, Nagammal walked on slowly, looking at each tree as she passed. As if a sudden thought had struck her, she began to put out the still smouldering cooking fires. Then she picked up the stones that lay beside the holes dug out to make the hearths and gathered them all up in a single heap.

There were seven or eight people gathered beneath a neem tree that stood next to the parched gram stall. An older man who sat among them said, 'If a single drop of rain were to fall today, that would be enough.'

The man sitting next to him added, 'If it does rain, I will arrange to have a bigger shrine built, before next year's pongal offering to the god.'

A young man wearing a red shirt, aged about twenty years, added, 'For my part, I'll contribute ten sacks of cement.'

At that moment someone exclaimed, 'I think I smell something in the breeze. Run and take a look at the sky!'

The youth in the red shirt ran out of the shade to take a look and called out, 'I can see clouds, Thaatha!'

The old man rose to his feet with unaccustomed haste and went to see, the others following. Wisps of cloud could be seen in the western sky. But they were absolutely white. Yet, when people saw them, a small ray of hope entered their hearts. They returned to their shade and resumed their conversation. The red-shirted youth pointed at Nagammal, saying, 'We gain merit by doing good deeds. Come on, let's all go and put out the fires. Let's fill up the holes that have been dug out. We'll pick up thorny sticks and twigs. We don't have the good sense that even an old lady has. Come on, da.'

After that all the men and women joined Nagammal in searching out the cooking fires which were still smouldering. Suddenly a woman called out, 'The sky is darkening!' Everyone ran out to look at the sky, including those who sat under the trees.

As they saw the clouds darkening minute by minute, two men

ran to the shrine, calling, 'Let's light camphor for the god.' In haste
they bought camphor, lit it, and made their obeisance. They helped
themselves to a handful of bangles which lay in a heap on the raised
stage, tied them at their waists and then returned. They began to
gather up the sticks which still lay beside the makeshift hearths,
hurriedly. All those who were still sitting beneath the trees and
those who had begun to bundle up their goods now joined the
others, clearing up all the cooking spaces, as if they were offering
a service to the god.

The sky continued to change colour. A cool breeze blew.
Nagammal took no notice of what the others did. She was entirely
engrossed in putting out fires and gathering up sticks and stones,
and heaping them up some distance away.

The cool breeze continued to blow and people became more
and more excited. Suddenly there was a more forceful wind. And
with the wind, the clouds began to dissolve away. The gathering
clouds changed colour once more. The people who were clearing
the area stopped their work to gaze at the sky. One man hastened
to the shrine, stood in front of the deity, and prayed, 'Mother, save
us; let not the wind blow away the clouds.' In the belief that his
faith and prayers would bear fruit, he seized hold of a handful of
sacred ash and smeared it on his forehead.

But the strength of the wind continued to dissolve the clouds.
Within ten minutes the clouds had turned white again. The clouds
vanished, like smoke. Disappointment spread over the faces of all
those who had been staring at the sky. A middle-aged man flung
away the stones he had gathered and spoke bitterly, 'A god should
grant the boon that we pray for. That's what a god should do. What
sort of god is it who doesn't know what's in our heart, who won't
act accordingly?'

A short, fat man answered him. 'It's very wrong to complain
against a god. If not today, it will definitely rain tomorrow. Is it
likely that it won't rain at some time? The wind came and spoilt it
all, as if a growing child were ruined by its own mother. So what

could the god do about it? Wait and see, it could still rain before it gets dark. Do you think she is an ordinary deity? This deity will never fail to fulfil a vow made to her. This is absolutely certain.'

At this, the middle-aged man spoke with great frustration, 'That's what we have believed and hoped since this morning, but it's all come to nothing. There's no point in believing any more that it might still rain. If you want, you can sit here, saying, "It will rain, it will rain." As for us, we're off.' Saying this, he told his wife to pick up their bundles. He refused to listen any more to the others, and began to walk ahead. Two other families, seeing him, followed suit.

The short, dark man tried to comfort the few people left. 'What is the need for the rush? The god is testing us, that's all it is. Should you rush off because of that? If it doesn't rain this year, it certainly will, next year. Four or five years ago, the same thing happened. This is all the deity's playfulness. Can man understand god's game?' But now, nobody paid him any heed. Even his wife had stopped listening, and stood up, her bundle on her head. The man didn't know what to do. He gazed yearningly up at the sky. Then he said, 'Wait, di, I'll be back.'

He ran up to the shrine, quickly. He prostrated himself at full length and prayed, 'Please, Mother, bring the rain next year at least. Don't send the people away, disappointed.' He took the sacred ash and smeared it on his forehead before turning round. His wife had started to walk away. He hurried after her. Nagammal went on at her own pace, picking up the stones by the cooking fires and taking them away. The western sky began to darken.

Translated by Lakshmi Holmström

CERTIFICATE!

ANBAATHAVAN

'Irulaandi, my dear son…please go and try again today. Here, take this for your expenses.'

She pulled the string of her cloth purse and opened it, took out an old, fifty rupee note, crumpled and soiled, and handed it to her son.

'In the pot there's some gruel I made for you. Finish your bath, drink the koozhu, and go and check….'

'What's the use of going again and again, Ma? Every time they tell me to go away and come back later.'

'Ayya, don't be so frustrated. They're all officials, they'll have a hundred things to do. We are only Irulas. They assume we have nothing to do. Even if we have to make four trips instead of one, no harm done. So just go, dear.'

'All right, I will go today. But if they say no again today…I don't know what I will do to those fellows.' Irulaandi gnashed his teeth.

'Don't get angry, my dear one. Can we succeed by getting angry? Do you remember, the other day when Tindivanam Kalesi Vadhyar was here, what did he say? That people like us, the depressed class, should make an effort to get educated. We should learn to write, we should absorb new ideas and knowledge…didn't he say that?'

A wave of memories flooded Irulaandi's mind….

Yes, yes…there was a lady Collector at that meeting. And Kalyani Sir also spoke.

He had said, 'Certainly you Irulas can continue to catch snakes and work in the forests, till the fields. But you must give your children a good education. Education is very important….'

He had gone on stressing that point.

'What is it? What's on your mind?' At the sound of his mother's voice, Irulaandi was startled out of his reverie.

'Nothing, Ma. I was thinking of what that Vadhyar said at the meeting.'

'That's right, Saami. Study well, try hard. I'm told that once you get this sutticate it will be easy for you to go for higher studies. So go and try again. I have to go to the Mekkalakattu to work in the western fields today, and it'll take me a long time to get back. I'm leaving now.' She picked up her basket, rope, and knife, and left.

The town bus sounded its horn in the distance.

Irulaandi got off the bus at the Pillayar temple stop itself. Otherwise he would have to go on to the new bus stop and walk all the way to the Taluk Office in the scorching midday heat. The shortcut through Kamarajar Road would get him there sooner.

The sun blazed down. Irulaandi felt tempted by the sight of the juice shops along the way.

'Mm…hmmm. No. It is money that Amma has earned by slogging in the forests and fields. I shouldn't waste it.'

'Oh…what a lot of jewellery shops, so many different kinds of jewellery. Once I finish studying and get a job I will buy jewellery for Amma.'

And so Irulaandi went on his way, conducting a conversation with himself as he walked. True to his name, he was very dark-skinned. Among the Irula families that lived around Vikravaandi, Irulaandi was the one with the most education.

'I've finished class eight. That's no small achievement. Next, I must go on to the ninth. Have to enrol in Vijayapuram High School. But I need a community certificate for that, and they're making me run around for it more than half a dozen times like this, back and forth. And I still haven't managed to get it.'

'Here is the Tahsildar's Office, Vijayapuram. They refer to it as the Taluk Office, but the board reads Tahsildar's Office. Oh well, let it be Tahsildar or any other "dar", somehow I have to get my certificate.'

Irulaandi greeted the peon at the gate, 'Good morning, sir'.

'Oh, hello, snake-fellow,' replied the peon. 'Go in and meet sir.'

Irulaandi entered.

'Sir, good morning.'

'What do you want, da?'

'Sir, a month ago we came and applied for a community certificate. I haven't got it yet. I need it to join my new school next week.'

'You are the snakecatcher fellow, right?'

'Yes, sir, we are Irulas.'

'Even educated people are not getting jobs. Now snake and scorpion catchers want an education.'

'Saami, why shouldn't I and my people get an education?'

'Mm...as if a fellow like you can study! Look at the fellow's face...as if he's just been dunked in a barrel of tar...' remarked the official. Then, turning to a woman official seated nearby, 'Hey, Madam A-3, look, this is the snakecatcher fellow.'

'Talk of snakes...we caught enough of that kind during the range survey. Why do you think I've been able to stay in the same posting for twenty years?' A-3's voice swelled with sly pride.

'Amma...madam...I don't want to get into this game with you now,' said the official hastily. Then, turning to Irulaandi, 'Sir is not here today. Come another day.'

'Sir, I've already come here six or seven times for this. Please have some sympathy for me....'

'Enda, once I say go, you go. Don't go on talking and creating a disturbance.'

'Sir...sir...next week I have to join school. Please take pity on me and help me, sir.'

'So...obviously you fellows won't understand when you're told something in a civil and polite way. After all, you're all savages.' Then he called out to the peon, 'Hey, Munusamy!'

'Coming, sir.'

'You let people from the jungles and mountains enter the office, and then you are lounging around outside?'

'Go away at once, da. Go!'

'What's all this? What's the commotion about?' asked the senior official, emerging from inside.

'Nothing, sir. He is an ST. It's a Community Certificate case. He is from the snakecatcher tribe.' Then, turning towards Irulaandi, 'What's the name of your tribe, da?'

'Ayya, we are Irulas. Ayya, please, please, take pity on me....' pleaded Irulaandi, falling at the feet of the senior official.

'Wait, wait, da…how can I be sure you are really a snakecatcher? Catch a snake and show me, then we'll see.'

All the office staff roared with laughter. Irulaandi cringed in embarrassment.

'Go, da. Go…go away.'

He managed to get out without being physically thrown out.

'Which village does this boy come from?'

'Sir, he is from Melakondhai, near Vikravaandi.'

'Melakondhai? Where's my jeep driver? Call him at once. Before that I have to make a phone call.'

The senior official seemed tense as he dialled the phone.

At Melakondhai, the aroma of chicken curry from Sambandam Reddiar's house was wafting all over the street.

The senior official jumped into the waiting jeep, and off it sped away.

'*Ey, make sure you cut the viral fish into nice big pieces for frying.*'

The jeep hurtled along the highway.

'*Yo…go into the garden and cut fresh end leaves from the banana plant. Fetch a jug of water.*'

The official wiped his hands with a satisfied air. The big burp he emitted emphasized his contentment.

'Enna, oy, how was the meal?'

'What a question, Reddiar! We're fortunate to have dined at Sambandam's house. It's a great honour.'

'Right, enough of the praise. Come to the point.'

'Reddy Sir, it's a very important matter. In spite of all the complications involved, I obliged you by altering your community status from Reddiar, which is a Forward Caste, to Kondareddiar, which is ST, that is, Backward Caste. Because the further education of your son depended on it, I took a very big risk and got it done.'

From the 'priority' file he was carrying, the official drew out a community certificate and handed it to Reddiar.

'I know, I know…de, Muniya, go and fetch two sacks of Ponni rice and put them in the jeep. Also load a plantain bunch and a basket of coconuts. Then go inside and tell Amma that I sent you. She will give you a bag. Bring it to me.' Then, turning to the official, Reddiar asked, 'Oy, what if your driver…?'

'I'll take care of that,' assured the official.

The servant brought the bag. It was duly handed over. The official left.

By the time Irulaandi boarded the bus, he had made up his mind. The urea bag hung heavy in his hand.

'Do you know how to catch snakes, da?' The questions that had been thrown at him in the Tahsildar's office, the waves of mocking laughter from all the staff…the images still tormented him. His hands curled into fists, mirroring the fury of his mind.

'I will show them…they'll see what sort of people we are.'

He alighted from the bus and walked into the same Tahsildar Office.

'Oh, it's the snake charmer again.'

'Sir, my certificate please….'

'Wait a second, da. Do you remember what we asked you the other day? We asked if you know how to catch snakes.'

Peals of laughter from everyone around.

'Well, I'm not an expert, but I know a little bit about it, sir. Look, here are the snakes I've caught over the past four or five days…they still have their fangs….' He reached into his bag, took out a snake, and held it up for everyone to see.

'De, de, what's this! Put it back in the bag. Put it back now!'

'Sir, this is a water snake. Like the people who work in your office, it likes to hiss a lot. But it doesn't bite. Here you are.' As he finished speaking, Irulaandi flung the snake across the room.

'Aiyyo, Aiyyo, snake, snake…!'

'This one is a rat snake. Enda…how many trips have I made to this office?'

'Thambi, please, please don't…please put them back inside.'

'You are raking in money in bundles, right? Like this striped viper here….'

'Aiyyo, one bite from this means instant poisoning.'

'Has anyone ever received anything from your office as soon as they requested it? Well, this is a nalla paambu, a good snake….'

'Kill it, kill it. See, it is hissing. It's going to bite….'

Irulaandi spoke passionately: 'Enda, you think a snakecatcher is an inferior creature? First learn to give a human being the respect he deserves. Now these snakes can be caught only by an Irulan like me. When you find one, send my certificate through him.'

As he spoke, Irulaandi flung baby snakes in all directions around the office till his bag was empty.

The snakes wriggled around all over in celebration of their liberation from the bag. The staff cringed and cowered.

Feeling liberated from his own burden of resentment, Irulaandi strode out with a light step.

Meanwhile, one of the banded vipers wriggled rapidly into the senior official's room.

Translated by Malini Seshadri

THE GOAT THIEF

PERUMAL MURUGAN

A minor slip occurred in Boopathy's plan. To silence the goat, his fingers clamped its tongue without getting caught in its teeth, but his grip slipped a bit. Adjusting his grip, he tried to choke its vocal cords. In the meantime, the goat opened its mouth with its quaking tongue and raised a lone bleat. Confident that the sound couldn't have penetrated the darkness, banged on the dew stiffened door and roused anyone from sleep, he hugged the goat to his chest and lifted it. It was somewhat heavy. The next moves of the goat— leaping and kicking to free its legs—were familiar to him. The way he held the goat gave no room for such manoeuvres. One hand was thrust inside its mouth, while the other held the animal tight against his body. *From now on, everything will go according to plan.* He walked rapidly towards the foot trail, landing his bare feet gently on the ground.

'Who is that?' He had gone barely twenty feet when he heard the commanding voice, along with the rustle of palm leaves behind him. He recognized the owner of the voice, and more people were beginning to join him. Boopathy couldn't decide whether he should drop the goat and flee or keep running with the goat on his shoulders. He came to an abrupt halt. Before his pursuers' eyes got used to the darkness and they started chasing him, he could cross the dirt trail and reach the road. Murugesan, who was waiting there on his moped, could ride so fast that he would cover a mile in the time a man tried to sit on the pillion. But if Boopathy ran with the goat on his shoulders, the noise would make it easy for his pursuers to nab him. He had never been in such a predicament before.

'Appov...our goat is missing!'

Boopathy trembled when he heard the agitated cry. He would be finished if they laid hands on him. He dropped the goat immediately.

Its tongue set free, the goat let out a scream. It was the primordial cry of an innocent animal stunned at being dropped like a rock on the ground. But Boopathy had run a fair distance by the time its cry fell on his ears. The bustle of men moving about and the barking of dogs had begun to come together at various spots. He sprinted, thrusting his body forward like a stone aimed at a tamarind pod by a boy. The sound of his feet thudding on the ground pounded in his ears. He also sensed someone running not far behind him. Turning back to look would slow him down.

The dogs in the neighbourhood barked in unison. Boopathy's earlobes tingled with fear. 'Thief! Thief!' 'Catch him!' He heard them scream in the distance as though from inside a well. All he had to do was reach Murugesan, who stood ready near the culvert with the engine of his soundless moped running. Boopathy sprinted single-mindedly towards the culvert. When his feet touched the pits on the tar road, they bounced and leapt. In the light of what he was able to see in the familiar darkness, he figured that he could catch up with Murugesan in four or five leaps.

With the goal so near, he tried to coax his legs to run faster. Just when he was feeling confident of jumping on to Murugesan's pillion in one more leap, a hand fell on his nape, pulled him back and pushed him hard. Tottering on unsteady feet, he was about to fall down. By now, Murugesan's moped would have travelled so far that no one could have gone after him. Before his pursuer came back from vainly chasing Murugesan's vehicle, Boopathy had recovered and assessed his situation. Both sides of the road were blocked. The men and their dogs had brought the road to life. Only the two ends of the culvert were still free.

He jumped into the torrent of sewage water that came swirling down the gutter. His legs sank in up to his knees like in the watery slush of a paddy field; drawing them out quickly, he took another step and waded in. The channel was wide and capacious. There was a lush growth of sedge grass and thorny babul trees all around. He could hear the sound of water swirling under the culvert. Boopathy entered the thicket of sedge grass and forged ahead. It was unlikely that any movements of the grass would be visible in the darkness from far away.

As soon as Boopathy jumped into the water, the fellow who was running after him stopped in his tracks, stunned. 'There he is, there he is', he shouted and clambered on top of the culvert. 'Come on, da! Come fast', Boopathy heard him calling out to the others. Boopathy had come very far inside the canopy of sedge grass. Raising a din, the men and their dogs surrounded the channel. Boopathy thought it might be wise not to risk any further movement. In the middle of that patch of sedge grass as tall as a man, he found a lone, sharply angled stone jutting out of the water. He climbed on to it and sat down. His legs were shaking. The slush and the water had drenched his body up to his waist. Sweat poured from his head on to his torso, making him feel as if he was just out of a bath.

Meanwhile, his pursuer was explaining the situation to everyone. Flashlights shone their beams inside the grass canopy. A large crowd of people had collected next to the culvert. There must have been thirty-forty people in the crowd. Some carried sticks in their hands.

The darkness would not betray any movements inside the sedge grass. If he walked further inside the canopy, he would reach the sluice gate of the lake. If he walked towards the banks, he would reach the coconut grove with a mud wall around it on one side and a sand track that led to the lake on the other. The moment they sighted any movement of the grass, someone might get into the channel aiming for that spot. He would not be able to sit for too long on that small stone. The soles of his feet were inflamed.

Amid the thickets of sedge grass he saw what appeared to be a sand dune. He got down from his stone perch and moved towards it. It was indeed a sand dune. A thorn bush had covered most of the mound. His feet stepped on a tangle of sharp, rough things. He took out the penknife tucked in at his waist and gently snipped away the thorny branches extending at ground level. The clearing held just enough space for him to lie on the ground. He lay down on his side. If he turned over on his back, the thorns would hover dangerously close to his eyes. If he stretched his legs, his feet would touch the water. He somehow curled up and lay in that narrow space. Nothing moved anywhere.

Now he could hear the voices from beyond the channel. Darkness added to the clarity of sounds.

Even a light rustle made his earlobes stiffen with fear.

'He couldn't have got away. He must be hiding somewhere inside this gutter.'

'He was moving so fast that he may have reached the lakeside by now, scrambled ashore, and made a run for it.'

'If a man entered this gutter, he must have been ready to risk his life.'

People milled about on all three sides of the channel. Flashlights swept the area relentlessly. Boopathy was sure that none of them would find him. He was at the centre of the channel, surrounded on all sides by the tall thickets of sedge grass. From a distance, his hiding spot wouldn't be visible under any amount of light. The engulfing darkness would make it seem as if the spot too was filled with sedge grass. What would he do if four or five robust youths like him dared to jump into the gutter to nab him? His imagination was running wild.

Just when he had nearly stopped perspiring, more beads of sweat appeared again. He appealed to his clan deity. 'Amma...Kariakali... save me, Mother,' he mumbled to himself. He didn't know what else he should pray for. Closing his eyes, he kept repeating 'Kalimma, Kalimma' like an incantation.

The chatter of voices kept getting louder and louder. The hour was past midnight, with its unique blend of darkness and dew, but everyone wanted to stay back and watch the fun. If the incident had involved merely the theft of a goat, it would have ended up as just another bit of news. Now it had grown into a topic on which interesting gossip could be exchanged for a few more days. He heard all kinds of voices now, including those of women and children.

Boopathy's ears grew erect, like a dog's. First he heard the sound of stones falling like rain inside the sedge grass. Then the abuses began and flowed freely: 'Come out, motherfucker!' Anticipating that a stone might fall on him, Boopathy curled his body further into a ball. However, not a single stone landed anywhere close. Like a palm fruit falling from the tree, they kept dropping into the slush with loud thuds. He was far enough away that he could not be approached by man or stone.

Even after dawn broke and daylight spread everywhere, no one would be able to find him if he remained in that position. Boopathy felt strong and confident again. The sound of stones falling subsided gradually. The crowd didn't seem to know what to do next. People made all kinds of suggestions. The owner of the goat kept describing his adventure to many people. He ended his narrative always with the same lament:

'I missed him by a whisker. I had pulled him back and flung him on the ground. If only I had caught his throat immediately, he couldn't have escaped. Instead I went after the guy on the vehicle... this one had recovered by then. How was I to know that he would jump into this stinking gutter and get away so fast, as if he was swimming in a well?'

The flashlights continued to scan the sedge grass with their beams.

'De, none of you pluck even a pubic hair of mine. Come here, da, if any of you has the guts.' As he became conscious of his mouth muttering the challenge, Boopathy chuckled to himself.

A woman said wearily, 'The goat is safe now, right? So why are you people loitering around in this cold? That man who entered this filth, do you think he will still be there? How do we know where he climbed ashore and in which direction he took off. The darkness is piled so thick that you can hack it slab by slab. Go and get on with your work.'

'Why don't you go home if it bothers you? How could a thief dare lift a goat from the doorway of a house? How can we rest without finding out what his face looks like? Even if we have to wait here till sunrise, we won't go home without catching him,' declared an energetic voice. 'Someone go and bring a fire torch,' commanded another. He could hear the bustle of a few men leaving. He could hear the bustle of a few men leaving. 'We have to go to work in the morning. Feeling very sleepy now.' A few women and girls seemed to be leaving for their homes as well. He didn't understand why they needed a fire torch. For a moment he was afraid that they might close in on him using the torch. 'Let them come. I'll see what they can do,' he thought boldly and stretched his legs. By now, the spot had become comfortable for stretching out. A few stars were visible from the sky through the gaps between the thorns.

'Ei, Marappa...keep a watch on that side. He might head for the lake over there and climb on to the bank and run away. The boys have gone to bring a fire torch. We'll wait for them to come.'

A message was sent from the sand trail side of the channel to the coconut grove side, which had very few men standing by; on the grove side there was only a foot trail, formed over time by villagers visiting a nearby field to defecate. No one could stay there for too long. He could clamber up over there, he thought. He postponed thinking about what would happen next and preparing himself for it. No trace of anger could be detected in the voices any more. Now they were mostly relating stories about the many cattle thefts that had taken place in the area earlier. Boopathy realized that a few of those had been carried out by him.

It was his father who had trained Boopathy in the art of stealing goats. Boopathy often felt that his own exploits were next to nothing compared to his father's. His father had never been trapped like he was right now. No man had waited with a vehicle to help his father get away. The goat across his shoulders had never made the smallest sound regardless of the distance it was carried. His father had told him about the most suitable hours of the night for stealing a goat—the time when Yama, the Lord of Death, having beaten all living creatures to sleep, played about freely: from midnight to three in the morning. Even old people and chronically ill patients shut their eyes during those hours. The period is a boon granted to us by God, Boopathy's father had told him often. 'Our actions must always be free of anxiety,' was one of his father's prime lessons. He had also taught Boopathy the technique of holding the goat's tongue as well as the knack of lifting the goat to one's shoulders.

The inaugural theft of Boopathy's career was carried out in the house of a frail old woman. She lived alone with two goats in a thatched shed in a field. One was a white male goat that had been castrated at the right age and the other was a black female kid. White goatskin fetched a lot of money. If there were two targets in one place, he had to choose the one that would earn him more income. This was also a lesson he had learnt from his father. He aimed for the ram. But he felt a qualm in his heart. Should he rob a lonely old woman of the fruit of her labours?

'There's hardship in everyone's life. If we start worrying about that, we'll never be able to practise our trade. Better keep *our* hardship in mind,' his father had said. Boopathy considered it no great achievement on his part to have stolen that goat. His hold was perfect. The old woman did not suspect him at all. His legs trembled, however. The trembling didn't stop even after he had brought the kid home. Still, he felt that his mind was strong. It seemed like all his fears had descended to his legs. After that first job, everything became easy and routine.

There was nothing special about holding the goat's tongue and lifting it to one's shoulders. Observing the daily routines followed in the target house before the theft was much more crucial. It was gathering intelligence on the various aspects—the shed where the goats were tethered for the night, the easiest way to get there, the distance between the shed and the house, the number of residents in the house, the spot where each resident slept daily, the person who had trouble sleeping—that required a lot of effort and legwork. One had to put on many guises, like a customer at the local toddy shop or a trader who bought and sold calves of water buffaloes and bulls. If everything was calculated properly in advance, the theft at night became easy to pull off. Before the owner of the goat even realized that the goat was missing, its meat would be cooking in many houses in the area.

After Boopathy teamed up with Murugesan, the work became even more of a breeze. Murugesan would ride his soundless moped stripped of its lights in pitch darkness. Once Boopathy got on the pillion with the goat, no one who came after them could catch them. Murugesan often said that it was best to practise moderation in everything. Once a goat was lifted and brought home, there must be a gap of at least one week before the next job. From the site of one theft to the next, there must be a minimum distance of ten kilometres.

Sometimes Murugesan too suffered a bout of enthusiasm, coming up with a host of daring ideas. Once, after they had handed over a stolen goat to the owner of a meat stall in the bazaar and collected the money, the butcher told them: 'I couldn't buy a single goat today. It's a festival day in most villages around here. If I can get another goat, it would be great. I am willing to pay fifty or hundred extra.' What could they do when it was already four in the morning? For stolen goats, the butcher always paid a fair price without haggling. He was a long-standing customer. If they brought him a goat, he slaughtered and skinned it immediately, regardless of how many goats he already had in his yard. Murugesan told Boopathy, 'We have to somehow help our man, pa.' He borrowed a vehicle from the butcher himself. It was a noisy machine fitted with lights. 'I'll try my best. After that, it's your luck,' Murugesan told the butcher.

He stopped the vehicle in front of a house on the outskirts of a village. A woman was milking goats in the cattle shed. Murugesan couldn't see her face in the dark. He went straight to her and said, 'Ammov, I've come to collect the goat.' He untied the goat and brought it to her. As she continued milking, the woman said, 'Take out the tethering peg and keep it on the floor before leaving.' He pulled out the peg, placed it on the pyol, and said, 'I've done it, Ammov.' It was believed that if a goat was sold along with the tethering peg, its progeny wouldn't survive.

'I'll come by at ten. Tell Natrayan that he should hand over the cash,' the woman shouted. 'You'll get the money at ten sharp, Ammov,' Murugesan shouted back as he lifted the goat, kept it across his legs, and sat on his vehicle.

The goat had already been sold to one Natrayan, who had promised to collect the goat that morning. When Murugesan and Boopathy went to the house, the woman had mistaken them for Natrayan's servants. The theft was discovered only when Natrayan's men went there after sunrise to take possession of the goat.

'You should listen keenly to everything that falls on your ears. After all, even a neem oil bowl may come in handy for some purpose,' Murugesan told Boopathy.

But so far, even Murugesan hadn't faced a situation like the one he was in. If this mob got hold of a thief, they would tear his limbs apart. After they were done with his body, he could only beg on the streets to survive. That was why Boopathy always packed a small knife in the knot of his lungi. He would be able to at least nick his adversary and get away.

Two or three fire torches were visible from his hiding spot. Those men might enter the grass thickets in the gutter holding those aloft. If they did, he would be forced to shift to another spot. Like a tadpole, he could find some nook or gap to hide in. If he crawled slowly across the channel, he could climb on to the opposite bank and take off. But no one entered the channel. Using the torches, they set the dry patches on fire. The fire didn't catch easily. Dampened by the dew, the reeds went out fast. After that, the men lost all interest in the chase.

'Let's go, da. This guy will surely be bitten by snakes.'

'Anyone who steals to survive deserves to die like that.'

'He will lie there all night with the thorns pricking his skin and die of the poison. We'll come in the morning and fish out his corpse.'

'There must be shards of glass in that sewage water from god knows where. Surely they will cut into his legs. Scavenging dog.

Instead of lifting goats for a living, he should pimp out his mother.'

After delivering lethal curses, the crowd began to thin out. All the curses of hate and intolerable anger flung at him seemed to melt away in the wind. Why so many curses for a theft he couldn't even pull off? He chuckled softly to himself. He closed his eyes. The crowd's chatter decreased gradually until it sounded like whispers from the road. From their voices, he could make out that even the couple of men left on the coconut grove side were moving away.

Playing a trick on him, a few men could still be hiding there. The moment he became visible, they might pounce on him and nab him. The owner of the goat had been somewhat bold. He had followed Boopathy without worrying that his adversary might be carrying a knife. The owner's hold and push still lingered on Boopathy's body. He decided not to get up from his spot for the time being. He had no option but to wait for everything to die down completely. Sleep weighed heavily on his eyelids and wore him out. Though he had instructed his eyes not to give in to sleep, they were in no mood to obey. But he was a light sleeper at night: if his head slumped just a little, he would wake up.

When he woke up finally, he could feel the wetness of the dew all over his face. He could not get up immediately. Thorny branches covered him like a blanket. The dried slush on his legs pulled sharply at his skin underneath. Moving his feet even a little was hard. He looked at the sky. Sirius, which deceived the eye by glowing exactly like the morning star, glittered in the low sky. He estimated the time to be around four. He crawled horizontally and came out of the net of thorns. As before, it was pitch-dark all around.

He could hear the strange sounds of unfamiliar insects. It was as if his ears, blocked until now, had opened up suddenly. He heard a rhythmic, deep-throated gurgle, which could have been a frog's croak or something else. He wondered if it could be the secret language of snakes. As far as the eye could see, the channel was covered with sedge grass. The reeds stood taller than a man. Who knew what dangers lurked inside those grass thickets? He jumped down from the sand dune and climbed on to the stone. He should not go back the way he had come. He had to find some other route. He looked around. Towering over the sedge grass, the thorny branches of the babul trees looked like skeletons. His eyes met the same spectacle on all sides.

Deciding to walk towards the coconut grove, he took the first step. His feet sank deep in the tangle of roots beneath the grass. His legs were buried in the mud up to the knees. He was frightened. The noise of insects around him seemed to grow louder. He tried to pull his legs out. He felt each leg rise, then sink again. He reached for the stone and held on to it. Pressing down on the stone with his hands, he lifted both his legs out of the slush. When he sat on the stone again, he felt enormously relieved. Though the dew still felt cold on his skin, he began to sweat.

He was trapped in a patch of quicksand from which there was no escape. The curses flung at him by the men had turned into the sedge grass, thorns, and quagmire that confronted him now. Was this not the way he had come in? How could the grass reeds, which had parted for him then, close up now? His legs began to shake involuntarily. It was the same trembling he had experienced when he had lifted the goat from the old woman's house that first time. He tried to shake off the tremors like they were slush on his feet and gather courage.

He looked at the sky. The morning star was twinkling like a yellow sapphire. His time was up. Now the bustle of human activity would begin. He heard voices from some place far away. The grass reeds around him had turned into human shapes that screamed at him. The thorn reeds had morphed into men who stood before him with their arms stretched wide to catch him. All the various sounds merged into a giant scream: 'Thief! Thief!' He felt a surge of anxiety. His legs began to leap forward.

Translated by N. Kalyan Raman

PIGEON FEVER

S. RAMAKRISHNAN

Goverdhan was leaning idly against his office window, when he happened to spot the pigeons. Across the road from his office was a warehouse of the Food Corporation of India, with very high walls. Atop one of these blackened walls sat the pigeons, all in a row. One pigeon was grey, the rest all white.

He counted them. There were sixteen in total. Goverdhan's years in this office had altered his nature. If he had seen these pigeons in his youth, he would not have thought of counting them. His mind would have instead immediately explored more amorous avenues, picturing pigeons as messengers of love notes. But, as a clerk in a government office awaiting retirement from service in just three years, such thoughts would not be appropriate, would they? And so he only counted the birds.

Those who work for the government for more than thirty years take on the characteristics of that very government. It's true. Their faces, bodies, behaviours, everything changes. Like the tables and chairs that populate the office, they too lose their individual characteristics and become part of the furniture.

If someone's job involves adding, subtracting, and totalling numbers all day and every day, is it any surprise that he would instinctively start counting things?

Goverdhan's children would tease him. Whenever they went to a restaurant for dinner, Goverdhan would have done the totalling mentally and arrived at the bill amount long before it was presented. 'Appa, the computer will calculate our bill. Why do you bother with it?' his daughter would ask. What could he tell her?

If the truth were told, it was not just the nature of his job that made him total bills in his head. It was also the way he had been brought up. Every paisa must be spent carefully; every paisa spent must be properly accounted for. That was the value system with which he had been raised. But who does that nowadays? He remembered how his mother had scolded him for leaving a five paisa coin behind at the grocery store. Today nobody cares for paise. Nor for rupees, for that matter.

So, since he had been brought up this way, and since he found it impossible not to total up the bills in his head, he continued to do so silently without talking about it to the others.

After finishing college, how thrilled he had felt at the thought of starting work in Madras. Yet these thirty-three years of his Madras life had not been all that great. He had bought a house, and his children were soon going to finish their studies. That was about all.

Chidambaram, Cuddalore, Karur, Rasipuram—his job had sent him to all these places. None of them had left an impression in his mind. Madras...this metropolis of more than a crore people... here he was a mere speck. A speck with no separate identity. Can anyone distinguish a single drop of water in a rainstorm? Doesn't every drop look like every other one?

When he landed his first job and came to Madras, he stayed in a rented room. In the evenings, after work, he would not head straight back home. Instead, he would roam the city. The temple, the beach. The bylanes of Triplicane. Public meetings, the library. Discourses, music concerts, shops that stayed open until late...the hours would slip by, unnoticed.

The room he had rented was in a so-called 'mansion', but had no facilities to speak of. Yet he did not see this as a drawback in any way. There were some Sundays on which he had managed to watch as many as three movies. Late at night, he would track down a place selling bilal biryani and tuck in heartily before going back to the room. And then, all of a sudden, he grew tired of it all. He got married. After he settled in Madras in a new home with his bride, it was no longer the same city to him. Its boundaries had shrunk.

Even a trip to the beach began to seem like a tiresome chore. On one occasion, there were hordes of people on the beach, and the din was so overwhelming that he began to feel suffocated. His little daughter urged him to take her up to the edge of the shore, where the wavelets lapped at the feet; but he was suddenly overcome with dread at the thought that a huge wave might roll in and wash them away. Not only did he not venture up to the shoreline, he also forbade his daughter from doing so. 'You've grown old,' chided his wife. 'That's why you have all these needless fears.'

He realized there was some truth to what she said. Were these fears really meaningless? Why is it that when one grows older even the smallest things in life begin to look like grave threats? One becomes afraid of anything and everything. Anxiety and anger are ever ready to erupt.

Once, at the office, the topic came up in general conversation. Typist Sundari said, 'Once our bodies no longer obey our commands, our minds begin to lose their balance. We obsess about the state of our bodies all day. Which twenty-year-old spares a thought for his body? At that age, we could eat and digest anything and keep going. Is it possible now? Just a vada takes half a day to digest.'

Everyone had laughed. But Goverdhan felt depressed. What she said was so true. The basis of all his fears was really the state of his body. And it was he himself who had caused the damage. And his office routine had played an important role in the process too. But what was the use of these regrets now? Day by day, life was becoming more tiresome.

Movies, newspapers. Temples, music. He could not turn to any of these. Nothing enthused him any longer. Earlier, he would play carrom in the office with his colleagues and chat for hours over endless cups of tea. All of that ceased when cell phones made their arrival. Playing games together, chatting in groups...all gone.

Goverdhan had to drag himself to work every day. He found office life increasingly tiresome. Every morning, when he placed his lunch bag under his table and opened the top drawer to start the day's work, it felt like he was tugging at thirty years of his life. The cobwebs he noticed were not confined to the office ceilings; he could feel them spreading all over him too, smothering him. These could never be swept away. He would forever be a man trapped in this spider's web.

It was on one such day, with its full quota of anxiety and depression, that he had started watching the pigeons.

After five minutes, he grew entranced by their whiteness. How perfectly white was that white! All the smoke and grime of the city could not mar its pristine perfection. They sat all in a row, as though awaiting something. Which one was the boss, which the steno, which the head clerk? The pigeons did not have these labels. One of the birds was preening its feathers, another crouched as though preparing to take wing and fly away. Another couple of birds sat rubbing their beaks together amiably.

One pigeon sat apart from the rest. Maybe it too, like him, was tired of this city.

As Goverdhan continued to watch, suddenly all the birds took to the sky. Where were they going? Where was each one's home? What was the urgency?

The opposite compound wall, now bare of pigeons, reminded him of a government office on a holiday. He continued to stare fixedly at it for a long time.

The Head Clerk, Arunan, turned towards him and asked, 'What is it, sir? Why are you looking so intently at the warehouse?'

Goverdhan wriggled out with a white lie. 'Oh, nothing. Just getting some air.'

That day, right up to closing time, his mind was full of thoughts of the pigeons. When he got home, he abandoned his normal routine. Instead he took out an old diary and tried to draw a pigeon. His wife assumed he was finishing some official work. The pigeon would not take shape on the paper. He made four or five attempts. No success.

The next morning, as soon as he reached his office, he looked eagerly to see whether the pigeons were back on their wall perch. They were not. He kept checking throughout the day. Still only the empty wall. Finally, at about three in the afternoon, the pigeons started arriving one by one. Soon they were all lined up in a row. The same sixteen pigeons...like inseparable companions.

At first he had assumed that they were there to feed on the grain at the warehouse. But close observation revealed that they were not eating anything. Why then this meeting place? What was the purpose behind it?

Suddenly the pigeons flew up, traced a circle in the air, and settled back on their perch. Was the wall their playground? A meditation centre perhaps? Which of them was the oldest? Which was their native place? There was no way to fathom these things. Yet, the more he watched them, the more energized he felt. He stood for a long time at the window, riveted by the pigeons. From behind him, the Head Clerk remarked, 'Earlier there used to be many more pigeons, sir. Now there are way fewer of them.'

'Have you ever watched them?' asked Goverdhan.

'Well, I would glance at them casually. How else to spend our office hours?' The Head Clerk was applying Amrutanjan balm liberally on his forehead as he spoke.

'Do pigeons come only to this wall? Or do they visit other places too?'

'There used to be plenty of pigeons in front of the mosque. Also opposite Safire Theatre. Maybe they were scared away by the American Consulate building nearby.' The Head Clerk laughed.

Why does this same set of pigeons keep coming? How did this strong bond develop among them? Why are the pigeons going around in a big bustling city like this instead of seeking the freedom of the forest?

He was overcome by a desire to view the birds at close quarters. He put on his sandals and went downstairs. There was no watchman at the gate of the warehouse. All he could see was some withered grass and a few nameless plants. As he walked further, a strong smell like that of boiling wheat assailed his nostrils. On a wall blackened by dripping rain there was a half-torn poster.

Goverdhan approached the wall on which the birds were perched.

He sidled up cautiously, lest the sounds of human intrusion disturb the pigeons, making them fly away. One of them seemed to notice him, but then turned its head away nonchalantly. He could clearly hear the distinctive sobbing sounds they were making. To his ears they sounded exactly like the dragging breaths of a patient with advanced tuberculosis. Then, as though suddenly deciding it was time to leave, they winged their way up into the sky and flew away past Goverdhan. One of the birds, which had been sitting a little apart from the rest, took a different route from the others.

As he turned away and started back to his office, the watchman of the warehouse appeared. 'Sir, why are you here? Whom did you want to meet?'

'Oh, I think I have it wrong. It must be the office next door,' he muttered, summoning up a false smile.

The watchman left it at that. But Goverdhan continued to ask himself questions. 'What folly! Why did I come down all the way here from my office just to look at pigeons?' His mind continued to dwell upon the pigeons long after he got back to his office.

That evening, instead of going directly back home from work, he went exploring. He was looking for other locations in the city where pigeons could be seen. It had appeared to be an absurd undertaking; but, against all his expectations, he actually managed to see quite a few pigeons. He counted them all. An inexplicable joy filled his soul.

Every evening he started taking diversions from the route home. Thousand Lights, Royapettah, Triplicane, Mylapore, T. Nagar, Saidapet, West Mambalam, Chromepet, Tambaram—all these he explored. He began to take careful note of how many birds congregated at which location, their appearance, their demeanour. The more deeply he researched them, the more his joy grew.

In order to keep an accurate record of his pigeon-related observations, he procured a small notebook. To Goverdhan's mind, it was as if the city had undergone a sudden transformation; as if, under the surface, there lurked undiscovered secrets. What else would explain why so many thousands of pigeons inhabited this city and yet went unnoticed by all?

Why do the pigeons prefer to inhabit ruined buildings? Are they ascetics who have renounced worldly comforts? Why do they never quarrel loudly? Why do they cluster around mosques, temples, and churches? Are they perhaps heavenly messengers? The more he studied them, the more extraordinary they seemed.

Once he got back home, he would flip through the TV channels feverishly, hoping to chance upon a programme featuring pigeons. He had scoured many sources to collect pictures of different varieties of pigeons. He would gaze upon these for hours. His wife, his son, his daughter...none of them could even begin to understand this strange transformation in him.

His Sundays were reserved for pigeon-watching. It is said that once two pigeons come together as a mating pair, they remain loyal and committed to each other for life. He believed this to be absolutely true. He was astonished to learn that even pigeons bred and raised in captivity had the homing instinct and would return home unerringly, no matter where they were released.

Could this mean that pigeons shared something in common with him? Was their home their whole world? But why were they so eager to be caged? Why, when the whole wide sky was up there for them to fly into, to disappear into? The watchman at the warehouse had once remarked, 'Even if that wall on which they perch is razed to the ground, the birds will still come there.' Was that a sign of stupidity on their part? Or did the wall mean something more to them than just a temporary resting place?

Caught in the grip of pigeon fever, Goverdhan would commute by electric train sometimes and at other times by bus, watching the pigeons on their perches as he went by. On one occasion, when he was in a share auto in Royapettah, a young woman in purdah was seated nearby. Suddenly, she shoved the men on either side and lunged forward as though trying to get off the vehicle. But no, she was only trying to get a better look at the pigeons perched on a tin roof by the roadside. Goverdhan was amused. The other passengers were not, and scolded her. She, however, seemed immune to their irritation and laughed merrily. Then, with no prompting, she remarked, 'I love pigeons. We've been raising them at home. My father takes part in pigeon race competitions.'

He merely nodded to signal his understanding. The share auto proceeded on its way. In a while, as a bend in the road approached, he told her, 'Look to your left. You will see a mechanic's shop. There will be pigeons on the roof.'

Exactly as Goverdhan had predicted, there were pigeons on the roof...a whole cluster of them. The woman began to count them hurriedly. Before she was done, Goverdhan announced the correct total.

'How did you know there would be pigeons here?' the woman asked.

He was rather surprised at the childish naivete of the young woman. He said, 'I have counted all the pigeons everywhere and recorded the totals.' He took his small notebook out of his shirt pocket and showed it to her.

She did not believe him, and so he handed her the book. She turned the pages eagerly. The pigeon census was laid out neatly, according to their location in the city.

'But why do you count pigeons?' the woman wanted to know.

He laughed. 'Oh, no particular reason,' he said.

'I would also love to do this. But my husband disapproves of this kind of thing,' she said, stroking the notebook longingly.

The share auto halted close to the bridge. Just before she got down, she handed the notebook back to him and said, 'It's not good to keep following pigeons. They will visit you in your dreams.'

Her words brought him joy. He yearned for at least one pigeon to visit him in a dream that night. But the truth was he never really had any dreams. Well, he sometimes had daydreams in the office, but never at night.

All the way home his thoughts dwelt on the purdah-clad woman and pigeons. At nine o'clock at night he retired to bed. No dreams, no pigeons.

A new feeling of elation had filtered into his life, such as he had never felt before. As he shaved in the morning, he would wonder whether he was destined to meet the purdah-clad woman again. He took a fancy to wearing white, like his beloved pigeons. He abandoned his earlier angry rantings and started speaking calmly. Pigeons have a discipline that is not readily evident. They don't await any signal; yet, in the blink of an eye, they rise into the air as one and fly away. Pigeons don't announce their hunger noisily the way crows do. The pigeons had opened a door to new experiences for Goverdhan and showed him novel ways to live his life.

A city doesn't contain just people. It also contains thousands upon thousands of pigeons. And other birds. And dogs and cats and rats and all kinds of microscopic life. They all live out their lives together. Each creature has to find its own sustenance. Nothing comes easily in the city. Nothing is permanent. One has to perch on any wall that is available. Goverdhan gradually began to shed the fears that had been plaguing him.

Some time later, on a Sunday, he was wandering near the Royapettah clock tower in a quest to spot pigeons. A voice called out, 'I saw you first!' It was the purdah-clad woman. She was carrying a basket.

He smiled at her. 'Do you live near here?' she asked.

'No, East Tambaram.'

'Oh, so you are roaming around here looking for pigeons,' she teased.

'Nothing like that,' he said, 'it's just that today is a holiday….'

The young woman laughed. 'My father is just like you. Pigeons, pigeons, pigeons…that's all he thinks about. He even talks to them. Do you talk to pigeons?'

'No, I don't know how to do that.'

'My father says that if we talk to a pigeon it will talk to us.'

'If you say so, then it must be true.'

'You trust me so completely?' she asked.

He did not know how to respond. He remained silent.

'Will you give me your little notebook?' asked the young woman.

'And if I do what will you give me in return?'

'I will buy you a cup of tea.'

'Really?'

'Yes. But only if you let me keep the book.'

'What will you do with it?'

'When I'm at home, I'll look at the book and picture the pigeons in my mind. After all, you've made detailed notes of how many pigeons visit each of the places.'

'Don't you want to go and see them for yourself?'

'How can I do that? I'm not a man. I can't be spending all my time following pigeons. I have to earn my living, you know.'

It seemed to have dawned on her that her remark could be construed as criticism. 'I wasn't talking about you,' she explained.

'Well, you only said what's true,' said Goverdhan.

'You're not angry?'

Goverdhan shook his head. 'No.'

'Then come on,' she said. She took him to a nearby tea stall and bought him a cup of tea.

'What about you?' he asked. 'Aren't you going to have any tea?'

'Ayyo, if they find out I stood on the road drinking tea, I'm finished.'

Goverdhan sipped his tea slowly, gazing at her all the while. Her hand reached out to take his notebook.

'I won't give you the notebook!' declared Goverdhan.

'Are you cheating me?' she asked, sorrowfully.

'No, no. I was joking. Here you are.' And he handed her the book.

She took it and just slipped it into her basket, unopened.

'What's your name?' he asked.

Without replying, she crossed the road and went her way.

Goverdhan stood for a long time outside the tea stall. A strange mix of joy and disappointment was swirling in his mind.

He took the last bus home. Even afterwards, he couldn't sleep. He got up from bed, sat in an easy chair, his thoughts full of the woman. At this moment, she would be at home, maybe turning the pages of his notebook and thinking about pigeons.

A city can do odd things. When, where it will bring people together, how and why it will separate them—nobody really knows.

It was as if he had momentarily turned back the clock and was twenty-five years old again. He took his old black-and-white photographs out of the cupboard and rummaged through them. The boy in those pictures....he is not me, he thought. I have travelled a long way since then. He didn't like the look of his own face these days. Still thinking about the woman, he went to sleep in the easy chair and slept in it all night. And that night, for the first time ever, a pigeon visited him in his dream.

After that, every time he saw a pigeon, he would see the woman in his mind's eye. Every time he began to count pigeons, a feeling of guilt would eat at him. He often worried, wondering if his wife would find out about the woman. But then he'd tell himself, it was just a meeting, that's all. Nothing more.

The more he thought of the purdah-clad woman, the more it felt as if a pigeon had descended to perch on his shoulder, only to fly away again. He was like a wall. Pigeons don't come and sit on a wall merely because that is what the wall wants. No, it is the pigeons that choose to beautify a wall by sitting on it. It seemed to him that walls were forever destined to yearn endlessly for pigeons that would never return.

In the office, some days later, Goverdhan overheard the Head Clerk saying, 'Is a human being meant only to eat and sleep? What about some happiness in life? What can this city offer? Everyone is after money all the time. Same thing at home, same thing everywhere else.'

'Very true,' remarked Goverdhan in a loud voice. The Head Clerk looked at Goverdhan, wondering what had made him shout out. But Goverdhan, head bowed to avoid his gaze, was silent. The window next to his chair was open. For some reason, this bothered him....

Translated by Malini Seshadri

PAYCHI TREE

S. THENMOZHI

Like a black column rising out of the earth, like a pillar left over from the Iron Age, stood a lone palmyra tree, a testimony to three generations of prayer. No sign of any spread-out hair on its head…indeed the head itself was missing, as if someone had pinched it off and tossed it away. Time, with the five elements as its hand tools, had stripped the palmyra of its rough native texture and given it an unnatural smoothness. Was the tree alive or dead? The truth was a secret as long and dark as the tree itself. Above ground, its life force had been extinguished. But under the ground…like a vast network of roots, its aatma had spread everywhere. Even though it had lost every last visible trace of life, the people of Thanjavur's Karuthattaangudi Sarukkai Street continued to believe that the tree was alive. In Sarukkai Street lived some people who had converted to Christianity, seeking self-respect and social recognition. These people worshipped the palmyra tree just as devotedly as they worshipped at the church of St Anthony and St Xavier. Except in the evenings, the sun and the moon would not allow a view of the pinnacle of the tree. On this treetop, which was hidden from the gaze of the human eye, some sparrows had created a world of their own.

It was a palmyra tree, a panaimaram. The people of Sarukkai Street called it Paychimaram. Ever since Amma can remember, the tree has been there. It had leaf fronds, but never any fruits, and so it had never yielded any toddy. Times changed, but the tree did not. Even when I first saw it, there were a couple of fronds still left on it. In the evenings, womenfolk would come by and light camphor to worship the tree. They would pick up some of the mud from near the foot of the tree and smear it on their foreheads and thaalis. Pregnant women smeared it liberally on their swollen bellies, their faces lighting up with joy when they felt the baby rolling and kicking inside them. Some day, somehow, no one knows precisely when, the remaining two fronds also disappeared, taking with them the only lingering signs of life from the tree.

Between this Paychimaram and my grandfather, Colonel Sebastian, was a long-standing, intimate relationship that was difficult to understand. Thaatha had served in the army and whenever he was posted to other states or to faraway places, it was to this Paychimaram that he always entrusted the responsibility of guarding and protecting his family and home. All his joys and sorrows and innermost thoughts, he would share with this tree. He would sit at its feet and open his heart and talk unreservedly—laughing and crying, talking and scolding. But no one in the village thought any the less of Thaatha for this. That Paychimaram is his wife, they would remark, in good-natured banter. But his real wife was Paanchaayi, also known as Mariyamma. Paanchaayi could sense that Paychimaram was Thaatha's closest confidante and soulmate, indeed his very life. But although Paanchaayi could see there was this very special relationship between her husband and this tree, she could not even begin to fathom the underlying nature of this strange bond.

To Thaatha, the sanctum of Paychimaram was imbued with the presence of his Aadhithai, Eve, unclad and in a state of nature. Paychi was a constant presence in his life. The tree was mother and friend, wife and daughter-in-law and grandchild—any or all of them. He was spiritually in thrall to Paychi. Without fetters or chains, she held him close. And Thaatha was only too happy to be her prisoner. During the day, and all through the night, Paychi would go away to wander around the village. So it was only at dawn or dusk that Thaatha could visit Paychimaram.

Paychi had enchanted and enslaved Sarukkai Street and its residents with her playful teasing, sense of mischief, and cajoling. Every house retained a mark of her presence. She would play hide-and-seek with the children, or pinch them to make them cry. Sometimes she would drag them away by force and abandon them somewhere else. As for the adults, whenever they were at fault she would appear in their dreams to admonish them. Drunkards or men setting out to indulge in any vice would feel her warning tap on the back of their necks. Like a village deity, she guarded the borders. She scared away burglars and thieves and alerted the public. If she spotted cattle thieves attempting to steal a cow at night, she would awaken the sleeping adults or pinch the sleeping children and set them crying so that the adults would wake. She safeguarded the street against diseases and ailments. Her spirit would possess someone and demand toddy or meat or cigarettes. Only after she was granted her wish would her spirit agree to leave the person in peace. No family's curry-pots did she leave unlicked. If someone called her with an offer of a full pitcher of toddy tapped from a toddy palm, she would rush there with a gleeful grin. The manners and modesty, propriety and decorum, that were traditionally expected of a woman...all these were foreign to her. She would sleep sprawled on her back, legs and arms flung wide apart. Her clothes would be in disarray. When she didn't feel like wearing any clothes, she would just take them off with no hesitation at all. She would suckle baby goats joyfully at her breast. Whenever it rained she would soak herself in it, from the first drop to the last. She would frolic and play in the puddles like a child to her heart's content.

The subtle art of awakening sexual desire and of extinguishing it—this was something that lived and coursed through her whole body. She would not approach even herself without permission. And that was the rule for others as well. She would revel in the fine art of arousing desire, almost as if she were drawing intricate kolams.

At other times, she wished to do the opposite; and then her very nakedness would be the flame that would incinerate kama to ashes. Her valour lay quietly at rest. But when it was needed, she could stir it awake into a terrible typhoon. Into every beseeching hand, she poured her largesse like the sea. Whatever anyone asked of her, she readily gave. And whatever she wanted, she took. What was there and what was not there...everything belonged to her. She would never weep. She would usually be found either on her feet, or crouching on her heels, or lying flat on her back. Only when she was in a serene mood would she sit cross-legged on the floor. All this was known from hearsay, from things that Thaatha and the other elders of Sarukkai Street said about her.

The village celebrated the presence of Vaasamba in their midst. Where she may have come from was a question that never entered their minds. Even if the question were to occur to them, it would be promptly forgotten at the sight of her, and they would not think of asking her anything at all. She accepted and ate whatever food was given to her, wherever she happened to be. At night she would sleep in someone's front yard or on the thinnai with the others. Very often she would sleep on the thinnai of St Xavier's Church. She had a good stock of stories and songs. Like a little girl on the seashore collecting shells and pebbles, she had collected these stories and songs. When the people slept, her stories stayed in their minds and melded with their dreams. Long stories that could not be completed in one night would be continued the following night. Between the instalments of the story, everyone would go around remembering the part of the story they already knew and speculating about the part that was yet to come. As for the songs she sang…her words soaked in emotion and were woven into the rhythm of music by relationships and the sheer beauty of imagination. Vaasamba's voice was majestic and powerful. She was tall, with a good stature; her body had a sparkle to it. Her complexion was as brown as that of a fawn. She wore her sari draped with the pleats at the waist. Her hair was so long that she had difficulty collecting it and tying it. Her smile was as bright as a freshly scrubbed brass pitcher. She would often laugh out loud.

Although there were so many houses in the street, for some reason Vaasamba chose to spend most of her time in Thaatha's house. After a while she started staying on there even at night. It did not occur to Paanchaayi to raise any objection to this. Besides, Vaasamba would help Paanchaayi a bit here and there with the household chores. She started accompanying her to the fields. Vaasamba would work only if she felt like doing so. Suddenly she would disappear for four or five days at a stretch. The whole village would be looking for her. But once she was back, every question that arose in the minds of the villagers seemed to find its own answer and die away. When it came to dealing with men, Vaasamba was like water. If a man were to merely tap her, she would tolerate it; but if he were to attack her, she would instantly drown him in the darkest depths of her being.

The bond between Thaatha and Vaasamba grew stronger each day. He seemed to pick up some secret signal from her. In a slow and subtle way, she was making him more and more aware of her. Thaatha, meekly adoring, rejoiced in her presence. Every encounter with her gave him the sense of fulfilment of a sexual union. Vaasamba was incapable of telling a lie and spoke only the truth. For his part, Thaatha never tried to restrict Vaasamba in any way. He had understood that she would never submit to being controlled by any rules. She was outgoing and energetic, or withdrawn and lethargic, all according to her own whims. But whenever Thaatha called to her affectionately, she would come running like a pigtailed little girl and stand smiling in front of him.

Quite often, Paanchaayi did not know what to make of all this. It was all a deep riddle to her. Yet, her trust in Thaatha was not shaken. She did not even think of seeing Vaasamba as 'the other woman'. In the beginning, a bit of jealousy would sometimes creep into Paanchaayi's heart, but each time it would fade away. Paanchaayi felt a kind of inner glow lighting up within her whenever she looked at Vaasambi. She became aware that her own sense of freedom was breaking free of its constraints and flowing free like a river. She realized too, that joy was in full bloom in that home, and prosperity had come to stay with them. The whole household revolved around Vaasamba. When she was not there, everyone was afflicted by a searing sense of loss. She was a companion to their eldest daughter. She also helped in the delivery of two of Paanchaayi's babies. Paanchaayi was not sent away to her parents' home to deliver her babies, as was the custom; Vaasambi looked after her entirely. She stayed awake at night to look after the infants. More and more, Paanchaayi came to look on Vaasamba as the very incarnation of Mother Eve...the joyful, free-spirited Eve of the Sunday sermons at church.

She was in awe of Vaasamba's spirit of restlessness and independence—surely Eve's attributes, before God's curse came down on her. Thaatha was very much aware of the situation. The relationship between Thaatha and Vaasamba was a private forest, embellished with unnamed and unnameable creepers. Thaatha yearned to be the foremost disciple of Earth's primordial mother, Eve.

Vaasamba would sit down with Thaatha for a game of cards, as his equal. She taught him the secret of how to drink liquor and yet not get drunk or betray the fact by a tell-tale smell. Thaatha gave up his habitual drinking, and made it an occasional pastime. She accomplished difficult tasks faster and better than Thaatha could. Thaatha would often stand and stare, in slack-jawed amazement, at her strength as she hoisted and carried big sheaves of paddy in the fields. She could fell a full-grown tree with no help from anyone. Whenever Thaatha went out of the village, she kept a careful watch over the family and protected them.

The days rolled by and the seasons came and went. Then came a day when Vaasamba was taken unwell. There she lay on the floor. Indeed, she had always preferred lying on the floor. Thaatha's universe was shaken. He was at a loss. He sobbed endlessly and hovered around Vaasamba in ceaseless circles. Five days of vomiting, diarrhoea, bleeding...five days when Vaasamba's end appeared to be approaching ever nearer. Thaatha took her sufferings into his own heart; he took the excrement from her body into his own hands. He forsook food and sleep in attending to her. As if the very purpose of his existence was to serve her, he never left her side. Paanchaayi too stayed near and helped to look after Vaasamba. She could sense a flickering flame within her own self gradually fading out.

When the gods were being called upon, Vaasamba appealed to Thaatha to stop, by putting her hand across his mouth. She laid her head on his lap and smiled as she made a vow. 'For ever more

I will serve your male heirs. My blood will be the milk that will nourish them. In my lap I will provide safety and protection to your children and your children's children. No affliction shall ever visit your family. I will ensure that they always flourish and prosper. But if I am ever ignored or disrespected, my very womb will turn into fiery sparks and scorch all these promises to ashes.'

That night Vaasamba was gone.

Thaatha and Paanchaayi saw three generations of their family prosper and thrive—children, grandchildren, and great-grandchildren. When a grandchild or great-grandchild, fresh from an oil massage and still unclad, would come running by, Thaatha would urge the child to dance. 'Come on, Paychi, dance...come on...' he would coax, and enjoy the little one's dancing. As Thaatha's family grew and flourished, the palmyra tree too flourished at the far end of the courtyard. This was the tree Thaatha had planted in memory of Vaasamba. Imbuing the tree with the spirit of his family deity, Paychi, he looked after it with the utmost attention and care. Gradually, the tree was adopted by the whole village. It became the repository of the joys and sorrows of the people of Sarukkai Street...their place of worship. As for Thaatha, he shared his life and his thoughts completely with Paychimaram. In his universe, everyone—man, woman, child—took on the guise of Paychi. Only after he had seen Paychi's shadow and heard the sound of her laughter would he even light the furnace of the brick kiln. Paychi, Paychimaram, and Thaatha...it was if all three were fused into one.

A long, long time later, one day Thaatha spread out his towel at the foot of Paychimaram and lay down. A sense of emptiness had taken over his mind and senses. His ribcage rose and fell with his breath. A feeling of unease stole upon him. 'Paychi!' he called aloud. Paanchaayi, unable to walk very well, came stumbling and staggering up to him as fast as she could. People young and old gathered around him. With no struggle at all, Thaatha's soul separated from his mortal body. Within and without, Thaatha's body bore the fresh imprint of Vaasamba-Paychi. Thaatha had embraced death with a serene countenance. The talk in the village was that it was surely Paychi who had taken the form of Vaasamba and lived with Thaatha; and surely it was the same Paychi who had swept by as a breeze and drawn his last breath so painlessly and peacefully away from him at the moment of his death.

Translated by Malini Seshadri

NOTES ON THE AUTHORS

S.V.V. (1880–1950) was the popular name of S.V.Vijayaraghavachariar, a noted writer during the 1930s. An advocate by profession, his writing career began with the publication of his humorous articles in English newspapers. He was persuaded by author-editor Kalki to write in Tamil and went on to publish numerous articles, short stories, and novels in the language. His writings, full of warmth, humour, and satire were immensely popular. Today, they give an insight into the life of the Tamil people of the time.

SUBRAMANIA BHARATHI (1882–1921) needs no introduction. A freedom fighter, social informer, translator, editor and, above all, a great poet, he pioneered every genre of modern literature. His timeless expressions indelibly mark Tamil phraseology. His prodigious output—poems, songs, essays, journalistic articles, translations, and children's writings—is too vast to enumerate. He holds the honour of being the first poet whose works were nationalized.

KALKI (1899–1954) was the pen name of R. Krishnamurthy, a famous writer known for his humorous and satirical articles and nationalist and historical novels, serialized in popular magazines and cherished by generations of readers. A nationalist and freedom fighter, he was jailed thrice during the Freedom Struggle. He launched and edited the magazine *Kalki* after having worked in *Ananda Vikatan*, another weekly, for several years.

KUMUDINI (1905–1986) was one of the earliest women writers in the world of twentieth-century Tamil literature. Named Ranganayaki Thatham, she was an autodidact, proficient in Tamil, Sanskrit, and English, with strong feminist leanings. In 1942, she wrote *Diwan-Magal*, which advocated for inter-caste marriage, revolutionary at the time. She was appreciated for the subtle wit and humour in her stories published in *Ananda Vikatan*, *Kalaimamagal*, and other magazines; a few of her stories were brought out in two collections. Apart from stories and novels, she also has a book on child psychology to her credit. An able translator, she translated the Gandhian writings of J. C. Kumarappa into Tamil.

PUDUMAIPITTAN (1906–1948) is the nom de plume of C. Viruthachalam, rightly recognized as the pioneer of the Tamil short story. True to his pen name 'Crazy about Innovation', he broke conventions and ushered in a renaissance in Tamil writing. In his short lifetime, he left behind a remarkable corpus of short stories, essays, poems, and translations, which are revered even today. His works were nationalized in 2002 by the Tamil Nadu government.

MAUNI (1907–1985), meaning 'the silent one', is the pen name of S. Mani. Hailed as the Writer's writer, he was born in a village in Thanjavur delta and completed his education in Kumbakonam. His lasting reputation rests on his twenty-four short stories, many of them published in the literary magazine *Manikkodi*. Thoughts, emotions, imagery, a weaving of the real and the dream state, render the stories inscrutable in the first reading. As the reader perseveres, the exquisitely crafted stories slowly unravel their import and leave a lasting impact.

C. S. CHELLAPPA (1912–1998) belonged to the *Manikkodi* literary movement along with Pudumaipittan, Mauni, and Ku. Pa. Ra. He founded the literary magazine *Ezhuthu*, which ushered in modern criticism in Tamil. As a young man, Chellappa adopted Mahatma Gandhi's creed of non-violence, and, in 1941, spent six months in jail for participating in the Batlagundu satyagraha. He wrote several novels, short stories, and critical essays, achieving wide acclaim with his novel *Vadi Vasal*. He was conferred the Sahitya Akademi Award posthumously in 2001 for his novel *Sudhandhira Daagam*.

LA. SA. RA. (1916–2007), or Lalgudi Saptarishi Ramamirtham, was known for his unique and inimitable style and his use of magical realism. He has 300 short stories, six novellas, and ten collections of essays to his credit. He was a contributor to the influential literary magazine, *Manikkodi*, which gave new direction to Tamil writers in the 1940s. Some of his famous novels are *Apitha*, *Puthra*, and *Prayachitham*. He won the Sahitya Akademi Award in 1989 for *Chintha Nathi*, a collection of autobiographical essays. His works were nationalised and brought into the public domain in 2008.

THI. JANAKIRAMAN (1921–1982), was an immensely gifted novelist and short story writer employed with the All India Radio. Few writers have captured the spiritual and artistic milieu of the Thanjavur district as he did. Even today his novels, which are nuanced depictions of life in the Kaveri delta, are considered classic examples of lyrical prose. The rich dialect of the Thanjavur delta lends a special flavour to his stories. Some of his famous novels are *Mogamul*, *Amma Vandhaal*, *Marappasu*, and *Chembaruthi*. He won many awards, including the Sahitya Akademi for his collection of short stories titled *Sakthi Vaidyam*.

KI. RA. (1923–2021), the shortened form of Ki. Rajanarayanan, began writing in the late 1950s. He was one of the first writers representing the 'karisal mann', the black loam soil suitable for cotton crop. Born in Idaiseval in Tamil Nadu, Rajanarayanan set a trend in writing in the native dialect of Tamil. He wrote more than thirty books of short stories, novels, articles, and folk tales, as well as a dictionary for the dialect. *Gopalla Graamam* (Gopalla Village) and its sequel *Gopallapurathu Makkal* (The People of Gopallapuram) were among his most acclaimed novels, and the latter won the Sahitya Akademi Award in 1991.

INDIRA PARTHASARATHY (1930–) popularly known as Ee. Pa. is the pen name of R. Parthasarathy, an award-winning novelist, short story writer, and playwright. He founded the Sankaradas Swamigal School of Performing Arts at Pondicherry University, and became its director, resuscitating the Tamil theatre scene with adaptations of the *Cilappatikaram* and Shakespeare's *King Lear*. He has published sixteen novels, ten plays, anthologies of short stories, and essays. He is the only writer to have received the Sahitya Akademi Award and the Sangeet Natak Akademi Award. He is also the recipient of Saraswati Samman and the Padma Shri.

ASHOKAMITRAN (1931–2017) was the pseudonym of J. Thyagarajan, one of the most revered Tamil writers today. A distinguished essayist and critic, he was the editor of the literary journal *Kanaiyaazhi*. He wrote over 200 short stories, eight novels, and about fifteen novellas, besides other prose writings. Most of his works have been translated into several Indian languages and English and other European languages. His novels like *Karaintha Nizhalkal* and *Pathinettavathu Atchkkodu* are hailed as masterpieces. A recipient of the Sahitya Akademi Award, he has also won several regional and national awards.

R. CHUDAMANI (1931–2010), though not formally educated owing to a physical disability, was a prolific writer in Tamil and English and started writing in the later 1950s. She has to her credit more than 500 short stories and thirty-two volumes of fiction. She began publishing in Tamil in 1954 and in English in 1962. Well known in both the world of literary journals and popular magazines, her felicitous and earnest writings made a significant contribution to contemporary Tamil literature, winning her the Tamil Nadu Government Award (1966), Lilly Devasigamani Award (1992), and Kalaignar Mu. Karunanidhi Award (2009).

SUNDARA RAMASWAMY (1931–2005) was an influential Tamil writer. As a native of Nagercoil in Tamil Nadu, in close proximity to Kerala, he represented the bilingual felicity of Tamil and Malayalam.

His literary career, spanning over five decades, included short stories, novels, translations, poetry, and criticism. He published poetry under the name Pasuvayya. His novel *Oru Puliya Maraththin Kathai* was a classic, presenting contemporary life in the dialect of the region. Much of his writing has been translated into Indian and European languages. The University of Toronto conferred on him the inaugural Iyal Award in 2001.

SUJATHA (1935–2008), whose real name was S. Rangarajan, revolutionized the style and content of writing in Tamil. An electronics engineer by profession, science and Tamil literature were his passions, and he was the first to introduce the genre of science fiction in a big way in Tamil. He tried his hand at all genres with versatility and ease. His prolific output with hundreds of short stories, scores of novels, and non-fiction, matched the wide and constant demand from the media and the public for his writings.

SA. KANDASAMY (1940–2020) was a prolific Tamil writer and literary critic. His first novel *Chaayavanam* was published in 1968. He has written more than 200 short stories, fourteen novels, and two works of non-fiction and his work has been translated into Hindi, Kannada, and English. An accomplished film-maker, his documentary *Kaval Deivangal*, which showcased the terracottas of South India, won the Angina Festival in Cyprus in 1989. He has won the Tamil Nadu state literary awards and the Sahitya Akademi Award.

AADHAVAN (1942–1988) is the pen name of K. S. Sundaram. Born in Kallidaikurichi in Thirunelveli district, he began his career as a writer for the children's magazine *Kannan*. He later became the assistant editor at National Book Trust of India. His publications include five short story collections and two novels. His novel *En Peyar Ramaseshan* has been translated into Russian. His stories have received critical acclaim and he was awarded the Sahitya Akademi Award posthumously for his collection of short stories.

AMBAI (1944–) is the nom de plume of C. S. Lakshmi, a historian, researcher, and creative writer, who has published short stories, novels, and articles. In 2006, she (along with Lakshmi Holmström) won the Vodafone Crossword Book Award (in the Indian language fiction translation category). She received the Iyal Virudhu (Lifetime Achievement Award) in 2008, awarded by the Tamil Literary Garden. A PhD from Jawaharlal Nehru University, she has been an independent researcher in Women's Studies for the last thirty-five years. In 1988, she founded SPARROW (Sound and Picture Archives for Research on Women) and NGO for documenting and archiving the work of female writers and artists.

THOPPIL MOHAMED MEERAN (1944–2019) was born in Thangapattanam, a small seashore village in Tamil Nadu, but was educated in schools where the medium of instruction was Malayalam. Among his published novels are: *Thuraimukam* (1991), *Koonan Thoppu* (1993), and *Chaaivu Naarkaali* (1995). His collections of short stories include *Anbukku Mudumai Illai* (1990) and *Thankaraj* (1993). Many of his novels and short stories have been translated into other languages. He received many awards and prizes, including the Sahitya Akademi Award in 1997.

BALAKUMARAN (1946–2018), one of the most popular Tamil writers, produced more than 200 books, including novels, short stories, and essays. Many of his novels were serialized in popular weeklies. His magnum opus was the historical novel *Udayar* on Rajaraja Chola. He was also an accomplished screenplay writer and has over a score of films to his credit. Drawn to spiritualism, Balakumaran also wrote several books on spiritual greats. He won the Raja Sir Annamalai Chettiar award and the Ilakkia Chinthanai for his contributions to literature.

POOMANI (1947–) is the pen name of P. Manickavasagam. A distinguished writer known for his use of local dialects, he has published six novels, six short story collections, and one collection of essays. He has also scripted and directed a film, titled *Karuvelam Pookkal*. His works have been translated into several languages. His novel *Angnaadi* has won several awards, including the Sahitya Akademi Award in 2014. Another novel, *Vekkai*, was made into a successful film.

FR MARK STEPHEN (1949–), or SJ, popularly known as 'Mark' in literary circles, became a Jesuit in the Madurai Province in 1972 and was ordained a priest in 1982. He is a people-oriented pastor and an effective social and Dalit rights activist. As a prolific writer, he has made a mark in different genres of literature, writing novels, short stories, theological articles, and biographies. Notable among his works is his well-researched and acclaimed book on the life and history of Arunthathiyars. Currently, he resides in Loyola College, Chennai.

MAALAN (1950–) is the pen name of V. Narayanan who started his career as a pharmaceutical chemist and later became a journalist and a bilingual writer. He has published novels, short stories, poems, and articles and his work has been included in anthologies published by the Sahitya Akademi. He has twenty books to his credit, many of which have been translated into various languages, including English, Hindi, Malay, and French. He is a recipient of several awards, including the Best Translator Award from the Government of Tamil Nadu, 2019.

DILIP KUMAR (1951–), whose mother tongue is Gujarati, is a well-known short story writer in Tamil with several awards to his credit. One of his stories, 'Theervu', won the best short story award of the year in 1977. He has translated poems, short stories, and plays from Gujarati, Hindi, and English into Tamil, and edited a collection of short stories translated from Kannada and Bengali into Tamil. He has also published a collection of short stories, *Moongil Kuruthu*, and a critical work on Mauni, *Mouniyudan Konja Thooram*. His stories have been translated into English, French, German, Czech, and many Indian languages, including Gujarati.

BAMA (1957–), as Bama Faustina is known, is a celebrated contemporary Dalit woman writer. She has been at the forefront of Dalit literary activism and has given Dalit aesthetics a visibility it had previously lacked. Besides *Karukku* (1992), her autobiography, she has published *Sangati* (1994), *Kisumbukkaran* (1996), *Vanmam* (2002), *Oru Thathauvm Erumayum* (2004), *Kondattam* (2009), and *Manushi* (2011) in Tamil. Her works have been widely translated. In 2000, the English translation of *Karukku*, translated by Lakshmi Holmström, won the Crossword Award, establishing her as a distinct voice in Dalit literature.

IMAYAM (1964–) alias V. Annamalai is one of the leading writers in South India, closely connected with the Dravidian Movement. He has six novels, six short story collections, and a novella to his credit. Of these, his much acclaimed first novel, *Koveru Kazhuthaigal* won several awards and was translated into English and other Indian languages. Born into a peasant family, he writes about the marginalized and their victimization by caste, religion, and politics. He was awarded a Junior Research Fellowship from the Department of Culture, Government of India. He received the Sahitya Akademi Award for his novel *Sellaadha Panam*.

ANBAATHAVAN (1965–), or J. P. Anbusivam, is a native of Villupuram. He commenced his literary career by contributing pieces to various small magazines. Till date he has contributed thirty-one written works to the oeuvre of Tamil literature, many of which deal with inter-caste conflict. He is the recipient of several honours and awards, including Tamil Nadu's Kalai Ilakkiya Perumandram Award and Dr Ambedkar Fellowship Award from Dalit Sahitya Akademi in New Delhi. He currently resides in Karnataka.

PERUMAL MURUGAN (1966–) is a Tamil author, scholar, and literary chronicler. He was a professor of Tamil at the Government Arts College in Namakkal. He has written ten novels, including

Nizhal Mutram, *Kanganam*, and *Poonachi*, five collections of short stories, and four anthologies of poetry. Many of his novels have been translated into English and other Indian languages. His best-known work is the novel *Maadorubagan* (*One Part Woman*), which attracted fierce controversy along with immense acclaim.

S. RAMAKRISHNAN (1966–) is a prolific, popular writer, who has written and published nine novels, twenty collections of short stories, and three plays, among other works. His short stories and articles have been translated into English, Malayalam, Hindi, Bengali, Telugu, Kannada, and French. Deeply interested in cinema, he has written several screenplays. The short film *Karna Motcham* with his screenplay won the National Award for Best Short Film. He is the recipient of several awards, including the Iyal Award from Canada and the Sangeet Natak Akademi Award for his novel *Sanjaaram*.

S. THENMOZHI (1972–) is a poet and short story writer hailing from Tiruvarur. A collection of her poetry was published as *Thuravi Nandu* in 2008. In 2009, she produced a collection of short stories as *Nerkkunjam*. She played a key role in establishing a literary forum called Ilakkiya Cholai in the Thanjavur region and has compiled the works of writers from the transgender community into an anthology titled *Maadavappilai*. She has postgraduate degrees in both chemistry and history and is currently researching virology at Thanjavur Tamil University.

NOTES ON THE TRANSLATORS

M. S. RAMASWAMI (1916–unknown) graduated from the Travancore (now Kerala) University, topping in English and Tamil. He went on to practise law in Tamil Nadu and retired as a Second Presidency Magistrate, Madras in 1971. His publications include *Painting in India and Bronze Icons of Tamil Nadu*, two pioneering works in Tamil. He also translated Sivaramamurthi's *Indian Painting* for the National Book Trust, New Delhi and his edition of Modern Tamil Poetry, which was published by the Writers Workshop in 1988.

LAKSHMI HOLMSTRÖM (1935–2016) was a British-Indian writer, translator, and literary critic. She is known for her translations of Tamil novels and short stories by important modern writers such as Sundara Ramaswamy, Ambai, Ashokamitran, Imayam, and Bama. Her translation of *Karukku* by Bama won the Crossword Book Award 2000. She was awarded an MBE in 2011 for her contributions to the field of literature.

VASANTHA SURYA (1942–) has written articles and reviews for major Indian publications, translated novels, short stories, and poetry from and into Tamil, and written children's books, and poems in English. Her translations from Tamil include novels by R. Chudamani, Sa. Kandasamy, Vaasanthi, and A. Madhaviah. *A Place to Live* is the second edition of a collection of her translations of outstanding contemporary Tamil short fiction. She has translated poems of Brecht and Rilke (German) into Tamil, and a narrative folk poem from Bundeli Hindi into English (*The Ballad of Budhni*). *The Stalk of Time,* shortlisted for the Commonwealth Poetry Prize, and *A Word Between Us* are her two poetry collections in English. Her works for children include *Mridu in Madras*, translated into Tamil by Prema Srinivasan and herself in three volumes as *Medraasil Mirudu*, and *Ramayana*, serialized in *Chatterbox* magazine.

C. G. RISHIKESH (1943–2021) was a former journalist, having worked with *Indian Express* and *Frontline*, and a translator. Referred to as the Gridman, he was on the panel of setters for The Hindu Crossword and has more than 1,000 puzzles to his credit from the time he joined it in 2001.

MALINI SESHADRI (1946–) is a freelance writer, editor, and translator based in Chennai. She has over three decades of experience writing newspaper columns and magazine articles on a wide variety of themes. Recently, she co-authored a series of value education books for schools titled *Living in Harmony*. She has translated Bama's novel *Vanmam*, and also ten Tamil short stories by various authors as part of an anthology. She has also written a work of fiction for children, and co-edited a textbook for an undergraduate programme.

C. T. INDRA (1947–) is the former Head of English, Madras University. She has translated short stories, plays, novellas, and critical writings from Tamil into English. Dr Indra's translations include *The Legend of Nandan*, *Cross Section* with Prema Jagannathan, *Internal Colloquies, Indira Parthasarathy: Three Plays* with T. Sriraman, and *The Solitary Sprout: Selected stories of R. Chudamani* with T. Sriraman. She won the Katha–British Council Special Mention Award for translation (1994) and the Katha Award for Tamil (1995).

PRABHA SRIDEVAN (1948–) is a former judge of the Madras High Court and the former chairman of the Intellectual Property Appellate Board. She writes regularly in English and Tamil on issues of law and life. *Seeing in the Dark* and *Echoes of the Veena and Other Stories* are her two books of Chudamani's stories. She has also translated Thoppil Mohamed Meeran's short stories for a collection.

GOWRI RAMNARAYAN (1950–) is a playwright, theatre director, journalist (formerly deputy editor, *The Hindu*, now freelance writer), vocal accompanist to legendary musician M. S. Subbulakshmi. Dr Ramnarayan's *Dark Horse & Other Plays* anthologizes her original plays. She has authored children's books and a biography of M. S. Subbulakshmi (*MS & Radha*), translated two plays by Marathi playwright Vijay Tendulkar, and the Tamil short stories of Kalki Krishnamurti.

P. RAJA (1952–), formerly a professor of English, Kanchi Mamunivar Centre for Postgraduate Studies, Pondicherry, is a bilingual author. Dr Raja has published more than 5,000 articles, short fiction, poems, interviews, plays, reviews, skits, translations, and features in no less than 350 newspapers and magazines, both in India and abroad. He has authored thirty-two books in English and fourteen books in Tamil.

N. KALYAN RAMAN (1953–) has been translating Tamil literature into English for over two decades and was conferred the Pudumaipithan Award in 2017 for his work. He has translated some of the finest Tamil writers, ranging from Ashokamitran and Salma to Devibharati and Perumal Murugan. Additionally, he has translated numerous Tamil poets, including forty poems by forty Tamil women poets for an anthology curated by Kutti Revathi titled *Tamil Women's Poetry: A Current of Contemporary Voices*.

AHANA LAKSHMI (1963–) received a PhD in environmental science from Anna University in 1990 where she serves as a guest faculty. She has been writing from a young age, and has published extensively. She writes stories for children and is on the Advisory Board for Rashtra Deepika's *Children's Digest*. Her translation of Prema Nandakumar's short story 'Roots: Extensive, Intrinsic' received the second prize in Muse India Translation Contest 2008 (Short Fiction). She lives in Chennai with her husband, Ramesh, and daughter, Mythili. She is also the granddaughter of Kumudini.

ACKNOWLEDGEMENTS

Grateful acknowledgement is made to the following copyright holders for permission to reprint copyrighted material in this volume. While every effort has been made to locate and contact copyright holders and obtain permission, this has not always been possible; any inadvertent omissions brought to our notice will be remedied in future editions.

'A Village Experience' by S. V. V.; translation used with permission of Malini Seshadri.

'The Story of a Crow Learning Prosody' by Subramania Bharathi; translation used with permission of P. Raja.

'The Governor's Visit' by Kalki; translation used with permission of Gowri Ramnarayan.

'Letters from the Inner Palace: Sita's Letters' from *From the Inner Palace: A Kumudini Anthology* by Kumudini, translated by Ahana Lakshmi. Published by Srirangam Srinivasa Thathachariar Trust, 2009. Reprinted by permission of the translator and publisher.

'God and Kandasami Pillai' ('Kadavulum Kandasmi Pillayum') by Pudumaippittan, translated by Lakshmi Holmström, from *Pudumaippittan*, (Katha, 2002), pp. 157–180.

'Kudumba Ther', Mouni, Lakshmi Holmström, © Gnanam Mahalingam (Rights sold by KALACHUVADU PUBLICATIONS).

'The Family Chariot' ('Kudumba Ther') by Mauni; translated by Lakshmi Holmström, from *Mauni: A Writer's Writer*, (Katha, 1997), pp. 53–63.

'The Door Closes' by C. S. Chellapa; translation used with permission of Malini Seshadri.

'Rivulets' by La. Sa. Ra., translation used with permission of Malini Seshadri.

We acknowledge with thanks permission granted by the copyright holder (Dr Uma Shankari, daughter of Late T. Janakiraman) for the story 'Mulmudi', translated as 'Crown of Thorns'. Translation used with permission of Malini Seshadri.

'The First Night' by Ki. Ra.; story used with permission of K. Shankar, R. Diwakar, and R. Prabhakar; translation by M. S. Ramaswami first published in *Modern Tamil Stories (Volume 1)*, Calcutta: Writers Workshop, 1991.

'A Disciple's Offering' by Indira Parthasarathy, translated by C. G. Rishikesh; story used with permission of author; translation published with permission from R. Raghunath.

'Let Me Sleep in Peace Tonight' by Ashokamitran, translated by Lakshmi Holmström; story used with permission of Rajeswari Thyagarajan, T. Ravishankar, T. Muthukumar, and T. Ramakrishnan; translation used with permission of Radhika Holmström.

'My Name is Madhavan' by R. Chudamani story used with permission of R. Chudamani Memorial Trust; translation by Prabha Sridevan from *Echoes of the Veena*, Delhi: Ratna Books, 2019, used with permission from the publisher.

'Nadar Sar', Sundara Ramaswami, Malini Seshadri, © S. R. Sundaram (Rights sold by KALACHUVADU PUBLICATIONS). Translation used with permission of Malini Seshadri.

'Snake' by Sujatha; story used with permission of Sujatha Rangarajan, translation used with permission of Malini Seshadri.

'The Slaying of Hiranya' by Sa. Kandasamy; story used with permission of K. Saravanan, translation used with permission of Vasantha Surya.

'Arrogance' by Aadhavan; story used with permission of Hemalatha Sundaram; translation by M. S. Ramaswami first published in *Modern Tamil Stories (Volume 1)*, Calcutta: Writers Workshop, 1991.

'Journey 4' by Ambai, translated by Lakshmi Holmström; from *Fish in a Dwindling Lake*, Delhi: Penguin Books, 2012, reprinted with permission from Penguin Random House.

'Space Travellers' by Thoppil Mohamed Meeran; story used with permission of A. Jaleela; translation by Prabha Sridevan from *Meeran's Stories*, Delhi: Ratna Books, 2021, used with permission from the publisher.

'Rain, Endless Rain' by Balakumaran; story used with permission of Suryaa Balakumaran; translation used with permission of Malini Seshadri.

'Change' by Poomani; story used with permission of author, translation used with permission of Malini Seshadri.

'Penance' by Fr Mark Stephen; story used with permission of author, translation used with permission of Malini Seshadri.

'The Door Opens' by Maalan; story used with permission of author, translation used with permission of Malini Seshadri.

'The Solution' by Dilip Kumar. Story used with permission of author, translation used with permission of Vasantha Surya.

'Ponnuthayi' by Bama, translated by C. T. Indra; story used with permission of author. Translation first published in *The IUP Journal of Commonwealth Literature*, Vol. 4, No. 1, 2012; reprinted with permission from the translator and publisher.

'The Binding Vow' by Imayam, translated by Lakshmi Holmström, from *The Oxford India Anthology of Tamil Dalit Writing* (2012), courtesy the editors of the volume, Ravikumar and R. Azhagarasan.

'Certificate!' by Anbaathavan; story used with permission of author, translation used with permission of Malini Seshadri.

'The Goat Thief' by Perumal Murugan, translated by N. Kalyan Raman, first published in *The Goat Thief*, Delhi: Juggernaut Books, 2017. Reprinted with permission from the publisher.

'Pigeon Fever' by S. Ramakrishnan; story used with permission of author, translation used with permission of Malini Seshadri.

'Paychi Tree' by S. Thenmozhi; story used with permission of the author, translation used with permission of Malini Seshadri.